300

THE MONEY S

Ian St James, ac
millionaire at the
merchant bank backing his enterprises suddenly
collapsed and took his business with it. In the
years afterwards he started a management
consultancy and later turned it into a small
investment house. In 1977 he retired to write full
time. His earlier novels include *The Balfour
Conspiracy*, *Winner Harris* and *The Killing
Anniversary*. Married with three children, he and
his family live in Ireland.

IAN ST JAMES

The Money Stones

FONTANA/Collins

To my old buddy David Hall,
who encouraged me in this madness.

PROLOGUE

'Too damn right it's a long time. Two years? Can't we hurry it up a bit?'

The grey-haired man smiled briefly. 'Perhaps – but I doubt by much. Anyway, why hurry? It's our last job together. And after this one you can retire. Not that you will. Con men never do. And even if it takes two, maybe three years to set up, it makes you more money than you could spend in a lifetime.'

'Ten million bucks!'

'Pounds,' the Englishman smiled. 'Ten million pounds.'

Part One

CHAPTER ONE

To be an accountant is to suffer a social disease. Take parties for instance. Tell someone you're an airline pilot or an actor and there's immediate interest. People ask questions or tell anecdotes about someone else in that line and inevitably end up with: 'and he was a fascinating man *too*.' Whereas own up to being an accountant and it's a conversation stopper guaranteed to start a panic. As if the entire gathering may be subjected to a lecture on Pythagoras or the law on income tax. I've always put it down to people's lack of numeracy. They figure numbers bore the hell out of them so anyone who spends a lifetime at it must be boring too.

I remember a party Bertie gave years ago. I was an articled clerk then and shared a flat in Belsize Park with two other refugees from the provinces, Bertie Marks and Terry Abbot. Bertie was in television, still is I expect, behind the cameras not in front of them, but always close enough to the action to be involved in press receptions and parties and the like. Not that we lacked for parties. London in the swinging sixties was full of them – half a dozen a night if you wanted, and more on weekends. But Bertie's were always the most boisterous and full of the weirdest people. Like this actress who was a big name then in some TV thing. Dreadful it was and I only watched it to gaze at her, wistfully and full of longing, like a dog at a bone in a butcher's window. In real life she was even more beautiful. All ash-blonde hair and the kind of tan which comes slowly on expensive holidays. For something to talk about I was asking her about the actors she worked with in the television series.

'Queers,' she said, her eyes scanning the room, watching who was there and with whom. 'All of them. Bent as a dog's hind legs.'

'Really?'

'Most actors are.' Her eyes turned back to me and I swear it was like being on the short end of an electric shock. 'Didn't you know?'

I didn't know many actors anyway.

'Lucky old you,' she said when I told her, her gaze drifting again. 'Queers or perverts. Take my word for it. Aren't you in this screwy business?'

I shook my head, dreading the next question, the one about what I did for a living, but instead she smiled, a big warm smile, so full of happiness that I might just have given her a present.

'I know,' she seemed suddenly triumphant. 'I know who you are. You're Bertie's friend. Er – no – don't tell me – Mike? Mike! Mike something or other. Mike Townley!'

'Townsend,' I corrected.

'And you're a fan of mine, aren't you? Bertie told me. You never miss an instalment.'

I was wondering what else Bertie had told her when she kissed me. I suppose initially I just clung on, but as it developed I must have taken over because when we parted she was looking dazed and shaken.

'Well!' she remained pressed tight against me and looked up with gratifying approval. 'That was going to be your reward.' Her gaze did another quick circuit of the room before she announced, 'I'm bored with this party. Come on – let's go.'

'Dinner somewhere?' I asked, all casual, as if kissing actresses at parties and dragging them off somewhere was something I had to live with.

'I've eaten.'

I hesitated. I couldn't afford night clubs then and they were not my scene anyway.

10

'And not dancing either,' she squeezed my hand. 'Good-looking men either dance badly or turn out to be gigolos. Either way's a disappointment. And *don't* suggest a quiet drink somewhere – I'm full to the gills already thank you very much.'

'What then?'

She seemed puzzled at that, and a bit put out, as if having second thoughts about the whole idea. 'The usual question, my pet, is simply my place or yours?'

'Oh? Well – er my place is here.'

'How convenient.'

Even then I must have looked bewildered because she fairly stamped her foot with impatience. 'Look, do you want to screw me or not?'

I imagine I conveyed my willingness to that all right and we fumbled our way through the crowd and down the corridor to my room.

Fifteen years later I can't even remember her name. Not her real name. Only the character she played in the TV epic. Sad in a way. Part of growing up I suppose. The only reason it comes to mind at all is because it typifies the kind of instant happening which passed for life in London and the sixties. But maybe if you're twenty-three and sharing a flat in Belsize Park it's still like that – I wouldn't know. All I know for sure is that Bertie's departure was a relief in a way, when it came some weeks later. Because along with him went all those fascinating distractions, leaving a vacuum to be filled. And Terry and I chose to fill it with work. Real work! So that within a month the flat acquired the calm of cloisters and we slaved at our respective disciplines with the fervour of novice monks. Not an evening passed without clearing the dishes by seven and attacking our books until midnight. And we kept that up for two whole years. It was amazing really, I think when we started neither thought it would last and after a while neither would be the first to give in. If ever two people sincerely wanted to be rich and successful, we did.

We qualified in the fullness of time, winning just about every prize going, but even after the exams, when we got back into the social swing, with girls and parties, and the occasional novel instead of all-consuming text books, work still came first if we were honest about it.

Odd really, considering what followed, but I sometimes look back and count those two years as the happiest of my life. Like the last days of a childhood summer, before raw ambition changed 'Consequences' from a child's game to an adult's reality.

CHAPTER TWO

After qualifying I stayed with the firm where I'd articled for a couple of years before two stints, three years at the first and five at the second, with two other outfits, both based in London. The first was another professional firm, specialists in liquidations. It was good experience, thickening the skin and toughening the gut for the business of taking risks which is what making money is all about. Then I joined Walpoles, the Merchant Bankers, partly because I'd learned enough about liquidations, but mainly to advance my reputation and increase my earnings.

I made a name for myself at Walpoles. It was said it was tough making a bargain with me and even tougher breaking one. Those who approved were given a cigar and a pat on the back. Those who didn't were told to try the church next door, money in our shop, compassion in theirs. I'm neither proud nor ashamed of it now, it was simply the way it was with me then. I was a young man in a hurry and I suppose everyone knew it.

The unprecedented happened when I was thirty-seven and the bank offered me a Directorship. Rumour was the offer had been made from fear and a divided board, some afraid I'd be tempted elsewhere, others prepared to risk it to maintain the boardroom as the preserve of the founding families. If it was true, I think I understood more than resented it. After all I'd no family background, no sizable capital of my own (though I'd accumulated a fortune by my old man's standards) and was regarded by most as something short of a gentleman. The strange thing was that when the invitation came I hesitated, and to everyone's astonishment, asked for a month to think it over.

It was during that month, and oddly enough through the Bank, that I met Rupert Hallsworth. He had a small block of shares in a business in which we also had an interest, and he had called at the Bank for some advice. Or so it seemed at the time. I took him to lunch at L'Opera. It was generally fairly quiet there at midday and far enough from the City to avoid bumping into any irritating casual acquaintances.

Describing Hallsworth is difficult on two counts. Firstly, it's rarely necessary. Those who meet him even once seem able to recapture his image as easily as seeing their own face in the mirror. Even people incapable of remembering their own phone number seem gifted with total recall when it comes to Hallsworth. The second difficulty is not in describing his similarities to others, but in catching whatever it is about him that's so different.

I suppose it begins with the eyes, though you were never immediately aware of them as being extraordinary. Quite large and dark brown, the colour old mahogany becomes with constant polishing. But I've known other eyes of similar shape and colour, so it's not that. More that when he spoke the eyes joined in, lightening almost imperceptibly, alive with intelligence, and adding persuasiveness to whatever he was saying. And when he listened they darkened and looked so deep in yours you felt him scrape the back of your brain.

He was my height, six foot or thereabouts, but more slightly built, weighing around thirty pounds less. Hair dark like mine, but nearer the colour of his eyes, healthy skin, well groomed and quietly but expensively dressed.

When I invited him to lunch I'd intended to make him an offer for his shares. I'd fixed a price in my mind; between three pounds and three-twenty a share, three thirty if pushed. But when I raised the subject he refused point blank, even advising me not to sell ours for as much as twice the price. I was suprised and said so, asking if he had any special information about the Company. But he smiled and shrugged, turning the talk first to the price of similar shares, then to the market generally, and finally even asking how I liked being at Walpoles.

By then we'd long since finished our meal. Most other people had left and waiters hovered, paying needless visits to nearby tables in hope of catching my eye. Yet I was only dimly aware of them. I found myself explaining things. Investment policies, opportunities, theories about the money market, the like of which I'd not even discussed in the Bank itself. Even my own ambitions. My next step, how I saw myself in ten years time. By no means a monologue either. He'd interrupt, agree, question, argue – and throughout displayed a knowledge of money quite as good as mine.

I was shaken. I'd been told I was good often enough for me to believe it. Some thought me a bastard, but none doubted my competence. Yet I was blabbing to Hallsworth like a schoolboy, bad enough in itself and quite out of character, especially as when I'd arrived at the Bank that morning I'd not even heard of the man.

Eventually, and to the undisguised relief of the staff, we left L'Opera and adjourned to his club. I made a brief phone call to my secretary, Jean, to clear the afternoon mail, after which Hallsworth and I found a quiet corner and continued our discussion over old brandy and fresh cigars.

He was thirty-five, two years my junior. He'd never worked. Not in the sense of having a job, going to an office, relying on a monthly pay cheque. He was divorced, without children, and as I understood, had been born comfortably off and grown rich, mainly by dealing very successfully on the London Stock Exchange. He estimated his current net worth at one point four million pounds, most of it liquid.

He recited details of his life in a detached, matter-of-fact way, much in the manner of a guide showing visitors over a stately home. I interrupted occasionally but not often; his narrative was so comprehensive where it touched financial matters that it made questions unnecessary, and I was so fascinated by his story that only as he neared the end did I wonder why he was telling it to me. He didn't keep me waiting long for an answer.

'I'm going into business, Mike.' He puffed the cigar until the end glowed red enough not to need attention for a few minutes. 'The Investment Business. Not as a Bank – the restrictions are too onerous. Too many damned civil servants sticking their noses into things that are none of their business. For want of a better title, call it investment counselling. Advising for investments in return for a fee. Big investments. And investing on our own account as well. Using a million of mine as stake money. And I want you in with me. As a partner. Fifty fifty.'

I was flabbergasted. 'You're joking! I don't have that kind of money. Nothing like. The bank might pay me well but –'

'No cash needed. We'll use my million as starters. Non-interest bearing loan stock if you like – whatever suits you and the lawyers. But we'll split the earnings down the middle.'

In effect I was being offered the annual income on half a million. Even with the market as sick as a dog it would yield forty thousand a year – double that when the index rose. And commission on top! I started to say something about not knowing enough about me when he stopped me with a wave of his hand.

'Born Darlington General, 4th April, thirty-nine. To

Gladys and George Townsend. Remmington Road Primary School, then Darlington Grammar. A brother two years younger – a sister sadly killed in a street accident when you were ten. Short service commission in the Army. Then Kingscotts – qualified – three years at Spencers – five at Walpoles, who offered you a seat on the Board three weeks ago.'

I watched him draw on the cigar and wondered how much I'd told him myself over lunch. But he hadn't finished.

'Recently you bought a house in Maida Vale for fifty thousand, with the help of a twenty thousand pound loan from your employer. You're white, fit, over twenty-one, heterosexual and unmarried. Need I go on?'

The eyes mocked as he waited. I suppose by then I wasn't even that suprised. Vaguely irritated perhaps. About being investigated without my knowledge. But it had happened and nothing I could do would change it. And the future sounded very rich indeed.

We talked it over for perhaps another half an hour and after refusing his offer of dinner I went home. Luckily I had nothing arranged for that evening, and even if I had I would have called it off. I needed to sit and think things through, the way I always did with big decisions. By the time I went to bed I'd made up my mind about Rupert Hallsworth, only for my plans to change the following morning. Hallsworth had been a step ahead. It was the beginning of a pattern.

CHAPTER THREE

There were five letters on the mat in the morning. I scooped them up on my way to the kitchen, putting them on the table while I made tea and toast. My morning routine had been perfected in the two year stint with Terry Abbot.

Forty minutes to bathe, shave and dress for the office, another five minutes for tea and toast, and by seven-thirty I was at the front door, complete with overcoat and briefcase. Invariably I collected the morning paper from the boy, on my way out; and during the journey I glanced first at the headlines, then the closing prices, and finally my morning mail. So that by eight o'clock I was behind my desk with a two hour start on most of the City. I'd work solidly then, free of interruption until ten when my secretary served the first coffee of the morning along with the office mail. It was a good system and by the time I'd swallowed a second cup I was ready for the round of telephone calls and meetings which mark a banker's day.

So that morning the cab was putting its back to St Paul's and labouring up Cannon Street as I turned to my five letters. The first was from a Chamber of Commerce asking if I'd give a talk in a month's time. I wrote a large 'no' in the margin which meant they'd get a polite refusal from Jean by return. The next was a note from my tailor telling me a suit was ready for collection. And the third was from a well known London bank. They wrote to inform me that the sum of one million pounds had been placed on current account by their client, Mr Rupert Hallsworth. And was at my disposal.

I read the letter again. Slowly. Chewing every word of it instead of gulping whole sentences. There was no mistake. I checked my own name and address at the top of the page, noticed the date and fumbled for the envelope to examine the postmark. Five p.m. yesterday. Typed, signed, sealed and posted at the very same time Hallsworth and I had been lunching together and drinking at his club afterwards.

I was stunned for a couple of minutes. Not till I choked on a lungful of smoke did I realize I'd lit the first cigarette of the day. Shock I suppose. But against the rules. My rules. Part of my precious routine which dictated that the first cigarette should be taken with coffee at ten o'clock. And I was at my desk before registering the collapse of another rule – that the rest of my mail was still unopened. Feeling like a drunk on the morning after, I reached for the other envelopes.

The first, from a well known firm of City solicitors, was respectfully worded to the point of servility. They wrote on behalf of their esteemed client and enclosed the first draft of a proposed partnership agreement. They stressed it was a draft, added they'd be pleased to consider any reasonable amendments and concluded by suggesting that if my solicitors contacted them, they felt sure the matter would be dealt with to my complete satisfaction.

The agreement was an exact resume of Hallsworth's proposals. He put all the money up, I took half the profits.

It was another five minutes before I turned to the final letter, my name and address handwritten on the envelope. I frowned as I tried to recognize the writing. Neat script, 't's' firmly crossed, 'o's' perfect circles. But the writing of a stranger I was sure I'd never seen before. But in the split second it took to unfold the single sheet of notepaper, I guessed it was from Hallsworth.

He wrote from his club.

'Dear Townsend,

I hope you'll forgive the presumption but in anticipation of our meeting and feeling sure we'd have much in common, I instructed my bankers and solicitors to write to you on the subject of our discussion.

Unfortunately, due to prior commitments, by the time you read this I'll be en route to New York where I'll be for the next ten days. Naturally I'm aware that Walpoles will require your decision before my return, and I hope that you'll weigh my proposals carefully against theirs. Regardless of which you choose, I'm sure you have a wonderful future ahead of you. I would suggest that my way offers a better chance of acquiring substantial personal wealth, but against that I know that the status and influence which will come your way at Walpoles can be seductive attractions to any habitué of the City.

I shall be back in London on the twentieth and wonder if you'll have dinner with me at the club? Meanwhile, I've instructed my solicitors to answer any questions you may have about my general finances, and they also hold my power of attorney, just in case you wish to finalise our agreement before I get back, or before you give Walpoles an answer.

With considered best wishes for your future. R.H.

I smoked another cigarette, past caring about rules, and read the letters again. All of them. Of course I was flattered, intrigued, interested. And above all, excited. But his trip to New York was a damn nuisance. He was right. I'd have to give Walpoles an answer soon. Certainly before his return from the States. Last night I'd banked on meeting him again. Now – to have to make a decision like this! In a vacuum.

Hallsworth's letter and the contract were still open in front of me when Jean arrived with the coffee. I'd lost track of time and was as startled to see her as she was by the cloud of cigarette smoke, so the looks we exchanged, hers curious and mine guilty, spoke volumes as I swept the papers into my briefcase.

The rest of the day was routine. Except that I telephoned Hallsworth's bankers and solicitors, Durbeville, Franz & Co., for appointments and arranged to be away from the office for the first three days of the following week. His American trip might prevent another face to face meeting, but I was itching to find out all I could in his absence.

CHAPTER FOUR

'What in particular would you like to know, Mr Townsend?'

Poignton was a senior partner, perhaps *the* senior partner, of Durbeville's. I judged him to be sixty, maybe older, though

I doubt by much. A few strands of hair combed neatly across his head showed as a dozen white trails on the pink of his scalp. He had a long face with a permanently mournful expression, and the manner of an undertaker to go with it. Black jackets and striped trousers, stiff collar and old school tie – the uniform of a traditionalist living in a changing world – and not much liking it.

He'd given me a halfway passable lunch in the partners' dining room and we'd spent the hour gauging each other's strengths and weaknesses. I found that I liked him without trusting him too much; our backgrounds were so different, his privileged and mine self-made, that we could never be close.

'Mr Poignton, if you were going into partnership with a man what would you want to know?'

Pale, tired-looking eyes crinkled. 'Everything I could find out about him I suppose.' He had a dry, precise voice, the inevitable legacy of a lifetime spent arguing the finer points of company law.

'Exactly. So I'd appreciate it if you'll tell me everything you know about Rupert Hallsworth.'

I felt no embarrassment at my bluntness. After all, Hallsworth's letter gave me a mandate to pry and Poignton had admitted he'd be equally curious in similar circumstances. So I was surprised when he hesitated. And even less prepared for the shake of his head.

'Oh no, Mr Townsend. I don't think I can quite do that.'

'But Hallsworth wrote to me – he said he'd given you instructions. Hang on. I've got his letter with me.'

'There's no need. I have a copy. And of course I'm happy to comply with our client's request.'

'Well then?' I gave him a hard look but the pale eyes remained unperturbed, perhaps even slightly amused.

'I suppose it's a matter of interpretation. You see, I take my instructions to answer specific questions. Where I can of course. Whereas a discourse on every single thing I know about our client would be a different matter entirely. You do see the difference, don't you?'

'But I'm sure he meant –'

'Whereas I'm only *sure* of what he said. I gave up trying to legislate for people's meanings years ago, Mr Townsend. It's dangerous ground. Full of assumptions. These days I prefer to –'

'Split hairs.'

He inclined his head as if in acknowledgement. 'Habit of a lifetime, Mr Townsend, but there it is. Now, if you've any specific questions . . .'

Impatiently I interrupted. 'Mr Poignton, your client initiated this partnership idea. Not me. A pedantic attitude now, on your part, could – well, could prejudice the whole issue.'

An eyebrow rose a fraction. 'My client's offer seems amazingly generous.' He paused managing to imply that I should jump at it. 'If I may say so.'

'And if I may say so, your attitude could jeopardize your client's best interests.'

'Your reputation for blunt speaking has preceded you, Mr Townsend. But I won't be intimidated.'

I drummed the tips of my fingers on the table, caught flat-footed by this unexpected obtrusion into the smoothness of our earlier conversation. But there was no doubting his determination to do this his way.

'Where was he born?' I asked, my surly manner out of place in the graciousness of the room.

'Allahabad. That's in India, Mr Townsend.' He contrasted his polished manners to good effect.

'Who were his parents? And don't say Mr and Mrs Hallsworth.'

'It had occurred to me. After all it combines the twin virtues of brevity and accuracy, don't you think?'

'Still alive?'

'Alas, no. His mother died when he was quite young. When

he was about four I think. His father died much later, when he was – um, twenty-four, twenty-five, something like that.'

'And that's when he inherited?'

'Yes.'

'How much?'

The slightest pause. 'Less than expected. About a hundred thousand after tax.'

'About?'

'Almost exactly.'

'Any brothers, sisters, cousins? Anyone share in the inheritance?'

'No brothers or sisters. I believe there is a cousin somewhere. The United States I think. But Mr Rupert Hallsworth was the sole beneficiary of his father's estate.'

'Do you know what he's worth today?'

'About one million four hundred thousand I believe.'

'How d'you know that?'

'It's what I'm given to understand by his accountants.'

'Who are?'

'Sorry?'

'His accountants?'

'Stevenson & Floyd.'

'Has he inherited any other money? From another source?'

'Not to my knowledge.'

'So his present net worth is what he's made of it from his starting capital?'

'That would follow surely?'

'Who are the brokers?'

'Leppard Peplow principally,' Poignton paused and thought about it. 'He may use others, but I think Leppard Peplow handle the bulk of his transactions.'

'Does he hold any current directorships?'

'None that I know of.'

'And you would know?'

'I might. I think so.'

22

'Any other partnerships, then?'

'He's a member of a Lloyds syndicate. I think that's all.'

'Which syndicate?'

'Aspreys. You may know of them?'

I smiled bleakly at his sarcasm. No one had a career in the City without knowing them. Aspreys were one of the biggest underwriters, long established and well respected. It was the same with the accountants and the brokers. Durbeville's too, come to that. All top firms. And were choosier than most bankers about whose cash they handled. Poignton puzzled me. Hallsworth had impressed me with his warmth and openness as much as his intelligence. Yet Poignton was as close mouthed as a clam and I wondered why? Perhaps he was just a professional secret keeper? A man who couldn't bring himself to volunteer information, even when authorised to do so. I tried another tack, in the vain hope of catching him off guard.

'What went wrong with Hallsworth's marriage?'

'I can't answer that question.'

'Can't or won't?'

'Does it matter, Mr Townsend?'

'If it didn't I wouldn't ask!' I snapped. Poignton's casual manner was beginning to get on my nerves. 'Dammit, all we're doing is cataloguing, when what I really want is to find out what the man's like – what makes him tick.' I glared across the table and growled. 'Perhaps his ex-wife can tell me? I presume you might know her name? And where is she now?'

'Johnstone, Mr Townsend.' His calm eyes didn't even flicker. 'Pamela Johnstone.'

'And her whereabouts?'

'Highgate cemetery. She's dead.'

'Oh!' Another blank wall. I shuffled my thoughts into some sort of order. 'Are there any relatives that you know of? Apart from the cousin in the States. Perhaps someone in the UK, someone I could talk to?'

'None that I know of.'

'Well, friends then?'

'I'm afraid I know virtually nothing about Mr Hallsworth's social life.'

'Virtually nothing?'

'Now I come to think of it,' he moistened his thin lips with the tip of his tongue, 'Absolutely nothing.'

He was enjoying himself, a fencing master toying with a novice, not mounting an attack of his own but making it clear he could defend the rest of the afternoon. Yet why? And defend what?

'Did you advise your client against going into business with me, Mr Poignton?'

The pale eyes registered a small triumph, but the voice remained as neutral as before. 'We do not advise Mr Hallsworth on anything. Not even the law. We merely carry out his instructions.'

'But you don't approve?'

'You misunderstand our function.' He sighed at my limited understanding. 'We neither approve nor disapprove.'

It went on like that for another thirty minutes or so and I was getting ready to leave, shrugging myself into my overcoat, when I asked one more question. Later I wondered why it had occurred to me. I think I was trying to imagine Hallsworth's childhood. To picture him growing up. His mother died when he was so young that I wondered what – who perhaps – had filled the void afterwards.

'What did Hallsworth's parents die of?'

'Pneumonia, I think, in his mother's case.' The level eyes met mine without wavering. We were both standing, about to walk to the door. 'Of course it was much more difficult to treat in those days.'

I nodded and half turned away. 'And his father?'

His hesitation stopped me dead in my tracks. After a moment he said, 'He committed suicide. Shot himself, poor devil.'

24

I wanted to ask more questions, but Poignton was looking at his watch and had already warned me of another appointment at three o'clock. It was five minutes to.

'Why?' I asked.

He shrugged. 'Why does anyone commit suicide, Mr Townsend? No one knows.'

He took a step towards the door and I followed reluctantly.

'Did . . . I mean, have any other members of the family committed suicide?'

'My dear chap, suicidal tendencies aren't inherited you know. It's not a disease. More a state of mind, don't you think? Despair I suppose.'

'So, it's the only instance in Hallsworth's family?'

We were at the door, his hand reaching for the door knob. I could feel him wanting to get rid of me. 'Yes, so far as I know. Now, if you'll excuse me –'

'What about his wife? What was her name? Pamela? Pamela Johnstone. She couldn't have been very old. How did she die?'

He had reached for my hand and was shaking it with a surprisingly firm grip. 'Ah? Um, case in point I suppose. Tragic business. Girl of that age. Not that I see it's any of your business. But as a matter of fact, she committed suicide too.'

We stood staring at each other, the handshake slowly coming to an end, our fingers parting. I felt stunned. Not just with the disclosure itself, but at catching Poignton out in an apparent lie.

'But you said? No other member of the family.'

'Well, she wasn't was she? Divorced – remember?'

'Splitting hairs, Mr Poignton?'

'Old habits, Mr Townsend.'

CHAPTER FIVE

The following day I went to Hallsworth's bankers and drank amontillado with the General Manager. He was attentive, discreet, urbane, and about as inscrutable as I imagine a Chinese whore might be. Yes, Rupert Hallsworth had maintained an account with them for a number of years. No, they didn't know him well, not personally, he rarely visited the Bank, transacting his business by letter or through his agents, Durbeville's or Leppard Peplow. Perhaps I knew them? I said we'd met.

As we couldn't discuss Hallsworth's character we did the next best thing, we discussed Hallsworth's money. The million on current account could be drawn out, every last penny, subject to my signature on one piece of paper. The note asked me to acknowledge receipt of the money as a loan pending the negotiation of a partnership agreement. If I withdrew the money from them I was to let them and Durbeville's know where it was, and if the partnership agreement failed to materialize the loan became repayable on demand.

I sighed. Mainly because I hate to see money idle when it could be working. Especially when it could be working for me.

The Manager's face brightened when I asked what rate of interest he'd pay if we switched the money from current to deposit account. He offered six per cent which I refused and then waited while he fought his conscience before coming up with another quarter per cent. I borrowed his telephone, spoke to Peter Warman who brokes for local authorities, and transferred the whole million to him for use as overnight money at eight and three quarter. It wouldn't make a fortune but as safe as houses, repayable on demand, and at least the three thousand pounds which would accrue before Hallsworth's return would replenish my wine cellar for the year – even split fifty fifty. After that the Manager said goodbye with less enthusiasm than he'd said hello and I left to keep my lunch appointment with Tommy Richardson.

I was pinning a lot of hopes on Richardson. A large, jovial man of about fifty, given to smoking Churchillian cigars and wearing red roses in his buttonhole. A man not easily overlooked. He had a round pink face more like a farmer's than a stockbroker's, honest eyes which were his fortune, and he was always happy. So should he be, with the money he made.

Of course, being top man at Leppard Peplow made Tommy a lot more than an ordinary stockbroker, but he was a kindly man who played himself down and gave credit to the efforts of others. I'd known him for about two years and we'd always got on. And his importance that morning was monumental. Not only did Leppard Peplow act for me at the Bank, but they also acted for Hallsworth. Richardson was the first shared acquaintance, the only shared acquaintance, I'd uncovered since I started.

I told him the whole story. I'd thought about trying to disguise the reasons for my interest in Hallsworth, even invented various stories, but they'd all sounded pretty thin and wouldn't have fooled Richardson for a moment. Even the truth sounded far-fetched.

'Lucky sod,' he said when I finished. 'I don't know what it is about you, Townsend, but you lead a charmed life. Only the good things happen.'

'And Hallsworth? You know him well?'

He shook his head. 'Not really. He comes to see us, what – three or four, maybe five times a year. We have a meal together, discuss his holdings, perhaps switch out of this to go into that, and he goes away again.'

'But you've known him for a long time?'

'About as long as I've known you. And I know you a damn sight better.'

Slightly disappointed I said, 'Still, you've advised him on his investments.'

'Christ no! Not really. Wish he'd been advising us – might have done better following him than he'd have done following us.' It was a brave admission, half joking and qualified a second later. 'Not that we've done too badly for people, you understand.' He sat staring at me, blue cigar smoke drifting between us, his eyes thoughful and pensive. 'Matter of fact, Mike, I doubt Hallsworth takes advice from anyone.'

I remembered the fleeting look of resignation on Poignton's face when he said that they didn't advise, not 'even on the law'.

'You mean he's invested in things against your advice?'

Richardson frowned. 'Not really that. He listens to what we say and then makes up his own mind.'

'And very successfully from what I hear?'

'Successfully yes. Very successfully?' He shrugged. 'I'd have said safe, steady, not spectacular.'

It was my turn to frown. 'But he told me he'd made a fortune on the market?'

'Maybe he has, but not with us. Good profits, yes. A fortune, no. Of course over the past year he'd been investing more heavily, using more money. God knows where it came from. Perhaps he made a killing with another broker and switched the bulk of his funds to us afterwards.'

'He wouldn't be the first to do that.'

'As we both know,' he chuckled.

I neither expected nor pressed Richardson to reveal the names of any of Hallsworth's investments, and at three fifteen he looked at his watch and said he must go.

'It's funny you know,' he said as we got up. 'We've watched him go liquid over the past three months and wondered what he was up to. Seems our loss is your gain, eh?'

I was planning to take a cab back to Maida Vale and he accepted my offer to drop him on the way. Just before the cab pulled into the forecourt of the Leppard Peplow building, he twisted his bulk in the seat and looked at me.

'What will you do, Mike?'

'What would you do?'

'Christ knows. All I wish is that someone had offered me something like that when I was your age.'

'You'd have taken it? In preference to the bank?'

'Spoilt for bloody choice aren't you?' He looked away, turning his gaze outwards to the crowded pavements. The cab stopped at a pedestrian crossing, the meter ticked above the muted street sounds, and I sat watching Richardson. Suddenly his advice seemed terribly important.

'Waiting for my pronouncement?' he turned back to me, a faint smile on his lips. 'Not on your life. Something as important as this – you make up your own mind. You know what you've got at the Bank. Stay there, and I dare say you'll end up running it one day – if the shareholders have got any bloody sense.' He shrugged. 'Hallsworth? What can I say. I've not heard any bad of him, I can say that. Of course, I've not heard any good of him either – that's the trouble isn't it? But as far as his dealings with us are concerned, he's been straight enough. Meticulous. Pure as the driven snow, as they say.' He thought for a moment and then added, 'But whenever I've thought about him I've put him down as a loner. And loners make difficult partners I've learned.'

'So you'd turn him down?' I felt disappointed as I said it.

'I didn't say that.'

The cab stopped and he heaved his bulk through the door and onto the pavement. He turned, thrust head and shoulders back in again, and slapped a meaty hand into mine. 'Thanks for lunch, Mike. You'll let me know, won't you? When you decide.' And he was gone before I could answer.

The cab moved off, along the Embankment, up Whitehall and into Trafalgar Square. The earlier greyness had turned to a drizzle, so that sudden gusts of wind dashed squalls of rain against the windows, distorting my view of the world outside. I grunted. A blurred view. It seemed appropriate somehow. Like the one I had of Hallsworth.

When we turned past the Garrick I remembered my date with Sue and cheered up. If anything would take my mind off Rupert Hallsworth for a few hours she would. Sue was from another world, ignorant of the ways of the city, oblivious even to the very existence of Hallsworth.

CHAPTER SIX

I arrived at Maida Vale at five past four. Sue's coat was thrown across the chair in the sitting room, her handbag and shoes were in the dining room, and I found her scarf in the kitchen. I was surprised. Not at all the untidiness. Sue could bring total disorder to the house from a range of thirty yards. But that she was there at all. Usually on a Wednesday she arrived at about seven and we had a panic to get changed and into the West End in time for the theatre.

'Sue?' I shouted from the hall.

'I'm in the bedroom.'

'Doing what?'

'Laying in wait for you.' The words bubbled through laughter, like water boiling in a saucepan. 'Laying I hope being the operative word.'

Sue Ballantyne had been part of my life for over a year, since her twenty-ninth birthday in fact. Tiny, no more than five foot tall, beautifully proportioned and, as my old man would have said, as bright as a button. She had black hair, so black as to be that almost blue sometimes seen in the plumage of birds, and ever since I'd known her she'd worn it short with a fringe at the front and full at the sides. Slate coloured eyes, cream tinted skin, and a gap between her front teeth as a result of refusing to wear braces as a child.

I went upstairs. She was in bed, creamy bare shoulders gleaming above the sheets, one arm beckoning.

'Suppose I'd been a burglar?' I kissed her forehead and narrowly avoided being pulled onto the bed.

'Don't be silly, it's still daylight. You wouldn't be burglaring, you'd be breaking and entering. And I'm looking forward to it.'

We had met on one of my rare visits to the provinces. The Bank had been owed money by a small engineering business in Winchester. Not a fortune, seventy-eight thousand to be precise, but it was showing all the signs of a loan going sour on us. I went to sort it out. The work took almost a fortnight to complete and I'd stayed at a small hotel on the edge of the City about a mile from the factory. And Sue had been staying there too.

I unstrapped my watch and put it on the dressing table, remembering the time as I did so. 'You're early. Did you catch an earlier train?'

'No train today. Car. I had a lift all the way. Door to door.' She looked at me, bright eyes inviting questions. I obliged. 'A young captain,' she said. 'Very dashing. Artillery. All fair hair and blue eyes. Nordic ancestors I should think – really dishy.'

I began to undress.

'Sports car too. New one. At least new to him – he thought the gear lever was where my knee was for half the journey.'

'Which half?' I took a coathanger from the wardrobe for my suit.

Oh very droll. Well he turned me on and you'll get the benefit won't you? You should be jolly grateful.'

'Great. So I'm to be used as a substitute now am I? Some bl–'

'He'd do as much for you. He said so. If ever my tycoon – that's what he calls you, darling – if ever my tyCOON –

31

GOD DARLING, your hands are FREEZING...'

During the first week of my stay in Winchester Sue and I had said little more than good morning and good night to each other. Until the Saturday. I'd finished with my engineers by mid-day and was drinking coffee in the hotel lounge, wondering whether to go back to Belsize Park until Monday, when Sue came in. We made polite talk for a bit and when I discovered that she planned to stay for a few more days, I asked her to have dinner with me that evening.

It was the first time I'd seen Sue really dressed up, off the shoulder gown, necklace glittering at her throat, the whole works. She looked enchanting, like a tiny Dresden china doll. Perhaps it was a bit much for Winchester, but I hadn't minded. Especially when of all things, it turned out to be her birthday.

I found out a lot about her that week. Her parents were dead, as were mine, though at least I'd a brother still in Darlington whereas she had no one, except an elderly aunt in Aberystwyth. She wrote books. History books for schools, the income from which supplemented the interest she received on some small investments, combining to provide a comfortable if unspectacular standard of living. And she was staying at the hotel while she looked for a cottage to buy in the area.

She enquired what I did and I told her, glad to be able to say banker instead of accountant; and she'd asked for some advice on her investments and been touchingly grateful to receive it. I'd probed, delicately but persistently, for some clue of a man in her life, but astonishingly there wasn't one. Not current at least – though I sensed there'd been someone once, a long while back.

A month later she phoned me at the office. She was due a weekend off from writing and planned to spend it in London, visit the theatre, do a bit of shopping, the usual sort of thing. We spent it together and soon after that it became a regular monthly date, sometimes a whole weekend, sometimes the afternoon train on a Wednesday, just for the evening and overnight.

I was still at Belsize Park when she started coming down, though Terry had long since gone and the flat was larger than I needed and scruffier than I could have afforded. I suppose I stayed because I'd grown used to it. I knew the local shops, the best pubs in the neighbourhood, everything was handy and organized. It meant not having to think about anything except work.

During her first two visits we'd kept to separate bedrooms, but I think we'd both decided by the third that we wanted something more than just sharing an evening together. Neither of us said anything but the atmosphere changed, a sudden pleasurable tension growing between us. I remember returning to the flat, locking the door and guiding her away from the living room. We stopped in the corridor and the kiss left us both breathless and trembling. 'Your place or mine,' I had said, nodding at the bedrooms and guiltily remembering the actress from years before. Sue had given me a long look and for a bad moment I thought she was going to say no. But she had smiled and opened the door to my room, and led the way to the bed.

'God, darling, I was ready for that.' She stroked my face and even with my eyes closed I could see her slate grey eyes watching me, sad and serious, soft and tender.

'Better than your soldier?'

'Better than the whole damned Army!'

'The Colonel's daughter didn't oughta –'

'Oh shut up!'

We should have got up then but we didn't, and consequently we arrived five minutes late at the theatre. Afterwards I took her to dinner at Au Savarin in Charlotte Street and found myself telling her about the decision I had to make. About staying at the Bank or joining Hallsworth.

'Can't you ask the Bank for an extension of time? Then,

when this man gets back from New York you can have another meeting and decide then.'

I tried to explain. 'Darling, the Bank was founded in seventeen eighty-eight, by the three richest families in England. Their descendants have controlled it ever since. Now, for the first time in history, they invite an outsider to join the board, and what happens? They're asked to wait! Some of the present Board must regret the offer and their ancestors must be spinning in their graves.' I shook my head. 'No – more time is out of the question.'

'Exceptional men merit exceptional treatment.' She sounded severe but her eyes betrayed her. 'I'd better give them a list of your finer points.'

'Physical attributes don't count.'

She pretended to be shocked. 'If you're implying that – that I only come to see you for your body – well, it's not true. I mean I do quite like talking to you as well. In between times. She giggled. 'While you're resting.'

I pulled a face and started telling her about my meetings with Mr Poignton and Tommy Richardson. And my visit to the Bank.

'You mean you've got a million pounds? In cash?'

I think everyone in Au Savarin heard her. Heads swivelled, women eyed me through narrowed lids, men laughed and made remarks about someone shooting a corny line. To make amends she became serious and we talked sensibly for the next half hour. On balance I think she favoured me leaving the Bank. Certainly the flow of her argument began to run in that direction. But I still hesitated, and we sat in silence for a while, turning it over in our minds.

'Look, darling,' she reached for my hand across the table. 'This man must be reachable. New York's on the phone for Heaven's sake. Why not find out where he's staying and phone him? It's his problem too, remember. He caused it by rushing off like that. Why not make a list of the things that are worrying you and ring him up? Just say

– "now look here Mr" – what's his name?'

'Hallsworth,' I said, thinking about the idea and wondering how many of my queries could be resolved over the telephone. 'Rupert Hallsworth.'

'Now look here Mr Hallsworth –' She stopped and took her hand away. For a moment I paid no attention, busy tracing lines on the tablecloth with a teaspoon, and wondering if Durbeville's would know Hallsworth's whereabouts. When I looked up, her face was as white as paper.

'What on earth? Darling, are you all right?' I reached across, putting a hand on the crook of her arm, alarmed that she was about to faint. 'Sue, you're not ill are you? What's the matter?'

'Rupert Hallsworth,' she said, dazed and looking straight through me. As if he was standing behind me and she was being introduced. 'After all those years.'

'You know him?' I couldn't believe it. I'd searched London to find someone who could tell me something about the man – and Sue *knew* him.

'I once knew a man of that name.' Her normally expressive face was blank, shocked, and still empty of colour. 'A long while ago.'

'When? What was he like? I mean, can you describe him?'

She took more than a sip of brandy and held it in her mouth, swallowing a drop at a time, taking an age to answer. 'Oh yes, I can describe him.'

She did. It was unmistakably the same man. As she finished she shivered as if someone had walked on her grave.

'When did you know him?' I asked.

She looked around the restaurant, people leaving, collecting their coats, another party arriving, waiters hurrying, clearing crockery, preparing tables afresh.

'Mike, can we go home?'

We'd finished anyway, and were just waiting for the bill.

'Of course. But Hallsworth?'

'Married my best friend. Pamela. Pamela Johnstone.'

CHAPTER SEVEN

We returned to Maida Vale. At around midnight it doesn't take long, about fifteen minutes by cab. I had a kitchenful of electronic gadgets, one of which switched the percolator on in advance, so we always arrived to the welcoming smell of coffee. I'd dim the lights, play soft music, pour drinks and we'd sit together, content that bed was waiting and not wanting to spoil it by hurrying.

But that night Sue spoke as soon as we were inside the front door. 'Mike, let's go straight up. Please.'

Perhaps because everything about her is so impish, her height, her provocative teasing looks, her sometimes salty sense of humour, whenever I picture Sue, she's laughing. So any other expression is set in sharp contrast and more startling as a consequence. At that moment she looked desperately sad. Too sad to even cry. As if drained of tears a long time ago.

We went silently to bed. My mind teemed with questions. Things I wanted to know. Answers she could give me about Hallsworth. But she was so obviously distressed that I cursed my earlier clumsiness and stayed silent. I cradled her in my arms and as the minutes passed her breathing became regular and measured, so that eventually, judging her asleep, I edged from the bed and fumbled my way across the darkened room to my dressing gown.

'Where are you going?' Her voice caught me at the door.

'Downstairs. I thought I'd have a night cap.' It was true, but most of all I wanted to think through the latest development. Though through to where I wasn't sure. 'Did I wake you?'

'I wasn't asleep. Not really.' Her voice was as low as a whisper. 'I'm sorry, Mike.'

'Don't be daft. Get some sleep. You'll feel better in the morning.'

'No I won't. Not unless I tell you. It wouldn't be fair. Not now.'

I hesitated, torn, wanting to know everything, but not if it meant causing her more pain. 'You don't have to, Sue. Really.'

She laughed and I was surprised at the bitterness in the sound. 'That's just it,' she said. 'I do. If things are ever to be the same, can ever be the same. Between us.'

'It's nothing to do with *us*.'

She didn't answer. Instead, seconds later, she said, 'Darling, if you're getting a brandy get me one too.'

I padded downstairs and returned five minutes later with brandy and glasses, cigarettes and astrays. She insisted that the lights remained out which made pouring drinks difficult, but I managed eventually.

'You remind me of my father,' she said. 'When I was small, he'd sit in the dark telling me stories until I fell asleep.'

'Now it's your story. And I promise to stay awake.'

'Yes,' she whispered.

I settled in the only chair, close enough to touch her, and sat watching the pale half moon of her face in the glow of the cigarette.

Suddenly she burst out with: 'Dear God, Mike, you'd think an old maid of thirty would have a cupboardful of secrets, wouldn't you? Instead of one. One that I'm ashamed of. Would rather no one knew about. You of all people.'

After a very long pause she spoke again, this time so softly that I found myself leaning forward to catch her words. 'Pamela's family were Army, like mine. Our fathers were great friends. Same school – Sandhurst together – you know the sort of thing – more like brothers in a way. And Pamela and I were very close too. Both only children; born in India within a month of each other. We grew up together – out there to start with before being sent home to school. Term time and holidays together, sharing everything and happy to do so. And we were like that until we left school.'

She sipped her brandy and sounded a shade more cheerful when she resumed. 'My family moved around a bit. The way they do in the Army. Quite a while in India, a spell in Germany. Then out to Singapore. That's where they were when I left school. I'd never been there of course and they wanted me to go out for a bit, so I did. Singapore was marvellous then. Oh Mike, you've no idea. Daddy had just been made up to full colonel and was a big shot locally. The social life was fabulous, and well, I had a great time of it I can tell you.'

I couldn't see her face but I knew she was smiling. She stubbed her cigarette out and said, 'Pamela and I always kept in touch. A monthly letter, birthday cards, that kind of thing. She was having a gay old time in London. Her parents gave her a proper coming out, the whole works, just the kind of thing she loved. Then – I'd been in Singapore two and a half years I think – she wrote to say she was getting married. I'd have loved to have gone to the wedding. But – well, Singapore to London and then back out again – it wasn't really on. But she sent me photographs, and I had a couple of letters afterwards, and she seemed happy enough.'

I didn't even move in the chair for fear of interrupting her. After a pause she said, 'Not long after that the troubles started in Singapore. Riots, killings, street bombings. Senseless and horrible. Then, one day, I'd gone to play tennis with some friends, and when I got back our house had been blown up. It was – indescribable. Rubble. Debris. Still smoking when I got there. My parents were killed outright. Both of them. And there was a young man. He and I – well I suppose we might have married eventually – he was very badly injured. Two days later he died. In hospital. He – he never even regained consciousness.'

I remained silent. Appalled by the story and knowing

nothing I could say would help. I'd guessed there had been someone, once, but it was the first time she had mentioned him. She was quiet for a while, with thoughts of him I imagined, perhaps wondering what kind of life they might have shared had he lived.

'I came back to England then,' she said eventually. 'Not that I had any family here, but I'd written to Pamela and she'd invited me to stay with her. With them I mean. Rupert and her.'

Abruptly she cleared her throat, and in a much louder voice she said, 'Oh God, Mike, you've no idea how hard this is.' Another long silence. Then, her voice soft again, 'I wish I could go home. Perhaps if I wrote it down? And sent it to you. I don't know. I'm sorry but I don't think I can go on.'

I didn't know what to do. After a moment or two I lit cigarettes and passed one to her, wondering if she would finish there and then.

'Look, their marriage wouldn't have lasted anyway!' she said with sudden fierceness. 'It was on the rocks then. Even the day I arrived they were having a furious row. And they never stopped. And – and, I just got caught in the middle. They should never have married in the first place. People like them. Priorities miles apart. She wanted a big social life with him forever dancing attendance. And he was always rushing off to some business meeting, arriving back God knows when, creating havoc with her arrangements. She hated business and he lived for the excitement of the big deal! Mike, they were incompatible. God knows she was a silly bitch with her garden parties and things. But he was an absolute work fanatic. Just like you I suppose.'

She stopped dead. As if the thought had just struck her and she wanted time to consider it. 'I remember,' she continued slowly, 'he'd invested heavily in a business in Scotland which had gone wrong, and sometimes he'd be away for days, weeks even, at a time. Oh, he sorted it out in the end of course. He's terribly clever with business things. Some kind of genius I'd think. But sometimes he'd get back, late at night, tired and worried – Pamela would have gone to bed in a huff – and I'd wait up for him. Just to be there. Give him someone to talk to. A chance to unwind. Scotland was Pamela's last straw. She upped and went home to mother. I'd been there six months then. Six rotten months of always being in the middle, of trying to keep the peace. A useless, thankless task if ever there was one.'

She finished her drink at a gulp and waved the empty glass at me, a pale shape barely visable in the heavy gloom. I flicked my lighter to see where I was pouring the brandy and as I tilted the bottle upright again our eyes met. She looked away. 'Oh, darling, for God's sake. Don't make me spell it out.'

Even then I didn't understand.

'Of course, when Pamela went I should have gone too. Or left before. Or better still, never have stayed in the first place.' Her voice fell to a whisper. 'A month afterwards she came back and found us in bed together.'

I think she was crying but I couldn't be sure.

'Oh Mike – I'm sorry. Darling, it was a long time ago. Nine years. From here it's like it happened to someone else. At the time Rupert fascinated me. His looks, his energy, his clever business talent. And I suppose I was lonely and a bit mixed up. But Mike, I'm thirty years old! And I've only been to bed with three men in my life. David and Rupert – and you. It hardly qualifies me for a lay a month club does it? The only reason I'm so upset now is – it's such a damned stupid, old-fashioned thing to say – is in case you think badly of me.'

I reached for her hand and she clung to me with the urgency of a child waking from a nightmare. Eventually she pulled herself together enough to finish the story. 'Preparations for the divorce were hurried through. Everything was hushed up as much as possible. I stayed on at Rupert's place. He was away a good deal. Much as before really. And living more or less alone didn't bother me. It was

40

a nice old house, peaceful and comfortable. I'd started to write by then. Articles, bits and pieces for magazines. Then – the day before the divorce became final – Pamela came back. Rupert was away of course, but she wanted to see me not him. It was all very unpleasant. She was upset – crying – hysterical part of the time. Calling me names, a whole torrent of abuse. God, it was awful! She wanted Rupert back. The divorce must be stopped. I was to leave the house that instant. I tried explaining that the marriage had failed. That I was unimportant. But she wouldn't listen. By then she'd reduced me to tears as well, so I wasn't paying much attention. Just wanting her to go, to leave me in peace. But I'll never forget her at the door. Screaming that we were murderers. That if I didn't stop the divorce, she'd kill herself.'

She shuddered at the memory and swallowed more brandy before saying, 'That's almost the whole story. The divorce became absolute the next day and she killed herself that night.'

I groaned at the horror of it.

'She drove her car over the cliffs near Eastbourne.'

'But that might have been an accident,' I protested. 'If she was upset – not concentrating –'

'She posted letters before she did it. To her parents and her solicitors. And – damn her – one to me. It came Monday morning. She killed herself Friday night.'

'Oh.'

'When I read it – all the bitterness and – Well I just knew I'd got to go away. Mike, I couldn't bear to look at him. Not any more. Every time I saw his face I heard her screaming – murderers.'

'Where did you go?'

'Rome. I was lucky I suppose. One of the magazines had talked of the possibility of a book. Italian history. I phoned them and they agreed. I stayed in Rome for almost three years.'

'And Rupert Hallsworth?'

'Went out of my life. Until two hours ago.'

CHAPTER EIGHT

Thursday moorning. I was back at my desk after a three-day absence. Once there, I listed what I had learned of Hallsworth. It wasn't a long list. Sue had added a little more, except that she never wanted to see him again, and making me promise not to as much as mention her name.

During the previous evening there had been a moment when I as good as decided to stay at the bank. Only Sue's unexpected revelations had changed my mind. Some of her phrases repeated themselves in my mind. Like the verses of a popular song. 'Some kind of genius', and 'absolute work fanatic'. With a chorus bouncing along to 'the excitement of the big deal'. Words which rekindled the excitement experienced first hand during my long talk with Hallsworth, prompting memories of Poignton's dry confirmation that his fortune was what he'd made of it, and Richardson's comment about investments being safe rather than spectacular – safe at the right time too, with the market turning sour as it had. Something else Richardson said? About Hallsworth being a loner. Well, what of it? Wasn't as much said of me? And wasn't it true? Didn't I believe he travels fastest who travels alone?

None had breathed a word of criticism. The worst discovered was that his marriage had failed. Even that he'd told me himself. And again, so what? Discarded marriages and coronaries – status symbols for ambitious men. Anyway, Sue had explained it, with 'priorities miles apart'. Even his wife's death, about which I had been so intrigued in Poignton's office, didn't rest at Hallsworth's door.

42

He'd been away, not known of her visit, never been told by Sue.

Sue? An unexpected twinge of jealousy. Unfair of course, I was fond of her but not in love and had never told her so. Naturally I was sad for her. About the awful time she'd had. Losing her parents and, what was his name, David? And after that her being attracted to Hallsworth wasn't difficult to understand. Nor him being captivated by her. She was fun, attractive, good in bed. Someone less selfish than me would have married her years ago.

I was still busy with my thoughts when Peter Marcus, one of the Directors, buzzed me: 'Big day tomorrow, eh Mike?' He meant the monthly Board meeting at which my acceptance was confidently expected.

'I can't wait.'

'I've been trying to think of a suitable initiation ceremony. You know – daub you with the blood of a sacrificial typist or something.'

'Do I choose the typist?'

'What? Oh yes, very good – you make the all-important first incision, eh?' He brayed with laughter and collapsed into sniggers before remembering why he had called. 'By the way, have you got the Baroni files in your office?'

We talked about the Bank's business with Baroni's for five minutes before he hung up, leaving me seething with irritation. The remark about the initiation ceremony was typical of Bank humour. A patronizing reminder to count myself lucky to be accepted into their club. Exactly the attitude which had stopped me accepting their offer in the first place. And a ceremony of some kind wouldn't surprise me either, however much I hated the idea. They were maniacs for charades. Half the time pomp and circumstance were more real to them than everyday business. It wasn't the first time that I asked myself if I'd settle for their silly jokes and endless committee meetings. But it was the first time I'd ever given myself an answer. At least with Hallsworth I'd be nearer being my own man. The biggest committee would be two. The pace would be fast and furious.

I phoned Poignton at Durbeville's and went round to see him after lunch, ignoring his warning that the most he could spare was half an hour of his time.

'Did Pamela Johnstone leave any money?' I asked, as soon as we were alone in his room.

'A will, you mean?'

'That's the usual way.'

'I've no idea. We acted neither for her nor her family. I rather doubt it would have been much if she had.'

'Why?'

'I believe her family had been Army for generations.'

'So?'

'Not many professional soldiers became millionaires.'

'Napoleon did.'

'Not a member of their family, Mr Townsend.'

'Pity.'

'We'd all cherish illustrious ancestors.'

'I meant about the money.'

'Why?'

'Just an idea – it doesn't matter.'

He fished the half hunter from his waistcoat and made a fuss of looking at it. I ignored the hint. 'You said Hallsworth was born in India, I believe. Were his family Army as well?'

'Indian Army,' he nodded. 'There was a great difference in those days.'

'You mean they were more likely to have money?'

'I mean that in the main they came from older families.'

'And that amounted to the same thing?'

'Sometimes.' His face dissolved into a patchwork of annoyed crinkles. 'I really am most exceptionally busy. I agreed to see you only because you said something about signing the agreement and I gave our client an undertaking to make myself available in that eventuality.'

'I have to let the Bank know tomorrow,' I said, almost

44

desperately. 'I wondered if you cared to add anything which might help my decision.'

He fairly snorted with impatience. 'Well, really! I feel I've done my share. Frankly another question and answer session is quite unthinkable. It's your decision, Mr Townsend, and I rather wish you'd hurry up and make it.'

'I might sign,' I blurted out. 'But I'd like a couple of clauses added to the agreement.' He had rattled me and I was annoyed with both of us. 'I need to discuss them with Hallsworth. Where can I reach him?'

'I've really no idea.' His blue watery eyes seemed interested. 'However, I am authorized to consider any reasonable alterations.'

I drew a deep breath. 'I want it stated that no investment may be made without my consent.'

'A power of veto?'

'If you like.'

'To veto what he does with his own money? Bit strong don't you think?'

'It will be the company's money, not his.'

'A loan, Mr Townsend – not a gift.'

'And that's the second condition. I want it written in that the loan is interest free and can't be called in for five years.'

There was a very long pause while I listened to the clock tick its heart out over the mantelpiece. I wondered if I'd gone too far.

'And those are your extra demands?' he said eventually.

'Yes.'

'The power of veto?' His pale eyes flickered while he considered. 'Perhaps if it was mutual. You both have to approve any investment in advance of commitment.'

'I'll agree to that.'

'Good of you,' he said drily. 'And as to the period of the loan itself? I suppose we might go to three years?'

'I'd rather we went to five.'

We stared at each other, hard-faced across the desk.

'We might just consider four years, Mr Townsend?'

'Might we, Mr Poignton?'

'Shall we?'

'Let's.'

The documents were amended, retyped, signed and witnessed, and twenty minutes later I was back on the street, with my copy of the agreement in my briefcase. I had become Hallsworth's partner. It all happened so quickly I could hardly believe it.

Sue phoned that night. It was unusual for us to be in touch between meetings. She had no phone at the cottage, regarding it as a potential source of interruption to her work, so for me to contact her was in any case virtually impossible.

'Are you all right?' she asked.

'Shouldn't I be?'

'Oh, I don't know. It's just that I've been worrying about you that's all. Me making a fool of myself last night whilst you were fretting over an important decision. It couldn't have helped and I wanted to say sorry.'

'There's no need. Honestly. And the important decision's made anyway.'

'Oh?'

'Don't you want to know?'

'You know I do.'

'I'm joining Hallsworth. I'll resign from the Bank in the morning.'

She was silent for a moment before asking, 'Are you pleased?'

'Yes. Now I've made up my mind.'

'Then I'm glad, darling. Glad for me too, I suppose. I can stop feeling guilty. Knowing that I didn't make things more difficult for you.'

'On the contrary,' I assured her truthfully. 'You helped me decide.'

CHAPTER NINE

The following year was one of the happiest in my life. At least the equal of the time spent with Terry in the flat at Belsize Park. But for the self-discipline learned then, the exhilarating freedom of becoming involved with Hallsworth might have gone to my head. He was virtually a sleeping partner and I was what I had always wanted to be. My own man at last. Even the business, when it was incorporated in March, was named simply 'Townsend and Partner Ltd.'

Hallsworth explained his function during the first month. And his New York commitments. We were sitting in our new offices on the corner of Hill Street and Chesterfield Hill, a stone's throw from Park Lane. The building was original Georgian, full of spacious rooms and long windows, Adam fireplaces and chandeliers. Four floors of gracious living, linked by a sweeping staircase and uncertain lift. I hesitated when I saw it the first time. For a start it was larger than we needed and certainly farther from the City than I considered ideal. But Hallsworth had insisted saying we'd grow into it in time, and meanwhile why not turn the top floor into a flat for myself. I thought about it, put the Maida Vale house on the market, sold it at a very good profit, repaid Walpoles, and by the end of the first month had settled very comfortably into Hill Street. It was one of the things I liked about Hallsworth. If an idea made sense, we did it. No messing about.

'Mike, I've got a problem in New York,' he settled himself in the chesterfield in my office. 'Oh don't look alarmed, nothing serious.'

I waited.

'It's just that some other arrangements I've been working

on seem to be materializing and they're going to require a lot of my time.'

'In New York?'

'There and Africa. I'm afraid it means I'll be away a good deal over the next year.'

'But what about us? Townsend and Partner?'

'I don't see a problem. You'll just have to make most of the decisions, that's all. After all, I trust your judgement — that's why I wanted you in the first place. Naturally I'll be in touch — be here once a month I'd think. But the day-to-day running will be all yours.'

I thought about it.

'Look, it's inconvenient and I'm sorry,' his dark eyes smiled and took over. 'Not that it's happened. Just that it's happening right now. Funny, but compared to what I've been used to in the past, the last couple of years have been pretty slow. Now, the three projects I most hoped for are all coming up together.'

'Will the other projects require any capital from here?'

'You mean any of the million pounds? Hell, no. Not a penny. As a matter of fact the New York thing might even generate a few opportunities for you, in time.'

I'll say this for Hallsworth, anything promised was as good as done. After that conversation, Townsend and Partner became for all practical purposes my own business. I engaged the handful of staff, devised and implemented policy and conducted the company's affairs, whereas even his attendance at the office was, to say the least, sketchy. Sometimes two meetings a month, then five or six weeks could pass before I even set eyes on him. Each time he would spend a day with me, examine our investments, discuss our growing list of clients, join me for a quick drink in the evening, and be gone again.

I learned a little about his two other schemes, in fact in a small way even helped with the African project. It was a simple, purchasing organization, buying manufactured goods – industrial machinery, drugs, that kind of thing – for various African countries. My involvement was limited to recruiting the man to run it, Paul Seckleman. That done, Seckleman engaged a couple of clerks, set up an office on the second floor and reported to Hallsworth in the same irregular fashion as I did. The New York job sounded bigger, involving a consortium of manufacturers engaged in equipping steel mills and blast furnaces in the States. I've no idea how Hallsworth became involved but it sounded like big business from what he let drop, though he never mentioned what his profit was to be at the end of it. Not that I enquired. It wasn't really my business. Townsend and Partner was, and I was more than pleased to have that.

Sue was away a good deal during the year as well. At the end of March she was commissioned to do a book on Greek history and early in April I was at Heathrow waving her onto a plane for Athens. We talked vaguely about spending a few weeks together in the Greek Islands during the summer, but as it turned out our work schedules never meshed and it wasn't until just before Christmas that I saw her again.

Sue provided the only mystery of the year. It puzzled me a good deal at the time. It was a throwback to the days spent wrestling with the decision to join Hallsworth. About a week after I signed the contracts at Durbeville's I ran into Bob Harrison, an old chum of mine from my days in the Army. He'd made Major by then, though he'd been a lowly lieutenant when we'd first met in North Wales. We had a drink together and arranged to meet again a week or so later. When we did he brought me up-to-date – on his new wife and their flat in Putney, and his current posting to Army records. I suppose I was still curious about Hallsworth and anxious to fill in the missing years, so I asked Bob to do a bit of research for me. Why I threw in the names of Johnstone and Ballantyne I'm not sure. I think because all of their fathers, Hallsworth, Pamela Johnstone's and Sue's, had served in India and I wondered if there was some kind of link from those days. Anyway I asked Bob to add their names to the list and he did.

A month passed. I was busier than a blue-arsed fly and I forgot old Bob completely. Also I suppose I'd stopped worrying about Hallsworth. So when Bob called I was only mildly curious as to what he had discovered. It transpired that Hallsworth senior had done rather well for himself. Retiring as a Brigadier no less. And even Johnstone had made full Colonel. But the strange thing was there was no trace of an officer having served in India or Germany, or even Singapore for that matter under the name of Ballantyne.

I protested at first, telling Bob he'd made a mistake or searched insufficiently. But he was adamant. He'd had the records traced back for the past forty years. Checked, cross-checked, and double-checked. There was no possibility of error.

The information embarrassed me. I could hardly raise the matter with Sue without it being perfectly obvious that I'd pried into her background. And pried without reason. God knows, I'd no claim on her. It wasn't that kind of relationship. And as she went off to Greece at about the same time, the incident slowly faded in my mind. But I never forgot it, not completely, and from time to time it popped up disconcertingly in my memory.

The year flashed past with astonishing speed, and by the end of it Townsend and Partner had acquired a good reputation, a string of illustrious clients and, if not a fat profit, then at least a plump one. It was a year of meetings, planning, decisions, and sustained hard work. And I revelled in every minute of it.

Then I met Aristotle Pepalasis.

It was Monday, the 3rd of April, 1977. The day before my thirty-eighth birthday. A messenger delivered a note from the Dorchester, a few hundred yards away from the Hill Street offices. The note was brief and to the point.

'Dear Mr Townsend,

Your name has been recommended as someone well known in the money market and I would greatly appreciate a meeting. I am in London for a few days with a need to raise substantial capital for a uniquely profitable operation. To explain the details will take several hours and since I have learned it is better to pay for service than to beg favours, I enclose a contribution towards the cost of your time for such a meeting. It is only a token gesture but I can promise you a much greater profit from a closer association with my affairs. I shall be at the hotel all morning and hope to hear from you.

Sincerely, Aristotle Pepalasis.'

The letter was handwritten on Dorchester notepaper and he had printed his name in block capitals below an indecipherable signature. Inside the envelope was a bank draft on Nat-West's Curzon Street branch and payable to Townsend and Partner. For one thousands pounds.

Bankers the world over suffer letters from cranks wanting money, half of them claiming 'Uniquely profitable operations'. And I'd had my fair share. But never before had someone sent me a thousand pounds for the chance to present his case. I read the letter a second time, my curiosity rising as I reached for my diary. A breakfast meeting was pencilled in for the next morning, and another immediately afterwards which would finish at about eleven – then nothing that couldn't wait, until my birthday dinner with Sue in the evening.

Part Two

CHAPTER ONE

Aristotle Pepalasis received me in his suite at half-past eleven the following morning. A powerfully built man of about fifty, with a mane of grey hair and a vivid smile. Quick clever eyes, deep set in a brown weathered face. The look of a man born on the shores of the Mediterranean. Immaculate clothes, grey suit, pale shirt, dark tie; worn with the casual assurance of international businessmen everywhere. We shook hands on the threshold of his sitting room. He was shorter by four or five inches, but the strength of his grip and the width of his shoulders told me plainly who was the stronger man.

'Mr Pepalasis, I'm returning your bank draft.' I went to hand it to him as we crossed the room. 'I assure you it's unnecessary. If you've got a worthwhile proposition I'll be happy to listen to it. If not –' I shrugged and pulled a face.

'Please, the cheque is unimportant.' He ushered me to an armchair. 'No more than a calling card. Let us agree you will take it if I waste your time. The point is you're here and we're talking at last.'

'At last?' I placed the draft on the coffee table next to me, my eyes following him to the sideboard. 'You've been trying to meet me for some time?'

He laughed and waved a hand at the bottles. I asked for a gin and tonic and he continued the conversation over his shoulder whilst putting ice into a glass. 'Often, Mr Townsend, I've thought of this meeting. So – in my mind – I've waited to meet you for a very long time.'

He poured a glass of white wine for himself and brought the drinks to the table, taking the chair opposite.

'Jammas, Mr Townsend.'

'Cheers.' I was frowning, wondering why he hadn't sought an earlier meeting if he'd wanted one. He read my mind.

'Of course, this meeting wasn't always with you,' he said by the way of explanation. 'Or even in London. Sometimes I would imagine it in Antwerp. Other times, the States. New York perhaps. You wouldn't be English then of course, but Dutch or American. But in the end – ?' He shrugged, using both hands. 'I came to London. After all, for much of my life London has been the financial capital of the world. So why not now? When I need additional finance and a lot of it.'

'What kind of business are you in, Mr Pepalasis?'

He set his glass carefully on the arm of the chair and fumbled in his jacket pocket. A second later a small chamois leather pouch landed in my lap.

I loosened the drawstring, opened the mouth of the bag, and poured the contents carefully into the palm of my hand. There were about a dozen stones, none larger than a fingernail. I weighed them in my hand, pretending expertise I didn't possess, knowing that the stones were more impressive than they looked from the expectant expression Pepalasis wore on his face.

'Do you know what they are, Mr Townsend?'

'Diamonds,' I guessed. Knowing just enough to know that whilst Amsterdam is big in diamonds, Antwerp's a hell of a lot bigger.

'Excellent, Mr Townsend. Diamonds. Bort to be exact. More commonly known as industrial diamonds. Those are worth about a hundred and fifty thousand pounds on today's market.'

I looked at the stones with new respect. 'So who needs money?'

He laughed softly. 'May I ask you something? Do you have

any knowledge of diamonds? Or mining perhaps? Any kind of mining? Coal? Iron? Gold, perhaps?'

I shook my head. Financial operators like me deal in paper and rarely have first-hand contacts with tangibles. We used them as securities, reducing a convoy of oil tankers, a new jumbo jet or a sugar crop to one common denominator. Money.

'Then if you'll permit me to sketch in a few facts. Relevant ones I assure you. Meanwhile – ?' He smiled and nodded at my hand. I replaced the stones, drew the string tight and returned the pouch to him.

For the next half hour he did most of the talking. He had a pleasant voice, made more interesting by his inability to pronounce the 'ch' sound which usually came out as 'th'. And while he talked, his fingers played restlessly with a string of beads, in one hand one moment, in both the next, endlessly twisting and turning snakelike, as if his fingers caressed instead of manipulated. He never looked at his hands, concentrating on my reaction to his narrative, and only once when he refilled our glasses, did he put the beads aside. Seconds later they were clicking in his fingers again.

A little before twelve a white-coated steward appeared at the door with a trolley and we adjourned to the tiny dining room for lobster thermidor and chablis. I complimented him on his choice and waited for him to reach the point of the meeting, beginning to feel slightly impatient at his long-winded approach.

'Mr Townsend, how much money do you think you could raise?'

My face went deliberately blank.

'Forgive me,' he said as my silence drew an explanation. 'But I'm trying to understand the scale of your operation. And I suppose of your experience. You are still a young man.'

My impatience curdled into irritation.

'Your company is very new, is that not so?' He didn't wait

for an answer. 'And before that you were with Walpoles?'

'You're well informed.'

'I've been in London a week and asked around,' he said without apology. 'I need someone with a name in the money market and yours was mentioned. What is the value of the largest project financed on your say so? At Walpoles for instance?'

I began to understand. 'Nothing's ever funded just because a finance man thinks it's a good idea. There are feasibility studies from the experts in the industry concerned and –'

'Yes, yes. I know. All the experts have their say and then the financier makes a decision.' It was his turn to sound impatient. 'What's the most you've ever raised for a single project?'

'I don't see what this has got to do with anything, but – ' Most of the final decisions at Walpoles had been committee jobs but a few times I'd put a deal together and the Board had merely rubber stamped it. 'I suppose about ten million pounds.'

He nodded. 'And at Townsends?

'We work on a different basis. We're not a bank. We advise the clients on their investments, but–'

'Yes, yes, of course. I understand!' He sighed as a frown settled around his eyes. For a moment we were both silent. He seemed to be trying to reach a decision and I was growing tired of the game. It was his meeting, not mine. And if he didn't get on with it I'd take the banker's draft and go.

Then, rapidly, he said, 'I need to raise twenty million pounds. Can you handle a transaction of that size? I'm sorry to be blunt but there's no other way of putting it.'

Twenty million was a hell of a lot more than Hallsworth and I had dealt with in that year. Twenty million was institutional money. Pension funds, insurance companies and the like. And when they put money out they wanted watertight security.

'It depends on the project,' I stalled. 'The kind of security, rate of return. I'm sure you know the rules, Mr Pepalasis. It's a lot of money.'

He seemed unimpressed, as if he'd not been listening. 'I should like your assurance that what we are going to talk about is in the strictest confidence. You will tell no-one, without my prior consent.'

'I have a partner. He has a right to know anything concerning the business. Even – if he asked – what I've been doing today.'

He sighed and poured the last of the wine into our glasses. 'Very well.' He looked at me and then reached his decision. 'Mr Townsend, I own what I believe to be the richest kimberlite pipes in the world.' My blank expression must have been a disappointment because he went on to define what he was talking about. 'Kimberlite pipes. Volcanic pipes, Mr Townsend. Stretching to the bowels of the earth. It is where diamonds come from.'

I sifted his words carefully. 'The richest diamond mine in the world?' I asked, quite prepared to have misunderstood.

'Potentially, yes.'

'And you own it?' I resisted an urge to laugh and said instead, 'But I thought – I mean surely the sources of the world's mineral wealth were discovered years ago. Last century almost?'

He laughed, a full deep chuckle which spread up from his belly and engulfed him. 'Last century? Mankind scratched the surface. That's all. No, Mr Townsend, more minerals have been torn from the earth *this* century than all the others put together.'

'But that's been exploitation of known resources surely?'

He was still laughing. 'Twenty years ago would you have believed Texas roustabouts drilling in your North Sea?'

I ran a hand through my hair. 'That's oil,' I said lamely.

'The world's bulging with minerals. Bulging,' He emphasized. 'Only the most obvious have been exploited.

Fifteen – twenty years ago, diamond pipes were discovered in the frozen wastes of Siberia. Today Russia mines about a quarter of the world's total output.'

'I didn't know that,' I said, beginning to concede ground.

'Why should you? Your business is money, not mining. And diamonds are mined all over the world. Africa, Russia, Borneo, Australia. Australian diamonds are the hardest in the world by the way.'

'But the biggest producer is still South Africa?'

'No, Mr Townsend. The biggest producer is Zambia. And then Russia. And then South Africa.' He smiled, like an indulgent adult explaining life's mysteries to a kid. 'Zambia's output last year was about five million carats. At current world prices about two hundred million pounds, Mr Townsend.'

'And your mine's richer than that?' I shook my head in disbelief.

'I haven't got a mine. Yet. That's why I'm here.'

'Let me get this straight. You own a site on which you've found diamonds.'

'If you like.'

'It must be a hell of a big site to rival the African mines.'

'Diamonds are not a crop grown in soil, Mr Townsend,' he said coldly.' You go down for them, not sideways.'

'And that's what you need finance for? To build a mine?'

'To sink a mine.'

'Twenty million pounds? Can't you sell some diamonds and plough the cash back into fresh equipment? Make the project self-financing?'

'It's more complicated than digging a hole in the ground.'

'Hell, that's what it boils down to doesn't it?' I snapped, nettled by his condescension.

'If you like. But it takes a big shovel. They've been a mile and a half down for gold in the Transvaal. Even the Kimberley diamond pipes have been worked to depths of more than three and a half thousand feet. You could drop the

57

Empire State Building down that hole. Three times over!'

Outpointed, I changed tactics. 'Look, this isn't straight forward bridging finance. This is a risk capital with a capital R. Why not take it to a mining company who'd understand the problems? Or a diamond group who'd understand the profits?'

'For exactly those reasons, Mr Townsend. The profits are huge. Much bigger than I think you realize at this moment. Mining companies would want an ongoing involvement, participation in future profits. I'd rather pay through the nose for borrowed money – pay it back quickly, say by the end of the year – and have a future alone. What would you do if you were me?'

I thought about it and saw his point. 'What was the output of the Zambian mines again?'

'About two hundred million pounds worth a year.'

'A year? How many years d'you reckon on getting for God's sake?'

He shrugged. 'No one can say. Maybe seven or eight, ten perhaps.'

I did the arithmetic and there was just enough room left in my head to figure some of the implications. One that wasn't difficult was that, if he was right, he'd be just about the richest man in the world. Past or present. My mind groped, his words barely audible above the uproar of my thoughts.

'The world's demand for industrial diamonds is insatiable, Mr Townsend. The Russians keep theirs for themselves and the West is reliant upon Africa for eighty per cent of its needs. Can you tell me more than two or three African states that are politically stable, Mr Townsend? What the Arabs did with oil the Africans could do with diamonds.' He paused long enough for the point to sink home. 'It's possible, don't you think? And if that were to happen I'd be the only man in the world with an alternative source. Imagine what that might do to the price?'

It seemed to me we were imagining a good deal too much already. 'Let's go through this one point at a time. First, what makes you believe your site's so rich?

He tapped his jacket pocket. 'You've already seen some of the evidence.'

'A hundred and fifty thousand pounds worth?' I almost sneered.

'Enough to make a point.' He seemed unworried. 'And I'm not without some experience in geology.'

I was without so much experience in geology that I wouldn't know a wrong question from a right answer. So I tried a different tack. 'And you've got clear title to the mineral rights?'

'I own the land itself.'

'Maybe. But often surface ownership doesn't extend to mineral rights. It's something the lawyers will want to be sure about when the time comes. *If* the time comes.'

He smiled, but remained silent except for the beads clicking in his hands. We were still at the dining table, the coffee pot cooling gradually.

'Of course, if you're right,' I said slowly, my brain still groping for something to hang on to. 'Even if you're a tenth right – you'll be taxed out of existence. Or nationalized. Or both.'

'But I own the land, Mr Townsend.'

'I know. You keep saying. But wherever it is the government will drop on you like a ton of bricks. Any government would.'

'But I am the government,' he said surprisingly. 'You see my kimberlite pipes have their surface point on an island.'

I stared at him. 'And you own the island I suppose?'

'People do, you know. I believe even off your own coastline there are many privately owned islands, and –'

'I daresay. But still subject to our law, our tax structure, our –'

'Are you sure? For instance, the island of Sark –'

59

I snorted: 'Let them claim the biggest diamond mine in the world and see what happens.'

He chuckled. 'I see you distrust governments as much as I do. Perhaps it's as well then that my island is in international waters. Free of any jurisdiction except my own.'

I felt punch drunk. 'Mr Pepalasis, I presume you can substantiate all this?'

'Most of it.' His eyes twinkled. 'Of course no geologist can ever guarantee what's in the ground, or the exact extent of a mineral deposit. He can only say when the signs are promising. After that it's a matter of sinking your mine.'

The interview had outstripped my experience. Normal questions, regular investment criteria, all seemed irrelevant. The situation was perfectly unique.

'This island,' I asked. 'Where is it?'

He answered slowly and carefully. 'If you'd left your house unlocked and it contained all your possessions, would you go around telling people?'

'What's that supposed to mean?'

'Only that a large part of the initial investment will be used to develop security systems. We live in a wicked world.'

'My father warned me.'

'The location of the island must remain a secret for the time being.'

'You can't possibly be serious?'

But he was. We argued for the next hour but he was adamant. Under no circumstances would he reveal the location of the island. He produced a map of the place, all lines of latitude and longitude suitably erased. He showed me his notes, and even offered the stones in the leather bag for appraisal by experts. Our exchanges grew increasingly sharp.

'Mr Townsend!' He snapped at one point. 'It strikes me you've led a very sheltered life. Perhaps you made your reputation with shop-keepers. But speculators, prospectors, are a very different breed. Believe me, I know. I've got a good title to this island but if its whereabouts become known before I can protect it, half the scavengers of the world will be crawling all over it. What do I do then? Appeal to the United Nations? Take it to the Human Rights Court in Strasbourg? Don't make me laugh!'

There was no danger of either of us laughing. We were both too angry. 'For Christ's sake!' I exploded. 'On that basis even letting people know it's an island makes you vulnerable.'

'Very few know that.' He permitted himself a tight smile. 'And there are millions of islands in the world. More than seven thousand in the Philippines alone – five thousand of them uninhabited.'

'But you said volcanic,' I pounced. 'That would narrow it down a bit.'

He laughed. 'There are volcanic islands off Iceland. Still active, some of them.'

I felt tired and confused. And still a little bit angry. 'So to sum up. You've got an island and all I've got to do is to raise twenty million pounds for you to sink a mine and build a defence system. Without telling anyone where it is.'

'I'm sure you'll find a way. If you're as good as your reputation.'

I tried very hard to keep hold of my temper. 'No-one – just no-one – is going to put up twenty thousand – let alone twenty million – on the word of – on unsubstantiated evidence. Even confirmed it's risk money, and they'll want an arm and a leg for security. And your balls for interest!'

'I'm prepared for it to be expensive.'

'For Christ's sake, you're not listening! It's not on at all. Not without proof. Evidence. Some solid, hard, concrete bloody facts!'

'I didn't think it would be.'

I stared at him.

'I'm prepared to take you to the island.' He smiled as if he was the most reasonable man in the world. 'And one other person. Perhaps a geologist whose authority is acceptable to your money people. Then they'll have your word and his that everything's exactly as I've said it is.'

I squeezed my eyelids together, opened them and shut them. And opened them again. He was still there, and I wasn't dreaming. 'Mr Pepalasis, may I be personal? What nationality are you?'

He didn't even seem surprised. 'My passport says I'm Greek.'

CHAPTER TWO

Hallsworth was at the office the next morning. I'd known he was coming and had set the day aside. We made an early start on the monthly review of our affairs and had as good as finished by the time we adjourned to Trader Vic's for lunch. During the meal I told him about my meeting with Aristotle Pepalasis, reciting the details in a flat monotone, anxious to avoid the impression that I'd already reached certain conclusions of my own. He listened without interruption, his dark eyes raking my face as I talked. I'm not a Catholic and I know priest and penitent are hidden from each other, but reporting to Hallsworth always had something of the confessional about it. What irritates me is I'm damned if I know why. I suppose because I imagine a priest to be receptive, uncritical, patient, encouraging; I don't know. Yet Hallsworth was certainly all of those when he chose to be.

When I finished he asked to hear it again. All the way through, as if it was a gramophone record being returned to the start. This time he bombarded me with questions. Describe Pepalasis. How much did the stones weigh? Describe their shape, size and colour. Did I study the map? Did I learn anything from the geology notes?

'An interesting man,' he said, when I finished, and

grinned. 'What happened to the draft by the way?'

'He offered it again before I left. I told him to hang on to it for the time being. Said I'd think about it. Talk it over with you and let him know.'

'And what shall we say to him?' His eyes mocked.

'Damned if I know. If it wasn't for the bank draft and the suite at the Dorchester, and the diamonds themselves – I'd say he was a nut. But they make you stop and think, don't they? Even so – ' I shrugged and dismissed it. 'The whole thing's mad. Or exaggerated out of all proportion. Can you imagine – a diamond mine bigger than the African mines?'

'I bet they said that before someone discovered diamonds in Siberia.'

I stared at him. 'You're not suggesting we take this seriously?'

'I don't know. But what you describe doesn't sound like a nut. The reverse in fact. The man sounds as if he knows his subject.'

'But what about the business of not disclosing the whereabouts of the island?'

'What about it? I don't think I'd tell you either. If it's not physically protected, it leaves him vulnerable as hell. Forget all about international law if you can't enforce it.'

I pulled a face, unsure of what to think.

'Mike, I know this though. The world's spending more on exploration than ever before. Take Canada for instance. Just the Hudson Bay Company. Do you know what they've budgeted for exploration this year? A hundred and fifty million dollars! Imagine – one company, one year. A hundred and fifty million – all for exploration.'

'For diamonds?'

'No. For oil and gas. But the principle's the same.'

'You mean you just dig a hole.' There was no reason for my mood to have soured but it had. Perhaps because his reaction was so contrary to mine, I don't know. In a gruff voice I said, 'Perhaps you should have seen Pepalasis yesterday. You'd have made more sense of it than I did.'

'We're partners, aren't we?'

'So what do you suggest?'

'Only that you don't turn the man down. Not yet. Not without further examination.' He looked at his watch. 'I wonder if he's in now? Perhaps I'll call round there for a chat.' He grinned at me and said cheerfully, 'It's about time I made some contribution to Townsend and Partner.'

I went back to the office and Hallsworth walked the fifty yards in the opposite direction to the Dorchester, and it was almost six o'clock by the time he returned to Hill Street.

'I take it that you saw him?'

He nodded and helped himself to a drink from the sideboard. We were alone in my office, the faint clicking of a typewriter sounding next door as Jean finished the last letter of the day.

'Mike, do you think you could raise twenty million in the City?'

I was astonished. 'You can't mean it's on? Not this –'

'Listen to what happened, will you? Before jumping off the deep end.' He put a drink on my desk and carried his own to the chesterfield.

'First of all I looked at the stones and arranged for a diamond merchant I know in Hatton Garden to call round at five o'clock. Then I looked at the map, and at his notes. Not that I learned much. Except it's a pretty big island. Did you realize that? It's about twenty miles along and ten or twelve wide at some points. Makes it about as big as Manhattan Island.'

'Should be easy to find then,' I said sarcastically.

He ignored the interruption. 'Pepalasis says he bought it a couple of years ago. Wouldn't tell me for how much, or even how he came to buy it, but I got the impression that the sum was quite sizable. Then he spent time and money prospecting – so he's got a hefty investment in the project already. Seems that the stage of proving diamonds coincided with him running low on funds, hence his visit to London. Anyway, we talked about a deal. I suggested he farm the mineral rights out to one of the big mining houses and take a royalty. He'd still end up as one of the world's richest men if what he says is true. But he wouldn't hear of it. Said he did that once twenty years ago with a tiny claim somewhere and got cheated. This time he's determined to find the money to go it alone – if not in London, then somewhere else. I can't blame him for seeing it that way and there's a chance he might raise it somewhere. So I asked what he'd pay on the money. He started at fifteen per cent and I started at sixty.'

'Sixty per cent?'

'Why not? He's Greek and used to haggling. And if you're going to raise that kind of money for a speculation, you're going to need some strong cards, aren't you? Anyway we spent an hour arguing before closing at forty per cent.'

'Forty per cent! *Per annum*?'

He shrugged. 'Stop thinking conventional business. X amount of capital invested to generate Y turnover to produce Z profit. Forget it. Mining's not like that. You sink a mine and if you're lucky then whatever you borrowed to begin with is peanuts.'

'And if you don't find anything. What's the security?'

'I covered that. The island gets put up as security. I know we don't know where the place is yet, but two hundred square miles of land anywhere's got to be worth something.'

I reached for my calculator. The worst way – if the loan was never repaid – the investors would have bought land for about three hundred pounds an acre. Compared with English farming land, changing hands at a thousand pounds an acre, it was cheap. But so was the land at the North Pole.

Hallsworth watched me fidget for a while, and then said, 'Oh by the way. As well as a high rate of interest, I knocked him for a commitment fee.'

Commitment fees are not uncommon. Providing all parties to the transaction know they exist. The borrower pays a fee, either to the lender or to whoever acts as broker, as a reward for organizing the loan. The fee is generally a percentage of the loan negotiated, very small of course, but even the not unusual one quarter of one per cent can amount to a tidy sum on a large loan.

'Okay,' I said. 'How large a fee?'

'Five and a quarter per cent.'

I was appalled. 'Are you crazy? The investors wouldn't stand for it. That's more than a million pounds! That much of *their* money – going straight out to us in fees. Christ, you know the rules. Never in a –'

'Townsend and Partner get a quarter of one per cent,' he interrupted. 'That's fifty thousand on a loan of twenty million. Sounds modest enough to me.'

'But you said –'

'That's right. But the five per cent gets paid to us privately. Half each.'

I was too stunned to answer immediately, and even when I'd recovered my breath I didn't know what to say. I know it's making excuses but wait till you're offered half a million tax free and see what you do. I finished my drink at a gulp and watched him pick up the glass and take it to the sideboard for a refill.

'A private transaction, Mike,' he said. 'Who's going to know? You open a numbered Swiss Bank account and collect half a million pounds the very day the deal goes through. Anyway, the investors get forty per cent on their money,' he said lightly, as if their profit made the whole thing legal and above board. 'And not a penny changes hands until everyone is satisfied with the prospects.'

I looked at him for an explanation.

'The offer Pepalasis made. About you and a geologist going to the island. Obviously it's got to be part of the deal, hasn't it?'

'But I don't know one end of a mine from the other!'

'You don't have to. That's the geologist's job. Whether the

66

deal's on or off rests on his report, not yours. You'll just be along as the investor's representative.'

I felt a shade better at that. It lessened my responsibility for actually parting people from their money. Twenty million of it.

'So I organize the cash on a stand-by basis?' I wanted everything straight in my mind. 'Pepalasis takes us to the island and if the geologist likes what he sees, the money goes in. Right?'

'That's it,' Hallsworth smiled happily. 'Anyway, let me finish the story. Once the business of interest rates and fees was out of the way, we waited for my Hatton Garden man to arrive. He looked at the stones and didn't say much in front of Pepalasis, but waited for me in the lobby downstairs. They're the real thing all right. In fact he offered to buy them at a hundred and sixty thousand if I could arrange a sale.'

I turned it all over in my mind, feeling excited and frightened at the same time.

'No one loses, Mike,' Hallsworth said patiently. 'And don't forget the responsibility for loosening the purse strings isn't even yours. That's up to the geologist. You help Pepalasis and he helps you. It's the Greek way of doing business, that's all. The point is, can you raise that kind of bread?'

'Let me think about it. Sleep on it. Give you an answer in the morning.'

But I knew then. Sitting at my desk and drinking my second whisky of the evening. I'd dreamt too long of total financial independence to pass up a chance like that. My expertise lay in making money and I earned a good living at it. But the real money went to the people with money to invest. The sort of people I'd spent years of my life advising. And with half a million in a Swiss Bank account I'd be in the game in my own right.

CHAPTER THREE

Raising money isn't easy. Not if you're looking for twenty million pounds to pour down a hole in the ground it isn't. It might have been easier in the sixties, when the City was buoyant and confident. Before it all went wrong.

Having Pepalasis for a client didn't help, either. There were times during April and May when I felt like telling him to stuff the whole deal. Forever imposing fresh conditions until the downright difficult became the damned impossible. Not to approach mining companies. The tour of the island to be limited to one week, one geologist and me. No rock samples to be brought back for fear of Customs enquiries about country of origin. The list seemed endless. At the end of May he and I had a blazing row and only Hallsworth's timely return from the States kept a Townsend and Partner interest in the venture. After that we agreed – as far as possible Hallsworth dealt with Pepalasis, and I dealt with the investors.

I've been in the money business all my working life, so I reckon to know investors. And believe me, they're the same all over. Threadneedle Street, or the Tokyo Bourse. To sell a deal you need five things going for you. First this thing mood, shorthand for a whole lot but mainly people sensing they're backing a winner. If they see someone else making a pile they'll join in, copy him, jump on the bandwagon. A few dozen doing that and you've got a buoyant market, a few more and you've got a boom. It's the herd instinct. In reverse, it causes runs on banks, depressions and people jumping out of skyscraper windows. Next, all moods are capricious, so you need timing. A good looking deal one day can turn sour the next, on a chance remark or a wife nagging over breakfast. Third, everyone on the borrower's side of the table must look as honest as freshly scrubbed schoolboys. Cards played up, nothing hidden. Fourth, a good proposition. And fifth, lots of luck.

Once Hallsworth got Pepalasis off my back things got easier. The market had been picking up slowly for months. Interest rates fell, the pound measured up against the dollar, inflation slowed down, and the Chancellor took one hand out of people's pockets. And all because North Sea oil had saved another balance of payments crisis. Oil fever! Five years earlier if you'd said 'gusher' to a City man he'd have thought he was talking too much. Now his eyes lit up like lemons in a slot machine and he dribbled enough to put his cigar out.

Hallsworth was at the office a lot more during those months. He kept clear of our other interests, happy to leave them to me, and concentrated solely on my progress in raising the twenty million. That and keeping Pepalasis happy. The Greek was away for a good deal of the time, but always back in his Dorchester suite in time for his meetings with Hallsworth. I assumed that they made an appointment each time for two or three weeks later, but I didn't pay much attention, just relieved that Hallsworth was keeping Pepalasis under control and had persuaded him to modify the more outrageous of his demands.

People don't realize how quickly money and power change hands. For instance, in the sixties there were many sources of investment capital, amongst them, but far from dominant, the pension and life assurance funds. But by the summer of 1977 the pension boys found themselves controlling assests of sixty thousand million pounds. They had grown big. Very big. And there were a lot of them.

I knew most of the trustees and fund managers, friends from my days at Walpoles. Lunch with one, dinner with another. Slowly I cobbled a deal together. They were a nervous lot that summer. Harold Wilson was sniffing round the City at the head of a Royal Commission. Rumour was he thought the funds were stifling initiative by investing too much in gilt-edged and blue chips, that they should become a shade more adventurous, use just a little of their muscle to help new ventures. I calculated that twenty million was just little enough to qualify, and that's what I meant about timing.

Harry Smithers of the A.W.F fund was the first to commit himself, promising to put up five million for three years, subject to a favourable geologist's report. I leaked the news and within a fortnight couldn't go into a bar in the City without being pointed out as Mike Townsend, the man heading up the new secret mining and minerals consortium. It worked. By the end of June I had pledges for the full twenty million. All conditional on the geologist's report.

It was round about that time that I began to see more of Sue. She was between books, and able to spend more time with me, coming down for weekends at least twice a month. I had kept my promise and never mentioned her name to Hallsworth. It was awkward at times, leaving a meeting with him to go straight to her, and making sure that their visits to Hill Street never coincided, but I managed. And she and I often talked about him. It was difficult not to. She took an interest in the business and I'd told her about Pepalasis and how Hallsworth had taken him over. Told her everything really – except the prospect of half a million in a Swiss bank account.

It was during July that I took her on a long weekend to North Wales. The company's affairs were in good order and July's a quiet month anyway, holidays slipping forward ahead of the August shutdown. And I was really marking time. Waiting for the consortium to pick their geologist and for Pepalasis to name the date.

We left Hill Street just after lunch on the Friday and headed west, the countryside shimmering in the full heat of a rare summer's day. But at the Welsh border the sky turned overcast and by the time we pulled into the hotel car park at

Barmouth rain was sheeting down and closing in for the night. We took dinner early, had a few drinks and adjourned to bed, thankful that wet evenings on the Welsh coast provided some compensation.

The rain persisted through all of Saturday, steady, relentless, and solid enough to veil the sea fifty yards from our bedroom window. In the afternoon I borrowed an oilskin and went for a walk; Sue stayed behind with a book. I splashed up and down the promenade, eyes slit against the rain, enjoying myself like a kid out of school. I'd not been back to Barmouth since my days in the Army and perversely liked the place better in rain than in sunshine. I would have walked for longer but for a sense of guilt at leaving Sue to amuse herself, so after half an hour of it I trudged back, my feet squelching in my shoes with every step. Upstairs Sue was on the phone. I could hear her talking even as I stood in the corridor, one hand on the door handle, rain dripping onto the carpet from my sodden clothes.

'No, he's out,' she said. 'But I wouldn't think for much longer. It's bucketing down outside.' There was a pause. I opened the door and went in, just as she added. 'No don't worry, we won't be back until late on Monday.'

Then she saw me. Her eyes rounded with surprise and a faint flush came to her cheeks. 'Darling, you're soaked!' Fleeting confusion, then quickly back to the phone. 'No, no, of course not you, Aunty. My young man's just come in, that's all. Of course he's got his own room. He's just come in to let me know he's back.' She pulled a face at me, one hand over the mouthpiece, her shoulders shrugging in a gesture of hopelessness as she whispered 'Maiden aunts.'

I grinned, pulled my clothes off, threw them into a soggy heap in one corner and went into the bathroom for a hot soak. And a minute or two later Sue came in, as naked as I was.

'My aunt in Aberystwyth.' She massaged my shoulders, sitting on the edge of the bath facing me, her hands sliding down my back and pulling my face forward into the softness

71

of her body. 'I thought, as we were so near, perhaps we might go and see her tomorrow. But she's going to visit friends and won't be back until late Monday.'

I grunted, my body already responding to the caresses of her hands, brain switching off, senses taking over. I remembered thinking that I'd misheard the scrap of telephone conversation and then was past caring.

Sunday. And the rain kept coming. Not as fiercely as the day before but a steady grey drizzle which could soak clothing through in ten minutes. I didn't know what to do. By myself I would have walked the hills and enjoyed it, but I could hardly leave Sue alone all day. So we had an enormous Sunday lunch, log fires burning unseasonally in the dining room, too much food and drink, leaving us doped and drowsy and fit only to snooze the afternoon away.

I stirred at around four o'clock and began to think about Hill Street. About the work I could do if we left tonight, a day early. We might as well. The weather looked set and Sue hadn't as much as put her nose outside the door since we arrived. I felt her move beside me and turned on the bed to find her grey eyes watching me.

'Feel like going home?'

'Mmmm, I am home.' She stroked my face and inched her body into mine.

'No, I mean now. Tonight. You could stay at Hill Street and travel down to Winchester in the morning.'

I felt her stiffen and sensed as much as heard the sharp intake of breath. A minute later she was kissing and stroking me, whispering and moaning, her lips and tongue and mouth and hands taking over and her movements building to a crescendo of urgency as she felt me respond. She had always been passionate in lovemaking but nothing we had shared together was as abandoned and inventive as those next hours. She became every woman of a man's imagination. Dominant and demanding one minute, slavishly submissive the next. In turn, as coy as a girl giving herself for the very first time,

72

then as practised as a whore in a waterfront brothel. It wasn't just what she did with her body, not even what she did with mine, though God knows that was unbelievable. But her language, the words, her voice, movements, mannerisms. Everything was designed to tantalize and arouse until I throbbed for release, tenderly and love warm at times, rutting like an animal an hour later.

I think we stopped at around ten the next morning. Of course, we'd slept from time to time, but not much, judging from my puffed eyes and blotched face in the bathroom mirror. And my body told its own story. Long scratches, bites and bruises. I bathed, dressed and inspected myself, feeling like a criminal concealing evidence.

At noon we had a brunch of eggs and bacon, and an hour later I was stowing suitcases into the trunk of the car. The rain had stopped and a few patches of blue sky were breaking through the overcast, as if to hint that summer might be returning to North Wales just as we were leaving. I left Sue in the car and went back to settle the bill.

Once an accountant, always an accountant. There's nothing you can do about it. Put a column of figures in front of me and I add them up. I checked the bill as I reached for my wallet and credit cards. One item jarred. I looked up to catch the manager speculating on the kind of night I'd had. 'Bit much isn't it?' I nodded at the bill. 'Three pounds for a phone call to Aberystwyth.'

He coloured slightly, as if I'd caught him cheating. Or maybe he guessed I'd read his thoughts. 'It is that,' he took the bill, frowning hard as if to frighten the truth out of it. I waited while he went to the operator's cubby hole in the alcove under the stairs. He returned triumphant. 'Aberystwyth? I thought it a bit much myself when I heard that. But it was a London call that Madam made.' He laid heavy emphasis on the 'madam'. As a matter of fact we have the number here. We record 'em, see. Just in case of queries.' He gave me the number and, awkward with embarrassment, I paid the bill and left.

It wasn't until an hour later, as the car pulled smoothly up the long escarpment north of Stafford, that I realized whose telephone number it was. The first five numbers were the same as mine at Hill Street, making it local to that part of Mayfair. I glanced curiously at Sue and watched in fascination as one grey, untroubled eye winked slowly and the red lips pouted in a kiss. My answering smile must have seemed poor response. But at least it covered my confusion. As I wondered if her aunt stayed often at the Dorchester on Park Lane.

CHAPTER FOUR

We arrived back in Hill Street at about seven-thirty and took the tiny lift up to the top floor. Sue had insisted on a leisurely drive back, stopping for tea at Warwick and later, because she hadn't been there for years, calling in at Jack Straw's Castle on Hampstead Heath for a drink. Not that I minded. I wasn't hurrying. Her train left at eight-thirty and after seeing her off I planned to go directly to bed.

The ground floor entrance hall looked much as usual and neither of us gave it a second glance as we crossed to the lift. Even the elegance of the fourth floor lobby was undisturbed. But inside, the flat had been hit by a whirlwind.

'Oh my God!' Sue was a few paces ahead of me, a yard across the threshold, her hands to her face.

The front door opened directly onto the sitting room. There were two doors off, one to the dining room and kitchen, the other to the bedroom and bathroom. I almost threw up at the mess. Overturned tables, drawers ransacked, paintings torn from walls, ripped cushions scattering more feathers than a fox in a chicken run. The other rooms were as bad. Even the kitchen cupboards gaped open, groceries littered everywhere, sugar granules crunched under foot. The sickness gave way to anger.

'What are you doing?' Sue's eyes followed me to the telephone.

'Getting the police.' I was already dialling.

'Mike, wait!' She reached quickly, tugging my sleeve, her other hand closing on the receiver, breaking the connection. 'Please. Just a minute.'

I put the phone down and looked at her.

'They'll want statements,' she said urgently. 'From both of us. Darling, don't you understand? I'll have to give my name.'

'So?'

'Rupert will find out. I mean you're bound to tell him aren't you? About – this – this burglary. And then the police will be back and forth. Questions. Statements. All their damned procedures. Well, Rupert's just bound to find out about me, that's all.'

I think I was still staring at her, not knowing how to answer, when she added, 'Darling, if I go now? Catch a cab to Waterloo? After all, it's not as if I can add anything to what you say?'

It was so obviously true as to be unanswerable. We went downstairs, collected her case from the car, and I kissed her goodbye through the open window of the cab. 'I'll phone tomorrow,' she promised as the cab drew away, 'to find out what happened.'

Ten minutes later I had called the police and was making a tour of the downstairs offices. They had all been given the same treatment.

Two plainclothes men arrived within the hour. We went upstairs and drank whisky amidst the debris. Afterwards they dusted for fingerprints, took mine for comparison, found a broken skylight and generally got on with being detectives, while I restored at least superficial order to the sitting room. They returned as I was stacking books on shelves, accepted my offer of another whisky and settled down to watch me work.

The sergeant spoke first. 'Any idea who did this, sir?'

'I imagined it might be burglars.' It was past nine, I was tired and irritated, and it began to show.

'These weren't ordinary burglars, Mr Townsend.'

'That's comforting.'

'Well, from what you say sir, nothing's missing.'

'So they were inefficient or disappointed.'

The constable joined in. 'Doubt that, sir. They'd have done a lot more damage if they'd been disappointed.'

I was standing on a chair, working along the top row of the bookcase. 'More than this bloody mess?' I waved a hand at the chaos.

'Oh easily. People we know would have urinated up your walls.'

'Or shit on your carpets,' the other joined in.

'Nice friends.' I climbed down from the chairs and poured myself another scotch. 'So where do we go from here?'

The sergeant shrugged, watching me closely. 'Leaves another possibility, sir. They were looking for something specific. Something in particular.'

'I'm damned if I know what. There's never much cash up here. A few bob in the petty cash downstairs perhaps, but – '

'We've checked that, sir,' said the constable. 'It's still there. The cash box intact and undamaged.'

'What, then?'

'We were hoping you'd know that, sir,' the sergeant said, the faintest hint of suspicion in his voice. 'Our guess is some kind of document – from the mess they've made of the filing cabinets downstairs.'

I shook my head. 'Only business papers. Nothing which might be, well, valuable to anyone else – valuable enough for this.'

They had finished their drinks and were going. 'We'll call back tomorrow, sir. You'll have had more chance to check everything by then.'

But I guessed. Even as I was showing them out at the front door. I could hardly get back upstairs fast enough. I remembered locking my briefcase away into the cupboard next to the bookcases in the sitting room on Friday. I had been working on papers when Sue had arrived and I'd shoved them back into the briefcase, knowing I'd need them again at the end of the weekend.

The briefcase was still there. Thank God for that! Gasping with relief I reached for it, springing the catches, lifting the lid. But the file had gone. *The complete bloody* file! All of my notes, calculations, minutes of meetings, everything. Everything I knew about Pepalasis. I groped for a chair as a new thought hit me. Now somebody else had the map of the island.

CHAPTER FIVE

'I still can't understand it. I left at five-thirty and you got here two hours later. Two hours? To create this!' Jean waved a hand at the mess in the general office.

I took her elbow and guided her through to my office, closing the door behind us. Jean Wilmslow was secretary, office manager, right hand woman and friend. She'd been with me at Walpoles for three years and had packed her bags to follow me as if it were the most natural thing in the world for her to do. If Jean had ever found a 'great man', to get behind she'd been living proof of the saying, but in the absence of one she made do with me and my life was a sight easier and a lot more productive as a result of it.

I never understood why she hadn't got a regular man in

tow. Twenty-five, honey brown hair, blue eyes, good figure, tall, I guessed five foot seven in her stockinged feet. We'd been out together occasionally. Dinner after working late, theatre when I'd got tickets and Sue hadn't been able to get down. I enjoyed our evenings a good deal more than I cared to admit and would have asked her out more often but for the rules. My rules. Never get involved with the hired help. And although Jean was a lot more than that, it was the nearest the rules got to classifying her.

She was everyone's favourite, too. Not just mine. Clients, business associates, staff, everyone succumbed. Even Hallsworth found time during each visit to spend fifteen minutes with her in the room next to mine. 'And you were the last to leave the office?' I was asking her.

'Aren't I always?' She crossed one long leg over the other, a hand automatically adjusting the hem of her skirt.

The ten o'clock conference with Jean. Coffee, the morning mail, a resumé of the day's appointments. Daily routine. Except that morning we were holding it an hour earlier because of the burglary, with the office cleaners waiting outside for instructions about what to keep and what to throw away.

'The police will be round later,' I said. 'To find out what's missing. I'll sort the mess out in here while you organize the staff in the other offices. After that perhaps you'll give me a hand in the flat?'

'You won't have time,' she shook her head. 'Have you seen your diary?'

I scowled at the desk top, strewn with papers ripped from still-open drawers. The diary was amongst them somewhere.

She saved me the trouble of finding it. 'Mr Hallsworth will be here at ten. And Harry Smithers of A.W.F phoned twice on Friday and again yesterday. They've appointed their man for the Pepalasis project and he's anxious for you to meet him. It sounded urgent so I slotted him in for two-thirty.'

I was both surprised and relieved. I'd not expected

Hallsworth until Friday, but at least his rearranged schedule meant I could tell him about the missing documents.

He arrived on the dot of ten, and as usual I told him everything. Except the bit about Sue being with me in North Wales. And still with me when I discovered the burglary.

'Pepalasis will throw a bloody fit,' he groaned. 'He never wanted to part with that map in the first place.'

'It's no damn use to anyone,' I said defensively. 'There's no reference to show where the island is.'

'But the areas are marked! Where he found diamonds.'

I shrugged. 'So? It's still useless without the island's location.'

He paced the room in a mounting fever of agitation.

'Suppose whoever's got the map follows him?'

'Are you kidding? Wherever the bloody place is, it's not in the middle of Hyde Park. How the hell can anyone follow him?'

He stopped pacing and stared at me as if I was being especially stupid. 'If they know where he is now they can follow him. It's that simple.'

'Rubbish!' I lost my temper, partly from guilt that the documents were stolen while in my possession, but mainly because I thought his theory ridiculous. It was the nearest we'd come to a full blown row since we started.

'I'd better let Pepalasis know.' He picked up the phone. 'I'll go straight round to see him.'

'Want me to come?'

He shook his head, waiting to be connected.

'Good,' I growled. 'I've got enough to do. What with the police coming and then this geologist from the consortium.'

'The police? What are you going to tell them?' He turned back to the telephone. 'Mr Pepalasis please, suite two eleven.' A pause. 'I see. Well, when he's free perhaps you'll give him a message? Rupert Hallsworth will join him for lunch. That's right. Thank you.' He hung up and looked at me. 'You were saying something about the police? Of course, you'll not say anything about the map or the papers to the police.'

'Why not?'

'Are you mad? Next thing the evening papers will have it and we'll have a bloody gold rush on our hands. We daren't risk the publicity.'

He was making a mountain out of a molehill as far as I was concerned and I told him as much, but after arguing for half an hour I agreed to say nothing to the police. And after that he left, no doubt as irritated with me as I was with him. So I was still in a sour mood when the detective sergeant and constable arrived, both seemingly hot with anticipation.

'Well, sir – discovered anything?'

'We left that for you.'

'With your help, sir,' the sergeant reproved patiently. 'Is there anything missing?'

I shook my head. 'Mind, we haven't sorted everything yet. We could use a bit more time.'

'Perhaps we could give your people a hand, sir?' the constable offered. 'We need another look round ourselves.'

I rang for Jean, glad to get rid of them. The sergeant checked himself as he followed her to the door. 'We'll want a formal statement from you later of course, sir.' I nodded and he half turned away, and then he added, 'By the way, you did say you were alone, didn't you? When you discovered the burglary?'

'That's right.' I feigned preoccupation with the papers on the desk, anxious for the police to be gone. After a second's pause I looked up, dismissively, and straight into Jean's eyes. There was no escaping the surprised disbelief in her expression. It was written all over her face. She hesitated, as if about to say something, thought better of it, and led them from the room.

I went to the sideboard in search of a drink. Lies are the refuge of incompetents. Or so I've always believed, priding myself on controlling my affairs so as to have little need of them. But now secrecy was leading to evasion and halftruths turning to downright deceit. Not telling Hallsworth about Sue. Misleading the consortium about the commitment fee. Two lies to the police about the burglary. At least one suspected by Jean. It was beginning to get complicated, one lie inevitably leading to another in the nature of things.

I was still nursing the drink when the telephone buzzed. 'Mr Townsend? My name's McNeil. Kirk McNeil. Harry Smithers will have mentioned me.'

I frowned, and was about to contradict him when I realized he must be the geologist. 'I've an appointment with you at two-thirty,' he said. 'But as I'm just round the corner now, and as it's almost lunchtime, I wondered if you were free to join me?'

I jumped at the chance to escape from the office. 'Where are you?'

'Right now I'm in the lobby of the Dorchester.'

Good God, was the Dorchester the only hotel in London? First Pepalasis. With Hallsworth there by now. And now Kirk McNeil. My memory stirred. *And* Sue's maiden aunt, if you believed fairy stories. Never had my preference for Trader Vic's in the Hilton been greater and after promising McNeil I'd be there in ten minutes, I told Jean and left.

With a name like Kirk McNeil I half expected a giant Scot in a kilt. But he was three inches shorter than me with something of the Greek's broad shoulders and strong arms about him. A brown weathered face, bright eyes webbed with wrinkles from searching a thousand horizons; wearing a grey suit and a friendly smile.

He told me about himself over lunch and I enjoyed listening, liking him from the start. His Scot's burr was almost undetectable after a lifetime spent overseas, and if anything his accent sounded more American for most of the time. He was totally without complacency, but exuded the confidence of a man who knows his own worth and doesn't waste time envying others theirs. His business card described him as a mining consultant and from the conversation, I gathered he'd mined anything and everything just about everywhere.

'How did you become a consultant?' I wanted to know. 'Presumably you're some kind of geologist?'

'What are my formal qualifications, you mean?' He grinned. 'None really. But I couldn't earn the fees I do without a fair knowledge of geology, petrology, minerology and geochemistry, for instance.'

It was a typical answer. A disarming disclaimer qualified by a whole slab of expertise which left me bewildered. I ran into another surprise when I asked how he became involved in our project.

'Harry Smithers cabled me. I was in British Columbia when he tracked me down. Then we spoke on the phone and he persuaded me back here to look at your job. Said it wouldn't take more than a month.'

'You've met Harry before?'

'Sure. Australia. Kalgoorlie and Boulder in seventy-one. I was retained by Western Mining then and they asked me to take Harry round their nickel interests for a couple of weeks. Nice fellow.'

I nodded. 'So Harry's briefed you on what's going on?'

McNeil grinned. 'Better than that. We couldn't get hold of you on Friday and Harry knew where your Greek was staying, so I've been to see him for myself. Just left him when I phoned you as a matter of fact.'

I began to feel out of touch. 'So now you know as much as I do,' I said, and then I asked, 'What did you make of Pepalasis?'

'Y'mean do I believe his story?' McNeil frowned. 'It's possible. Just.'

My hopes soared sky high and it took an effort to keep the excitement out of my voice when I spoke to him. 'But what about this refusal to disclose the location of the island? Doesn't that strike you – as, well – odd?'

He shook his head. 'Don't you believe it. In this business secrecy's everything. Everyone will tell you stories about claim jumping and most of them are true. And it gets worse. You can be a couple of hundred miles deep in Western Australian desert, drop your pants for a crap and some flaming helicopter will buzz over from the next hill to see what's going on.'

Excitement flickered into alarm as I remembered the missing map and the tongue-lashing Hallsworth had given me earlier. I decided not to mention it, at least until I knew McNeil better, so I settled back in my chair and encouraged him to tell me about the mining business. And I couldn't have found a better teacher.

'What about Pepalasis?' I asked at one point. 'From the way he talks he's done some mining in his time hasn't he?'

'Superficial,' McNeil sounded positive. 'Oh, I daresay he's knocked around a few mines. But he's more real estate than prospector.'

I must have raised my eyebrows because he went on to explain. 'There are lots of guys calling themselves prospectors who are mainly pegging blocks, you'd call it staking claims I imagine. And then selling on. Reckon our friend Aristotle's one of them.'

'But he told me he wants to mine himself?'

'Yeah, he told me that too. Damned if I believe him though.'

We talked for a couple of hours and it was past three-thirty by the time we left the restaurant. McNeil was catching the evening flight to Glasgow and spending a day with relatives, but he promised to call me as soon as he got back to town on Thursday. And on the way back to Hill Street I was more excited than I'd been since I met Hallsworth. Whatever my earlier reservations had been, they weren't shared by the experts. That much was becoming increasingly obvious. Suppose it came off? And we discovered the biggest diamond field in the world? There'd be an absolute fortune on the

83

table. Just waiting to be picked up. Suddenly the prospect of half a million in Zurich stopped being a pipe dream and came a whole lot closer to reality.

Then I ran into Pepalasis. He was sitting on the chesterfield in my office, worry beads clicking like a demented cricket and looking sadder than a man in a condemned cell. And Hallsworth was doing his pacing bit. Up and down the same stretch of carpet like a ploughman digging the world's deepest furrow.

'So who's having the baby?' I asked, and wished I hadn't.

'Ari's worried sick about this burglary,' Hallsworth snapped. 'To the point of calling the whole deal off.'

I sat down. Ari now, was it? Ari and Rupe no doubt. Very pally. But the threat to kill the deal worried me. Just when I was getting used to the idea of being a millionaire. 'Look, I know it's a hell of a shock,' I said, trying to calm him down. 'But I can't believe the burglary had anything to do with the map. Dammit, hardly anyone knew I had it! Something else must have been taken. I can't think what, but Jean's still checking.'

'Jean's finished,' Hallsworth shook his head. 'Nothing else is missing.'

'Oh,' I sagged in the chair. 'Does Jean know?'

'She thinks you've got Ari's stuff in the flat if that's what you mean. And I suggest she's left thinking that.'

'Yes. I suppose so. I've been out. Meeting the consortium's geologist.' I wondered why I was making excuses.

'We know,' Hallsworth said, and to my relief he sat down. But he still looked very angry. 'We've got an ultimatum on our hands. Ari's leaving for the island on Saturday. The deal with the consortium must be wrapped up by then. And you and this McNeil guy have to be on the same plane out of London. Otherwise no deal.'

'But it's Tuesday now,' I complained. 'Maybe Harry Smithers won't agree –'

'He'll bloody well have to agree,' Hallsworth interrupted hotly. 'And there's something else. A few other conditions. I've made a list of them. It's on your desk. As I said, we're dealing with an ultimatum.'

I glanced at Pepalasis who scowled back. 'My island's threatened,' he said simply. 'I must get there as quickly as possible.'

'I've been on to Durbeville's,' Hallsworth interrupted with brisk efficiency. 'Poignton's standing by if you want him. And Jean phoned Smithers and he'll see you at ten in the morning. Meanwhile, I suggest you say nothing to the police and the minimum necessary to Smithers, providing he understands the urgency. And drop everything else until we've put this one together.' He stood up. 'I'm going to walk Ari back to the Dorchester now, but I'll phone you later. Okay?'

Okay or not, they were going, Pepalasis rising to his feet as if controlled by a string from Hallsworth's pocket. At the door, Hallsworth hesitated, let Pepalasis walk ahead into the lobby, half closed the door between them and whispered to me, 'He's more frightened than a virgin at a gang bang. I think I can calm him down, if you can swing the consortium into line. But Christ, Mike – we've got to deliver. And fast!'

He was gone before I could reply. I settled behind the desk to read the handwritten list of new conditions, knowing I wouldn't like any of them and expecting the consortium to like them even less. And by the time I reached the last one, the optimism I'd felt earlier had vanished. As far as I could see, the deal was as dead as a lost island.

CHAPTER SIX

Wednesday passed in a flurry of meetings. Harry Smithers first, then round to Durbeville's, and finally a six hour marathon back at the A.W.F. offices as Poignton, Harry and I tried to reconcile ourselves to the Greek's extra demands. Harry didn't like them and I can't say I blamed him. But he didn't turn them down out of hand the way I imagined he would, and by six o'clock Poignton was dictating the basis of a compromise to an assistant, while Harry and I sipped sherry and listened. The lawyer earned his corn that day, stripping the agreement of the inessentials and simplifying it to a dozen clauses. Most of them gave Pepalasis what he wanted and about all we had salvaged was our right to withdraw if McNeil's report was unfavourable. Still, it was the best we could devise. Harry would have to sell it to his members. McNeil would need to confirm his acceptance. And I had to persuade Pepalasis that it was the nearest anyone in their right minds would go to meeting his terms. If everyone said 'yes' together, the agreement would be signed on Friday and I'd be on a plane to God knows where on Saturday.

I phoned Pepalasis at the Dorchester. He sounded more relaxed than I had expected and invited me cheerfully enough to join him for dinner, even mentioning that Rupert might be calling in as well. I accepted and said I'd be there by seven-thirty, glad that Hallsworth might be along in support. After that I had another sherry while the draft was typed, caught a cab to Hill Street, had a quick wash and brush up, changed my shirt and walked the two hundred yards to the Dorchester.

I went directly up to suite two-eleven. Surprisingly there was no answer to my knock, and I stood uncertainly in the corridor for a minute or two. I wondered if Pepalasis might be waiting in the American bar downstairs, then I knocked again, harder this time, hearing music from the other side of the door. But apart from that, nothing. I half turned, thinking to check at the desk in the lobby. A final rap on the door with my knuckles, a quick rattle of the handle. And surprise – as the door opened under the pressure of my hand.

The sitting room looked much as mine had when I returned from North Wales. Ransacked! I stepped inside and closed the door quietly behind me, half imagining the burglar still in one of the other rooms. Then six paces at a charge to take me through the open door into the dining room. The same chaos. Four quick steps into the bedroom. Music blared full volume from the bedside speakers, wardrobes gaped, drawers hung empty on their runners, clothes piled high on the bed, linings ripped from jackets, laundry scattered. I fumbled with the radio, turning the switch the wrong way, making it worse before killing the noise. I sensed someone. But saw no-one. Only heard the sound of water. Cascading water. Torrents of water. Bath water.

Pepalasis lay on his back in the bath. Fully dressed except for his jacket. The water around his body was stained red. I looked at the taps, stupidly expecting to see them pouring blood. The level of the bath was chest high and rising. The Greek's eyes were closed, his nose was bruised and swollen, and a deep gash spewed blood from his forehead. There was *no chain?* A chain to the bath plug? I plunged an arm elbow deep to find the plug and felt only smooth metal, unyielding under my prising fingers. At the other end of the bath I got both hands under Pepalasis's armpits and heaved, not knowing whether he was dead or alive. His body rose a few inches, sliding up the back of the bath, but the weight was too much and I let go, gasping for breath. The level of water lapped his chin. A second's panic. The taps! Turn the bloody taps off! I sat panting on the edge of the bath, water and blood dripping from my clothes. The bath stopper? Of course! Controlled by the lever between the taps. I pushed it, choking with relief as the level fell rapidly, my ears pounding with the sounds of my rasping breath and the escaping rush of water. Pepalasis groaned.

Then I heard another sound. From the bedroom? I froze. Only my eyes moving, hunting in vain for some kind of weapon. A muffled curse from outside. Chance it. Count on his surprise being greater than mine. I moved quickly back into the bedroom, fists balled and ready. The room was empty. But there had been a noise. I was sure of it. The dining room? The door, closed when I'd left it, was now half open. For the love of God, find a weapon! but I was already throwing the door wide open and charging through. A man with his back to me in the opposite doorway. Tall, my height. He began to turn the instant I decided to hit him and ask questions later. And he was turning fast as I crossed the room. Turning just fast enough to stop me dead in my tracks. Hallsworth!

'What the bloody hell?' I think we both said it together. I did a quick about face. 'The bathroom. Quickly. Pepalasis – beaten up.'

A few minutes later we had Pepalasis on the bed, sodden clothing ruining the silk cover. He was conscious now, groaning and swearing in Greek as Hallsworth sponged his face to examine the cut on his forehead. I got the brandy bottle from the sitting room and hurried back with three glasses, not knowing whose need was the greatest.

We got the whole story fifteen minutes later, Someone had knocked on the door at about seven. Pepalasis opened it, thinking it was me running early. Two men, both wearing stocking masks, had hit him before he could even cry out. After that he couldn't remember much. Except noises – music blaring, rushing water, more punches – and then oblivion.

Hallsworth took over. Using the telephone in the sitting room he made all the arrangements while I helped the Greek to find a suit with a lining to its name. His wound had stopped bleeding and though unsteady on his feet he was strong and recovering fast, helped by the brandy and a hand from me.

Ten minutes later we left. Crossing the main lobby, experiencing the same sensation as I used to have on Army night patrols. A burning conviction that someone would jump me at any second. But no-one did. And minutes later we were both in a cab heading towards Sloane Square.

Hallsworth paid for three rooms he had booked at the Carlton Tower, and after showing ourselves around reception for five minutes, we went upstairs. Not that we stayed for long. The bell boy had hardly whistled back down the corridor when Hallsworth was on the phone to the desk, telling them to get a cab down to the underground car park.

'Order food and drinks for three, Mike,' he said to me. 'And stay in your room all evening.' Suddenly his expression softened into a smile. 'By the way, I forgot to ask, how did your meetings go today?'

Wordlessly I fumbled for the draft agreement and handed it to him.

'I'll phone you later,' he said, turning to Pepalasis. 'Come on Ari, let's get you out of town.'

'Hang on – ' was about as far as I got, before the door closed. I was *fuming*! And pretty mixed up about Hallsworth. His behaviour seemed absurdly melodramatic. He'd even spent the cab ride staring out of the window – in case we were being followed! And now this business? Taking three rooms here when I had a perfectly comfortable flat a mile away. Crazy! All right, two burglaries and a beating up were reasons enough for caution, I'd agreed to that. So call the police. Instead of this cloak-and-dagger nonsense. But he'd taken over so completely, muttering all the time about publicity, that I'd never had time to finish the argument.

I was still simmering two hours later when the phone rang.

'Comfortable?' It was Hallsworth.

'Where the devil are you?'

'Tell you tomorrow. Any callers?'

'Oh sure. I'm having a bloody party up here.'

'It's only for tonight. Anyway I've got some good news for you. Better dust your passport down. Pepalasis has agreed the contract.'

I tried to hide my exasperation but only succeeded in sounding grumpy. 'Let's hope Harry Smithers talks his people round. And that McNeil buys it.'

'You'll persuade them.' He sounded full of confidence. 'Well have a good night – and pleasant dreams.'

But the dreams came later. I was too excited to sleep. Two days and we could be on our way. I could be on my way. To half a million.

CHAPTER SEVEN

'Pepalasis must be stark, staring mad!' McNeil snapped, not even bothering to sit down. 'It's like asking a doctor if you're sick and then refusing an examination. I'm not allowed to take so much as a bucket and spade to this island. You know that, don't you? No instruments! No facilities! Damn all! How the hell does he think I work? Sniff with my bloody nose?'

I sighed and let him shout at me for half an hour. It was to be expected, and in truth my sympathies were on his side. It would be his name and reputation on that report. He had good reason to be nervous.

He had telephoned as soon as he had arrived back from Glasgow, and then had come straight round to Hill Street. Well, almost straight round. Unfortunately Harry Smithers had got to him first with news of the added restrictions.

I replayed some of Hallsworth's arguments. 'Look at it this way. Who loses? If you turn the project down Pepalasis doesn't get his money and he's wasted a hell of a lot of time for nothing. He must be damned sure he can prove it's viable.'

'Crap! Either way I lose. Suppose there's some evidence, I tell Harry to go ahead. On little more than a qualified guess. Then we strike out. Mine proves a dud. What happens? My name stinks. Right? On the other hand I can't test properly, so I tell Harry to cop out. Then your Greek raises the wind elsewhere and hits a bonanza. Result? My name stinks again. No, I'm sorry, Mike. No way. Count me out!'

He meant it. Jean brought coffee and I did my soothing best to persuade him to change his mind, but he was sticking. And still sticking when Hallsworth phoned. I reported the state of play and he promised to get tough with Pepalasis and call back. McNeil and I waited in silence.

Hallsworth was back within half an hour. 'I've put an idea to Ari and he's bought it. Let's simplify things. If you actually discover diamonds and bring them back, the deal goes ahead. Fix a figure. Say a hundred grand's worth, or whatever McNeil thinks reasonable. Actual diamonds. Makes it easier all round.'

'And Pepalasis agreed?'

'As a fiinal concession. But Mike, he's at the absolute limit.'

'I'll call you back. Where can I reach you?'

'Don't worry. I'll call you. In about an hour. Give you time to check it out with Harry Smithers.'

I told McNeil about the new proposals. 'Takes the pressure off you,' I pointed out. 'Pepalasis puts his proof where his mouth is.'

McNeil turned purple. 'I'm going to tell you a few things about mining diamonds,' he snarled, jabbing a finger at me. 'It's not your subject, so I won't bore the pants off you with a goddamned lecture, but it's time you learned the facts of life. To start with, have you got any idea of the diamond content of diamond ore?'

I squirmed. 'Kirk, is this necessary?'

'Necessary!' he roared. 'I'll say it's damn well necessary. Because it strikes me you think we're going on a bloody picnic. The average content of diamond rich ore is something like one part in twenty million. Get it? One in twenty million. Can you imagine –'

'But surely – ?'

91

'Jesus! Grant me patience. Will you listen? In two thousand years of mining about a hundred and thirty tons of diamonds have been recovered. That's all. And to get it about three thousand million tons of rocks, sand and gravel have been sorted. Begin to get the picture?'

'Of course, I understand –'

'Understand!' His roar rattled the windows. 'You don't understand a pick from your prick. But you bloody well will. Listen, looking for diamonds is hard and I'll tell you why. For a start they aren't found in the rocks in which they were formed, like most minerals. So you've got three types of deposit. Alluvial, conglomerate rock and volcanic pipes. All alluvials are derived from undisclosed pipes. Pipes whose mouths are covered with more recent strata – maybe the result of geological upheaval at some time – follow me?'

I nodded and remained silent, thinking that if I didn't add fuel to his temper he'd burn himself out.

'For instance,' he said, his voice dropping to a level which would at least let them get back to work again in Grosvenor Square. 'Diamonds have been found in the States. Not many, but some, and all over. But there aren't any pipes there. So how'd they get there? Most geologists will tell you that they were carried down by ice-age glaciers from Canada. That's possible. Pipes *have* been discovered in Canada. But none worth mining. So you see the next problem? Finding kimberlite pipes doesn't guarantee finding diamonds. Christ, I've known pipes as barren as a doctored cat. So our Greek's pipes prove nothing. It's just a starting point, that's all.'

'So you make tests?' I suggested.

'Tests!' he slammed a fist on the desk top. 'Damn right we make tests. *Magnetic* tests. *Gravitational* tests. *Electrical* tests. *Radioactive* tests. How many tests d'you want, for God's sake?'

'You're the teacher.'

He scowled, still angry. 'And after testing we sink shafts.

And boreholes. Shafts for shallow tests – boreholes deeper. Some go down as far as seven *thousand* metres! And d'you know what a borehole costs? Anything from fifty to a hundred quid a metre. You're the accountant – you work it out. And while you're doing it, remember this. Even the oil boys, with all their muscles and experience, reckon to drill twenty dry holes for every one that strikes oil.'

He slumped into a chair, red-faced and truculent, but drained of the hot blast of temper. 'So getting back to our tricky Greek,' he growled. 'We're to go to an island. Make no tests. Sink no shafts. Carry no instruments. And find ourselves some bloody diamonds.'

'If we don't,' I pointed out tentatively, 'it's his loss.'

Jean brought fresh coffee and I stuck at it like a politician on the hustings. Accountants and bankers generally make bad salesmen but I read Dale Carnegie once, and maybe it helped. I plugged away with the argument that the only loser could be Pepalasis himself. And I tinkered up some compromise clauses of my own, lumbering the Greek not only with the expenses of the trip but a fifty thousand pound penalty if we came back empty-handed. Only a mad man or someone super confident would sign a deal like that. And when we phoned Smithers, with McNeil on an extension for a three-way conversation, Harry jibbed. Accepting my items but adding one of his own. If we were not to be allowed to take instruments, we would have to come back with diamonds *and* a general assessment from McNeil, before the money went in.

Hallsworth phoned on the dot of twelve. I gave him the good news. And the bad. Then listened while he relayed it to Pepalasis in the background. Even McNeil, more than a yard from the phone, heard the explosion of temper at the other end. But Hallsworth could charm the birds from the trees when he chose and ten or twelve minutes later he had actually got agreement. Provided that we left on Saturday. We arranged for all parties to meet at the A.W.F. offices the next afternoon to sign the contracts, and then he hung up. I felt relieved and triumphant – and prepared to believe it when it happened. After which McNeil thawed out enough to stand me lunch at Scotts to celebrate, and then he left in a cab for the City.

I walked back from the restaurant in Mount Street, and was climbing the steps to the front door of the office when, quite suddenly, the hairs on the back of my neck pricked. Odd feeling, the sensation you get when you look up expectedly and catch someone watching you. I stared back across the street. A postman, passers by, a female traffic warden. The normal scene. Dismissing it, I hurried up to the offiice, planning a busy afternoon with Jean. She was on an outside call when I buzzed, so I left the key down, which meant a light would show on her desk telling her that I wanted her when she finished.

Idly I looked out of the window, lighting a cigarette, thinking what might crop up during my absence. And then I saw him. Medium height, brown hair, middle thirties. Getting into the passenger seat of the car parked fifty yards away. Pointing down Hill Street towards Berkeley Square. Facing our building. I knew I'd seen him before. Recently. And seconds later it came to me. The Dorchester lobby yesterday. And Trader Vic's on Tuesday when I had lunched with McNeil. Something twisted in my stomach and I sat staring out of the window, almost sweating with alarm. It was minutes before I got the nerves sufficiently under control to look for a rational explanation. Probably just someone else who worked in the area? There were dozens of half-familiar faces around the place. People who used the restaurants and bars locally. I grunted and turned away, telling myself to forget it before I ended up in the same stupid state as Pepalasis.

If the car had driven away I'd have thought no more of it. Jean came in and we immersed ourselves in work until three-thirty when the office junior brought tea and Jean went back to the office to get a file. I looked out of the window. The car was still there. Complete with its two occupants.

Jean returned as I reached a decision. 'I'm going out for a minute. Forgot to get cigarettes.'

'I've got some. And a spare pack in my desk.'

'Oh.' There was nothing for it but to tell her. 'Look, I think someone's playing a joke on me. All very silly really. Come over to the window a minute, will you. No, not too close. See that car down there? The blue one? Well watch what happens when I go out. I'll only be ten minutes.'

I walked quickly. Crossing to the south side of the street, passing the blue Fiat close enough to touch it, eyes straight ahead, resisting the urge to sneak a quick glance. Across South Audley Street into Park Lane, left fifty yards and into the tobacconist's. I paused, browsing through magazines, half hoping that the man I had recognized would follow me into the shop. Nothing. I moved round the racks to get a better view of the street outside. The usual scurry of pedestrians against a backcloth of red buses and black cabs. But no eyes peering curiously in through the plate glass window. I bought a newspaper and moved from the counter pretending to read an inside page. A woman bought some tissues. Followed by a man for cigarettes and a boy for chocolate. I reached for a magazine, thinking that I had walked too quickly, needing to allow time to pass, give him a chance to catch up. My eyes darted from the glossy page every time the door opened. A smartly dressed matron with blue rinsed hair, buying a road map of London and asking the whereabouts of the Tate in flat American. A thin man in a shiny suit buying cigarettes. Then a gap. Minutes passed, five, ten. Nothing. Except the probe of the assistant's eye hostile with suspicion.

Suddenly the whole performance seemed absurd. I bought a couple of packs of cigarettes and left, continuing on round the block, back to Hill Street and up the steps to the office. Hurriedly I climbed the stairs to my own office, feeling incredibly stupid, embarrassed by my own behaviour.

'You were longer than ten minutes,' Jean said, accusingly. 'Nearer twenty-five.'

'Sorry.' I almost blushed as I sat behind my desk, anxious to resume work.

'Well? Who is he?'

'Who's who?'

'The driver of that car. The man who followed you?'

CHAPTER EIGHT

Jean and I worked until six when I asked her out to dinner. I felt the need of company, and hers would be a bonus. Being followed had left me edgy, and I cursed Hallsworth for not letting me know his whereabouts, oddly sure that he would know what to do about it.

While Jean went home to change I waited in the flat. She promised to be back in an hour but I allowed an hour and a half; efficiency personified in the office was one thing, a woman getting ready for an evening out – another.

The car had gone. I watched from the fourth floor windows and wondered about it. About them – who they might be – what they wanted? If they were the burglars why hang about watching the building? If they were the men who attacked Pepalasis what did they want from me? I remembered Hallsworth's agitation. It had seemed ridiculous at the time. Now I wasn't so sure.

Jean arrived at about eight. A cab door slammed in the street seconds before the door bell buzzed. The flat was fitted with a security lock and an intercom so I could open the front door from upstairs after identifying the caller. She looked stunning, more elegant than I'd ever seen her. We had a couple of drinks and then walked across to the Twenty-One Club to dine on the terrace.

'You still haven't told me,' she said, 'who that man was?'

'I don't know.'

'But you said? Someone playing a joke?' Her blue eyes rounded with suspicion. 'Not that I believed you.'

'Oh?'

'Something's going on, isn't it? The burglary. Then that man Pepalasis in the office the other day – as nervous as a kitten. You're the boss of course, but –'

There was no-one I liked more, trusted more, who was more discreet, more loyal than Jean. So I filled in the gaps. About the missing map. Pepalasis being worked over. Even me staying at the Carlton Tower last night.

'Mike, you've got to go to the police.'

'Hallsworth's dead against it. Afraid that news of the Pepalasis project might get into general circulation.' I cheered up and tried to make light of it, as much for her benefit as mine. 'Anyway, if this thing's signed tomorrow and we go off to the island, no doubt it will be all sorted out.'

I was glad to talk to her about it. You can't work closely with someone for four years and start having secrets. Not someone you like as much as I liked Jean. It doesn't work. And she was nobody's fool, and if she was going to be in charge while I was away, it seemed only fair to put her on her guard.

We had a coffee and brandy, but when I suggested one for the road she shook her head. 'But you could twist my arm to have a coffee back at the flat.'

I was surprised. It was past eleven and whenever we'd been out before she'd refused any suggestion of coming back afterwards.

At Hill Street she fixed coffee while I poured brandy, fiddled with the hi-fi and considered our relationship. Dinner had been a tonic and I felt relaxed and unwound for the first time that day. And she looked especially beautiful. She had done her hair differently and the dress she wore had been exciting me all evening. The dress and the way she moved inside it. Rules seem damned silly at times and the urge to break one had never been stronger.

She might have read my mind because she blushed when she spoke. 'Don't misinterpret this, but I've got a proposition to make. Suppose I stay here tonight? It seems silly not to. Trudging back to Fulham and turning round first thing in the morning.'

I was delighted. Triumphant. The flat only had one bedroom and Jean knew it. The perfect ending to a pleasant evening. I moved closer on the sofa, an arm encircling her shoulders. When we kissed, her lips were soft and yielding and responding. But as it ended she pushed me away. 'You're doing it,' she said, eyes amused, her hands intercepting mine like Spitfires climbing to meet Messerschmitts.

'So were you.'

'I meant that you were misinterpreting.'

'I'm easily confused. Besides I've only got the one bedroom.'

'I've slept on sofas before.'

'But I couldn't permit it. It would be – unchivalrous.'

'Thank you. Then I'll have the bed, and you can have the sofa.'

I glared as she kissed me lightly and darted back out of reach. 'Complications,' she said shaking her head, slowly, sadly almost.

Then the telephone rang. I got up and crossed to the bookcase, cursing the interruption. It was Sue.

'Oh hello.' I started guiltily, my eyes finding Jean, wondering if she guessed who it was. Jean knew Sue, at least knew of her, from occasional messages left at the office, knew she'd stayed at the flat, at least guessed she'd been with me in North Wales.

'I'm sorry it's late, darling,' Sue was saying. 'I've been working – didn't notice the time. I phoned earlier but you were out.'

'Yes – dinner – er, how are you?'

Jean smiled knowingly, blew a kiss, mouthed the word 'complications' and went into the bedroom. I ground my teeth as I watched her go.

Sue prattled on for a minute or two before reaching the point. 'I was thinking of coming this weekend? Unless you're frightfully busy.'

'I don't think I'll be here. The Pepalasis project.'

'Oh, darling, how wonderful. Treasure Island at last. You must be thrilled out of your mind. Do you know where it is yet?'

'No, and I don't think I will until we get there.' I was only half concentrating, my mind back in Barmouth and her telephone call to the Dorchester. It seemed such a silly, unnecessary lie.

'Darling, is anything wrong?' Sue was asking. 'Are you worrying about anything?'

Always damned questions. Forever wanting to know. Once it had flattered me. Now it seemed a perpetual inquisition. I watched Jean emerge from the bedroom, toss sheets and blankets onto the sofa and disappear out to the lobby. Then I heard the hum of the lift door. I frowned, wondering why she was going downstairs when she was staying.

I spent a few minutes finishing the one-sided telephone conversation. Sue was bubbling as usual, but my responses were flat and stilted. It wasn't just because Jean was in the flat, but ever since the Barmouth episode I had been plagued with memories of Bob Harrison's red face as he protested that no Ballantyne had ever served in Singapore – let alone died there. The discovery of her lies had helped me to decide to end a relationship which had spluttered on for a couple of years without really going anywhere. But not, I decided, over the telephone.

She promised to call again in a fortnight and giggled her

way to the finish. 'And send me a card. Or a least bring me back a parrot. And some pieces of eight.'

I replaced the telephone as Jean returned, carrying a suitcase.

'You planned to stay?' I was amazed, realizing that the suggestion hadn't sprung from the mood of the moment.

She blushed furiously, holding me at arm's length as I took the case from her. 'Mike, don't rush it, please. It's just that I knew something was wrong. Even before you told me.'

'And you've come to protect me?'

'And don't laugh either. But sometimes, two people together –'

The phone rang again. Twelve-thirty at night and suddenly the whole blasted world had to speak to me!

'Mr Townsend?' A man's voice, not one I recognized.

'Yes – who's this?'

'My name doesn't matter, Mr Townsend. Just a well-wisher. With a proposition.'

My night for propositions! I threw a quick glance at Jean, knowing whose I preferred. 'Look, who is this?'

'Patience, Mr Townsend. And a chance to earn some money. Big money.'

Something prompted me to wave at Jean, pointing to the telephone, then the bedroom, hoping she would understand. She left as I asked, 'Do you have any idea how late it is?'

He chuckled. 'It's never too late to make money. A great deal of money.'

I heard a click as Jean picked up the extension. I said, 'Look, whoever you are, I don't do business with people who withhold their names. Especially at this time of night. I suggest you telephone my secretary tomorrow to make an appointment, stating your business and –'

Again the chuckle. 'Unless I'm much mistaken, your secretary has just joined us. Good evening, Miss Wilmslow.' A great gust of laughter this time, the sound distorting over the line, empty of humour and laced with cruelty. Once, as a kid, I'd seen a boy blind a kitten while making the same sound. 'But to get to the point, Mr Townsend. You have the location of an island. Know the place I mean? We'd like to know where it is. That's all. And we're prepared to pay generously for your help. Very generously. Maybe as much as a hundred thousand dollars.'

I dragged the phone to an armchair and sat down, my legs suddenly weak under me. 'I don't know what the hell you're talking about.'

He laughed. 'Pepalasis would be proud of you. But is he worth dying for? Shall we say, two hundred thousand? Our final offer, Mr Townsend. Don't disappoint me by saying no. Because you'll tell us in the end. One way or another.'

'Is that a threat?' I croaked, dry-mouthed.

'It's a fact, Mr Townsend. Think about it.'

The line buzzed. He'd hung up.

I was still in the armchair when Jean appeared in the doorway, white-faced and trembling. 'Mike, that man! What kind of people? For God's sake, Mike, aren't you frightened?'

I hoped it didn't show, but yes I was frightened. And my hands shook slightly as I rummaged through the telephone directory.

'That laughter.' She sat hugging herself to stop the trembling. 'Awful. And that great thick accent. Oh Mike, please. Let's call the police.'

'There *was* an accent, wasn't there?' I paused in mid-stretch to the telephone. 'What the hell was it?'

'That's easy. Three years in Jo'burg as a kid. South African. Didn't you catch the way he clipped his vowels?'

I was dialling the number. South African? It didn't help. Except that whenever I thought of South Africa I thought of diamonds –ever since meeting Pepalasis.

Hallsworth wasn't at his club.

'I think he's staying in the country,' Jean frowned. 'Hampshire or Wiltshire somewhere.'

'Why on earth do you think that?'

'Oh, there was a bit of a tiff in the office the other day. All very silly. Nothing to worry about. But he rang Muriel and asked for the dialling code book to be sent to his office. Well, you know what she's like. Anyone gets their own number and it's an insult. So she offered to get it for him. And he refused, saying he just wanted to look something up. So, of course, she said she'd look it up for him, and – I don't know, it must have touched a nerve or something – because he got quite nasty. Perhaps he thought she was being cheeky but honestly she wasn't. It's just that, without knowing it, he was breaking one of her rules. We all have them, don't we? Our own set of rules?'

She gave me a sly, amused look from beneath her eyelashes, the colour of her face quite back to normal.

'Him staying in the country,' I reminded her.

'Oh yes. Well, I was standing next to Muriel while this was going on, and just about to pick up the book and take it to him, when he must have relented. Or seen the funny side of it, because he told her where it was that he wanted.'

'And?'

'She had a job tracing it. It wasn't listed for STD and she had to check with Enquiries. It's a village. Near Winchester.'

I stiffened. 'Called?'

'I'm sorry,' she shook her head, 'it didn't seem important. Perhaps Muriel will remember.'

I got up, heading for the bedroom. 'Get onto Enquiries. See if anything's listed under Hallsworth in the Winchester area.' It was worth a try. In the bedroom I searched for a weapon. Something I could take a swing with. A club of some kind. But all I could find was my squash racket, which seemed stupidly inadequate, but better than nothing.

'Oooh!' Jean grinned, quite recovered. 'Anyone for tennis?'

'Try the name of Ballantyne, as well,' I said, suddenly wondering how Sue made phone calls at half-past midnight from a country cottage without a telephone.

Jean repeated the name while her eyes tracked me across the room to the lobby. 'Mike?' I looked at her. 'Be careful.'

I started at the front door and worked my way up. Floor by floor, office by office. Checking windows, opening cupboards, daft things like that. The lower floors had false drapes at the windows instead of proper curtains so I worked in the darkness, wanting to avoid a sudden blaze of light. On the second floor I paused long enough to look out of the window. It was a fine night, and I was reaching into a pocket for a cigarette when somebody else had the same idea. And struck a match.

He was perhaps thirty yards away, in the cab of a van parked in Chesterfield Hill. But the flare of the match was as clear as a shooting star from the window. I left the cigarettes in my pocket and watched the end of another one glow down the street. Nearly one o'clock. Just someone having a quiet smoke? But facing the building? Watching? Waiting? I shuddered, remembering the laughter and straining my eyes to see if there was a second person in the cab. But the shadows defeated me.

Not that one o'clock was late for the West End. People were still about. A couple sauntered up from Berkeley Square, stopping on the corner to embrace, the man stooping, his hands going to the girl's hair. Light brown hair in the lamplight. Another figure on the far side of the street, a measured pace, like a policeman's. Then the sound of an engine and I felt a surge of relief and surprise as the van pulled away, shifting into second gear as it passed below the window and turned the corner. I mocked my nerves and continued the tour of inspection.

On the third floor I checked the skylight. The building changed shape above the level and the stretch of flat roof was the way the burglars had come before. It took a while to get a table beneath it, and a chair on that, but I managed. It was firm and secure, Jean having had it repaired and strengthened the day after we had discovered the burglary.

I finished at the small office on the corner of the third floor, and paused at the window, peering into the street, looking for the lovers and the girl with hair like Jean's. Instead I saw the van. It was slowing to a halt and back in the position of five minutes earlier. It stopped. The driver cut the engine and killed the sidelights. It must have circled the block. Perhaps the driver had seen me at the window? Or heard the policeman as I had? Suddenly I felt more angry than frightened. Angry with whoever was playing silly bloody games at this time of night. Angry with Hallsworth for disappearing. Angry with Pepalasis for his way of doing business. And angry with myself for turning into an old woman. Defiantly I lit a cigarette and smoked about a third of it before going upstairs and leaving the driver to the loneliness of the night.

'Nothing listed for Hallsworth,' Jean reported in the sitting room. 'Or Ballantyne.'

I nodded, not surprised, not anything really – just tired.

Jean undressed in the bathroom and emerged tall and glowing and Grecian in a long white nightgown. We lay together on the sofa for a while, her folded into my arms as if we went to sleep like that every night of our lives. Then she left for the bedroom, leaving the door open behind her.

I closed my eyes and a minute later I was fighting Pepalasis on the sea shore. He hit me and I fell in the sand, got up, only for him to knock me down again. Kirk McNeil bobbed in and out shouting something in a South African accent. And there was another man. With his back to me, a wooden leg and a frock coat and a parrot on his shoulders. Then I caught Pepalasis a real haymaker. He was below me in the sand and I was swinging wild punches in the hope of landing another one. Swinging and falling. And falling and . . .

'Mike, are you all right?'

I was on the floor, looking up at the sofa, Jean crouched over me, an arm under my head, her nightdress dipping away from her breasts. She kissed me gently and the dream went away.

'You'd better come to bed. But I warn you,' she added sternly, 'if I ever find out that this was some kind of act on your part, you'll never see me again.'

She needn't have worried. I was asleep within seconds of hitting the pillow.

CHAPTER NINE

Waking up beside Jean was a good start to the next morning and after that it was as if she'd blessed the day for me. The van had gone from its overnight position. I checked to see if the blue car had taken its place, but there was no sign of it. All morning my eyes were drawn to the windows, expecting to find someone watching me from the street. And whenever the telephone rang I jumped, half anticipating the threatening voice of the night before. But nothing happened. Someone had called the dogs off. And I wondered why?

I wished that Hallsworth would make contact. But there had been no word from him when I left for lunch with an investment client, nor when I returned. So at two-thirty I caught a cab to the A.W.F offices in Holborn, creased with worry that Hallsworth and Pepalasis would miss the meeting.

'Mr Pepalasis?' Harry Smithers peered behind me as if expecting the Greek to materialize out of thin air.

'Coming separately,' I hid my concern. 'With my partner.'

Kirk McNeil was already in the Boardroom, along with a couple of Harry's assistants and Peter Emanuel from A.W.F's Merchant Bankers. And five others arrived a minute later, all members of Harry's consortium.

It was exactly three o'clock. I avoided the question in McNeil's eyes and concentrated on the small talk of the man next to me. Until five minutes past, when there was a knock on the door and Harry's secretary ushered Pepalasis into the room. Alone.

It was the first I'd seen of him since the Dorchester. His nose was slightly swollen and he wore a strip of plaster on his forehead, but apart from that he looked his usual smooth self. 'A thousand apologies,' he began, 'my cab was delayed. The more I fumed the slower he went, and the thicker was the traffic.' He laughed easily, going from place to place around the table, shaking hands, smiling affably. When it was my turn he greeted me like a long lost brother, dropped into the chair on my left and beamed about him like a boy at a birthday party. The beads appeared in his hands as if by magic.

'Hallsworth?' I muttered amid the general clearing of throats and rustling of papers which has preceded every meeting I've ever attended.

'Another appointment, I believe. Said he'd phone you later.'

I felt annoyed enough to pursue it but he turned away and addressed Harry Smithers at the other end of the table.

'Mr Chairman. May I be permitted a word before we begin?'

Harry conjured a smile out of a surprised expression and everyone sat back expectantly, except me. I had a minor heart attack. The Greek in normal form would scatter a room of investors faster than Jews leaving a pork buffet. But I needn't have worried. Pepalasis proved his birth that day. He spoke for six or seven minutes. Smooth, honeyed phrases.

Beginning with an apology for the difficulties in getting the agreement to the table and ending with a lavish compliment on their commercial judgement in backing the venture. In between, he praised Harry for his skill as Chairman, McNeil for his reputation, the whole consortium for their wisdom and me for my efforts to find a formula acceptable to all. By the time he finished they wore the bright-eyed, flushed-face look of brides on honeymoon. And when Harry passed copies of the agreement down the table a minute or two later, Pepalasis signed with a flourish.

'Aren't you going to read it first?' Harry was appalled.

'Why should I? I'm in the City of London doing business with gentlemen. Who's going to cheat me?'

It was a perfect finishing thrust, earning murmurs of approval just short of an outright burst of applause. Everyone signed with great good humour and Harry rang his secretary to bring in the champagne.

The room took on the atmosphere of a cocktail party; several of Harry's colleagues stopped by for a drink, and contributed their good wishes.

I found myself with a glass in my hand talking to Pepalasis and McNeil. 'So we're leaving tomorrow?' I said, still only half-believing.

'But of course,' Pepalasis smiled hugely. 'I'll make a prospector of you yet.'

McNeil's expression doubted it, but instead he asked, 'Now it's all signed, suppose you tell us where we're going? I haven't even changed any currency yet.'

'First stop Sydney,' Pepalasis said, as if Sydney was half an hour's walk away. 'And don't worry about money – you're my guests.'

I'd not been to Australia and the prospect pleased and worried me at the same time. 'I thought we'd only be gone a week?' I said, trying to calculate travel time.

The Greek laughed. 'My island's not in the middle of Hyde Park, you know.'

The phrase struck a chord somewhere but I couldn't immediately place it, and minutes later the party was breaking up and we were on our way. I found myself walking down the steps to the street with McNeil.

'You'll have a better night tonight than last, I reckon,' he said casually.

I swung round, wondering what the hell he meant. The dream flashed back. McNeil chanting something. The phone call. Being followed. Just how much did he know anyway?

He caught my look. 'An end to all the messing about. Everything signed at last. It must have been a worrying time for you.'

I gave a confused laugh, arranged to meet him for lunch the next day, and caught a cab to Hill Street.

'Mr Hallsworth phoned,' Jean said. 'From Heathrow. He was on his way to New York.'

'Oh Christ! That's the bloody limit.'

'I know. He sounded awfully upset about missing you. Said he'd got a crisis over there which he just had to deal with. Apparently he should have gone on Monday but stayed to lend a hand with Pepalasis.'

'Did you tell him about the phone call last night?'

'Oh Mike, how could I?' She was blushing and looking very pretty.

I groaned aloud. 'What else did he say?'

'Wished you luck for your trip. Said Pepalasis was staying with friends tonight so you don't have to worry. Oh, and that he'll be back the week after next, all being well. That's about all, I think.'

I sipped the tea she'd put on my desk and thought about it. Hallsworth had every right to give priority to his New York deal. After all he'd dropped everything to help at this end during the week. And even if he had known about me being followed, and the phone calls, there was nothing he could do about it. I went to the window and looked for the blue car. There was no sign of it. Nor the van. Nor any prying eyes peering up from the street. Suddenly my anxieties evaporated, like a mist dispersed by sunshine. After all, it was the end of the day. The end of a week. A day and a week nearer the Pepalasis diamonds and my half million. Memories of Jean's fragrant softness lingered from last night and I felt totally happy for the first time in weeks.

'I catch a flight to Sydney tomorrow evening,' I said grandly. 'So I'll pack in the morning, lunch with McNeil, and travel out to the airport in the afternoon. But tonight I'm free. So how about coming out to dinner again?'

Disappointment must have been written all over my face when she shook her head. 'I'm sorry, Mike, but I've got somebody coming to my place tonight.'

'Oh.'

'As a matter of fact I was going to ask if I might leave on time? I've a meal to prepare and I wanted to bathe and change into something slinky before he arrives.'

'Sounds – sounds very pleasant,' I said grimly, savagely jealous of the 'he' and remembering last night with unexpected bitterness. It had seemed special somehow, for reasons I wasn't sure about. But special for her too. As if we'd discovered something about the way we felt for each other after all this time.

'Will that be okay then?'

'Yes – I suppose so,' I grunted, black with disappointment.

'Good. You do remember where I live, don't you? Shall we say about seven-thirty?'

I looked at her. I had dropped her at her flat once, but never been inside.

She smiled, blue eyes dancing above the faint blush on her cheeks. 'Oh, and Mike – why not pack tonight? After all, you could leave from my place just as easily as from here.'

Part Three

CHAPTER ONE

Singapore Airways' departure SQ86 cleared Heathrow at 17.30 hours and within a short time McNeil and Pepalasis were swapping yarns like prospectors round a camp fire.

'Of course things have changed a lot,' McNeil reminisced. 'When I was first in the Aussie goldfields we spent more time looking for water than for gold.' He squinted at Pepalasis. 'Ever seen any water flies, by the way?'

'Actually flying, you mean?' Pepalasis laughed, shaking his head. 'And I never believed a white who said he did either.'

McNeil's eyes puckered. 'Water was a hell of a problem,' he said to me. 'They've got it licked now in most places but, Christ, it was murder then. Even then you always took some Abo trackers with you – in case a water-hole had dried up or got polluted. Odds were you'd had it if that happened. Unless your natives found a water fly.' He took a pull on his drink, as if just remembering made him thirsty. 'It was the damnedest thing, but only the Abos could see the blasted things in the air. They're maybe a quarter the size of a bee but a hell of a lot quicker. Anyway, water flies spend their lives flying to water and grow a size bigger with a gutful on board – and the natives could even spot the full ones from the empty ones, so they'd track 'em back to the flywells. And they *were* tiny – less than the diameter of a pencil. But once the Abos had found one they'd search for more, until they could tell you the size of the underground water supply from the number of flywells they found.' He grinned triumphantly. 'Saved my life once, that trick.'

My face expressed disbelief but Pepalasis was nodding so I was left in two minds about the story. The conversation ebbed and flowed without help from me, but the more I heard the more apprehensive I became. The implications of the journey hit me for the first time. Not just London to Sydney and on from there to somewhere else. But from one way of life to another. From mine to theirs. And their casual chat, about hardships endured and dangers experienced, provoked thoughts sober enough to deaden the effects of the whiskies I'd sunk since take off.

We talked for hours, alone in the first-class cabin except for the fluttering of the stewardesses. Occasionally we napped rather than slept, ate regularly and drank constantly, made dry by the chat and too many cigarettes. It seemed a time to get to know each other – weigh one another up for what lay ahead.

It was the longest I'd ever spent with Pepalasis since we'd met five months earlier and I found myself watching him with more than casual interest. After all, if his claim proved true he'd be one of the world's richest men in a short time, and would at least set me on the road to fortune. I'd been aware of his physical strength ever since the first crunching handshake, but listening to him field McNeil's questions was the best insight I'd had into his artful intelligence. He had the politician's knack of rephrasing questions to suit his answers, appearing to reply to everything but never telling McNeil what he most wanted to know – the location of the island. McNeil plugged away, all the time testing the Greek's knowledge and experience, and if that was as superficial as McNeil suspected earlier, it certainly fooled me.

During the last lap, Singapore to Sydney, just when I was thinking the journey would pass without incident Pepalasis produced his surprise. McNeil had gone to freshen up and the stewardesses had retreated behind their screen, so the Greek and I were quite alone when he handed me the slip of paper. It was a bank paying-in slip. I noticed yesterday's date

111

but took a second or two to realize that it recorded money paid into my personal account at the Barclay's I used in South Audley Street. But the amount – fifty thousand pounds – registered immediately.

'A down payment,' Pepalasis murmured. 'Ten per cent. On account.'

'But you haven't got a deal yet? If we don't find diamonds –'

'We will.' His smile was full of confidence. 'Then you'll get the rest. In Zurich as promised.'

I was still telling him it was generous to the point of lunacy when McNeil's return ended the conversation. After that they dozed for a bit while I pretended to, as my mind did handstands about my good fortune. And hurriedly reclassified Pepalasis from a slippery Greek to a man of his word. It occurred to me to ask how he'd found out where I banked but McNeil's presence made the question impossible, and when an opportunity did occur later, the whole matter had completely gone out of my mind with so much else happening around us.

We landed at Kingsford-Smith Airport, 06.45 local time, stale, tired and talked dry from our twenty-seven hour flight, and went directly to the hotel. Pepalasis had no need of us during the day so McNeil and I went to our rooms to catch some sleep, leaving the Greek rattling off a list of telephone calls to a startled receptionist. He made a productive day of it too, because his warning over dinner later of a dawn start caused McNeil and me to settle for drinks at the bar instead of the promised tour of Sydney's night life.

At six o'clock breakfast was followed by a ride across town to Sydney's second airport to board a charter DC3. Pepalasis paused just long enough to tell us where we were going – Tontouta, New Caledonia – before disappearing onto the flight deck with the crew.

McNeil shook his head in disgust: 'It's like drawing teeth – getting information out of him. Bet the bastard wishes

112

he could blindfold us half the time.'

We were the only passengers. The plane was mainly freight anyway, half a dozen seats set in two rows facing each other, an open galley and a closed toilet comprised all there was before the bulkhead separating passengers from cargo. I crinkled my nose at the stink of fish while McNeil wiped a spy hole in the film of grease which lined the ports.

'No pretty hostess flashing a handful of cleavage this trip.' He swung his case onto the seat opposite, extracted a bottle of Scotch and went to examine the galley.

'How far's New Caledonia?'

'Ah, coffee!' He found a tin in the cupboard. 'About twelve hundred miles I reckon – north-east from here.'

'And what's there?'

'Plenty of mining for a start.' He waved a packet of sugar. 'It used to be the biggest producer of nickel and chrome in the world – cobalt too, come to think of it. And there's other stuff – the Japs were mining iron ore there in the thirties, and sending it back home as fast as ships could carry it.'

'Any diamonds?'

'None I've heard of.'

The port engine crackled, paused, spluttered and blazed into life, joined a minute later by its starboard twin, producing enough shock waves between them to tear the wings from the fuselage. McNeil said something which lost itself in the din and seconds later the plane was rolling forward and gathering itself for take-off. I'm no expert but that noisy heap seemed years past retirement age, and never more so than at maximum throttle for what promised to be more of a fast cross-country drive than a smooth climb upwards. But we lifted – eventually – though it was a good five minutes before I *felt* airborne; and an hour later the co-pilot joined us long enough to brew coffee, a mug for each of us and three carried back to the flight deck. And Pepalasis stayed out of sight for the whole trip.

Tontouta greeted us with the oven heat of mid-afternoon.

McNeil's warning about moving closer to the equator proved singularly inadequate. A roasting hot, Turkish bath of a place, the sun blinding the eye, heat waves bouncing head high from the blistering surface underfoot, and the humidity gluing my shirt to my back within a minute of standing there. I mopped my face and watched a red Honda van pull away from a cluster of buildings to drive out to meet us.

'Customs,' Pepalasis shouted from a patch of black shade under the nose of the aircraft. 'Better get yourselves a drink – I'll join you later.'

We crossed a hundred yards of shimmering concrete to a prefabricated building which had started life as an aircraft hangar, and entered a crude bar full of red metal tables and chairs set on bare concrete. But the drop in temperature was luxurious, and the beer – cans of Fosters bought with Aussie dollars changed in the hotel last night – ice-cold when we got it.

'Where next?'

'Christ knows.' McNeil punctured a second can, beer frothing onto my hand as I took it from him. 'There're plenty of islands along the coast from here, but none that I imagined privately owned. Still, I've only been here once, and that was nine years ago – daresay plenty's happened since.'

'So, if not here – where?' I persisted.

'I'm right out of guesses.' He shrugged, his attention wandering around the bar before returning to me. 'Truth is, I don't know. Take this place – we're halfway to Fiji here, another thousand miles or so. They've got gold there, and silver at Vatukoula, though mostly worked out from what I've heard. But maybe an island off the coast somewhere? Or north to the Solomons? There's gold there. And more gold and manganese in Guinea west of here.'

'Everything but diamonds.' I took a long pull on the beer.

'Sure – but they reckon Aussie's the biggest undiscovered store of minerals in the world and I've believed that long enough. The point is these arcuate islands in the Western

114

Pacific are geologically similar, younger of course, but there's a good deal of sedimentary rock and andestic volcanic material about. Start going east from here into the Central Pacific – say towards Easter Island – and there're thousands of islands, they're even called the Strewn Islands.'

'So we're getting close?'

'On the doorstep, mate,' he grinned. 'I'd say anywhere inside five thousand square miles of ocean.'

I was about to question him further when Pepalasis arrived, hot and sticky and swearing in Greek. McNeil passed him a beer and we waited for him to cool down.

'We've a couple of hours to kill while they transfer the cargo.' He wiped a mixture of beer and sweat from his mouth with the back of his hand. 'Thought we'd go down to Noumea for a decent meal and a clean-up.'

'Transfer what cargo?' McNeil asked. 'To where?'

'Our cargo.' Pepalasis enjoyed his secret. 'For the last leg of the journey.'

Noumea had streets full of Indonesians and hotels bursting with Vietnamese, but we found a place for a wash and brush-up, had a meal and, two hours later the same green VW cab picked us up to take us on our way again. I'd expected to head back to the airport but the cab turned off the main road and bumped down towards the harbour which I'd glimpsed from the hotel windows. The French-style houses gave way to a shanty town of corrugated iron lock-up shops, cafés and cheap living quarters, and the ever narrowing road became thick with people contesting our right of way.

'Used to be a French penal colony, this place,' McNeil observed.

The unfriendly faces half convinced me it still was. But it got better some minutes later when we reached the harbour walls and looked out across the bluest stretch of water I'd ever seen in my life.

'See that?' Pepalasis pointed. 'It's a Widgeon and all mine.'

I followed the direction of his arm, uncertain of what to look for. The harbour wall ran a hundred yards before swinging left to form the half horseshoe of the breakwater. A cluster of small boats were moored nearby but Pepalasis was looking beyond them. I located a tramp ship, held together with brown rust, black pitch and its owner's prayers; and beyond that more small boats. Then I saw it. The clue was the Honda van from the airport now parked on the quayside, its red paintwork flickering through the forest of bamboo masts. An aircraft, amphibious, fat canoe-shaped floats which formed obvious black blobs on the surface of the water as we drew nearer. A Widgeon.

'Jesus,' McNeil blasphemed, suitably awed. 'Which museum did this come from?'

But it looked better than the DC3 to me. McNeil and I inspected it from the jetty, while Pepalasis dealt with the two men in the Honda.

'Wonder what range it's got?' McNeil speculated. 'Although those pods under its wings are auxiliary tanks. He'll have doubled up on the original specifications.'

He was running on about amphibious aircraft in that part of the world but I missed most of it, suddenly too drowsy to concentrate. God, but I was tired! My eyes could barely focus on Pepalasis as he took the two men from the red Honda along the rope-sided gangplank and onto the sea plane. Then the men returned and began to transfer some crates from the van to the aeroplane.

'What's up?' McNeil asked.

'Dunno. Just damned tired that's all.' The words slurred, I was too drained of energy to even speak straight. I blinked my eyes to get the weight off the lids and drew deep breaths to force more oxygen into my lungs. But it was no good – if I didn't sit down, I'd fall down. Somehow I stumbled across to the Honda and collapsed on its bonnet.

'You're not sick are you?' McNeil was already at my elbow, his voice concerned.

116

'Dog tired.' Just to shake my head was an effort. 'Sorry – making a fool of myself.'

'Anything wrong?' I *heard* but couldn't see Pepalasis, my lids clamped firm over my eyes. A chuckle before he said, 'It's the local wine – strong stuff in this heat. Let's get you on board – you can sleep it off.'

God knows how they got me onto the plane, Pepalasis shuffling one side of me, McNeil guiding me from the rear. I opened my eyes long enough to register four seats in the cabin – cockpit I suppose – two at the controls and two behind; and I clambered into one at the back just as my eyes gave out. I sensed someone take the next seat, felt fingers fumble with my seat belt, heard the click of a safety buckle.

McNeil asking: 'Where's the pilot?'

Pepalasis laughing: 'You're looking at him.' He sounded a long way off.

The sound of metal running in a groove – a rush of warm air – the slam of the cockpit closing. McNeil again: 'Ari, are you sure you're okay?' The Greek answering: 'Go to sleep – don't worry.' The stutter of engines, muffled, less noise than the DC3. McNeil muttering something and tugging at my arm. Something important. Then I heard him – understood his words. 'Mike, we've been drugged. Bloody well drugged!' I was nodding, agreeing, trying to get my eyes to open. But it was no good – I had to sleep.

CHAPTER TWO

Semi-darkness. Stiff-necked from sleeping strapped to a seat. Mouth like an open drain. Pain as stretching arms struck metal. The original rude awakening. My mind registered McNeil asleep and my memory pieced the rest

117

together like parts of a jigsaw. The sea plane? The Widgeon! Empty seats in front, the view through the cockpit obscured by some kind of sacking. Neither sight nor sound of Pepalasis. In fact nothing. No movement, no engine noise, no bobbing on the sea. Just a faded brown light turning everything the sepia of old photographs. But the sea was somewhere – I could smell it, hear it as the faintest noise in the background – the measured pulse of waves breaking gently on an easy shoreline.

After releasing the seat belt I pushed the back of the seat in front, hoping it might fold forward to allow me to climb over without disturbing McNeil. It didn't, but as I squirmed in search of a safety catch, he groaned conscious.

'Jesus! My head. What happened?'

I told him as best I could while we helped each other forward into the front seats. The sliding hatch of the cockpit was already open a few inches and it was a moment's work to push it back on its runners and to claw at the sacking. Except the sacking was layers of finely woven net, masses of it extending all over the plane, trapping us like flies in a spider's web. I heaved myself out and onto the wing, using hands and head and shoulders to fend off the suffocating weight of the netting; McNeil did the same on the other side, catching his shin and swearing like a trooper. The mud turned to grains of soft sand when I landed on it, and half stooping, half crawling, I edged sideways like a crab, the netting closing in relentlessly until I reached the tent pegs at the perimeter. And a minute later I was through.

Sea. Fifty yards away. More water than I'd ever seen in my life. Vivid blue near the shoreline, flecked white a hundred yards out, then emerald and back to blue again in time to meet the sky. And sky everywhere – sea and sky for all eternity. Half turning, my gaze tracked the white ribbon of beach to a rock a hundred yards away; the rock rose to a cliff which continued up and behind me. I continued to pivot in the sand to register the base of the cliff twenty-five yards

118

from where I stood. Then I saw Pepalasis. He was wearing a skin diver's wet suit but without a skull cap, his mane of grey hair falling forward into his eyes as he bent over an open packing case.

'So – awake eh?' He straightened and trudged barefoot across the sand to greet me, a broad smile breaking on his face.

'You bastard!' McNeil lurched from behind the camouflage netting. 'I should have known. Never trust a Greek! You drugged us, didn't you?'

They stood a yard apart in the sand, facing each other. I remembered my dream about fighting Pepalasis and wondered if this was the place. Except one look at McNeil said he was going to do the fighting for both of us.

'No ill effects – I promise.' Pepalasis was still smiling. 'Come. I've made coffee – after that you'll feel wonderful.'

McNeil moved quickly, his hand gripping the Greek's shoulder. 'Ever do that again and I'll break your bloody neck. Understand?'

The Greek looked along the arm to the angry face at the other end of it. 'I understand. I would be angry too. You have a right to lose your temper. But I have a right to protect my island.' His eyes met McNeil's without wavering and, slowly, he prised the fingers loose from his shoulder and stepped backwards.

McNeil hesitated – the Greek turned on his heel – and the moment passed.

We followed Pepalasis to a spot at the foot of the cliff where he had built a lean-to with more of the netting, ten foot square and high enough for us all to stand beneath. A spirit stove supported an enamel pot which puffed coffee-scented steam into clean air.

'So this is the island?' McNeil said as much to himself as anybody, sipping coffee and looking back down the beach.

'No,' Pepalasis surprised both of us. 'But it's as near as we can get by plane. And it's not far from here.

119

Finish your coffee and I'll show you.'

Half an hour later we clambered over the rockfall at the edge of the beach for a view of what lay beyond, McNeil and I sensing the Greek's excitement and sharing it. But sights were disappointing. Land – five or six miles away, rising no more than seventy feet above sea level, nondescript and undistinguished. My eyes traced its outline against the sky and I guessed it four or five miles wide at that point.

'There's the problem,' Pepalasis pointed. The surf was barely visible at first glance, but as the eye concentrated the white line seemed to extend to the width of the island. 'A barrier reef. The Widgeon would be smashed to pieces within a mile of it and the lagoon is too short to land in.'

'So what do we do?' McNeil shielded his eyes from the reflected glare of the sea. 'Swim?'

Pepalasis threw his head back, delighting in the excitement of the moment, waving a hand back up the beach. 'Help unload the cargo. Then you'll see.'

It took two hours, McNeil and I stripped to the waist, the Greek still in his wet suit. The third crate revealed everything needed for the last leg of the journey – three yellow inflatables – each the size of an overnight case in its special container. Other crates included all manner of things: endless coils of nylon rope, a first-aid pack, spades and picks, canned provisions and three large outboards, about which McNeil became very curious. I was more intrigued with the metal tubs, shaped like fruit bowls but large enough to sit in, three sets of six, fitted into each other like Russian dolls.

We stacked the contents of the crates alongside a small inlet, ten yards wide and running almost to the foot of the cliff, before returning all packing materials to the hold of the Widgeon. When we had just finished, McNeil stood watching Pepalasis adjust the camouflage. 'We on an airline route?' He squinted into an empty sky.

'The occasional plane.'

'What type?'

'Too high to see.'

I grinned at the never-ending game. Now it seemed unimportant. If we found diamonds Pepalasis was contracted to reveal his secret. Until then why worry?

The dinghies were the type used by Air Rescue the world over – self-inflating when they hit the water. Pepalasis heaved them into the inlet and jumped in after them, water rising waist high as he linked tie ropes to secure them to the bank. Fully inflated they seemed enormous, fifteen foot long, five or six wide, shaped at the prow.

'How about some coffee?' The Greek grinned up at me. 'And some food. I'm hungry.'

So was I come to think of it. I left them fitting the first of the Gardner outboards and went back to the lean-to to get the coffee going.

'The next step is both difficult and dangerous,' Pepalasis said, an hour later, as we were finishing our meal. He drew a rough circle in the sand. 'This is the island. My island. Or rather the reef which surrounds it. There is only one access point – a rock-lined passage, maybe thirty metres wide. Once through, we're clear of danger. The risk is getting through.'

McNeil and I looked at him and waited.

'The surf hits the reef at an angle – like this.' He drew a line in the sand which almost missed his circle. 'See the problem? Line up with the passage and the current will sweep you past. If you're lucky right past. If you're unlucky onto the reef itself.'

McNeil's eyes widened. 'With engines that size?'

'Twenty horse power. Any more weight would tear the inflatables apart – any less and the power wouldn't be worth bothering with.'

'Jesus! Some current.'

Suddenly I felt cold, despite the heat through the netting. 'But if we can't line up on the passage?' I asked.

'Line up on a point a hundred yards up current and a hundred yards out. Then full throttle on the Gardners.

Under normal circumstances – on flat water say – do that and you'd hit fifty knots inside sixty metres. Out there – with the current running part behind and part across you'll be going even faster but not in a straight line. Get it right and you'll go through the mid point of the passage like a bullet down a rifle barrel.' He smiled thinly. 'And you've got seventy metres on the other side to slow down.'

'And get it wrong?' McNeil's eyes narrowed.

'You'll break your back on the reef.'

He was deadly serious. McNeil and I were silent for a full minute before I asked: 'Have you done this before?'

'Three times. Each time I think it will be easier. It never is.'

'*Now* you tell us.' I stifled my irritation and asked: 'How do we get back? If the outboards won't take the current going in they sure as hell won't take it coming out.'

'There's a point here.' He marked his circle forty-five degrees from where the passage was indicated. 'The current races past this corner of the reef leaving an area of calm water. Coming out we paddle to the reef, drag an inflatable across and launch from there. We're a hundred metres out before the current catches us and then it's taking us away from the barrier and out to sea. It's a matter of riding the current for a mile or so and then swinging back in an arc to get back here.' He shrugged. 'It takes time but there's no danger.'

Most of the afternoon was spent stowing cargo aboard the inflatables and by the time we finished, there wasn't a spare inch in any of them. It put enough of a fresh light on the argument about test equipment to make me wonder about it, but if McNeil was struck by the same thought he kept it to himself. After Pepalasis satisfied himself with the weight distribution in each boat everything was lashed into place and made waterproof with protective covers zipped kayak style around the passenger. Then, all now in wet suits, we paddled out of the inlet and into the sea.

Forty yards from shore Pepalasis gave the signal to pull

start the Gardners and the big engines blazed to life with an ear-shattering roar. Even at half throttle, racing inches above the water surface, the sensation of speed was electrifying, so it was an hour before McNeil and I dared use anything like three-quarter power. And the thought of full throttle seemed suicidal.

We did a series of test runs parallel to the beach, going endlessly up and down, spray flying like mist turned to rainbows by the sun. At five o'clock Pepalasis signalled us back to the inlet. 'Brandy.' He handed us each a hip flask as we came ashore. 'A toast to success.'

McNeil unscrewed the cap and sniffed cautiously. 'Last time I drank with you, Greek, I slept for twelve hours.'

Pepalasis exploded into laughter. 'But this time I need you awake.'

We drank while listening to his final instructions. 'We'll go in convoy, me first, Kirk last. Boats twenty metres apart. No closer – we daren't risk a boat running wild and colliding. When I'm lined up I'll signal – like this.' He raised an arm quickly above his head and dropped it smartly back to his side. To me he said, 'Come in dead astern of me and you'll be okay. As soon as I've signalled I'll hit full throttle and go. You do the same when you've made up the extra twenty metres. But signal Kirk first, understand?' I nodded and he continued. 'Turn your rudder into the current as soon as you feel it. Gently at first, gradually, but as it bites harder keep turning – you'll have full lock on just before you reach the barrier.'

'Full lock *and* full throttle?' McNeil shook his head in astonished disbelief.

'Full lock *and* full throttle,' Pepalasis repeated sharply. And don't try it another way. If you miss the opening do what you can to ride the current. And pray to God that you stay off the reef. If He answers you send a flare up to let us know you're all right. Then run out to sea, turn and try again.'

He'd spoken urgently, his expression more serious than I had ever known it. Now he paused and his voice dropped to little more than a whisper as he added, 'If you hit the reef we'll get you. If we can.'

We climbed into the boats, stowed the flasks and followed the Greek out into the open sea. The weather was perfect. A cloudless blue bowl of sky, a slight breeze, water breaking gently from the bows of my inflatable as it followed the arrow-straight course of the Greek's wash. I turned and got a cheerful answering wave from McNeil, the beach receding behind him, the Widgeon already invisible beneath its camouflage.

Eyes front, correcting my course to stay in line, I smiled, thinking there was a bit of the old woman in Pepalasis after all. No doubt a lot of fuss about very little. McNeil had obviously thought so too. The whole thing was probably exaggerated out of all proportion. Another ruse to add to the bloody mystery of his precious island. I remembered Army manoeuvres off the Welsh coast in the middle of winter and laughed aloud. Now that *really* was tough going.

We remained at half throttle, twenty metres apart. The sea began to run a noticeable swell, not rough or frightening, but a nudging reminder that the Pacific is the deepest ocean in the world. I could see the breakers now, still a long way off, a mile away, maybe more; a long white line dipping in and out as the horizon divided the solid blue of the sky from the flickering, heaving mass of the sea below. And the volume of noise increased so steadily and undramatically that I hardly noticed it. Earlier the sound of the Gardner had swamped everything, now its sharper note was insistent but no longer dominant above the growl of the sea.

We had travelled another half mile when the rudder line jerked unexpectedly in my hands, swinging me off course. We had reached the current. I made the necessary adjustment and brought her round, surprised at such a strong pressure this far out. Pepalasis glanced quickly over his shoulder, checking to see that McNeil and I were still on station. I waved a hurried acknowledgement and hastily returned both hands to the rudder line as the current tugged again.

The swell grew relentlessly, long oily washes of water dipping and rising like a switchback, down into a trough and then twenty feet up to the crest. And the sea changed colour. No longer blue, but green where it wasn't grey and knotted with white veins of spume, hissing and spitting like a wild cat. And running faster and faster.

Then I lost the Greek! One moment he was there, in line, twenty metres ahead – the next moment gone, nothing, no sign of him. Instead a wall of solid water reaching to the sky, racing upwards like an avalanche going the wrong way. Over the top. How high? Forty – forty-five – fifty feet? The Gardner was suddenly clear of the water, its blades biting empty air as the boat stood on its prow and threatened to somersault forward. *God, where was Pepalasis?*

I was climbing again – higher this time and even faster. And then I saw him, glimpsed him; a small black figure in a yellow boat on a mad green sea, still in line – twenty, maybe thirty yards ahead. A weird half sighting, all fragmented through the towering wall of spray. *Thank God!* An arm raised quickly up and down. Was that it? The signal? So soon? It had to be. I hit full throttle. Signal McNeil. I did, and hoped he saw it. Go – go – go! For the sweet love of God – *go!* I hauled on the rudder line and set my strength against the current, abandoning any pretence of steering, of being in control. Look for the gap – the gap in the. Visible soon? The air shook with a pounding a hundred times more deafening than the wake of jets on a runway, swamping the sound of the Gardner so completely that it might not have been there. Pepalasis cleared the next ridge, going fast and straight for the rocks. He must have miscalculated! There was no gap! Just iron toothed rocks smashed by the sea. I glanced to my left, a fury of spray and more rocks – and beyond them more again. *Then I saw it.* A gap – no spray –

just water flowing as fast as the top of a waterfall. We're too far right? Dammit, *we must be*! Pepalasis – dead ahead now – crouching low in his boat. Running faster than ever. A split second's view before the sea's spume-laced fingers snatched his boat and hurled it forward. Pepalasis was no more, and I was forty yards from the reef – travelling faster than an express train without a prayer of stopping. Where was the sodding gap? Twenty yards – the rocks as pale as old bones streaked green by the sea. Ten yards. Five. Then – suddenly – unbelievably – mercifully into open water and going fast enough to slip off the edge of the world. No waves – just a mirror flat surface with me skimming over it like a pebble on a mill pond, easing the rudder, slowing the engine, slowing everything.

Calm. Only my hands still shaking, my heart pounding, my mind trembling. A different world. A sky I could see again. Soft water – quiet – the dramatic stillness which follows the battering of a storm. And Pepalasis – waving excitedly forty yards away. I twisted to look back, terrified McNeil had failed to make it. But he was close by, shouting, grinning, waving. Pepalasis signalled to cut engines and we called across the water to each other like excited school-boys, and never was the sound of a human voice so sweet.

After a few minutes rest we lined up again behind the Greek and followed him towards the shore. Even inside the barrier it was a cruel looking coast line. No white sand here, just a strip of shingle strewn with boulders. We edged slowly past a bluff gouged hollow like a rotten tooth and paddled across shallow water through which strings of weed, like knotted ropes, reached up from patches of greenish white sand on the sea bed.

Pepalasis pointed to a slab of rock – a hundred feet wide and maybe half as high, garnet streaked grey at irregular intervals, its face as bare as concrete except for a gap like the slot in a machine gun turret. A cave of sorts? The opening three or four feet high and three times as wide. Our entrance to the island?

McNeil drew alongside, convulsed with sudden laughter. 'Jesus – why bother to keep this place secret? There's not a bugger alive who could get in without the guided tour.'

After that we unloaded the equipment and supplies, McNeil and I waist deep in water, heaving items one at a time up to Pepalasis in the cave. Last to go were the inflatables themselves. The Greek had rigged up a primitive winch which swung out from the mouth of the cave, but even so it was two hours of backbreaking effort to unhitch the Gardners and raise the still inflated craft from the water. Night had fallen when we finished, and both McNeil and I were close to exhaustion as we climbed out of the sea, and onto the island.

CHAPTER THREE

There was so little to distinguish the next day from the seven which followed, a cruel, punishing, inflexibility about all of them, a subterranean existence like moles in runs, in that cave and those adjoining. The caves stretched for miles, some as large as a concert hall, others no more than tunnels with overhangs low enough to force us to our knees. All in darkness except for the entrance cave itself. I hated it from the start, glad of the dark only when it hid the fear in my eyes from the others.

Pepalasis had prepared the site well, equipping it with ropes, hoists and winches where possible, but no amount of preparation could have made the work easy. At all levels below the entrance cave we wore mining helmets, and our daily routine was established on the very first morning when Pepalasis led us to the two points in the underground system at which he had found diamonds. To reach the first we followed a tunnel a hundred yards long to an opening twenty yards square – square counting that half of the floor area which was an open hole, with the next level five hundred feet below.

We abseiled down, clamping a harness around our bodies and hooking it to a single rope secured to the rock face with climbing pitons. The fast drop through darkness was terrifying and I met the ground with a spine crunching jolt which still had me winded five minutes later. After that, another rock corridor, the ground sloping away all the time so that it was difficult not to break into a trot, to reach the second rock chimney. It was as deep as the first but I made a better landing, helped unexpectedly by falling onto softer ground. Another walk, the rock ceiling closing in at intervals, progress made in a single file amidst curses and warnings about the overhang, until we reached a pear-shaped opening some thirty yards wide.

'This is where I found my first diamonds.' Pepalasis squatted and felt the ground with his hands. 'Once a year it's flooded down here. Hurricanes drive waves across three-quarters of the island's surface – in January and February.'

I was still shuddering at the thought when McNeil asked bluntly: 'So where's the kimberlite?'

'Look at the walls. And the ground here – and here.'

We looked. I'd learned enough by then to have a vague idea of what to look for. Kimberlite – blue ground which goes yellow near the surface due to the oxidation of the iron content in the rock. But how blue was blue? The rock walls had blue in them right enough but other colours – browns, reds and charcoal, gleamed back under the probe of our flashlights.

McNeil grunted and walked further down the passage, stopping every few yards, the beam of light from his helmet exploring the surface like a prodding finger. He came back to where we waited. 'And you found diamonds here?'

'On the ground,' Pepalasis nodded. 'My guess is water

carried them down from higher levels.'

McNeil swung the short handled axe and began to work an area a few feet wide. I watched and waited, my excitement growing by the second, knowing that most of the world's diamonds have been found in the alluvial terraces of river beds, and that's exactly what we were standing in – the dried up bed of an underground river.

'So what's the plan?' McNeil asked, still crouched on his knees examining the rock, not looking up.

'We take diggings from here back to the base camp and pan there.'

'Without a conveyor?' McNeil stood up. 'Jesus! How much d'you plan to shift? A tub a day?'

'We can manage the vertical lifts easily enough with simple gravity hoists. The real sweat will be the haul down the tunnel and I can rig up drag lines of sorts using the Gardner engines. Hard work of course, but – ' the Greek shrugged, 'but I'm planning to shift a ton or more a day.'

McNeil thought about it and then grinned at me. 'I hope you're fit. Because you will be, after a week of this.' His teeth gleamed white in his dust-stained face. 'Or dead.'

I drew the worst job. Mainly because I lacked specialised knowledge, but there weren't any soft jobs going anyway. So I worked at the rock face filling the tubs, with the other two taking turns to help me. We'd fill nine of the tubs and then one of us would make the journey to the bottom of the rock chimney on the third level to start the Gardner engine. The Greek had rigged up an ingenious pulley system which dragged two lines in from the workings – the lines threaded around the tubs so in theory all we had to do was to guide them over the uneven ground with the Gardner doing all the work. But in practice the tubs kicked and bucked like wild things, catching outcrops of rock and smashing against our shins as we fought to keep them upright, spilling a regular ten per cent of their contents on each journey. At the bottom of the shaft the Gardner was switched off to conserve fuel and

Pepalasis or McNeil would strap on the abseil harness and begin the climb upwards. The ascent is made up the rock face, hauling body weight all the time until the top is reached. Even the Greek lacked the strength in his shoulders to make the journey without one rest, taken by clamping the harness tight on the rope, fixing the feet firm on the rock face and hanging back in mid-air, allowing tired muscles to gather themselves for the final assault upwards. Once one of them reached the top I sent the first tub of ore upwards, on the end of a rope which led over a pulley to another tub filled to a compensating weight which was lowered at the same time. When all nine tubs were raised I climbed up and we worked our way to the other chimney and hoisted to the first level in the same way, a second Gardner pulling drag lines in to the foot of the shaft. Then I returned to the digging alone, leaving them to make the final shift to base camp while I set to filling another nine tubs. McNeil and Pepalasis took turns at panning the ore at the entrance cave – base camp – and generally I had filled most of the next quota by the time one of them joined me to begin the whole process over again.

Each lift took two hours and we did six a day, twelve hours of unrelenting punishment, straining muscles which screamed for rest after the first two lifts. At night we slept in hammocks, exhausted and still in our wet suits. Base camp was well organized with plenty of evidence of the Greek's previous visits – coils of ropes, more tubs, even an oil stove for cooking an evening meal.

In two days we shifted three tons of ore. And found nothing. Depression applied its own drag to tired muscles, heartache added to backache, and the drudgery of the work seemed unending. Pepalasis took it in his stride, talking of the next day with the unfaltering optimism of a born prospector, but McNeil's reaction was different and difficult to interpret. I expected him to crow a bit – after all, he'd been sceptical from the outset and results so far justified his opinion. Yet he seemed more puzzled than anything, as if something troubled him, something he couldn't quite put his finger on. Whatever it was he kept it to himself, and I was too tired to be more than casually curious – until the third day, when something happened which turned my interest to suspicion, and suspicion to downright hostility.

It was mid-morning. We had made two lifts and I was alone at the rock face, coaxing aching muscles and preparing to start again, when I saw a light at the far end of the tunnel. At first I assumed it was McNeil coming to join me, Pepalasis having worked the previous lift. *But then the light stopped.* For a minute or two it reamained perfectly still, maybe sixty yards away. And then it went out. My skin prickled under the wet suit. I fixed my gaze on the point where the light had been and tried to keep my imagination from playing tricks on me. Then, a minute later, the light was back on again, farther back in the tunnel this time, stopped or moving so slowly that I was unsure which. For no reason I could think of I extinguished the light on my own helmet and sat in total darkness, my eyes staring back down the tunnel.

Whoever it was was taking his time. Four, five minutes passed, and still the light drew nearer. Mines, tunnels, caves – the whole damn lot are the same as far as I'm concerned – are spooky, unnatural places, and for the hundredth time I promised myself I'd never set foot in one again. I debated whether to call out, a greeting of some kind, or a challenge, but instead I just sat there, watching and waiting, until a minute later I heard the sound of steel clashing on rock and saw the light jerk in time with the swing of a pick. Ten minutes passed. I timed it exactly, the luminious dial of my watch bright in the pitch black. Then the noise stopped and without further hesitation the light started towards me and I heard the positive crunch of footsteps in the stillness.

'Mike?' It was McNeil.

I switched on my lamp. 'Over here.'

He saw my light and walked over. 'Sitting in the dark? What are you doing?'

'Watching you.'

I made no attempt to get up and waited for an explanation. None came, so eventually I asked: 'Find any diamonds back there?'

'No bloody chance.' He sounded disgusted. 'You couldn't swing a Woolworth watch on diamonds found here.'

I choked back my disappointment: 'So what were you doing back there?'

'Nothing. Forget it, eh.'

We resumed the back-breaking work of filling tubs and lifting them to the higher levels, and two hours later I was alone at the rock face again. According to the system Pepalasis should have joined me for the next lift, leaving McNeil at base camp sifting ore. But – *when* he came – it was McNeil, and again he spent half an hour deep in the tunnel before joining me.

The following morning we transferred to the second site, hopes dying an inch at a time with each successive lift. McNeil and Pepalasis must have arranged a change in the schedule because from then on McNeil made all the journeys and Pepalasis stayed at base camp. It made no difference to me of course, and I wouldn't have questioned it if McNeil had not gone missing so often. But his increasing absences made my job even harder, and bone weary as I was, my feelings towards him hardened and soured with resentment.

By the end of the fourth day I was bruised and aching all over, and bitter with disappointment. The wonderful dream was fast fading and we all knew it. *Yet Pepalasis had been so confident!* Every mile of the journey out from London had seemed certain to bring him closer to a fortune and me nearer half a million in a Swiss Bank. Now I felt as cheated as the man who won a lottery and lost his ticket.

But the next day we found a diamond. It was in the ore taken up on the third lift. Pepalasis came scrambling down to the diggings alive with excitement. But when I looked at the stone, smaller than a shrivelled pea, all that registered was that we had a long way to go to meet the requirements of the contract. Still it was a start, and drawing encouragement from it we worked an extra shift, seven instead of six, before collapsing after fourteen hours of non-stop grind.

The next day, day six, I made two lifts as good as single-handed. McNeil disappeared for hours on end, and joined me just long enough to help with the hoists, a two-handed job anyway. And finally three days of pent-up resentment boiled over: 'Where the bloody hell are you going now?' We were at the foot of the chimney leading to the second stage and I'd caught him moving off towards another tunnel instead of returning to the diggings with me.

'Prospecting,' he avoided my eye.

'Prospecting *be damned*! Staying clear of the work more like. For God's sake! It's hard enough for two – damn near impossible for one.'

'Mike, it may seem that way but –'

'But nothing. You've been swinging the lead for days now. Prospecting? You've found damn all and –'

'Who says so?'

'Well?'

'I'm not sure – yet. It's inconclusive and –'

'Oh, go to hell!' I swung round and stormed back down the tunnel, leaving him to follow or not. *Not sure!* He'd been bloody sure enough in London. Full of how clever he was. How experienced. I threw myself at the rock face – spiked with the gut ache of disappointment – and filled the tubs in half the usual time before trudging back to start the Gardner. I met McNeil on the way.

'Mike, I'm sorry about this but –'

'Just answer one thing. Have you found diamonds and kept quiet about it?'

'Jesus, no! What the hell –'

We stood facing each other, the lights from our helmets bright enough for me to watch his expression. He was telling the truth – I was sure of it. I shrugged, turned away, started

133

the Gardner on the second pull, and walked back with him following behind.

That one tiny crystal of diamond was all we ever found. Eight days of back break to move the best part of seventeen tons of ore for a crystal worth a few hundred pounds. The Greek's gamble had failed and we all knew it. And my hopes died at the same time. A dream of a half a million. Enough to bank-roll me for the big time. But, as we discussed plans to break camp early the next morning, I was just too damned tired to care any more.

CHAPTER FOUR

If McNeil and I were exhausted when we left the island, Pepalasis was on the verge of collapse. On the way out from London he'd been shot full of adrenalin. But now his yesterdays weighed heavily on his shoulders and his tired face was lined with bitterness. He'd gambled, maybe with all he had, and lost. And it showed. Even his passion for secrecy had exhausted itself, and the flight back to New Caledonia was made without any attempt on his part to disguise the route. We flew south-south-west for five hours at an air speed of about a hundred and fifty knots, and although neither McNeil nor I said anything, we both knew that we had a good idea of the island's location.

Yet if the Greek's disappointment was easily understood, McNeil's behaviour was downright puzzling. It began as we were leaving the island. With the business of the rucksack. Each of us had one – standard sort of things, army surplus probably. During the week I'd left mine at base camp. It contained soap and a razor, a couple of towels, odds and ends, nothing of value. If I thought about it – which I didn't – I would have imagined the contents of theirs to be much the same. And I would have been wrong – at least about McNeil's.

We were climbing from the shallow water into the single inflatable to be used for the return to the other island, and McNeil couldn't pull himself aboard. He'd got this pack strapped on his back and it was absolutely bulging. I was already in the boat so I stretched out an arm to help, but the weight he was carrying almost had us both in the water.

'Good God – what's on your back – half the island?'

One look at his face told me I was right. The pack was loaded with rocks.

'Shut up, can't you? Mind your own damn business.'

It seemed an astonishing reaction for which he instantly apologized, but it showed how tense he was. And at exactly that moment the Greek appeared at the mouth of the cave, took a look over his shoulder like a lover saying farewell, and slipped down into the water. He gave no sign of having overheard the exchange, nor did he remark on McNeil's pack, though he could hardly have overlooked it. And McNeil kept that pack close by him all the way to New Caledonia.

It was early afternoon when we berthed at Noumea. The fact that there was no Customs intervention seemed unimportant at the time, but looking back on it McNeil must have blessed his good fortune. We took ourselves up to the hotel we used on the way out, staying overnight anyway, to pick up the scheduled Qantas to Sydney in the morning. After a late lunchtime meal the Greek excused himself and went to his room and I did the same, taking my aching body to the luxury of a hot bath and a soft bed as quickly as I could get there. But McNeil went out, saying he'd see us at dinner.

I slept the rest of the afternoon away, bathed again, dressed and went in search of a drink at about seven, and on the way to the bar tapped on McNeil's door, only half expecting an answer.

He ushered me in and returned to the bathroom to knot

135

his tie, while I turned to examine the view from his window. The rucksack was on his bed, as bulging and misshapen as ever, and obviously not yet unpacked. But on the dressing table were more rocks, a dozen or so of various shapes and sizes, next to a small pot of paint with a still wet brush resting on its closed lid. And all of the rocks had been daubed white.

'You expecting C.O.'s inspection?'

'What?' He emerged from the bathroom, shrugging himself into a linen jacket.

'Painting rocks? I haven't seen that since I was in the Army.'

'Oh those.' He was dismissive but uncomfortable, as if embarrassed that I'd seen them. 'They're from the hills round here. I collected them this afternoon. Come on – let's get a beer.'

Pepalasis had done better than that. He was a third of the way down a bottle of white wine when we found him and, if you excused his hangdog expression, seemed well on the way to recovery. 'So, Kirk?' he grinned. 'Enjoy your afternoon as a tourist?'

McNeil smiled back but saw me watching and I knew he would have to mention what I had seen in his room. 'I've been gathering rocks. Just a few. It's a hobby – a collection – I try to add to it on my travels. And I've arranged a Customs certificate of no commercial value – so it won't hold us up in the morning.'

I was quite certain that we weren't hearing the whole story, but if Pepalasis shared my view he gave no sign of it. 'You must have rocks in your head.' He growled. 'To do that – after what we've been doing.'

Over dinner the Greek tried hard to put a brave face on things but his mood of depression was never far from the surface. Even returning to London seemed in doubt. 'What's the point?' he asked at one stage. 'Mike's consortium won't do business now. Not when we return empty-handed.'

'I dunno,' McNeil said surprisingly. 'Sometimes as one door closes another opens. And unless you're washing your hands of the whole thing London's as good as any place to cook up a deal.'

Under the circumstances it seemed an astonishing thing to say. It was as plain as a pikestaff that the consortium wouldn't want anything to do with Pepalasis now. And neither would anyone else. I would have pursued the point but for rubbing salt in the Greek's wounds, so I stayed as non-committal as possible. But after half an hour's chat Pepalasis decided to return to London anyway, mainly, I sensed, because he didn't know what else to do and McNeil's comment about London being as good as anywhere seemed to convince him. That resolved, McNeil produced his own surprise: 'I've got a few calls to make in Sydney. Old friends. You know how it is – if they found out I'd been in town without looking them up I'd never hear the end of it. So I'll stop over for a day or two – see you guys back in London next week.'

'See if she's got a couple of friends,' Pepalasis suggested. 'And Mike and I'll keep you company.'

But McNeil smiled and shook his head, so that's how things worked out. We arrived in Sydney at four the next afternoon and the Greek and I caught the evening Jumbo to Heathrow – leaving McNeil 'down under'.

The long flight home couldn't have been more different from the outward one. No excited talk. No reminiscing. No sense of adventure. Just the stale tiredness of defeat. We drank too much, over-ate, and slept. But I suppose that it gave me a chance to think. To see things in perspective again. My 'get rich quick' dream was behind me. I'd enjoyed it and wasn't sorry to have had it, and I comforted myself with the thoughts of Hill Street and the resumption of a life spent earning money my way. Instead of gambling with holes in the ground. I smiled. I wasn't really cut out to be a prospector. An adventurer. At the end of the day I'd settle for what I was

– an accountant – and for perhaps the first time in my life I felt truly happy to be one.

Two miles above London I wrote Pepalasis a cheque for fifty thousand and that was an end of it. Generously he protested, saying that I should keep it, but I insisted and felt good doing it.

It was late afternoon when we touched down. Friday the twenty-sixth of August. McNeil had promised to let Jean know our flight details and I hurried through Customs knowing that I'd discovered something else about the things I wanted from life: that Jean was one of them.

CHAPTER FIVE

It was Bank Holiday weekend. Jean and I spent it together and without doing anything spectacular it became a special time for us both. We never as much as stirred from her flat until Sunday morning, when we roused ourselves for a drive out to Marlow for lunch, and then spent the afternoon downriver in a boat, just looking at each other and talking. God how we talked! Two people who had known each other as long as we had should have learned everything there was to know about each other long ago. But our new curiosity was boundless. And every revelation added to my enjoyment of her. The weather was balmy; we trailed bottles of wine in the water and made a honeymoon of it.

But Tuesday came and we were back at the office, trying hard to pretend that nothing had happened when all the time everything was fresh and exciting.

Things had been quiet during my absence, August always being our slowest month, so that by the end of the day I had brought myself up to date and started to plan September's work. Hallsworth had phoned to say he would be in the next afternoon and I pulled a face about breaking bad news whilst busying myself with other things. The day ended, Jean and I went out to dinner and back to her place afterwards. And the Greek's island seemed a million miles away. Until Harry Smithers phoned us on Wednesday.

'Recovered from your exertions?'

I misunderstood, my mind too full of last night with Jean, fumbling an answer to his question with one of my own: 'I thought you were holidaying in Bermuda?'

'Don't remind me. I was all set to go Saturday when I got Kirk's cable. Marion and the kids had gone and I'm supposed to join them at the weekend. Not that they're speaking to me right now.' He laughed without sounding amused. 'Still that's life. How're you feeling about this island?'

'Sick. I'd have sent you a report but I thought you were away.'

He paused before asking: 'Mike, is there someone in your office with you?'

'No. Why?'

Another pause. 'Perhaps we shouldn't discuss it on the phone anyway. Can you get across here? Kirk's with me now as a matter of fact – got back last night and stayed at my place.'

'It sounds urgent, Harry?'

'It is urgent.'

'How about lunchtime?'

'Sure – but don't plan on getting back much before the end of the afternoon.'

I finished the figures needed for my meeting with Hallsworth and then took a cab across town to A.W.F., curious about the mystery in Harry's voice.

Harry's secretary led me directly to the Board Room where Harry was waiting with McNeil and Peter Emanuel from the Bank. The table was laid out with a map of the Western Pacific, marked up with enough pencil lines to suggest that

McNeil had been pinpointing the island for them. We shook hands, Harry mixed me a drink and ushered me to a chair, while I tried to work out what all the excitement was about.

McNeil broke a nervous silence. 'Harry tells me I owe you an apology, Mike.' He hesitated. I guessed apologizing didn't come easily to a man like McNeil and he was wondering how to phrase it. Then he said: 'Well – I may as well come right out with it. As a matter of fact – I did find something on the island.'

I kept a tight rein on my reaction and my silence forced him to continue. 'I was pretty sure at the time, but I wanted an analyst's confirmation,' he said. 'Harry says I should have confided in you and – er, well I'm sorry I didn't. But for one thing I wanted my findings checked in a lab, and – ' he hesitated. 'And, well I didn't know whose side you'd be on. Harry's or the Greek's.'

'I thought it was a joint venture,' I said coldly.

He gave me a stubborn look and said, 'My function was to report my findings to Harry.'

'Are you saying that you found diamonds and kept quiet about it?'

'Jesus no! That *would* have been unethical. Forget diamonds. Pepalasis has a one-track mind. I've seen it before in prospectors – they get their heads fixed on something – like maybe they're after gold for instance – and that's it. They'll turn up copper and iron and every damn thing imaginable, but because it's not gold they'll go right past it without a second look.'

'But we found a diamond,' I said firmly. 'Disappointing I know but – '

'Forget it, will you. Okay there's a bit of kimberlite there – but tiny – not worth mining in a thousand years. Not commercially.'

He was as near hugging himself with excitement as I've ever seen anyone get and throwing quick, sideways glances at the others as if seeking approval. 'Shall I tell him, Harry?'

'It's nickel, Mike,' Harry announced. 'Kirk reckons the biggest strike since Poseidon.'

'Maybe even bigger,' McNeil burst in. 'Look at the map.' He hurried around to my side of the table. 'The island's somewhere in that triangle there, agree? New Hebrides, Fiji, New Caledonia. That's the clue. Manganese and gold at Fiji and just about everything under the sun at New Caledonia. But mainly a hell of a lot of nickel. They're still the second largest producer in the world, even now.'

'The point is,' Harry interrupted. 'The assay results of Kirk's samples are, to say the least, exciting.'

'Exciting!' McNeil's grin almost reached his ears. 'Some of the results made their hair curl back in Aussie I can tell you.'

I raised an eyebrow.

'Oh yeah, that's right.' He avoided my eye. 'That's what I did as soon as you left Sydney. Went down to the School of Mines with the samples. Now get this – this is the mindblowing bit – the first official figures out of Poseidon showed assay results of 3.5 per cent nickel and .55 copper. September 1969, remember? And stock markets went crazy the world over – right? Well, we *averaged* 4.8 nickel! Averaged! And 1.22 copper. Can you believe that?'

I shook my head, bemused by the whole thing. Harry freshened my drink and took the chair next to me. 'Poseidon, Mike,' he said, bright-eyed with excitement. 'There's been nothing to touch it in *my* life-time, let alone yours. Remember their shares on the London Stock Exchange? Opening at 7s 6d old money – and four months later you couldn't buy them for a hundred pounds each.'

I nodded absently, my mind still full of the island. 'But don't you have to drill or something?' I asked McNeil. 'For confirmation.'

He shook his head. 'Those caves did most of our drilling for us. How far down do you reckon we went? Seven hundred – eight hundred feet? My guess is a good eight fifty

141

on the first site, and maybe a thousand on the second. And I sampled at both points. And other places, as far as four or five miles apart. There's a lot of other stuff there of course, not usually associated with nickel. Conglomerates, basalt and stuff. Threw me at first, I don't mind admitting. But I know this Mike, that place is Aladdin's cave it's so rich.'

'So we found a fortune after all?' I said, trying to take it all in. 'By accident.'

'Happens all the time,' said McNeil happily. 'They nearly missed it in Aussie I can tell you. Hitting nickel at Kambalda was a pure bloody fluke. Everyone was uranium crazy then. That's all they wanted to know about. Then this bloke Cowcill finds nickel in his garage and they all get excited about nickel instead.'

'But the island's under water for two months of the year,' I remembered. 'What good's a mine that floods regularly?'

McNeil shook his head. 'Don't worry. My guess is that the surface only gets swamped to a couple of feet or so. We could build sea fences against that. Even if we can't – and I think we can – the Canadians are mining nickel and copper in ocean three miles deep.'

I think I sat shaking my head through most of this – the world of mining seemed utterly unpredictable to me. 'So what happens now? I asked. 'Presumably you want to go back for a second look?'

'Would Pepalasis buy that?' Harry sounded doubtful. 'After all he's entitled to wave the contract at us – say it's time we put up or shut up.'

'Well hardly – after all, he short delivered at his end didn't he?'

'The point is,' Harry said, 'Kirk's already convinced – even without another look. The size of the find is enormous.'

'*Probably* enormous,' McNeil qualified. 'Big certainly. Probably very, very big.'

'Pepalasis will be over the moon.' I remembered his face when I'd left him at Heathrow.

'Ah?' Emanuel cleared his throat and spoke for the first time. 'We were coming to that. You see he's got no idea of what's there, has he? And from what Kirk says he's a bitterly disappointed man at the moment. Fed up with the whole thing, eh?'

I had wondered why Emanuel was in on the meeting. Now he was going to tell me.

'Seems to me,' he said slowly, as if trying out a new thought, 'A man in that frame of mind might be persuaded to sell pretty low. Know what I mean? Sort of peanuts.'

I was prevented from answering by the arrival of Harry's secretary with a tray of sandwiches and coffee. We nursed our drinks in silence until she left.

Harry resumed immediately. 'You see Mike, contractually we're under no obligation to tell Pepalasis what we know, and subject to what he found to be prepared to invest short term finance.'

'And if we *do* tell him,' Emanuel joined in, 'he's under no obligation to work with us. Not in developing a nickel mine anyway. That's the problem.'

'He'll still need cash,' I pointed out.

'Huh, that won't be difficult,' Emanuel said positively. 'Not if Kirk's findings become general knowledge. Your Greek could go and find himself a whole new ball game. Without us. We'd have helped pinpoint a fortune for someone else.'

'So what do you suggest?'

'That we buy him out and control it ourselves.' Emanuel delivered his conclusion like an ultimatum.

'But why? Why not work with him?'

'We daren't risk telling him, that's why!' he snapped back, as if I was being particularly stupid. 'Tell him what's there and he might choose not to work with *us*.'

Harry shook his head in agreement. 'You said yourself he can be a difficult man, Mike. Look at all the problems we had coming to an agreement in the first place.'

I nodded, remembering, but also remembering how fair the Greek had been about the fifty thousand.

'What do you think, Mike?' Harry sounded anxious.

'Are you asking me to find out?' I reached for a sandwich.

'What's his mood like at the moment?' Harry countered.

'Depressed as hell last time I saw him. But he's the resilient type. I bet he's bounced on his arse before and come back.' I had another thought.

'Anyway any offer now would convince him that McNeil found diamonds and held out on him.'

Harry thought about that and then said, 'It's not that we want to cheat him of course.' He sounded like an extortionist apologizing for his high prices. 'But I really don't see that we can play it any other way. And what the eye doesn't see the heart doesn't grieve over.'

'My point exactly,' Emanuel nodded enthusiastically. 'Right now I bet he'll be only too pleased to wash his hands of the whole project.'

'Yeah, I know,' I said. 'We'll be doing him a favour.'

'Look Mike, this is going to be big. Really big,' Emanuel bubbled. 'But we've got to do it *our* way. The Greek would just complicate it. Let's pay him a profit and get him out.'

'And then?'

'Then the big sell. Profit projections. The Poseidon experience. Forecast recovery of the world commodity prices. The whole bit. I can tell you the City's *ready* for another Poseidon. Hell, maybe the whole world's *ready*. We launch as a public company from go. Simultaneous placements in London, New York and Tokyo. Can you imagine? Whatever the offer price of the shares we'll be over subscribed a hundred times. Follow me?'

'It's not difficult.'

'Sure it's not. But you're the key, Mike. You're the promoter. You're going to have to negotiate with Pepalasis. For which you'll want a fee. And we convert the fee into shares. How's that sound?'

144

'Fine. *If* Pepalasis sells.'

'It won't be easy. We know that. That's why the fee's substantial.' He looked pleased enough for both of us. 'We thought five hundred thousand shares, Mike.'

'One pound shares?'

'Sure one pound shares. One pound at placement. After that, who *knows* what they'll fetch? Three pounds. Five pounds. A hundred pounds.'

'It's *that* big?'

'Bad word,' he shook his head. 'Try enormous. Take the tax angle alone. Any mining group – anywhere – Australia, Canada, anywhere – pays a lease to the host government for all ore extracted. Then local taxes on top. Company tax on top of that. One way or another a host government snatches better than seventy per cent of the mining company's true take. Whereas this island – ' He shrugged and let the sentence hang in the air.

I remembered Pepalasis the first time we'd met, equally excited about his tax haven.

'How much do you reckon to pay for the island?' I asked. '*If* he'll sell.'

'That's for you to negotiate, Mike,' Harry raised an eyebrow. 'What's two hundred square miles of derelict land worth in that part of the world?'

'Especially when it floods two months of the year,' McNeil added.

We talked about it some more before I took my leave of them and journeyed back to Hill Street. However hard I tried, it was *impossible* not to get excited. This Pepalasis project! There was something about it which just wouldn't lie down. Another chance to earn a fortune. If Pepalasis would agree to sell.

CHAPTER SIX

It was past six when I got back to Hill Street. Hallsworth was slumped on my chesterfield with Jean perched on the arm of the chair opposite. They both nursed drinks and were so deep in conversation that I startled them when I opened the door. There was something about the scene, both of them so obviously relaxed in each other's company, which made me feel like an intruder in my own office. And possessively jealous about Jean. Of course, it was damn silly. The feeling came and went in a split second. But I felt it all the same.

We said our 'hello's, Jean fixed me a drink before returning to her own room, and Hallsworth and I got down to business.

'Which first?' I asked. 'Good news or bad news?'

He groaned. 'The day I've had and you've got *more* bad news?'

I wondered which of his interests was causing the problem but didn't dwell on it. 'No diamonds,' I said brutally. 'At least nothing worth mining.'

He was even more shocked than I had expected. So I gave him the good news and sat in pleased silence whilst he digested it. Then he was positively delirious with his recollections of Poseidon and had me almost laughing with excitement.

'But I *still* can't believe it.' He shook his head. 'I mean, Pepalasis was so damn certain about diamonds. And now nickel? Nickel of all things. It's amazing – I bet Ari can't believe his luck!'

'He doesn't know,' I said and finished the story. He listened as carefully as always, asking the occasional question until he was satisfied that he'd learned all there was to know. And then began to laugh.

'What's funny?'

'My bad news.' He was still laughing. 'My bad news – is – is suddenly very funny.'

I sipped my drink and waited.

'The big deal I've been working on,' he explained eventually. 'The one in the States. It as good as fell apart this week – today as a matter of fact.'

'That's funny?'

'Hysterical. When you know about it.' He was still grinning hugely. 'Our end was to supply plant for a new mill for U.S. steel. A *lot* of plant – worth twenty-eight million dollars. Tenders accepted months ago, all set as far as we were concerned. Then U.S Steel started wetting themselves about the future stability of the world nickel market. Two things worry them – supply and price. If the world economy revives in the mid-eighties they predict demand for nickel could outstrip supply. So they've been trying to buy forward. Problem is the producers pool output and market collectively, and the marketing boys, both here and in the States, won't guarantee price or volume more than a year ahead. A lot of crap about their responsibility to the mining houses to maintain a stable market – in reality a price ring. Now, my problem. U.S Steel want guaranteed price and volume for the next five years to calculate the return on their investment. Given that they go ahead – and I get my contract. Without it? Well, they've been pussyfooting around for months now with my order getting colder every day. And today they more or less buried it.'

I whistled aloud and then got ahead of him. 'So we put the two together!'

'Do you think we *could*?'

'If Harry's consortium buy the island?' I asked. 'Will U.S. Steel sign a five year contract?'

'They'll sign terms with the devil to get that nickel.'

'Guaranteed prices? Large quantities?'

'Gilt-edged on vast amounts!' He nodded.

'So if we get the right price they'll as good as finance the whole operation.' I whistled again. 'The consortium would be onto a fortune. Without risking a penny!'

'And I get my order for plant at the same time.'

It would be hard to say who was the more excited. We poured fresh drinks, calmed down as much as possible, and started looking for snags. Pepalasis was certainly one but timing was another. 'That could be the killer,' Hallsworth said. 'Vince Pickard – he's the V.P. in charge of the project – is in London now and this morning he was worried sick that his Board will shelve the project. You know what that means – mutually exclusive investments – tying cash up elsewhere – it could be five years before Vince gets it back on the table.'

That would be a blow. 'How long's he here for?'

'Vince? Never sits still long. Maybe a week. I can find out, I'm meeting him for dinner. Want to come?'

I decided against it. A meeting now would be premature. But another chat with Harry Smithers seemed a good idea. So I phoned to suggest he and McNeil join Jean and me for dinner, and Hallsworth left to hold U.S. Steel's hand for the evening. And I was just pouring myself a fresh drink when Jean came in: 'Weren't you ever told it's bad for you to drink alone?'

I took the hint and poured one for her while telling her about our dinner date. She seemed pleased. It was a new role, social contact with business associates. She fooled about for a few minutes, fluttering eyelashes and asking what special duties would I like her to perform now that she was a 'hostess'? Then when I told her that Harry and McNeil would be arriving within half an hour she fled to Fulham to change.

I went upstairs to the flat to wash and had just got into a clean shirt when the phone rang.

'Hullo, you're back then!' Sue said. 'How marvellous. I'm dying to hear how it all went. Give me the outline now but save the juicy bits for Friday.'

'Friday?'

'Umm, I thought I'd come up for the weekend.'

I struggled for the right words, not really wanting to see her but feeling I owed her that much. After all I had enjoyed her company and her body for more than two years in a relationship which had been part friendship and part affair. Now it was over. Except she didn't know that.

'Hallsworth's around a lot at the moment,' I said lamely. 'He might be around on Friday evening.'

'Oh.'

I *felt* disappointment come down the telephone and cringed with embarrassment.

'Mike? You're still there?'

My finger nails dug hard into the palm of my left hand and I was clammy all over despite the fresh shirt, but yes, I was still there. 'I was thinking – perhaps we could meet somewhere else? Have dinner?'

'Only dinner? Darling it's been *weeks*!'

'Sue, there's something I've got to tell you. It's –'

'Oh, don't spoil it. I want to hear all about it, properly, when we meet. Dinner on Friday then?'

'Friday? No – it's difficult – we've got this big deal on, well *possibly* we've got this big deal on. Conceivably we'll be working all weekend and –'

'Oh, you and work! Don't you ever stop? Well Monday then – you've got to take a break sometime. Okay?'

'Yes, okay, but –'

'Fine. But where, I mean if Hill Street's still difficult?'

God, I was making a mess of it! Other men seemed to cope with this sort of thing without much trouble. Off with the old and on with the new. Why not just come out with it? Tell her it's all finished.

'I know just the place,' she was saying when I tuned back in. 'Remember that hotel at Windsor? We had lunch there once. Overlooking the river. Why not meet there? It's perfect.' Suddenly she was giggling, that throaty chuckle which was so much a part of her. 'And bring an overnight case, I'm counting on more than dinner.'

'Windsor?' I was still trying to find the right words. 'Oh yes, I know where you – –'

'Right. Eight on Monday then. Take care, darling – 'Bye.'

And I was still opening my mouth to protest when she hung up.

CHAPTER TWO

'So you're the young man with the mining deal?' Vince Pickard pumped my arm. 'Say, am I glad to meet you.'

'Mike's not in commodities, Vince,' Hallsworth corrected, anxious to protect me from technical questions. 'He's a money man.'

'Shit, when wasn't money a commodity? Get me a bundle at a discount will you, Mike?'

Pickard's office two days later. Except *office* is misleading. But then everything about Marlborough House was misleading – including its name. A pile of Victorian red brick standing in fifty acres of Hertfordshire, just north of St Albans. From the outside, a well preserved country house set amidst manicured lawns and rhododendrons, protected from public gaze by twelve foot walls, wrought iron gates and security guards. And from the inside, the most impressive display of corporate muscle I've ever seen.

The first hint of it being a meeting out of the ordinary came when Hallsworth announced us at the gate-keeper's lodge and Pickard's security men took the car apart with stares like lasers.

'I'll vouch for him,' Hallsworth grinned at one of the men and nodded at me before explaining: 'Normally you're asked for identification – and even the most respectable submit to having their briefcases searched.'

150

I passed mine out of the car door for inspection but the man shook his head: 'Pardon me but that won't be necessary, Mr Townsend.' To which I said 'thank you,' and he answered 'you're welcome,' in that unexpectedly gracious manner Americans have. After which we crunched the car wheels over the hundred yards of gravel drive to the front door.

The oak panelled reception hall was bigger than centre court Wimbledon and smothered with the trappings of the British aristocracy. But the rooms behind were a revelation, stuffed with Cape Canaveral electronics and operated by men talking fluent Harvard Business to girls listening with the fluid poise of MGM. The entire staff of fifteen were American and the offices buzzed with the business of U.S. Steel. Yet no one would have known, from the outside.

I asked Pickard why the secrecy.

'Politics,' he said. 'With you Brits its always politics.'

He answered my puzzled look with a pitying one of his own: 'We *have* to keep a low profile. If your unions even suspected we were here you'd have a General Strike on your hands. And why, for Chrissakes? To protect British Steel.' He shook his head as if the puzzle baffled him. 'We could supply this country with all the steel you need and then some. But no – your politicians *have* to be in the steel business. Not for money – hell no – but for what they call the national interest. But can you tell me what kind of interest allows British Steel to piss away two million bucks a day?'

The hired help might be Ivy League but Pickard himself was plain, old-fashioned American business. He was also just about the fastest thing I've ever seen outside a race track. Rapid fire speech, a jerky laugh and quick darting eyes. I ducked the political debate in favour of a feigned interest in the electronics.

'Everything works overtime, Mike. Gives us the big picture. Globally. Right round the clock. Howie!' He summoned an assistant. 'Show Mike the main com-

151

munications set up, will you. He'll be real pleased to see it whilst he's here.'

Pleased or not I saw it. And listened to a highly technical explanation from a whizz kid ten years my junior while Pickard and Hallsworth moved off to say their goodbyes. Hallsworth was bowing out after the introductions fearing a conflict of interest if he participated more fully. Of course I had agreed, despite a hunch that I'd miss his skill as a negotiator before the day was over.

'Your other boys on their way?' Pickard asked when he rejoined me. His speech was so fast that I had to replay it in my mind to make sure I had the sense of it.

'Any minute,' I looked at my watch. 'I believe you said twelve noon, Mr Pickard, it's a couple of minutes to.'

'Swell – Vince by the way. You want a drink or something?'

Harry Smithers, McNeil and Emanuel arrived in time to give their requests to the white-coated steward and, while we waited for the drinks, we did the grand tour all over again. Pickard may have been hidden behind a CIA style security screen but he took his responsibilities as a host seriously. Everything was explained – the computers, the video satellite with Pittsburgh, the charts, statistics, and the unceasing flow of telex messages arriving from every corner of the globe.

The tour ended at a cold buffet table set up in a small dining room. 'You men help yourselves,' Pickard waved at the tables. 'All I have for lunch is a piece of cheese and an apple.'

Our meal was more substantial and having served ourselves we sat around a low table and did the business small talk bit, world trade, the American economy, that sort of thing – until Pickard could restrain himself no longer: 'Mike's partner tells me you boys can help me with my problem?'

'Maybe,' Harry answered for all of us. 'How big's the problem?'

152

'Big enough to bury me,' Pickard's grin dared anyone to try. 'Harry, I'll tell you – unless I find a guaranteed source of fifty thousand metric tons of processed sulphide every year for the next five, I'm in big trouble.'

McNeil's eyes popped. 'Starting when, Mr Pickard?'

'Like I said – Vince. Starting any time. But not later than a year from now. 'Course that means tying up contracts a whole lot sooner.'

'What price structure did you have in mind?' Emanuel asked.

'You tell me.' Pickard grinned, too wily to be first bidder at an auction.

Emanuel avoided telling him any such thing and it was one-way traffic for a while as Pickard listed his requirements and rapped out answers to our questions. It was an impressive performance and we showed badly by comparison, Harry and McNeil especially vague at times. Of course I knew why – without an agreement with Pepalasis in our pocket we could hardly play it any other way – but Pickard grew visibly irritated when his open way of doing business wasn't reciprocated: 'For Chrissakes, what's the problem? It's a straight choice who you get into bed with – me or those shits at the Metals Exchange.'

McNeil glanced anxiously at Harry. 'Delivery could be tight, Vince. We've got a lot of construction work to contend with, building a processing plant, you know how delays crop up.'

'Is *that* all? Shit, we won't argue over a couple of lousy months. Give me warning and I'll work round it. If you fall short at the start you'll make it up, won't you? Say by the second year?'

'So no penalty clauses in the contract?'

'Screw you if you come in late? Where's the percentage? I want sulphide not blood. Guaranteed prices and total delivery over five years. Gimme that and I get my new plant.'

And Hallsworth gets his order I thought.

Harry looked pleased. 'So we write a contract at today's market price. Two thousand pounds a ton, with, say, a ten per cent per annum price riser and an escalation clause to take care of any increase in world freight costs.'

Pickard's face was expressionless. 'All other cost increases, your problem?'

Harry nodded.

I held my breath while I multiplied tonnages by price and sagged with the weight of the answer. If Pickard said yes, we had stitched together the biggest deal of my life in less time than an average housewife would take to buy a week's groceries.

But Pickard didn't say yes. Instead he unleashed a battery of questions about our ability to meet his requirements which left us gasping. Answering was like feeding a computer. Black eyes blinked at each reply and stored it away in a memory bank. Until finally he asked Harry: 'You really got that much nickel?'

'We think so.'

'Who's we?'

'Well, Kirk here has just completed the initial survey.' Harry wilted under the steady gaze. 'I don't know if you're aware of Mr McNeil's reputation –'

'Yeah, we've checked him out. You're good, McNeil. At least everyone says so. But the rest of you guys are money men, aren't you?'

Emanuel shrugged. 'We're businessmen, Vince.'

'Yeah, I know. Just trying to make an honest buck.'

There was a murmur of faint laughter while we waited for him to continue. 'Tell you something though,' he said thoughtfully. 'You've sure got yourselves a valuable piece of real estate. Wherever it is.'

We had refused to divulge the location of our source, but the pressure of his questions had trapped us into revealing its off-shore potential. And he stayed with it like a dog sniffing a bitch on heat.

'Howie!' Pickard raised his voice and the whizz kid appeared in the open doorway. 'Get yourself in here a minute will you. And bring Charlie – there's maybe something you can do for me.'

Charlie astonished us by being a well constructed brunette with a notebook and a hemline that swivelled our eyes as she took her place next to Pickard.

'Boys, I'm turning you down.' Pickard didn't surprise, he *stunned* us. 'And I'm real sorry. How's that saying? It hurts me more than it hurts you? Never more true. Let me tell you what I don't like about it. Apart from McNeil here there's not a mining man among you – which makes me vulnerable. Sure, you'll bank-roll the operation. Mike's partner's already vouched for that. But the whole thing hinges on McNeil getting stuff out of the ground. And how well he sweet talks you when things go wrong. Suppose you get knuckle-headed? Argue about more cash when he comes in over budget? Cut back on his expenditure requirements?' He pulled a face. 'See what I mean? Who needs it?'

Of course we protested – McNeil could hire all the technical expertise he wanted, we'd be receptive to his needs at all times, and a lot more besides – but Pickard had made up his mind.

'On the other hand,' he rewarded us with a quick smile. 'You're all men of integrity so when you say you've discovered a field with my kind of quantities, I believe you. The nickel's in the ground and I want it bad enough to cry. The trick is to get it at minimal risk to me and allow you boys a profit – right? So I'll put it to you straight. I'll buy you out. I'll buy all rights in your field. Outright purchase. And maybe some kind of royalty deal above certain output.'

It was so obviously the best possible outcome that we kicked ourselves for not seeing it to begin with. We'd neither have to raise working capital to go into the mining business, nor to be involved in the risks that went with it. And U.S. Steel would have their own source of nickel under their own

155

control. Everybody gained. And our profit came fast – the simple difference between buying from the Greek and selling to the Americans. With maybe royalties to come later as the icing on the cake.

Pickard was talking to McNeil when my mind refocused on the conversation: 'Kirk, if we can deal on this basis I'd sure like you with us. Get that field under your management and our control and that's *real* muscle at work. And I tell you this – we've a way of looking after our own that beats running your own cat house.'

We spent half an hour batting the idea round before Howie interrupted: 'Mr Pickard – your next appointment –'

'Yeah? Already? Oh shit!' Pickard pulled a diary from an inside pocket and began leafing through its pages. 'Harry, if you're interested in doing things my way here's how it runs. Monday afternoon I leave for Frankfurt, then Turin for a week and on to Osaka for another week. So I get back to Pittsburgh on the twenty-third and my big meeting's on the thirtieth.' He snapped the diary shut. 'So if we're going to put a deal together, it's gotta be this weekend. My feeling is that a letter of intent oughta hold it until I get back Stateside. Then why don't you and the boys here get out to Pittsburgh for say the twenty-sixth, twenty-seventh, and we'll wrap it all up then?'

It was a lifeline and we grabbed it. The weekend to clinch agreement with U.S. Steel and then three weeks to patch a deal together with Pepalasis.

'Now you keep real quiet about this, Mike.' Pickard squeezed my elbow as he walked us back to the reception hall. 'That's a condition – understand? Whatever we put together I want under wraps until I get back. So top secret, eh? A lot of people would like to see me fail with this project and I wanna see their faces when I pull it off.' He turned to Howie. 'Know who I mean?'

Howie was still ecstatic when we left, having arranged to return at eleven in the morning.

We spent the evening discussing tactics, closeted in my office at Hill Street until the overpowering fug of tobacco smoke drove us out in search of fresh air and food. It was an education for me. The economics of mineral recovery are very different from the more predictable areas of industrial activity. Some of the figures are staggering. Texaco for instance, spending two hundred and fifty million on the Tartan oilfield. Shell laying out one thousand, two hundred and fifty million on one field alone in the North Sea. Of course, nickel's not that rich, but it's got its good points. Like the States importing four hundred million pounds worth of processed ore every year because they've none of their own.

But negotiating with Pickard and his 'in house' lawyer Clem Atkins was like chewing leather, and there was a point on the Saturday when I thought we'd never reach an agreement. So after eight hours of it we adjourned until the following morning.

Sunday began well. Emanuel got a price of seventy million on the table, based on McNeil's qualified estimate of the likely yield, and we started from there. By noon were arguing between Pickard's highest offer of forty million and our 'sticking point' of sixty. And half way through the afternoon we reached the inevitable compromise. U.S. Steel would buy the island for fifty million pounds outright and we would waive any claim to royalties. Once again I was on the road to a fortune. After all, as McNeil said on the way back into town, 'All you've got to do now, Mike, is to buy the island from Pepalasis.'

Part Four

CHAPTER ONE

The very next morning, Monday, Hallsworth and I opened negotiations with Pepalasis. It went badly, worse than I'd feared. The Greek was furious. McNeil and I were accused of finding diamonds and not disclosing them. He'd taken us for gentlemen and we'd taken him for a ride. And a lot more in the same vein. It was a bit too near the truth for comfort but there was damn all I could do about it. Especially as Hallsworth had come down heavily on Emanuel's side concerning the need for total secrecy.

The three of us lunched together, Pepalasis glowering, me defensive, and Hallsworth as smooth as silk. And after the meal Hallsworth took me to one side and quietly suggested he'd make more progress without my help than with it, so with a sigh of relief I left them at the Dorchester and retreated to Hill Street to get on with other things. Until the evening, when I went to Windsor to keep my date with Sue.

Jean knew where I was going. It would have been difficult not to tell her, what with me having as good as moved into the Fulham flat. The previous evening, on the way from St Albans to Jean's place, feeling tired and mangled but triumphant after the marathon session with Pickard, I had rehearsed how I'd handle it. Just slip it in. Casually. Between news of Pickard and everything else that was going on. But Jean had prepared my favourite dinner; the wine was chilled and she looked enchanting. And it seemed a pity to risk spoiling a perfect evening. So I left it till later. When we were in bed, dozing in that relaxed twilight which exists between lovemaking and sleep.

'Of course you must go,' she'd said, wide awake suddenly, and using a voice straight from the deep freeze. 'I know you'll have a *lovely* time. See you at the office shall I? On Tuesday morning.'

I groaned in the darkness, knowing that I'd planned to return to Fulham afterwards. But there seemed little point in prolonging a discussion about it. So we sighed our way to sleep, restlessly, instead of drifting into it in the way we were getting used to.

I went to Windsor and Sue turned every head in the bar when she arrived. And the kiss of welcome she gave me left every man watching it gasping for another drink, me included; so it was another half hour before we moved to the seclusion of a corner table in the restaurant. By then I'd told her all I could think of about the visit to the island, but nothing of what had happened since.

'So, your adventure's over?' she asked, grey eyes as round as saucers. 'Poor darling. All that work for nothing. And the *risks* you took! Mike, that awful man could have got you *killed* in that dreadful place.'

I spent a while defending 'that awful man' until I could put it off no longer. 'Sue, I'm getting married.' I wasn't sure whether I was or not – really I'd not thought that far ahead. But 'getting married' seemed to have the ring of finality needed at that moment.

'Oh?' Her slate eyes registered surprise, shock, even doubt. But thank God, she didn't break into hysterics, or cry, or any damn fool thing like that. 'How sudden,' she said coolly, and moved her knee away from mine as if she had just diagnosed something contagious.

'Well – yes – in a way. But not in another. You see I've known Jean for four years. I mean it doesn't seem sudden when –'

'Jean? Your secretary?'

'That's right.'

I got the strangest feeling that the news alarmed her. Not

159

me getting married – it seemed that after all I could have married anyone without breaking her heart – but marrying Jean appeared to worry her. For a moment or two she was almost angry, a small spot of red touching her each cheek before she got herself in check again.

'So, no overnight case tonight?' Her earthy humour came to the rescue, peeping out from beneath lowered lashes, while I, like a bloody fool, said: 'Well, it's not that I don't – ' and shut up, having made things even worse.

She laughed then, a low chuckle with a touch of brittleness in it somewhere. 'Well – we've always been "just good friends", haven't we, Mike – so stop being so damned embarrassed about everything.'

It got rid of the awkwardness and we both cheered up, relaxing enough to have a couple more drinks to take us well over the legal limit. Of all things, she seemed curious about Jean, wanting to know how much I told her about my business life and things generally. Had I, for instance, told her where I was going tonight? And then, just as we were leaving, she said: 'I'm sorry, Mike. Sorry now, that it was you. Remember that, eh?'

I puzzled about that all the way back to town. Sorry? Not sorry that we were perhaps seeing each other for the last time. Not sorry that I was getting married. But 'sorry now, that it was you'. Strange thing to say. Still I suppose there are times when the words don't quite come out the way we mean them. Especially when we're embarrassed, or upset. Or something.

Looking back, those weeks seem like a view glimpsed from a speeding train. Everything happened so quickly. For the first few days Hallsworth kept after Pepalasis, returning to Hill Street every evening after long sessions at the Dorchester, tired and talked dry, but far from dispirited. And the breakthrough came on Thursday, when the Greek conceded that he *might* sell if the price was right. Establishing

160

just how right took another day, so it was Friday evening when I heard about it.

'Thirty million? Pounds?' I was shattered. 'It's a hell of a lot more than we'd bargained for.'

'It's a hell of a lot less than he wants,' Hallsworth retorted hotly, as if detecting criticism of his handling of the negotiations. 'But I think it's what he'll settle for.'

Normally it would have ended there. I'd have said ditch the whole thing. But not when we were sitting on U.S. Steel's written offer of fifty million. We were still looking at a profit of *twenty million*! If Pepalasis was being greedy, so were we. So we stifled our disappointment and Hallsworth held the Greek's hand while Emanuel and I got on with the job of raising money. Even today, thirty million's a lot of cash, and finding it quickly and quietly is damn difficult. But we had a few things going for us. Like Harry's original consortium sticking by their commitment for twenty million, and of course just having Harry around helped. A twenty-year track record as good as his was something that investors liked rubbing shoulders with. And something of the same could be said for Emanuel's bank. Even me I suppose, to a lesser extent.

But what usually clinched it was the letter of intent. The one Pickard delivered by hand following our Sunday meeting at Marlborough House. Generally one look at that was enough to swing the waverers. Typed as it was on U.S. Steel letterhead and signed by Pickard as Vice President and Clem Atkins as legal advisor to the board. Even Poignton was convinced that it was a binding, *provided* we delivered our end of the bargain by the thirtieth of the month. Of course Pickard's letter contained some provisos, but not many and the only one of importance was a warranty about the minimum nickel content of the site. That one really put McNeil on the spot. Naturally he would have preferred to make another visit to the island, normally he would have sought a second opinion, ideally he would have saturated the site with a whole team of experts. But Pickard's deadline and the need for secrecy killed those options stone dead. So McNeil spent the best part of two nights on the phone to the most experienced quantity surveyors in Australia until the general opinion emerged that the location of his nickel discoveries had been so far apart, both laterally and vertically, to suggest a field of enormous dimensions, at least four times larger than Pickard's minimum qualifications. So, given that, we all breathed a sigh of relief and got on with chasing the money.

Emanuel's bank came in with two million on their own acount, and some of my clients formed their own 'mini consortium' to provide another one. I flew out to St Tropez for a day, interrupting Tommy Richardson's holiday to persuade him to bring the Leppard Peplow crowd in for two more. Mind, there were strings in Tommy's involvement. He agreed to commit his money if Townsend and Partner put money in as well. So I pledged Hallsworth's million and flew home to get his approval.

'All of it? Every penny?' He was more than a bit taken aback.

I shrugged. 'We've got to show confidence. Anyway it's the best investment going. That's what I've told those clients who'll keep quiet about it. What's good for them should be good for us too.'

He argued for a while, about trusting all of his eggs to the Greek's basket, but in the end he agreed and we called Jean in to take a minute of the decision. Despite that, the days slipped by and with fifteen left before Pickard's deadline, Emanuel and I were still four million short of the thirty needed to pay Pepalasis. Our daily conferences became increasingly desperate.

'Hell, all we're looking for is a short term bridging!' he said one evening. 'We've got corporate finance for the best part of the deal and we're still stuck.'

We combed our combined contact lists for the tenth time before admitting that we had tried everyone we could rely on

162

to keep quiet about it. Or who wouldn't take too long making a decision. Or who had access to that kind of money. The constraints of time and secrecy seemed to be combining to cheat us of a once in a lifetime opportunity. Until Emanuel surprised me by saying: 'There is one man I know.' We had been at my office for a couple of hours or so, and had sunk a few drinks while searching for inspiration. 'Not top drawer banking, or anything like that, but I think he could raise the money.'

'All of it?' I gave him the kind of look I normally reserve for the slow-witted.

He nodded, and then said: 'Simmy Drachman.'

'You know him?'

'The bank's even done business with him.' His smile was a shade selfconscious. 'Kept bloody quiet about it, mind you.'

'I bet.'

Drachman's name had the aroma of an open sewer. A North London jobbing builder who had moved into property at the right time, converting rat infested tenements into bijou residences for short haul commuters. After that he had blossomed out into betting shops for a while, then he had sold out, and funnelled his cash into strip joints, sex emporiums and porn. And those were his *legitimate* interests! There were plenty of rumours of his involvement in the drug scene around Soho and out in the provinces. I had never met the man, but his reputation would send Harry Smithers and Tommy Richardson racing each other for the front door. I said as much to Emanuel.

'So we keep his name out of it,' Emanuel didn't even hesitate.

'Let Drachman put the money up through us. You and me. We get a cut on the profit and no one's any the wiser.'

We drank whisky until it made sense and once Emanuel had latched onto the idea he fell in love with it. 'He's not as bad as he's painted and it's the sort of deal he'd jump at. And he's used to keeping his mouth shut. We wouldn't be marrying the bastard. Just this one transaction, that's all.'

I thought *what the hell*? No one else that I knew would be able to find four million in a hurry.

We went to see Drachman the following evening. I was sober by then and a good deal more hesitant than the night before, instinct telling me that I was a fool to get involved with a man like Drachman. But as the same instinct failed to provide a source for the other four million I went along – especially as Emanuel had fixed the appointment.

Drachman's office was the basement of a club he owned in Paddington. We were shown into a big, square room, artificially lit, well furnished in ultra modern on knee deep carpet. The air conditioning, set at morgue temperature, just failed to dispel the combined smells of cologne, sweat and fear. But the room itself was less arresting than the people in it. Drachman peering up suspiciously from behind a six-foot-wide desk, a little man of around fifty with a bald head, broken nose and strong eyes; and flanked by two men capable of winning the world heavyweight championship single-handed.

Emanuel outlined the proposition so casually that investing four million sounded less important than borrowing a car for the weekend. Still, it was his way of telling the story and he knew best how to hook a man like Drachman. When he got to the other participants he listed them like a roll of honour and produced the letter from Pickard with a conjurer's flourish.

Drachman feigned indifference while his fish eyes psyched me out: 'I've heard of you,' his voice was a soft growl. 'You've a nice reputation Mr Townsend, yes, very nice – very nice indeed.'

I tried to return the compliment but gagged on the words.

'Are you interested?' asked Emanuel bluntly.

'I might be.' Drachman was still studying me. 'What's my cut?'

Emanuel pretended to consider the matter for the first time. 'Well, we'll only need the money for a month or so. And it's safer than houses. Shall we say ten per cent?'

'Say that and you can go fuck yourself.'

Emanuel barely blinked: 'So – you got any ideas?'

Drachman took a cigar from a sandalwood box on his desk and spent a long time working it over with a steel-bladed gold cutter. We watched as the plump white hands fluttered about their task, gold rings on two fingers of each hand picking up light signals from the desk lamp. 'A deal this big?' His eyes remained fixed on the cigar. 'I'd want to double my money.'

'In a few weeks?' I snorted. 'We're wasting each other's time, Mr Drachman. Come on Peter.'

Emanuel's feigned indignation extended to half rising from his chair, as the goon on Drachman's left glared at me and his mate busied himself lighting Drachman's cigar.

'Too much for you, Mr Townsend?' Drachman asked, invisible behind a cloud of blue smoke.

'Too much time,' I answered quickly, 'putting this thing together, to throw it away now.'

'I doubt you've any alternative.'

'And I doubt you could raise four million.'

The left hand goon stopped filing his nails long enough to fix me with a look of total disbelief before the smoke parted and Drachman beamed out from the other side. 'Four million? For a few weeks? Difficult, but it could be done. It would need organising though, and that costs money Mr Townsend – which is why it's so expensive.'

'So? You were offered four hundred thousand profit. Take it out of that.'

'It's not enough. Really it's not.' His thin lips removed themselves from the cigar and split into a wolfish smile. 'You wouldn't be here now, Mr Townsend, if the profit wasn't very big. Or if you could raise the money elsewhere.'

There was no answer to that.

'And there's the risk factor to consider,' he added.

'What risk? U.S. Steel won't go broke. There's no risk and you know it.'

'There's *always* a risk.' His face flushed angrily. 'U.S. Steel pay your consortium, they pay you, you pay me. I'm tail end Charlie. Anything goes wrong and I'm bad luck Charlie.'

'What could go wrong?'

'You might forget to pay me?'

For Emanuel's sake and the sake of the deal I kept hold of my temper. 'So sue me.'

His lips smiled, but the amusement never reached his eyes. They stayed as hard as ever while he said: 'Of course, I know that wouldn't happen – not with gentlemen like you involved.'

We skirmished for a while longer and then the hard bargaining began. The weekend arguing with Pickard must have sharpened us up a bit, though, because an hour later Emanuel and I had a deal we were a lot happier with than showed on our faces.

'Before you go, Mr Townsend,' Drachman said as we stood to leave. 'There's something I'd like you to see. Please don't be offended, but I show it to everyone I do business with. After all, it was you who mentioned the possibility of legal action.' He pushed his chair back and stood up, adding less than a foot to his height but giving me a chance to inspect the sharp tailoring of his suit as he moved from behind the desk. He slid back a panel in the wall behind him to reveal a display case, its glass front reflecting the lighting in the room and making it impossible to see the interior. I crossed to the desk for a closer view.

'You see I don't much hold with the processes of law,' he stood me to one side. 'They're too slow. Too risky. If someone forgets to pay me I deliver my own judgement.'

I was still having difficulty seeing what was in the case, so I put both hands to the glass to make a spyhole. And at exactly that moment Drachman switched on an interior light to reveal the contents with nauseating clarity. For an instant my mind rejected the evidence of my own eyes, until a second look convinced me of what I had seen. Even then I prayed that it might be some macabre piece of sculpture, a black joke of some kind.

'The genuine article, Mr Townsend,' Drachman murmured in direct answer to my thoughts. 'Sprayed with quick drying cement within minutes of –' he hesitated, and then smiled his thin smile, 'within minutes of the operation taking place.'

Sickened to the pit of my stomach, I turned my eyes away from the sight of a man's genitals nailed to a block of wood and glimpsed Emanuel's white face next to me. 'Legal agreements,' my voice croaked unnaturally, 'drawn up by my solicitor.'

'Of course,' Drachman was still smiling as he slid the panel back into place. 'But you'll remember my views on the courts, won't you?'

We left.

'Gave you the creeps, did he?' Emanuel asked on the way back. 'Me too. But I knew he'd have the cash.'

'This one deal – that's all. Then I never want to see that filthy bastard again. And another thing, Peter, keep this to ourselves, eh? I wouldn't want it known that we're keeping company with a man like that.'

CHAPTER TWO

So that's how we put the money together. It took exactly two weeks and by Friday the sixteenth of September we were as good as ready.

People abuse lawyers – and I'm as guilty as most – forever complaining that they charge too much, take too long, do too little. But in the days and nights following the meetings with Pickard, Poignton and the team of A.W.F. lawyers worked non-stop – forming the enlarged consortium, drafting the agreement with Pepalasis, and preparing another one for U.S. Steel. I got my own man to draw up the agreement with Drachman and sat back to count my profit.

'There's a tide in the affairs of men which taken at the flood leads on to fortune.' It's always been true of business. Most of the world's commercial empires were founded on just one deal – and this was to be mine. Not just mine of course; Hallsworth, Smithers, Emanuel, even McNeil to a lesser extent, all stood shoulder to shoulder with me in the land of the big profit which stretched all the way from Pepalasis to the United States Steel Corporation.

U.S. Steel's first million pounds was to be paid jointly to A.W.F. Weisman's (Emanuel's bank) and Townsend and Partner as a management fee, after which the remaining nineteen million pounds would be divided between the investors in the proportion of just over six hundred and thirty thousand for every million invested. Thus the true earnings on Drachman's four million was a staggering two and a half million. And he'd settled for one and a half which left Emanuel and me with a personal profit of half a million each. So add the hundred and fifty thousand which would come my way from Townsend and Partner, and I reckoned I'd just about got it made.

Only one surprise occurred and predictably the Greek produced it. All along I'd been nervous about his title to the island but when it came to it, providing ownership was quite simple. The whole area of the Pacific had once been a French protectorate, then British with Australian trimmings. And finally something called the Central and Western Pacific Commission, and that had more or less disintegrated in the fifties with the surge towards independence by the larger, more populated areas. About then, dozens of the smaller islands had passed into private ownership. The Greek's island had even changed hands twice before he acquired it in seventy-four. Poignton despatched an assistant to Noumea and another to Sydney and both cabled back satisfaction of clear title as far as Pepalasis was concerned. So I breathed a sigh of relief and forgot about it.

No, the surprise came when Pepalasis announced that he had formed a British company to handle the transaction. Everyone had assumed that he would want the purchase price paid to a Greek outfit or at least paid outside of the U.K. It made no difference to us of course. In a way it even removed a complication. The lawyers had anticipated holding our money in escrow until Bank of England consent was obtained to transfer funds outside the sterling area – which, apart from the time it would take, was not considered a problem – not with fifty million pounds worth of very acceptable U.S. dollars flowing back within the same accounting period. But it puzzled me when I heard about it. A British company could only complicate life for Pepalasis later when he wanted to move the money abroad. And if he didn't want it overseas what the hell was he going to do with it here? Still, it was none of my business and it quickly lost itself in the pace of events.

And so the afternoon of Friday the sixteenth of September. I was alone in my office, tired and triumphant, and looking forward to a weekend off for a change, when Paul Seckleman put his head round my door. He managed to look even more worried and flustered than usual, and every bit as exhausted as I felt.

'Sorry to trouble you, Mr Townsend, but I need Mr Hallsworth urgently. Do you know where he is?'

'Yes, but telling you won't help. He's gone until Monday.' Hallsworth had taken the Greek off for the weekend. Grouse shooting in Scotland I think, though I hadn't paid much attention when he'd told me. I looked at Seckleman's worried face and said, 'Can I help you?'

He hesitated, a study in indecision, until shuffling forward and closing the door behind him. 'I'm not sure. Er, well perhaps. With advice if you wouldn't mind. It's about this shipment. I've had Leyland on three times this afternoon. They must have our confirmation that we'll take the Range-Rovers definitely next week. Otherwise they'll re-allocate them.'

'I didn't know what the devil he was talking about, but he was in such an obvious state that I reckoned talking might help.

'So what's the problem?'

'I can't give it to them. Not definite confirmation. All I can say is what I've told the other suppliers. Shipping is imminent – probably the end of next week. Stand by for firm delivery instructions.'

'That sounds pretty positive.'

'But Leyland insists on knowing this afternoon,' he said, almost plaintively. 'Seems that if we don't take the vehicles definitely next week they'll be re-allocated. And we'll be three weeks back in the queue.'

I didn't know what to do. Hallsworth's export order was none of my concern but I felt obliged to help if I could. And clearly Seckleman was out of his depth. So when I offered to speak to Leyland's he grabbed the suggestion like a drowning man.

'You'd better tell me more about it.' I waved him into a chair while we waited for the call to come through. 'How many vehicles are we talking about?'

I'd no preconception of his answer but when he said three hundred, I nearly fell out of my chair.

'And spare parts,' he added proudly. 'All together it's about two million quid's worth.'

The call came through and I succeeded in persuading the man on the other end to hold his decision until Monday – winning equal measures of his bad temper and Seckleman's admiration in the process – and when I put the phone down, I asked Secklman, 'What's the hold-up anyway?'

'Shipping. Mr Hallsworth is handling that himself. I've worked to a provisional date, but as it gets nearer all of the suppliers are getting nervous about exact confirmation.' He looked greatly relieved, as if his weekend now wouldn't be ruined by worry. At the door he said. 'It's bound to be all sorted out next week. Thanks very much for your help – I suppose I flapped a bit.'

'So did Leyland,' I said, trying to cheer him up. 'How big's the total shipment, by the way?'

'Oh, it's huge. Biggest thing I've ever worked on.' He brushed his hair back from his forehead with the back of his hand. 'Almost thirty million pounds worth now.'

After he had gone I sat thinking about Hallsworth. Sue's description came to mind – about him being some kind of business genius. He was certainly that. A thirty million pound export. His contract with U.S. Steel. The Pepalasis project. Townsend and Partner. I grinned, remembering his answer to my question about all of his business interests. 'Just juggling, Mike,' he'd said. 'Just juggling. Keeping all the balls in the air without losing your own.'

'Do you often do that?' Jean startled me from the open door.

'Do what?'

'Sit grinning at yourself.'

'I was thinking. And looking forward to the weekend. Three nights and two whole days without as much as a single thought about business.'

It was true. We were taking Bob Harrison and his wife to see 'Chorus Line' and out to supper afterwards. It promised to be a pleasant evening, I liked Bob and Amy and I was still enjoying showing Jean off to my friends. And as for the rest of the weekend, Jean and I planned to do nothing. Except lounge around in her flat. Eat and sleep, talk and make love.

CHAPTER THREE

'Chorus Line' was everything they said it was and afterwards we had a supper at the Twenty-One before going on to Churchill's for the floor show. Bob had just got his half-colonel's pip and was out to paint the town red and I suppose I was celebrating too. After all I had just been made a Director of the new consortium, my bank account promised to groan with riches, and Jean looked like a million dollars. So we danced and had fun until two in the morning. I think I had just about everything I wanted in life that night. Money, status, an exciting enough life style, and the most wonderful girl in the world. Until Bob gave me his news.

He dropped his bombshell while the girls were collecting their coats. He and I had just been arguing, in a bantering sort of way, about who was who's guest as far as the bill was concerned, when he said, 'Remember some time back, asking me about a Brigadier Hallsworth?' His words slurred slightly, but we both had had a few. 'Well, I ran into someone who knew him the other day. Did you know that he committed suicide?'

I said yes, while keeping an eye out for the girls.

'Oh?' His voice echoed the disappointment of discovering that his gossip was already known. 'Bloody funny business. What d'you make of it?'

I admitted to knowing none of the details, signed the bill and left a tip.

'All his son's fault apparently. Involved in a big fraud case and implicated the old man. Bad business from what I heard.'

I froze while something unpleasant twisted in the pit of my stomach. I *swear I knew then*, immediately, instinctively, in that split second, that something was wrong. Even now I can see Bob's face, his eyes blinking as if focussing was difficult, before his expression changed to one of concern as he saw the look on my face.

'You all right, old boy? Tied one on tonight, eh? Dunno about you but I'm inches off being pissed.'

'Hallsworth?' I was sober as I would have been with a bucket of water thrown over me. 'What's this about his son? Bob – it's terribly important.'

'Can see that – from the look on your face. Quite a scandal apparently. Feller I know says the son should have gone to jail. In Italy of all places.'

'Are you sure? When was this?'

'End of the sixties I think. Buggered if I remember now. Certainly happened though. Awfully sorry old boy, but I really am pie-eyed. That last bottle I shouldn't be surprised. Oh, I say, doesn't that rhyme? Pie-eyed and –'

'Hallsworth, Bob – Hallsworth!'

'What? Oh yes. Big fraud job. All I know. Find out if y'like. Come round Sunday and I'll have all the gen. Suit you?'

It had to, the girls were returning with wraps over their shoulders and the commissionaire was signalling news of the cabs he had waiting at the kerbside. I kissed Amy goodnight, said we'd be round for Sunday supper, and Jean and I left for Fulham.

'Darling are you all right? You look awfully white and a bit green round the gills.'

I never answered. Just held her hand – and felt sick. Not booze sick. Thankfully she neither asked questions or chatted the way some women might have done, but sat perfectly still with my hand in hers until we were home.

In the flat she made coffee while my mind played tricks with my memory. Wild guesses like it being a different Hallsworth or another son? But Poignton's account of Hallsworth's background made him an only child and confirmed his father's death by suicide. Then my brain exploded with memories of Sue Ballantyne. Sue's whole story – how she'd met Hallsworth, fell in love and left him. Nine years ago, she had said. Nine years? Which meant that Hallsworth would have been about twenty-six. And he inherited when? When he was twenty-five, twenty-six? Old Poignton had been vague about it. Odd for him, that lack of precision when he was so pedantic about everything else. And Poignton himself? Must have known of a scandal and hadn't said a word.

'Something's wrong, Jean. Bloody wrong.'

She lit cigarettes for both of us and passed one to me.

'Hallsworth was mixed up in a fraud case. In Italy. Apparently he nearly went to prison – or should have.'

She sat there in shocked silence for a moment before answering. 'I don't belive it.' She laughed nervously. 'Oh Mike – it's nonsense. Where on earth did you get this?'

'Bob. Tonight.'

'Now I *know* it's nonsense.' I could hear the relief in her voice. Then she added, 'After all, he was three parts gone wasn't he?'

'Not gone enough to have made it up.'

'Well when then? I mean, *when* was this supposed to have happened?'

'I'm not sure. Nine or ten years ago I think.'

'You *think*? Darling, shouldn't you be certain? Getting in a state – jumping to conclusions –'

'Christ, Jean, it's more than that! His father committed suicide and it was his fault – Rupert's. And he never said a word about it to me.'

'Oh, be fair, Darling. Why should he? A thing that personal. After all there are things you wouldn't tell him.'

'What for instance?'

'Well – things. *Us* for instance.'

'Oh, come on! It's hardly the same sort of thing is it?'

'It's exactly the same. Your personal life – nothing whatever to do with business. I should think that's how he feels about his father – only more so.'

174

I squirmed, recognising truth when I heard it, but plagued by a gut feeling that something was wrong. We sat facing each other, me almost angry, her seeming to be defensive where Hallsworth was concerned. She reached for my hand. 'Mike it's got to be nonsense. Have you ever known him do anything even remotely dishonest?'

I groaned, remembering the Pepalasis kickback. 'No more than I have.'

'Oh Mike – no?' She slid to the floor at my knees, her grip tightening on my hand and her face turned up to mine. 'I can't believe it.'

I told her everything – well almost. The meetings I had had with Poignton were easy enough, but I was more cautious in telling Sue's story. Not what she had said as much as where she had said it – instinct preventing me from describing to one woman the implied intimacies of a bedroom scene with another. The Barmouth telephone call was omitted for the same reason, but at least I told her about the side deal with Pepalasis.

'I can't understand why you're so worked up,' she said. 'After all you gave him his money back.'

'It's not that,' I shook my head. 'It's Hallsworth. There's something about his background. The story doesn't fit. When we first me he told me some of his history – made a point of telling me. But there was nothing in it about Italy. And Sue told me that she went to Italy to get *away* from him – nine years ago. Nine years ago, *don't you see*? According to Bob that's exactly when Hallsworth was there – nearly being sent to prison.'

Her doubting expression slowly dissolved to one of bewilderment. 'Darling, we're too tired to make sense of it tonight.' She stifled a yawn, brown hair lifting from her shoulders as she shook her head. 'Let's leave it till the morning, please.'

'No – there's more.' I had to make her see. 'Bob did some snooping for me about a year ago. About Sue's story – her

being born in India and growing up with this other girl –
Pamela Whatshernname. Army families and all that stuff.
But when Bob dug through the records there was nothing to
show a Ballantyne having ever served in India. Or Singapore
for that matter.'

She stood up and took the cups to the kitchen for a refill.
I sensed her impatience, even shared it in a way, after all
nothing I said seemed to make sense. So when she came back
looking every bit as puzzled and worried as I felt, I was
surprised as much as anything.

She put the cups on the carpet and sat at my feet again,
her hand finding its way to mine. 'As you've brought it up,
there is perhaps something you ought to know.' She
hesitated, fumbling with her cigarettes and avoiding my eye.
'Except *ought to know* is probably the wrong expression. It
happened last summer. I spent a week of my holidays in
Malta with my parents, and on the last night we had dinner
at an hotel they use – the Dragon's Lair it's called. Well, it's
probably nothing at all – ' she paused, drew a deep breath,
and then said: 'But Hallsworth was there. Having dinner.
With Sue Ballantyne.'

I was so surprised that I slopped half the coffee in the
saucer.

'It's probably nothing at all,' she repeated, as if regretting
having told me.

'*Nothing at all?* When she was supposed to have spent all
summer in Greece? Christ, Jean – why didn't you tell me this
before?'

'Oh, *Mike*! What was I supposed to do? Come running to
tell you that I saw your girlfriend out with another man?'

'Another man? *Hallsworth*? The man she never wanted to
see again – ever!'

'Well, I didn't know that did I? For all I knew you might
have known about it – about them I mean. She could have
been a sort of shared perk – strictly partners for the use of.'

'Oh, don't be so damn ridiculous! I'm amazed. Amazed,

that's all. *You* knowing something like that – and not telling me.'

'Mike, that's unfair.' She pulled away angrily, her cheeks flushed, temper flashing in her eyes. 'Remember last summer? I was someone you took out occasionally and returned to her cubbyhole afterwards. No ties – no strings – no obligations. Whereas she –'

'You should have told me.' I was practically shouting now.

'How *could* I tell you? She was number one girl and I was someone who worked for you. Someone to be given a treat when the rules allowed – your rules, Mike, not mine.'

'They're not written down.'

'They damn well don't need it! They're that obvious!' Tears flickered at the back of her eyes as she shouted back at me. She changed her position on the floor, kneeling now so as to give her more height. 'Mike, there are times when I don't know what to think. I mean if I hadn't stayed at Hill Street that night? Dammit, I almost threw myself at you. Suppose I hadn't? Would we be here now? Would any of this have happened? Between us I mean?'

At least I had sense enough to know an important question when I heard one. For an instant we were like figures frozen in a photograph, me leaning forward from the edge of my chair, Jean kneeling but straight backed, so that her head was almost level with mine. And then I reached for her. 'Perhaps not when it did – but it would have happened. Even I'm not blind stupid all the time.'

Her body was still tensed under my hands as she pulled away. 'But all *this* fuss?' She said warily. 'About Sue Ballantyne and Hallsworth?'

'Not fuss about, fuss about why. She's not important – really she's not – but her lies are, especially when they involve Hallsworth.'

'But she told you they knew each other. Perhaps they met again? By chance? And, well, didn't tell you in case you'd be upset or something?'

It didn't ring true and we both knew it. I could even hear the lack of conviction in her voice. But the hurt gradually faded from her eyes and she gave the tiniest grin before resting her head in my lap, our hands clasping in reconciliation.

A few minutes passed before I risked re-opening the subject. 'Last summer? You'd only met Sue once – and Hallsworth was away so often that you'd not got to know him. You might have been mistaken?'

She snuggled into a more comfortable position. 'I *might* have been, about him. But I don't think so. And I certainly wasn't about her. Women don't make mistakes like that, my darling.' She was quiet for a moment, and then she added, 'No – it was them all right.'

'Did they see you?'

'No. We'd finished our meal as they arrived. I'd have missed them altogether but for my father running into some people he knew. We all went off for a drink and you can see the restaurant quite clearly from the bar. But they were staying there. At the hotel I mean.'

'How do you know?'

'It's a sort of local for us – I know the layout of the place quite well. They walked into the restaurant from the direction of the lifts.'

She yawned and stretched, so I took the hint and we went to bed. But as soon as she fell asleep I returned to the kitchen for some fresh coffee and cigarettes. I'm not sure which alarmed me most, Bob's unfinished story about fraud or Jean's revelations about Hallsworth and Sue in Malta. One was enough to shock – both together stunned me as effectively as a blow on the head. Hallsworth and Sue? It didn't make sense. Them seeing each other. Not when only a few days ago the prospect of a chance encounter had been enough to stop her from visiting Hill Street. And Bob's story? What if they were both right? Jean *and* Bob. I felt threatened and vulnerable, as if a disaster I couldn't define was looming over me. After the feeling grew to mammoth proportions an hour later, when I traced Jean's holiday back to the time of one of Hallsworth's trips to the States. Lies from Sue was one thing. Deceit from Hallsworth another.

It was past six when I finally fell asleep in the chair, Saturday the seventeenth of September, and when Jean woke me three hours later I did the only thing I could think of. Within an hour we had packed our bags and left.

CHAPTER FOUR

'We could have booked into the Dragon's Lair,' I grumbled, flicking the steering wheel to move into the fast lane. Staying with her parents meant separate bedrooms, and the loss of pleasures to which I had happily become accustomed.

'Don't be silly, darling. I'm going home. We couldn't possibly. Anyway, after last night I was beginning to think my physical charms had lost their appeal.'

'I had something on my mind.'

'So did I, and it's not a good place for it.' She giggled at her little joke, then said, 'Anyway, you still haven't told me. Why this sudden dash to Malta?'

'The Dragon's Lair. To find out if you were right. About last summer.'

'But why? I mean I know perfectly well what I saw. Why is it so red hot important?'

'If I knew that I wouldn't need to go,' I snapped. The words were out before I had time to check them. I got my nerves under control again and threw her a quick glance of apology. 'This hotel, how well does your father know the people who run it?'

'Mr Tonelli? He's the manager. Oh, he's a great friend. You'll like him.'

I hoped so. The whole trip depended on him.

There are three flights to Malta from Heathrow on a Saturday. The first was bursting with holidaymakers, but we got stand-by for the second and struck lucky – helped by Jean ogling a ticket clerk and a twenty pound note changing hands at the right time. And Luqa three hours later seemed as hot as Noumea had been a month earlier, but fanned by a salt breeze which swept the tarmac as we crossed to the Customs Hall. Jean's father was waiting for us, a tall silver-haired man dressed in fawn lightweights; about sixty, keen-eyed and bronzed by the sun. We sized each other up as we walked to the car, his look curious and mildly suspicious, the sort of look that fathers everywhere reserve for the escorts of only daughters. But for all that he had a straightforward, no-nonsense manner which appealed to me, and I found myself liking him as I got to know him. Altogether an interesting man, with a distinguished naval career behind him and a half share in the biggest marine business on the island. Successful, shrewd, and nobody's fool.

They lived a few miles beyond Sliema in a big white house surrounded by bougainvillea, full of gracious archways and Italian marble; set high on the cliffs and only a mile or so from the Dragon's Lair itself.

'Yes, I know it well,' he said when I asked him about it. 'Too well I think sometimes.' He patted the barely discernible bulge about his waistline. 'I eat there three or four times a week.'

'And the manager?'

'Alberto?' his eyes flickered with curiosity. 'Yes – he's something of a friend.'

'Friend enough to open his records to us?'

He hesitated. 'Do you mind telling me what you're looking for, Mr Townsend?'

Jean and her mother were off supervising the domestic arrangements and the two of us were alone on the terrace, sipping iced drinks and soaking up sunshine. Late afternoon, a perfect sea under an empty sky, and all so tranquil that I wondered if I wasn't being stupidly melodramatic about the whole thing.

'I'd be pleased if you'd call me Mike,' I answered clumsily. 'After all, Jean and I are practically engaged.'

He raised an eyebrow and waited, making me feel a perfect bloody fool, as if I should be expounding on my future prospects and asking for his daughter's hand in marriage.

I drew a deep breath and plunged into the story. 'Jean thinks she saw my partner here last summer. Having dinner at the Dragon's Lair. With a girl. Well – the odd thing is I know the girl too, and according to her she hasn't seen my partner for years. If Jean's right – and the two were together last summer – well, someone's been telling me a pack of lies.'

It sounded thinner than strained soup. He waited for me to continue but there was nothing to add which didn't make me sound like a hysterical schoolgirl, so I sipped my drink and hoped he'd settle for what he'd been given.

'And *that's* important enough for you to catch the first plane out here?' Some of the warmth went out of his eyes in a look which told me all about his opinion of his daughter's choice in men.

'You've a partner, haven't you? In your business.' I groped for another angle. 'Suppose you found out, quite by chance, that he'd consistently misled you about something? Wouldn't you be anxious to find out why?'

Hostility was replaced by a look of concern. 'Any man with a dodgy partner has got trouble. Big trouble.' His grey eyebrows straightened and dropped until they almost hid his eyes. 'I should know,' he growled. 'Did Jean tell you?'

I shook my head, relieved to have struck a vein of understanding.

'It happened when I first started out here. Bastard cleared the bank account and vanished. Clean off the island. Took me five years to straighten out.

'I vowed then I'd never have another partner for as long

as I lived.' He looked thoughtful for a moment, then he shrugged: 'But a chance came up to buy someone out and I needed a spot more cash, so I took another fellow in with me.' He grinned suddenly, making the eyebrows lift again so that he looked ten years younger. 'Best move I ever made. Never looked back. But picking a partner is tricky – reckon I've had the worst and the best of them – so I should know, eh?' I nodded and he said, 'And yours is up to no good, is that it? What can Alberto do for you?'

I wished I knew. 'Confirm Jean's story I suppose. Or refute it. She thinks they were staying at the hotel. A look at the register might help.'

He nodded. 'Got photos of them?'

I cursed my stupidity and felt myself drop another notch in his estimation.

He shrugged. 'Their names are probably enough. The hotel collects all passports on arrival, so at least they couldn't have registered under false names.' Jean and her mother were coming to join us and he threw me a quick glance as he stood up to greet them. 'Unless they're travelling under false passports of course. In which case you've got more trouble than you bargained for.'

I winced at the thought and felt a moment's panic as I remembered Bob's abortive search of another set of records.

We lazed away what was left of the early evening, enjoying the salt air and the sunshine, and each other's company. Jean's mother was as tanned as her husband, a tall, graceful woman who'd once been an actress. It showed occasionally, in a graceful movement or a lively expression. They were an interesting couple and I liked them, she with her fund of stories about playing the Palace during the blitz while husband Jack hunted U-boats from the bridge of a destroyer in the North Sea. Malta must have seemed an oasis of calm after the lives they had led and they seemed as happy with it as they were with each other.

At about eight-thirty we summoned up enough energy to

go to our rooms to change for the evening, and an hour later we were at our table in the dining room at the Dragon's Lair.

'Alberto's going to join us for a drink after dinner,' Jack told me. 'You'll be able to get what you want then without being interrupted every five minutes.'

And Alberto joined us in due course, two hundred pounds of smooth Italian charm, flashing white teeth and ready compliments. He made a great fuss over Jean and would have spent the rest of the evening improving on it, but for my scowl and Jack's amused reminder about my questions.

'Ah yes – you wish to talk business, Mr Townsend? Then may I suggest we adjourn to my suite. More comfortable and more private.'

It was: a discreet sitting room full of soft lights and large brandies.

'But of course I know Mr Hallsworth,' he said in answer to my question. 'And his charming wife. Such a nice couple – yes?'

'His *wife*?'

'But of course.' He saw my look of astonishment. 'You do not know her perhaps?'

'But I thought,' I began. 'I mean, I'm not sure –'

'Forgive me, but then you cannot. With her, no one is not sure.' He shook his head emphatically. 'She is someone you either know or you don't know. You never forget. Like him too – yes?'

'Can you describe her?'

'Can I describe a beautiful woman?' He used both hands and most of his body in a shrug, and then closed his eyes to picture her. 'What do you see first? Her size, no? Small. Very small, but the figure of a Venus. Skin the colour of a peach ripened slowly in the sun. Dark eyes that dance and laugh and share secrets – and make impossible promises without a word being spoken.' He blinked and beamed about him in triumph.

'Is that your girl?' asked Jack.

'It's like someone he knows,' Jean corrected with her deep frozen voice. 'Though it's not the way I would have described her.'

I looked at her. It *was* Sue and we both knew it.

'And she's his *wife*?' I persisted.

'But of course.' Tonelli sighed. 'A man must be blessed by the Gods to have a wife so beautiful. Waking every morning to – to a face like a Botticelli angel on the next pillow. Oh, can you imagine?'

'Try him,' Jean nodded at me. 'His imagination's lousy but his memory's perfect.'

I scowled, uncomfortably aware of Jack's eyes narrowing as he watched me.

'And they stayed here, last summer?' I pressed Tonelli.

'Last summer – the one before – the one before that.' He shrugged and was about to add something when he stopped, his look flicking from my face to Jack's with sudden nervousness. 'Please – Mr Hallsworth, he's not in any kind of trouble?'

Jack was positive. 'Nothing to worry about, Alberto. You can trust Mike. And you'll be doing me a big favour.'

It seemed that Tonelli was in the business of doing Jack big favours so that settled it. 'They stay here perhaps once every six months,' he said. 'Most times for just one night at a time.'

'Since when?'

'Since years. Two, three, four maybe.'

I shook my head in bewilderment but Tonelli mistook the gesture for one of disbelief. 'Oh, but I am certain,' he protested. 'I will show you the records.'

And he did, leading me first to his office, explaining the hotel's record-keeping system on the way. Guests registered on four by six index cards, supplying their name, nationality, home address – the usual kind of thing. Hotel booking clerks compiled a daily record from the cards, listing all guests on a pre-printed form. At the month's end all daily forms were photographed side by side and put onto microfiche, so an entire month's traffic appeared on a single piece of film. The film was viewed through enlargers like television receivers and twelve screenings gave the bookings for an entire year.

'So to go back three years will not take long.' Tonelli was pleased to demonstrate his efficiency. 'Half an hour is all.'

He was wrong. We did it in twenty minutes. Mr and Mrs Hallsworth had stayed once earlier in the year, three times in seventy-six, and twice in seventy-five. I cursed the pair of them, hating them for their deception, and feeling more frightened than ever.

But it was while I was making a written note of the dates – my eyes on the screen as my head throbbed with questions – that I saw the other name. Whatever the shocks earlier, nothing could have prepared me for that. I felt disorientated before. Confused as a consequence of people important to my life being where they had no business to be. But now the feeling of unreality exploded to the edge of hallucination.

Tonelli saw the look on my face. 'Something is wrong, Mr Townsend?'

I swallowed hard to clear my throat. 'Aristotle Pepalasis. You know him too?'

Aristotle Pepalasis had stayed on the tenth of January seventy-five. *The very same date as the Hallsworths*. I searched for the other date in that year. September fifteenth. It was the same. Two dates, eight months apart. Still dazed, I turned the controls to the next year. January the eighth – August the tenth – December the second. Hallsworth, Sue and Pepalasis. *The very same date every time*!

'Pepalasis,' Tonelli was repeating the name, frowning as if it meant nothing to him. 'Ah, but of course.' His face cleared. 'The Greek gentleman. Another who stays with us whenever he's in Malta.'

'But they know each other? They're friends. Hallsworth and Pepalasis?'

He seemed surprised at that. 'No. I think not.' He thought about it a moment longer and then made up his mind. 'No, this time you are wrong, Mr Townsend.'

We rejoined the others in the sitting room, Tonelli describing Pepalasis on the way. There can't be too many men in the world named Aristotle Pepalasis. Especially ones who twirl worry beads from morning to night.

Not long after that we left, and went back to the white house on the cliff.

'Did it help?' Jack wanted to know.

'*Help*? That was the last thing it did. But it proved something. Though God knows what so don't ask me.' I shook my head, still in a state of shock I think. 'Anyway, Jack, I'm grateful – good of you to use your influence.'

We went to bed. My room was at the end of the corridor, a guest suite separate from the rest of the house, and I was already in bed when the door opened and Jean slipped in.

'It's all right.' She kissed me and slid under the bedclothes. 'Mother approves.'

'Mother doesn't worry me. But any second Captain Blood will the kick the door in and come after me with a cutlass.'

She giggled. 'He's not that fierce.'

'No, I like him. Let's keep it that way.'

'Well, even he can't object, can he?' She was making snuffling noises as she unbuttoned my pyjamas. 'After all we're practically engaged.'

'Oh? You heard about that?'

'We're a close family. Anyway, they like you. Except for your habit of taking married ladies to bed.'

'Yes.' I raised myself on one elbow. 'What the hell d'you make of that?'

'Oh, we approve. We're going to give you one of your own.'

CHAPTER FIVE

The telephone interrupted breakfast the following morning. Tonelli for me.

'Mr Townsend, last night I forgot, but I have a meeting in Gozo today. But the other information you wanted – Ricardo will have it by the time you get here.'

I thanked him for his help, promised to convey his warmest best wishes to Jean, and was on the point of hanging up when he remembered something else, 'Oh, by the way,' he said quickly, 'Mr Hallsworth, he has friends in Malta yes?'

'What makes you think so?'

'Because of his meetings.'

'Meetings?'

'Whenever he stays – he holds a meeting in his sitting room.'

'With whom?'

'Ah, that I don't know. My staff tell me two people.'

'Pepalasis being one of them?'

'No, no – *not* Mr Pepalasis.'

'Who then?'

'I've no idea. Mr Hallsworth says always he is not to be disturbed.'

'But you know it's two people?'

'Only from the dining room. They send a luncheon trolley for four people and Mrs Hallsworth takes it at the door.'

I pressed him for details until realising that he had none to give, said goodbye for the second time, and returned to my breakfast. After which we had a holiday. Jack's big motor cruiser took us off to the deserted north coast of the island. We moored well clear of the rocks and enjoyed a morning's swimming and fishing and lazing in the sunshine. Correction, they enjoyed it while I pretended to have stopped worrying for a few hours. But however hard I tried it was impossible. During less than forty-eight hours the whole structure of my life had been changed. Relationships I had believed in proved to be not what I thought they were: people, events, memories, everything had to be re-evaluated. And all the while I was cursed by a premonition that time was running out, something wrong was happening, someone, somewhere, was about to bring life crashing down around my ears.

In the afternoon Jean's parents drove us to the airport, stopping briefly at the Dragon's Lair. They took Jean off for a coffee while I kept my appointment with Ricardo.

'Hallsworth did not stay with us before seventy-five,' Ricardo was positive. 'Neither did Mr Pepalasis.'

'Oh, but Mr Tonelli thought –'

'He was mistaken. I myself checked the records this morning.'

'I see. Well, thanks for the help and –'

'You are a friend of Mr Hallsworth?'

Something in the way he asked made my hackles rise. 'Yes, that's right, we're in the same line of business. Mr Pepalasis too. We're all *old* friends.'

He smiled and shook his head. 'Excuse me, but that cannot be. Mr Hallsworth and Mr Pepalasis have stayed together – no, no – not together, at the same time, yes? They have passed each other – without speaking – I have seen this happen, in the lobby, in the bar. I am sure they do not know each other.' He gave me a sly look

'Perhaps *another* Mr Pepalasis?'

It was difficult to be sure about Ricardo. He was either intent on being accurate or as good as calling me a liar to my face. Whichever, there was damn all I could do about it, but whereas Tonelli had been anxious to help I got the strong impression that Ricardo resented giving me the time of day. I shrugged, said goodbye, and went in search of the others – thinking Jack wasn't the only one with a friend in the hotel.

I told him as much on the way to the airport.

'Why didn't you tell me back there? I could have done something about it.'

'Like what? Cause a fuss? You live here, remember. You've done plenty already.' I screwed up my eyes against the glare of the sun reflected from the white dust of the road. 'But if you ever get the chance to look at the records for yourself – perhaps you'll let me know.'

We said our goodbyes and Jean and I boarded the plane for the flight home.

'You're worried sick, aren't you?'

'That's an understatement,' I snapped, nerves making me irritable. 'Sue Ballantyne *equals* Mrs Hallsworth. Pepalasis *equals* old friend. And –'

'They didn't say that. About Pepalasis I mean. They said he never knew them.'

'And you believe that?' I sneered. 'Come on, Jean. The same dates every time. Business trips. Private meetings. Of course they know each other!'

'But they –'

'All pretend otherwise. I know, I know. What the hell's going on?'

'Mike, if only I knew I'd –'

But I wasn't really listening. Too many pictures were in my mind for me to concentrate on anything else. Sue, at the old flat at Belsize Park. At the house at Maida Vale. The flat at Hill Street. Sue in restaurants. Sue at the theatre. Sue in bed. Barmouth! *Sue in bed like never before*. When only hours earlier she had telephoned the Dorchester. *And spoken to Pepalasis?* I could see him sitting there taking the call, Hallsworth in the chair opposite, all of them laughing. I could even hear the laughter. I could sense their triumph. But triumph about what for God's sake?

'Mike, you are all right aren't you?' Jean was saying. 'You look so, so bleak.'

'It's got to have something to do with this bloody island.'

'Malta? But why?'

189

'Christ, not Malta. The Greek's island.'

'Sorry.'

I knew I had offended her, that she was getting the brunt of my frustration, and knew that later I would apologise.

But right then there wasn't time.

'Suppose it happened this way.' I had taken her hand, turned her in her seat to face me, anxious to get every ounce of concentration from her. 'Hallsworth and Pepalasis know each other from way back. They make some private arrangement to sell the island. But then McNeil discovers not diamonds – but nickel. The biggest strike since Poseidon. If you were Hallsworth – what would *you* do?'

She frowned. 'Oh, Mike – *you're* the businessman. I don't know –'

'Think about it, Jean. *Think, think, think*! You'd do one of two things.'

'One of two things?' She repeated, staring at me. I sensed I was frightening her and relaxed my grip on her hands as she said, 'Mike, I *can't* think.'

'Yes you can. Come on now, Jean – you would have a choice of action.'

'A choice? You mean sell or it or mine it?'

'Right. Now which one would you do?'

'Oh God knows. Darling, it's a commercial decision. Find out which was the most profitable I suppose and –'

'*Genius*! And then what?'

'Are you making fun of me? All I said was find out which was the most profitable – why the excitement?'

'Because you're still Hallsworth, remember – now you're going to tell me *how* you would sell it – most profitably.'

She gave a blank look so I prompted her by saying: 'To *whom* would you sell it most profitably?'

'To whom?' Suddenly she was smiling. 'Of course. To U.S. Steel.'

'Exactly.'

'Well, that's just what you're doing.'

'That's what *we're* doing. The consortium. But you're Hallsworth. You and U.S. Steel have been buddy buddy since God. They want nickel and you've as good as got some. So what would you do?'

'Darling, I've said it already. Sell them the island.'

'*You* would sell *them* the island. You, you and Pepalasis. *Direct!* You don't need the consortium! So why involve them? Why throw away an extra profit so fat that you'd live like a sheik for the rest of your life?'

We asked ourselves that all the way to Heathrow. All the way through the plastic meal and the white wine warmed by the sun through the ports. All the way through the interruptions as stewards delivered drinks and cleared trays and offered us duty free goodies from a trolley. We asked – but I'm damned if we answered it.

Just before the descent over London the picture show started up in my mind again. Meeting Sue and then Hallsworth and then the Greek. All about a year apart. While all the time the three of them were meeting in Malta. No, *not* the three of them? What had Tonelli said? A luncheon trolley for *four* people. Four people. I could hear Tonelli saying it. 'Mr Hallsworth, he has friends in Malta, yes?'

'Next time we go we must see more of the place, darling,' Jean was saying. I stared at her. 'Malta I mean,' she smiled. 'I've got lots of friends there.' She laughed. 'Or I used to have. Trouble is, for the last couple of years I've only been able to get back there for the odd day or two. Every six months or so. You know how it is.'

I closed my eyes and prayed that I did. It would make a nice change.

CHAPTER SIX

'Mike, you look as if you've been in the south of France,' Amy said when I kissed her. It was true. I've got that kind of skin. The few hours on Jack's boat had given me a bronzed sheen which would last just about until morning.

'I've been sunbathing.'

Bob snorted. 'It's rained buckets all weekend.'

'In Malta,' I said. Whether I wanted to or not I would have to tell them.

'Malta for the weekend?' Bob sneered, and led the way to the sitting room. 'Business must be good. Mike – let me introduce a friend of mine – Claude Jenkins.'

I was surprised, expecting Jean and me to be the only guests. Jenkins was a tall, spare-framed man, casually but expensively dressed in a lightweight suede. His name rang a bell but there was no time to work on it as Amy completed the introductions and Bob poured drinks, while we arranged ourselves in armchairs.

'Bit sudden, wasn't it?' Bob cocked an eyebrow. 'Malta? You didn't say anything on Friday?'

I glimpsed Jean's quick look and sensed that she wanted them to know her news. Our news. And it was a relief to have a reason which had nothing to do with Hallsworth. 'We went to see Jean's parents,' I said gruffly. 'Jean and I are getting married.'

The next five minutes were spent listening to congratulations and 'about time too's' and all the other daft things people feel compelled to say on such occasions; but in the middle of it all I stole at glance at Jean and felt well pleased with myself. And not long afterwards the girls went off to the kitchen, leaving Bob and me to entertain Mr Claude Jenkins.

'Sorry about Friday night,' Bob said, bleated almost, he

sounded so sheepish. 'Had a drop too much. Got a right bawling out from Amy afterwards.'

I said we'd both had one too many and wished that Jenkins would push off somewhere so that Bob could give me his news.

'Still, I wasn't so plastered that I forgot this Hallsworth business.' Bob read my mind. 'Matter of fact that's why Claude's here.' He checked himself. 'Sorry Claude, I meant you know all about it and wanted to meet Mike anyway – so here we all are.'

Jenkins gave me a cautious smile.

'Claude's a journalist,' Bob added, by way of concluding the introduction, and the bell rang again as I placed him. He was a journalist all right, the sharpest pen in Fleet Street, looking for commercial Watergates, real or exaggerated.

'Of course,' I said. 'Didn't you do a piece on the Crown Agents a few weeks ago?'

His gesture of modesty was so blatantly false that I disliked him instinctively.

'How do you two know each other?' I asked.

'Much as you do, I imagine,' Jenkins answered. He spoke slowly, lazily, but I guessed he was probably a lot quicker asking questions than answering them. 'Bob and I met some years back,' he said, 'while I was doing a piece on defence costs, and we've kept in touch ever since, in a vague sort of way.' He gave me a vague sort of smile to prove it, while Bob grinned like an uncertain bridegroom introducing new sets of in-laws.

'Anyway this Hallsworth thing,' Jenkins drawled. 'Bob wanted whatever I had on the file, which isn't much; the press here didn't give it coverage at the time. But it made headlines in Italy. They labelled it the Frascari scandal and a lot of people got very excited about it. I was based in Rome then, and a great pal of mine was Carlos Pinero – and it's really his story.'

After Bob had interrupted just long enough to refill our

glasses Jenkins continued. 'The background to it was simple con,' he said. 'The three card trick using businesses instead of cards. A company called Frascari got a massive order from a firm in Scotland – A. H. Haldane. Frascari was a small electronics outfit in Milan employing about a hundred and fifty people, and the order was so big that they had to raise the additional working capital to handle it. Seven hundred million lire worth. Difficult, but not impossible – thanks to the Italian Government who were underwriting all sorts of export business for balance of payments reasons. So once Haldane's payment had been guaranteed by the Italian ECGD, Frascari's raised their money fairly easily, and started buying the components they needed. But their biggest supplier, a German outfit called Mullers, got the wind up about lire being devalued, so they insisted on advance payment. Frascari's needed the goods desperately and the German source promised the fastest delivery, so they paid. Two hundred million lire. Follow me so far?'

I nodded and waited for him to continue.

'Next thing you know, Mullers goes out of business. Goes bust overnight. Of course Frascari screamed blue bloody murder but the money had gone and that was that. But either by luck or smart lobbying the Italian government heard about the jeopardised export contract and stepped in with a non-repayable grant to make up the loss. Frascari found another supplier, worked every hour God sent, delivered to Haldane's a month late and got paid.'

He ended with such a finality that I was left wondering what on earth it had to do with Hallsworth. 'And that's the story?' I asked.

'It would have been. But for Carlos Pinero. Pinero was industrial correspondent to *La Stampa* and running a campaign about the misuse of government funds. So when he heard about the grant to Frascari he followed it up – much as he investigated other stories. But I think he was also intrigued to find out how a little outfit like Frascari landed such a big order in the first place. So he flew to Glasgow to interview Haldane's Purchasing Director.'

He paused, partly to sip his drink but mainly, I sensed, to watch my reaction. And he was still staring at me when he said, 'Who turned out to be a Brigadier Hallsworth.'

I blinked; Jenkins scratched the side of his nose and watched me. After a bit he said, 'Of course, there was no real story in Glasgow, Haldane's was thoroughly sound and the Brigadier had neither heard about Frascari's troubles with the German supplier nor about the government bail-out. But Pinero's journey wasn't entirely wasted. He did discover *something* of interest.'

There was no mistaking his curiosity now. It became a battle of wills as he fought for the reaction I sought to deny him. And it was getting harder all the time. Especially when he said, 'Pinero found out that the man who had introduced Frascari into Haldane's was the Brigadier's own son, Mr Rupert Hallsworth.'

It was impossible to guess what Jenkins was leading up to but I kept quiet and after a long pause he continued. 'Pinero sniffed a story and back in Rome and Milan he checked up on Hallsworth junior, and found him to be a bit of a playboy – forever in the casinos and the night spots – along with his glamorous wife and their industrialist friend – Mr Bruno Fascari. Pinero figured Hallsworth got a bankhander on the Haldane order and stayed close, even going to Hamburg for an interview with Mullers' liquidator. Mullers' demise hadn't caused a ripple in Germany. There was nothing to the company anyway, just a couple of rented offices, and no German businessman had lost as much as a Deutsche Mark. In fact there was only one creditors' meeting.'

I was still imagining Hallsworth at the gaming tables when Jenkins added, 'The big surprise was finding out who owned Mullers to begin with. Care to make a guess, Mr Townsend?'

There was no doubting the inference, he *expected* me to know.

'I suppose you're going to tell me it was Hallsworth?'

He stared, as if trying to decide whether it was a genuine question or an attempt to conceal knowledge. 'No,' he said eventually, shaking his head, a thin smile on his lips. 'Though I think Pinero was beginning to suspect it might be. But Mullers had been owned by a *woman*, Mr Townsend.'

Dear God it was like a maze. Ever since Friday night I had been twisting and turning to find a way out, only to meet a new nightmare around every corner. I looked at Jenkins and waited.

'Mullers had been owned by Miss Pamela Johnstone,' he said.

At precisely that moment Amy announced supper and the diversion of moving to the dining room robbed Jenkins of the astonished reaction he had been looking for. *Pamela Johnstone*! I knew nothing about her except what Sue had told me. And according to her Pamela Johnstone had *hated* business. I was still trying to make sense of it when Jenkins finished the story at the dinner table. 'Of course Pinero didn't see the connection. Not at first. He'd got a good story about tax payers' money being used to support bad business decisions – and that's all Frascari was guilty of – nothing illegal.'

Bob mopped his mouth with a napkin. 'I'm sorry, Claude, but I don't see the connection either.'

'Miss Pamela Johnstone's other identity.'

Bob frowned and cocked his head to one side, looking from Jenkins to me in search of an answer.

'The ex-Mrs Rupert Hallsworth,' I said evenly.

'*Good Lord*!' Bob was suitably shocked and the silence engulfed all of us until he asked, 'What happened then?'

'*La Stampa* ran the story,' Jenkins said. 'And within weeks people started to disappear. Hallsworth dropped out of sight first and soon afterwards Frascari sold up and left Italy like a bat out of hell.'

'Can you describe him? Frascari?' I asked urgently, too

late realising that his feigned casualness had lulled me into a false sense of security. Now his eyebrows twitched and the cunning eyes below them screwed into slits of speculation.

'Why, Mr Townsend? Do you think you might *know* him?'

I squirmed. 'It's just that it might help to follow the story. If I could visualise him.' Miserably I pushed a potato to the edge of my plate, knowing what I was going to ask, had to ask, but alarmed by the prospect of Jenkins knowing too much. 'Did he look Italian?' I said. 'You know, Mediterranean. That look some Italians have, Greeks too, come to think of it.'

'*Come to think of it*,' Jenkins mimicked. And then he smiled. 'No, as a matter of fact he didn't, Mr Townsend. Bruno Frascari went back to the States. He was an American. Third generation Brooklyn. Came to Europe at the end of the war.'

We stared at each other. A partly formed theory collapsed in the back of my mind. He smiled and turned to Bob. 'Other people in the story just died off. Strangely, in my opinion. Pamelas Johnstone, for instance. Committed suicide. Just four weeks after the poor old Brigadier had done the very same thing.'

'Ugh,' Amy pulled a face. 'What a grisly tale.'

'Isn't it,' Jenkins turned to her. 'But it didn't end there, Amy. You see I have a theory. I think they all stayed in touch. That the three of them never really split up at all.'

'The *three* of them?' she repeated, puzzled.

'Yes.' He looked back at me. Because there was a *third* man. Bruno Frascari's cousin. Now he did have the look you were describing a minute ago, Mr Townsend. You know, the look of the Mediterranean.' He mimicked me again. 'That look some Italians have, Greeks too , come to think of it.'

Even the slight tan I had acquired didn't help. I felt my face blaze as the others watched Jenkins bait me. 'What makes you think that they – ' I gulped helplessly. 'That they still know each other?'

'There was a share scandal in Sydney five years ago.' His

eyes were slits of suspicion as he answered. 'Again, nothing illegal. Not on the face of it. But a lot of people lost a packet of money to some speculators who moved in and out over a six-month period. A couple of Aussies were involved of course, but somewhere on the sidelines was an Englishman. And an American. *And someone with the look of the Mediterranean about him.*' He smiled, before asking in a suddenly crisp voice, 'How much of this did you know, Mr Townsend?'

'How much do you think I knew?'

'I wasn't sure.'

'And now?'

'I'm still not.'

For reasons which had a lot to do with not liking him I felt pleased.

'Will one of you tell me what's going on?' Amy asked bluntly.

'I'm sorry.' Jenkins warmed his smile up for her. 'Bad manners – my fault. I do apologise Amy, darling. This is quite delicious by the way.'

'And cut out the soft soap.' Amy was tougher than her soldier husband if the truth were known. 'There's an atmosphere and I won't have it at my dinner table. Who's needling whom and why?'

'I suppose I was,' Jenkins sounded quite unruffled. 'But I *do* apologise, really. Professional curiosity, I suppose, got the better of me, and –'

'There's nothing about Mike for you to be professionally curious about,' she told him.

'Oh, but there is. If you'll pardon the contradiction.'

'What then?' she demanded ahead of me, colour rising like a tide up the column of her throat.

'Because, though not for publication, Mr Townsend is in business with a man I believe to be at least guilty of fraud. If not something worse.'

Bob's gasp and Amy's flame-red cheeks were evidence

198

enough of their embarrassment. Jean started to say something but spilled her wine in her agitation and her words ended as a muffled cry of dismay. Only Jenkins and I appeared to be in control of ourselves.

'Care to comment?' he drawled. 'As I said – not for publication.'

I had had enough of Jenkins. 'Yes, I'll comment. And you can publish and be damned. Everything you've told us tonight is second or third hand, even first hand it's nothing but speculation. There's not a scrap of proof, there has never been any prosecution, no official action of any kind has ever been brought against Hallsworth. But I'll give you some facts, Mr Jenkins. Something which *ought* to interest you as a newspaperman. I've been involved with Hallsworth for over a year now, and during that time our business transactions have been not only perfectly legal but totally ethical in every respect. And I warn you – publish anything damaging to Townsend and Partner and I'll bring proceedings against you to leave you penniless. Do I make myself clear?'

If anyone had dropped a pin it would have deafened us. Eventually Jenkins broke the long silence. 'Perfectly,' he said, his face empty of colour but his expression holding the ghost of a smile. 'And I've behaved badly. I can only hope that you'll thank me one day.' He turned to Amy. 'And that my hostess will forgive me.'

It was an odd kind of apology but I took it as such, and everyone set about repairing the damage of a wrecked evening. But we never effectively salvaged it, and Jean and I left as soon as we decently could.

'What an objectionable man,' was her verdict on the way back to Fulham. 'But you put him down beautifully, darling. I almost cheered.'

'The trouble is,' I said bleakly, 'I think he was trying to warn me.'

'About Hallsworth?'

'About being set up – used – screwed – however you want to put it.'

'But you've done nothing wrong, darling, even that thing with Pepalasis. Mike, you've got nothing to worry about.'

'That's probably what the Brigadier thought.'

She was quiet for a moment, and then she said: 'Poor man.' She shuddered. 'And – and Pamela Johnstone. What a terrible death.'

But I was already nursing an even more terrible thought.

'If it *was* Pamela Johnstone,' I said, 'in that car.'

CHAPTER SEVEN

I was half way to Fulham before I decided. Hell, I wasn't going to be able to sleep anyway. I swung on the wheel and changed direction, causing a cabbie behind me to brake hurriedly and Jean to ask where we were going.

'Hill Street. We've got work to do.'

I knew she was tired. Dammit, so was I. But in a sense I had slept too long. Much more of it would finish me.

'Then you believe Claude Jenkins?' she asked softly.

'How can we not believe him? Except that all he's got is a string of assumptions. We got more hard facts at the Dragon's Lair. Add what we *know* to what he *suspects* and it's terrifying.'

'I still can't accept it.' She stared in front of her, out into the night. 'Rupert Hallsworth. I mean, he's such a nice man.'

'Yeah,' I sneered bitterly. 'And Sue Ballantyne's such a nice girl.'

'Oh, well, *her*. She's different.'

'And Jolly Old Pepalasis. He's bloody Father Christmas, isn't he?'

'Mike, there's no need to –'

'And Frascari? Bruno Frascari. *WHO* is Bruno Frascari? *WHERE* is Bruno Frascari? Will the real Bruno Frascari please stand up?'

'You're driving too fast. Mike, please, slow down.'

I suppose I slowed down. No one booked me anyway. At Hill Street the first thing I did was to pour myself a double brandy while Jean made coffee. She thought I was behaving badly. Not that she said anything. I think she was frightened of the way I had been driving, frightened of the situation, frightened of me. And I was too worried, too tensed up, too full of my own fears to spend time soothing her. I was angry too. God, I was angry. It swamped through me so that my hands shook and my teeth clamped and I couldn't sit still for a minute at a time. I *hated* them. I would have denied the capacity to hate before that night. To *really* hate. But it burned me up that they had used me, that they were still damn well using me, that they planned to go on using me. And for what? What was the deal? Hallsworth was making a fortune as an honest businessman. Where was a deal big enough to warrant this? This *charade* – this expensive, elaborate farce they had made of my life for more than a year.

It took Jean an hour to calm me down. I don't know how she did it. Let me rant and rave, and curse and swear, and pace up and down. Agreeing with me, never too quickly or too openly, but pretending to give everything I said due thought and consideration before accepting the wisdom of it: making coffee, lighting cigarettes, and just being there. Thank God for her being there.

Then I went to work. By that time it was two in the morning. I searched Hallsworth's office first. *Everything*. His desk, filing cabinet, wardrobe, drinks cupboard, the whole bloody lot. It was uncanny but not one scrap of personal identity was to be found anywhere. My own room was a jumble of personal bric-a-brac, every drawer containing something identifiable as mine, bills, receipts, club memberships, all the impedimenta of everyday living, whereas Hallsworth's office could have been a hotel room prepared for an incoming guest.

Back in the flat I listed every investment and transaction entered into as a result of a recommendation from Hallsworth. There weren't many so it didn't take long. Then I analysed them, looking for some decrepancy, some anomaly, something which might provide a clue about what was going on. But it was a waste of time and at four o'clock we went to bed, as tired and worried as ever; only to face the whole wretched business all over again in the morning.

Jean went home first thing, to change into something more suitable for the office, while I slumped behind my desk and pretended to work. But it was no good, my mind was gripped by the discoveries of the weekend and couldn't settle on anything else. So after messing about for half an hour I went off to find Hallsworth, uncertain of what to say to him when I found him.

The export shipping date had apparently been finalised because when I poked my head into Seckleman's office the scene was one of almost feverish activity. The whole place had been transformed into a fair copy of a war-time operations room, with Seckleman and his two clerks hopping from phones to wall charts, updating information with a series of red ticks and blue crosses. And amidst it all sat Hallsworth, juggling telephones and barking instructions at two secretaries who scribbled away furiously. Despite everything I couldn't repress a twinge of admiration. Hallsworth had put a thirty million pound export order together in this room – with just the help of Seckleman, a couple of clerks, and two part-time secretaries.

'Hi, Mike.' He caught my eye. 'Nothing urgent I hope? I'm a bit, er – engrossed.'

I shook my head and left him to it, half planning a word later and still unsure of what I would say. Back at my desk I telephoned Poignton at Durbeville's to tell him that I would be over later, and I was just about to make another call when Hallsworth came in.

'Phew!' He slumped into a chair. 'I need a breather – it's a madhouse up there.' He did a quick double take at my face. 'You look fit. Get away to the sun this weekend?'

I grabbed the opening. 'Malta as a matter of fact.'

'Really?' He sounded interested, but not in the least concerned. And for a crazy moment I found myself wondering if I had got it all wrong.

'Went to see Jean's parents,' I said. 'We're getting married.'

His face shone with goodwill, but his congratulations lacked the spontaneity of surprise I had expected. Until I realized that a little bird had probably passed that snippet of information on to him already.

'Thanks,' I said when he had finished. 'Nice place, Malta. Do you know it at all?'

Despite my pretended casualness it was the most important question I had ever put to him. I tensed while I waited for his answer. He shook his head. 'Can't think why. Never been there on a holiday. And never had to go on business.'

A provable lie! All weekend I had searched for a *provable* lie. And here it was. Somehow I stifled the automatic contradiction and said. 'It's worth a visit. Of course, Jean's parents know it well. All the right places, that sort of thing. Took us out to dinner on Saturday. Place called the Dragon's Lair. It's an hotel. If you ever go I'd recommend it as the place to stay.'

He didn't as much as bat an eyelid. 'I'll remember,' he said.

For a moment we just stared at each other. There was something so confiding in his manner that I wondered about telling him everything , confronting him with it, straight out. He even helped me by saying: 'Look, I just called down to find out what you wanted? Can't stop long. The shipment goes out this weekend and it's panic stations till then.'

I don't know whether I lost my nerve or changed my mind. Whichever, something told me that the time wasn't right. So I said: 'Oh, nothing really. Just to tell you about Jean and me, that's all.'

'*That's all?*' He stood up and crossed to the door. 'Quite a week! *My* export order. *Your* getting married. The *Pepalasis* contract.' He smiled one of his fat, conspiratorial smiles. 'We must have a night out to celebrate. Make it a night to remember.'

I was still staring when he closed the door behind him. His confidence was insufferable! That, and this contemptuous assumption that he could fool me forever. The mood of angry alarm simmered for the next hour. It stayed with me during the cab ride to Durbeville's. And came nicely to the boil as I was shown into Poignton's office.

'Did you know that Hallsworth remarried?'

'No. As a matter of fact I didn't.' Poignton's manner was its usual bland self but his eyes betrayed a flicker of curiosity.

'But you're not surprised?'

'Should I be?'

I was in no mood to debate the issue. I wanted Poignton rattled. Shaken out of his normal complacent smugness. So I snapped: 'I know all about the Frascari scandal,' and waited for his reaction.

'I see,' was all he said, very softly.

'You're not going to deny knowing about it?'

'What is there to deny?'

'Oh, come off it, Poignton! What kind of lawyer are you? You knew about *that*? And you didn't tell me. The whole thing stinking of fraud. You had a duty, a responsibility – '

'To my client,' he interrupted sharply. 'My only obligation to you was to answer your interminable questions.' He sighed for effect and added, 'And Heaven knows I discharged that. At some considerable length I seem to remember.'

'It's a pity you didn't remember a few other things,' I said angrily. 'Like Frascari and Hersch. With Hallsworth and Pamela Johnstone shuffling cash between them.'

'I'd really like to know –'

'So would I, Poignton. I'd *really* like to know. The only thing I'm certain of is that I've been tucked up. And that you helped. You put me into bed with a con man and –'

'Any bed was of your own making,' he retorted furiously. 'And any other suggestion is pure invention.'

'Invention? I bet your fees were real enough,' I sneered. 'Christ, Hallsworth must have paid a fortune for your help.'

'My fees are my business.'

'We'll see if the Law Society think so. Or the Old Bailey.'

His usually waxen face went crimson with temper and his voice hoarse with outrage. 'How dare you! Neither my client nor I have any reason to reproach –'

'Save it, Poignton. Don't hand me any crap about Hallsworth making one mistake and turning over a new leaf. Your precious client is all set to pull the biggest con the City's ever seen. Savundra and Stonehouse were choirboys by comparison.'

'You're mad,' he said with conviction. 'Or sick. Whichever it is you'd better go.' He reached for the telephone. 'Perhaps your doctor –'

'Leave it!' I slammed a hand on his. 'I'll go when I'm ready. And that will be when we've had our talk.'

Outrage dissolved to alarm as he recoiled, nursing a bruised hand and watching me as if he feared for his life.

'For the record.' I reached across and slid the dictating machine to my side of the desk. 'A blank tape. Quickly!'

He found one in the bottom of his desk drawer and handed it to me without saying a word, his expression a mixture of curiosity and apprehension. It took a minute to fit the cassette in the machine, dictate the date and play it back to make sure that everything was working properly. Then I switched the machine to record and set the microphone on the desk between us.

'Hallsworth and Pepalasis are in this together,' I begun, more calmly now, using my head instead of my nerve ends. 'They've been meeting in secret for years, planning it, scheming and –'

'Preposterous!' He recovered enough to drag his gaze away from the tape recorder to face me. 'Pepalasis was your discovery. If anyone arranged anything with him it was you. Hallsworth's hardly been involved.'

'Don't you believe it. He's been pulling the strings all along.'

'And you've danced to his tune?' The sarcasm was biting. 'A man with your reputaion for tough bargaining? I'm sorry, but I can't see you doing that. Unless it suited you, of course.'

'Meaning?' I wondered if he knew about the promised kickback.

'Meaning something's gone wrong. I can't imagine what, but clearly something has. So now you decide it's all your partner's fault. But Hallsworth didn't hawk this deal round the City as if his very life depended on it. Hallsworth didn't visit the island. Hallsworth didn't get elected to the Board of the new consortium.'

'Hallsworth planned the whole bloody thing!'

'Ridiculous. Something's gone wrong. Own up to it like a man. You're not the first man in business to make a mistake.'

'And that's how you see it?'

'That's how the world will see it. That's how it is. You'll make things a damn sight worse by –'

'They planned it I tell you! Will you listen? Secret meetings in Malta. Every few months for the last couple of years.'

His face twisted into a smile designed to humour me. 'Naturally, you've got proof of this, Mr Townsend?'

I reached to an inside pocket for the list. 'Those are the dates,' I said triumphantly. 'When they all met at the

Dragon's Lair Hotel in Malta.'

He accepted the piece of paper and sat staring at it, turning it over in long thin fingers, as if thinking rather than reading it. Eventually he asked: 'When they *all* met?'

'Mr *and* Mrs Hallsworth. And Aristotle Pepalasis.' I paused until his eyes lifted to reach mine. 'And Bruno Frascari.'

It took ten minutes to relate the details of the weekend's discoveries. The machine recorded it all and the tape was still turning as I finished and reached for a cigarette.

'It's hardly proof of anything is it?' he snorted. 'In fact quite the reverse. There's no evidence that anyone actually met anyone. And Frascari's presence is total assumption on your part. So is the claim that it's the same Mr Hallsworth, or the same Mr Pepalasis.'

'Oh, for God's sake! What is this? A cover up? How many Aristotle Pepalasises do you know?'

'It's not an uncommon Greek name. I've seen it over shop windows in Athens and I even enjoyed holidaying once at an hotel owned by a man of that name.' His smile was infuriating. 'After all, a Greek might not know many Townsends but there's hundreds of them in the London phone book.'

'You're dismissing *this*?' I snatched the list from his fingers. 'You asked for proof, and –'

'You've given me assumptions. That's all. That's not proof. Coincidences perhaps, but . . .'

'Coincidences? The *same* names. The *same* dates. The same out of the way hotel in Malta?'

'Adolph Hitler and I stayed at the same hotel,' he said surprisingly. 'In 1935 and again in 1936. It was a large hotel and we never met but *you* might infer our nights were spent together planning the Second World War.'

'Don't be so bloody stupid.' It seemed an absurd argument to me but he seemed pleased with it. He sat with his chin cupped in both hands, with the mildly curious expression of an entomologist watching a scorpion sting itself to death.

I tried again. 'So how do you explain Mrs Hallsworth?'

'Any number of ways. The most obvious is that she's additional proof that *this* Mr Hallsworth isn't the man we know. The next is –'

'Her real name's Ballantyne. Susan Ballantyne. I told you –'

'Oh yes. What was it? "Eyes that dance and make impossible promises." Your Mr Tonelli missed his vocation. Writing lyrics for popular songs earns more money than running hotels.'

'Treat it as a joke, Poignton, and you'll laugh your way right into the Old Bailey. Four people Tonelli said, four people meet whenever Hallsworth goes to Malta. Well, I'm damn sure I know three of them and I'll take short odds on the fourth being Bruno Frascari.'

'But you don't *know*.'

'I'll damn soon find out. I'll phone Jack and have him check the records. Will you act then?'

'I've a very good mind to act now,' he answered quickly. I could hear the temper back in his voice. He'd once told me that he couldn't be intimidated and I believed him. 'By phoning Hallsworth immediately,' he said, waving a hand in disgust. 'You barge in here, commandeer my dictating machine, make a lot of wild accusations about the man who's been largely responsible for your recent success. It's not on, Townsend. Hallsworth's dealings with you have been greatly to your benefit. After all, Townsend and Partner has been pretty much your own show hasn't it?'

'Has it? Maybe on everything except the Pepalasis project. And that's where the con is, Poignton, I'm convinced of it. And you'll be convinced too. When I tell you the name Frascari uses these days.'

'Oh, you know that too, do you?'

'I know someone with an American accent. Whose involvement would be crucial. And his name is Kirk McNeil.'

'McNeil?' Poignton's astonishment was completely genuine. No one could have faked the eyebrows climbing into the hairline and the mouth gaping in amazement. It took him almost a minute to recover and then, very quietly he said. 'You really are mad. Quite, quite, mad.'

'Am I? I'll tell you about it. Pepalasis found an island of dubious value, McNeil exaggerated the amount of nickel there, and Hallsworth used me to persuade people to invest in it. It's the only way to make sense. It's a perfect set up. They pick up thirty million from the consortium and disappear when U.S. Steel's experts contradict McNeil's findings. U.S. Steel withdraw and I'm torn limb from limb by the consortium for persuading them to invest in the first place.'

'And you *really* believe that?'

'I know it's incredible. Don't think I don't,' I admitted. 'But it fits.'

'Incredible?' he shook his head. 'It's more than that. And as for fitting . . . ' Words failed him for a moment, then he said, 'Kirk McNeil is an acknowledged expert in the mining industry. And isn't he a friend of Harry Smithers? Wasn't that how he became involved? They knew each other in Australia.'

'So who more likely for Harry to send for when he has a mining problem?'

'But the man's got a lifetime experience behind him. It was largely because of his reputation that U.S. Steel moved so quickly. And you claim that the man's an *imposter*?'

I tried hard not to back down. To meet Poignton's look of utter disbelief with one of conviction. But it was damn near impossible. The truth was I wasn't convinced myself. Not about McNeil. Dammit, I *liked* the man. But the problem had an answer somewhere, some theory seemed better than none at all.

'And as for Hallsworth and Pepalasis skipping with the money,' Poignton said derisively. 'Of course you *know* that

Pepalasis has set up a British company to handle the transactions, don't you? So think what's involved in moving thirty million out of the country in a hurry. It will take weeks. Months probably, to get Bank of England consent to move that much. Consent might even be refused. And then what happens to your moonlight flit theory? Not to mention that during those weeks and months you and U.S. Steel will have experts crawling all over the island.'

'And suppose they don't come up with nickel in the right quantities?'

He shrugged, and then smiled. 'The only person you won't be able to blame is Pepalasis. After all, he's never claimed there was any nickel. If anyone's being deceived by the present arrangements, he is.'

'So it all rests on McNeil?'

'It always did surely?'

'I'm still not satisfied,' I said, conceding the argument but stubbornly resisting the outcome of his logic.

'It's a bit late in the day for that isn't it?'

'Not too late.'

'So what will you do?' There was no temper left in his voice now, only a kind of malicious curiosity. 'Call the deal off? There's still time. Though God knows how you'll explain it to your consortium. And I'm bound to say that in view of the letter of intent sent to Pepalasis he must have the basis of a massive claim against you for breach of contract.'

But it wasn't Pepalasis I was worrying about. Not at that moment. I was picturing a Paddington cellar and wondering how I would explain the loss of four million pounds to Simmy Drachman.

'I'll let you know,' I answered, bleak with defeat, switching off the microphone.

Poignton was watching the tape re-wind itself. He said: 'I'll have to consider reporting this conversation to Mr Hallsworth. I'll sleep on it. Decide in the morning. But some of the allegations you've made . . .' He stopped abruptly. 'What the devil are you doing with that tape?'

But he was too late. I had already slipped the cassette into my pocket and was half way to the door. 'Maybe I'll save you the trouble,' I said over my shoulder. 'And give him this to play with.' And I left.

CHAPTER EIGHT

I went for a walk. Not for the exercise but to digest Poignton's attitude. Loyalty to a client was one thing; conspiracy to defraud, another. It was of no consequence that he had demolished my arguments. After all, even I was sceptical about some of them. All I was sure about was that something was wrong. Very wrong. Despite his refusal to see substance in the coincidences. That alarmed me almost as much as his forecast about the consequences. And *that* was beginning to scare the hell out of me. Pull out now and Pepalasis would ruin me with a writ for breach of contract. Stay in and, if I was right, I'd never be trusted in the City again. Not that *that* mattered. If I was right, Drachman would murder me anyway.

A dozen cigarettes later I reached the only conclusion possible. Face Hallsworth when I got back to Hill Street. If I was wrong I'd leave the office on the toe of his boot. If I was right I might just persuade them to pull out of Wednesday's meeting. Just in time for me to play the jilted bridegroom, with thirty million pounds worth of presents to return.

It had turned five. For an hour I had sat on the Embankment, gazing moodily across the Thames, my mind a turmoil of fear and uncertainty. But now the decision was made, and I shifted my eyes from the river to the road as I looked for a cab. Instead I found a long, low, black limousine

211

parked by the kerb. With Drachman's face peeering out at me from the open rear window.

'Mr Townsend. What a pleasure.' He nodded at the parapet. 'Not contemplating jumping I hope?'

One of the heavy mob was already opening the door and guiding me into the rear seat. It was a very practised manoeuvre which I found disturbing and then alarming, as he followed me in and closed the door.

'You worried about something?' Drachman searched my face.

'Just getting a breath of air. You know what it's like – meetings all day in stuffy offices.'

'Sure.' The car had already pulled away and was beginning to nudge a path towards Parliament Square. 'Can we drop you somewhere?'

I felt the relief well up inside me. 'Hill Street. If it's not out of your way.'

'Timbuctoo wouldn't be out of our way. Not for you. Right now, Mr Townsend, you're our most valuable property.'

I wondered if I should ask him to call me Mike but decided against it. Instead I laughed nervously. 'Coincidence. You passing just then.'

'Yeah, wasn't it?' There was a glimmer of humour in his expression. 'You'd be surprised how carefully we watch our investments.'

I understood and almost let it go, overburdened with enough worry without dwelling on the thought of Drachman having me watched. But it prompted a memory. 'Have you ever had me followed before, Mr Drachman?'

'Before when?'

'Before now. About a month ago for instance?'

'I had no business with you a month ago. You think my boys need the practice or something?' He laughed and everyone in the car laughed with him. Except me, and I pretended to watch the grass grow in Green Park.

212

'Everything set for Wednesday?' he asked.

'Yes.'

'No last minute hitches?'

'Should there be?'

'Legitimate business?' he shrugged and looked a picture of misery. 'Always screws me up. Can't sleep for the worry of it. Know what I mean?'

I knew exactly what he meant.

They dropped me at the corner of Hill Street and Chesterfield Hill and Drachman said goodbye through the open window. 'You'll let us know if you plan to move around, eh? Like the filth say – notify us of your travel arrangements.'

'I'm not going anywhere.'

'That's best,' he nodded soberly. 'This time of year – all those crowds. It ain't healthy.'

It was six o'clock and the front door was closed. I unlocked it and walked up to the first floor to see if Jean was still working. She wasn't. So I continued on to the floor above, half expecting to find Hallsworth and Seckleman still involved with the export deal. But that office was empty too, so I climbed the final flight of stairs to the flat, hoping that Jean would have finished the packing and be ready to leave. We planned for me to move into Fulham while we searched for a suitable house. I reached the landing, crossed it, and was just about to open the door to the flat, when somebody opened it for me. From the inside.

'Come in, Mike. We've been expecting you,' Sue Ballantyne said as she stepped back into the doorway to allow me to pass.

Part Five

CHAPTER ONE

'Oh Mike – thank God!' Jean threw herself at me like a frightened child. Beyond her was Hallsworth and someone else, just inside the room – a big man, very big, someone I had never seen before. Sue Ballantyne closed the door behind me and the small sitting room seemed suddenly crowded as everyone stood looking at each other expectantly. Alarmed at Jean's trembling, I looked to Hallsworth for an explanation. But he merely smiled and raised the glass he was holding. 'To the happy couple.'

The mockery of his toast added to my confusion and I was about to ask what the hell was going on when the doorbell interrupted me. One short ring, twice more – three bursts followed by a longer one. I sensed Sue look to Hallsworth for instructions as the big man closed in from the left and placed a hand on my shoulder to propel me towards the centre of the room.

'Mike, meet Albert,' Hallsworth said casually.

Closer inspection confirmed first impressions. Albert was a giant, easily six inches taller than me with the weight to go with it. A battered, moronic looking face, hands like bananas; second cousin to the men with Drachman in the Cadillac. For a fleeting second I wondered if, after all, this was Frascari. But a second glance into the dull eyes convinced me otherwise.

'Champagne for Mike please, Albert.' Hallsworth might have been speaking to a child. 'Answer the door, Pamela, there's a good girl.'

Jean and I sat on the sofa, while Albert filled the glass from an open bottle.

'He said it was a surprise.' Jean's voice was barely a frightened whisper. 'A celebration. For us. Then that other man arrived – with *her*.'

I put an arm across her shoulders and watched Hallsworth, conscious that he had called Sue 'Pamela' and grappling with the significance of it.

'So?' I said. 'True colours at last.'

But any reply Hallsworth might have made was cut short by the arrival of Pepalasis who almost wrenched the door from its hinges in his hurry. Sue followed him in, a pace behind, her face as worried as his. His gaze flickered briefly from Jean to me and on to Hallsworth. 'Why are we meeting here?' Temper blazed in his voice. 'This is madness. I could hardly believe your message –'

'Mike and Jean have been to Malta,' Hallsworth interrupted. To the Dragon's Lair. Asking questions. Putting two and two together and making four.'

Pepalasis stifled an oath and turned accusing eyes at me. 'An accountant's mentality, I'm afraid.' I faked the confidence which I lacked, and added, 'Making things add up.' I let that sink in and then asked: 'Where's Frascari by the way?'

Pepalasis plunged a hand into his jacket pocket and I could hear the kombolois clicking even before he withdrew them. Sue's eyes rounded and Hallsworth almost dropped his glass. Their surprise really was most gratifying and I used their silence as an opportunity to counter-attack. 'Perhaps I'm not the idiot you've all taken me for. The dream's finished. This is the one con job you're *not* going to get away with.'

'Get away with *what*, exactly?' Hallsworth recovered first.

For the obvious reason that I did not know I turned to things I did. 'The game's over, Hallsworth. I've got it all. The meetings in Malta. That girl there – Sue, Pamela, whatever you call her – phoning from Barmouth that time for you to burgle this place.' Nerves wagged my tongue. 'And

215

you had me followed, didn't you? And staged that beating up in the Dorchester. *You* all the time. What was it supposed to do? Chivvy me up to put the cash together?'

'Well, it didn't take you long, did it?' He might have been paying me a compliment.

I looked from face to face and it was as if scales had been lifted from my eyes. I saw them afresh – the smooth playboy, an aging adventurer, a white-faced girl who was neither as young or pretty as I remember.

'Come on, Jean.' I tucked a hand under her elbow and pulled myself upright from the sofa. 'Let's get out of here.'

But Albert moved first, two quick steps, blocking my path like a stone slab in a tomb.

'Shouldn't you consider your own position?' Hallsworth asked quietly and I heard a threat in his voice.

'Which is what?'

'Blow the whistle on us and we'll beat you to it with details of the fifty thousand in your Barclays account.'

So that was it! I looked at Pepalasis. 'I paid it back.'

'I forgot about your cheque,' he smiled. 'And never presented it.'

'That fifty thousand came from here,' Hallsworth added quickly. 'And by the time the books are rearranged it will look uncommonly like embezzlement. Fifty thousand, milked from the day to day running of Townsend and Partner, of which you had sole charge.'

His sneer of triumph was the last straw. All the worry and the hate and the feeling of betrayal, erupted into action. I launched myself at him, catching a shin on the coffee table as I went over, arms outstretched to grab his lapels, cursing as his knee caught me, momentum carrying me on until one hand made contact with his jacket and gripped hard as my other arm swung in a punch. Then Jean's rising scream as the roof fell in and Albert took over. A huge, chopping blow delivered from behind, his other hand lifting and turning me, backing me to the wall and doubling me with quick punches to the ribs and stomach. I would have fallen, *tried* to fall, anything to escape the power of those hands, but other punches straightened me, lifting me from the floor as one hand groped for my throat to pin me to the wall. I jerked from outstretched fingers, my watering eyes catching a blurred glimpse of Jean, her mouth opening to scream as Pepalasis swung his arm with a crack like a pistol shot to send her toppling backwards beyond my view. Another punch, expelling every ounce of breath from my lungs, sent me to the floor, fighting for air through a haze of pain before Albert dragged me back to my feet and pushed me contemptuously into a chair. I heard Jean sobbing and Pepalasis shouting at her, the sharp sound of a blow followed by her cry of pain – and then silence, broken by the rasping of my strangulated breath.

'Come on, we need a meeting with – ' Pepalasis checked himself. 'Leave Albert here with these and – '

'No.' Hallsworth sounded positive, an order, crisp and businesslike. 'The closer we stick to original plans the better. Get her up, Albert.'

Her could only mean Jean. Even without seeing the direction of his glance I knew that.

'Leave her alone!' I started across the room, legs buckling under me, my eyes on Jean, oblivious of all else, not seeing Pepalasis turning, not realizing – until the red hot stab of pain as his shoe smashed into my knee cap. I dropped, crawling, dragging the dead leg, desperate to reach Jean first. But we were there together, Albert already pulling her upright, rough fingers at the shoulders of her dress, fabric tearing, the sound joining her cry of protest as she struggled against him.

'Get him back here,' Hallsworth commanded.

They came together, two men in a hurry, the Greek trapping my arms from behind as Albert brought his knee up hard into my groin. I think I screamed. I was incapable of thought, writhing and kicking, conscious only of savage

217

pain tearing my body in a blazing merciless ache as they dragged me across to a chair.

Pepalasis used my own necktie to bind my hands twisting my arm like a child working Plasticine. I glimpsed Jean in a chair opposite me, eyes wide and frightened, the entire lower half of her face covered by Albert's hand.

It was all over so quickly. A few minutes before I had been confused but still capable of rational thought. Able to speak, make decisions, to reason and to behave like a human being. God, was this all it took? Five minutes? To reduce me to this! Bathed in sweat, twisted with pain, humiliated, afraid.

A minute passed and predictably it was Hallsworth who broke the silence.

'Jean, I want you to listen carefully. We shall avoid violence if we can. Believe me, it's not our style. But if you scream, Albert will hit you. Very hard. Understand? Do as you're told and you won't be hurt.' He paused, while Jean's eyes sought mine and I found myself nodding to do as he said.

'Very well,' he turned to Albert. 'Release her.'

Jean sucked air into her lungs and wiped her mouth clean of Albert's grip, while her other hand reached for the shoulder of her torn dress.

'It suits us best,' Hallsworth spoke to me as normally as he would in a business meeting, 'if things stand as they are. Contracts exchanged on Wednesday as planned. You and Smithers sign for the consortium. Ari collects the bank draft and it's all over.'

It was incredible! I couldn't believe they still intended to go through with it. 'It's all over now,' I answered bitterly. 'The deal's off. I'll make *sure* that the consortium never sign.'

'Never say never,' he said and the threat was back in his voice. 'And I think you'll change your mind. After all, there's nothing illegal about our transaction. Whereas embezzlement? If we release details of that –'

218

'You'll do that anyway,' I interrupted, never more sure of anything in all my life.

'How perceptive of you.'

'That was the plan, wasn't it? You scream embezzlement – I disappear – presumed skipped the country.'

'There are many plans.' He smiled, all his confidence back now, the situation well under control. 'An operation like this. Three years is a long time to work for something. Contingency arrangements exist for all manner of things including –'

'Including me not signing?' I jeered. 'Try planning your way out of that.'

'We're wasting time,' the Greek complained to Hallsworth. 'We must have a meeting to –'

'Not yet.' Hallsworth silenced him, then turned back to me. 'I'll tell you once more, it suits us best if you co-operate and –'

'And I say never!'

They stared at me, Pepalasis scowling and truculent, Sue white-faced, a vein pulsing at her neck, and Hallsworth as calm as a judge. The loudest noise in the room was the clicking of the Greek's worry beads. Almost a minute passed. Then Hallsworth turned his gaze away from me and looked at Jean.

'Stand up, Jean, will you please,' he said softly. 'And don't forget my warning about Albert.'

Jean turned enquiring eyes to me and my brain jammed in a panic of indecision.

'*STAND UP!*' Hallsworth shouted suddenly, so that we all jumped.

Jean stood, one hand still at the torn shoulder of her dress.

'Now turn around, will you.' His voice lowered to little more than a menacing whisper. 'That's right – right round. And now back again – to face me.

'No, don't sit down, not yet. Jean, I've never told you before, but you've got a magnificent figure. I've often thought it, of course, but I've never told you. Have I?'

She blushed, unsure of what was expected of her. Her cheek still bore the imprint of the Greek's hand and her face slowly reddened to cover the mark. The room was suddenly very still.

'HAVE I?' Hallsworth shouted at her.

'No – no – you haven't,' her answer was almost a sob.

'No, I've never told you,' Hallsworth whispered, almost to himself. His dark eyes devoured her and his expression was set and tense. Then, without looking away from Jean, he said: 'Albert, don't you think Jean's got an exciting body?'

I swung my gaze to Albert, the hairs along the back of my arms and neck rising and alarm knotting my stomach as I watched his eyes widen and a slow greedy smile spread on his face. Hallsworth was still looking at Jean. 'There's only one thing wrong, Albert, isn't there. Too many clothes spoil the view, don't you think?'

Albert's hands opened and closed with a child's anticipation. It was enough. Tied or not, I was moving, kicking the chair backwards, half rising to my feet. But the Greek had anticipated me, an arm already locking over my neck and snapping my head back until air rasped from my windpipe.

'Let him go!' Jean was shouting. 'Damn you – ' But even as my head bent backwards I saw Albert grab her, blotting out her words with a huge hand. Seconds later a noose was around my neck and knots jerked into place as my arms were wrenched high up my back. I glimpsed Pepalasis' face, sweat stained above his open shirt as he linked his own tie to mine to truss me like a chicken on a butcher's slab. By the time he had finished any attempt to free my hands jerked my head backwards and my efforts to free my head forced my arms an inch higher up my back.

'Remember what I said, Jean,' Hallsworth was saying, and I squirmed into a position to see him. 'One sound.'

He nodded at Albert who removed his hand and took a step backwards, while Jean and I exchanged helpless glances across the three or four yards separating us.

'Now take your clothes off, Jean,' Hallsworth said. 'All of them.'

'No!' It was my shout and the edge of the Greek's hand which thudded into my throat to kill the sound of it as Hallsworth continued, 'A word from me, Jean, and Albert will strip you. The choice is yours.'

I swear before God that there was nothing I could do. Just twist in the chair as my eyes sought hers in an unspoken plea for forgiveness. And never once did she look away.

'Beautiful,' Hallsworth murmured a minute later. 'Quite enchanting. But I knew you would be. And I did say *all* your clothes, Jean.'

He might not have been there for all the notice she took of him. I sensed more than saw her nakedness, filling my consciousness with the blue of her eyes, knowing that to as much as blink would be the biggest act of betrayal of my life.

But Hallsworth's little drama still had its climax. 'The bedroom's behind you, Albert. Take her there for a while. Play with her if you like. We'll look in later and –'

Even silk biting deep into my windpipe and Pepalasis fighting hard to hold me down couldn't keep me in that chair. 'Stop it! For Christ's sake –' I was up, then down again as my curiously hunchbacked position toppled me to the floor, conscious only of Jean struggling and kicking as Albert half pulled, half carried her through the doorway.

Hallsworth stood over me. 'Well? The deal goes ahead?'

'You bastard! Get that – that animal away from her. D'you hear me? You fucking . . .'

'An appropriate word I would imagine – in another minute or two. You're wasting time, Townsend. The deal? On or off?'

'Anything. Get her back. For the love of –'

'The deal. Goes ahead. Right?'

'Right. Get her –'

But he had gone. I shut my eyes to blot out the memory

and listened to Hallsworth shouting commands like a man with a trained dog. And then they were back. Jean wrapped in my old dressing gown, so big on her that she could have camped in it.

'Nothing happened?' I began as she leaned over me, cradling my head in her arms, her cheeks still wet with tears. She put a finger to my lips, shaking her head, her eyes brimming with tears and trying to smile at the same time.

'Cut him loose,' Hallsworth said above me. 'I doubt we'll see any more heroics. But a warning, Michael. Albert's been denied a pleasure beyond his wildest dreams. He'll bear you a grudge for that, for the rest of his life.'

'Or yours,' Pepalasis muttered as he rolled me over to untie the knots.

Jean helped me to a chair like a nurse guiding a geriatric, whilst I scraped my ribs back together and rubbed the circulation into my wrists. When I was settled, Hallsworth began to dictate the terms of my surrender.

'Ari, you and Albert will take Jean to – ' he checked himself. 'To where you were going when you got my message.'

'No!' I snapped. 'Jean gets on a plane and goes home to her family.' I thought about her grizzled old sea dog of a father. He wouldn't thank me much for sending his daughter back to him in such a state but at least she'd be safe.

'Don't be a fool, Townsend,' Hallsworth said coldly. 'Without her we can't control you. She'll come to no harm. As long as you behave yourself.'

'How the hell do I know that?'

He hesitated. 'She'll speak to you. Once a day.'

'*Once a day?* For God's sake! How long's this going to last?'

'Until the agreement's signed. And the money's handed over.'

'That's Wednesday. Then we go free?'

'Not immediately.' He glanced quickly at Pepalasis. 'In

fact you'll come with us. We'll put you down safely, a few days later, outside the country.'

The prospect amused Pepalasis enough for him to smile. 'A nice sea voyage. Just what's needed.'

There was no more argument. Not with Hallsworth rattling out orders and Albert standing a foot away waiting to finish what he had started.

We collected Jean's clothes and went to the bedroom for her to dress – Albert watching hungrily from the open doorway. I kissed her and a few minutes later she left, walking between Pepalasis and Albert, Sue Ballantyne leading the way, the bedroom door closing as I was locked in. I wondered when I would next see her and for the first time in years found myself saying the Lord's Prayer.

CHAPTER TWO

Sleep cheated me when it came, the sought-for refuge turning to a chill nightmare, until waking lifted the mists of unconsciousness and my mind ran away to hide, terrified by the discovery that it was all true – real – had happened.

Something had disturbed me. I held my breath, not daring to move, waiting and wondering. Seven o'clock in the morning, bathed in sweat in my bed in Hill Street after an hour's troubled sleep. Every nerve in my body listening, almost certain that the noise I heard was outside the door. A board creaked and I *knew* I was right. Someone was in the corridor. Doing as I was – waiting and listening. Then the key turned slowly in the lock, and raw nerves and bruised muscles screamed in unison as I jerked upright. Albert was framed in the open doorway, dressed in the same sweater and slacks as last night, crumpled now from sleeping in them, his greasy hair uncombed, and the lower half of his face dark with stubble. He looked slyly satisfied, like a tiger watching a tethered goat. I wasn't going anywhere and we both knew it. Neither of us spoke. I was in no mood for conversation and he couldn't if he tried. It was one of the things I had found out last night. He was a mute. Or as near being one as makes no difference; with a repertoire of noises, grunts mostly, the deep threatening sounds being the ones to watch for. But he couldn't actually say a word.

It had been midnight when I had made the discovery, when he returned, alone and seemingly tired from a long journey. Hallsworth had explained the rules to both of us. I was to be locked in my room by night and given the run of the building in the daytime, shadowed by Albert in the flat and Hallsworth in the offices. Outside phone calls were forbidden and incoming ones accepted only with Hallsworth on an extension, ready to break the connection on an ill-judged word. That apart, I was to act normally – or try to. Any move to escape, or show of defiance, would be punished by an act of compelling simplicity. They would kill Jean.

Kidnap may have become a part of everyday life in the seventies, but not part of mine. No newspaper headline ever prepared me for the dreadful hopelessness of it all. The frustrating impotence. The haunting, worrying fear for the safety of a loved one. I was *terrified* for her safety. And Hallsworth knew it.

Albert followed me to the bathroom, staying so close that I could smell him. I soaked in the bath for a while, with him squatting on the floor watching me like a trained Doberman waiting to rip my throat out. I ignored him, or at least pretended to, while I splashed in the water and hummed the refrain from 'Chorus Line'. Not a memorable performance but the warmth of the bath eased enough of the ache from my body for my mind to function again.

My only bit of comfort was the thought that Jean would be safe until morning at least. Whatever they threatened, they wouldn't harm her until the contract was signed. Which gave me twenty-seven hours to find a way out. It was a good thought to start with because there wasn't much to follow. Except the reverse of the coin. Three years to plan, Hallsworth had said. And it could all go wrong in the next twenty-seven hours. Which would make them as jumpy as I was.

I dried myself and returned to the bedroom, telling myself to put a brave face on things, even if it kills, and laughing aloud at the absurdity of everyday language.

Hallsworth and 'Sue' were already in the kitchen, drinking my coffee and eating my toast. Her appearance surprised me. She had done something different with her hair and was dressed in a tailored business suit, quite unlike the casual clothes she usually wore.

'Good morning, Pamela.' The new name felt strange on my lips. Odd really, how difficult it was to call her Pamela, and yet how impossible to think of her as Sue. But I knew who she was for all that. I took another look at the suit and asked, 'Going for an interview?'

'High spirits?' Hallsworth cocked an eyebrow. 'Different from last night?'

I grinned at him. 'A good sleep and an easy conscience. My remedy for anything. What's yours?'

'Thirty million pounds.' His smile was so warm and friendly that last night might never have happened.

I looked at the girl. Half the night had been spent thinking about her. Wondering how I would feel when I saw her again. Trying to make sense of her life, all that deception, all those lies. Making guesses about how much of our relationship had been genuine and how much fake? Windsor came to mind. 'I'm sorry, Mike,' she had said. 'Sorry now, that it was *you*. Remember that, eh?' I remembered all right. The bitch!

Turning my back on them I filled the kettle to make tea. 'Whatever became of Susan Ballantyne?' I asked over my shoulder. 'Remember her? The girl who lived quietly in the country, writing history books. The church mouse with an honours degree.'

There was no reply. I carried a cup and saucer to the table and caught the girl watching me. Something in her expression was startling enough to jog my hand and rattle the cup and its saucer. Except expression is quite the wrong word, the opposite in fact. Her face was motionless, as still as stone. The cool grey eyes looked back into mine totally without feeling. What had I expected for God's sake? Remorse? Guilt? Even embarrassed, perhaps. Anything but cold detachment. I recovered enough to say: 'Sue Ballantyne really existed you know. Once. About your size and not unlike you to look at. She was a real church mouse though. No family, little money, few friends. You were probably all she had.'

She turned her face away to study the kitchen clock.

'We've a busy morning,' Hallsworth began, but I cut him short. 'Not till I've breakfasted we haven't.' I put bread in the toaster and collected marmalade from the larder. 'Anyway we were talking about Sue Ballantyne. I'll tell you about her if you like. After all, the story almost begins with her, doesn't it?'

He made no reply. Just sat and watched me. But he was curious all right. I said, 'About the time you married. A young man with a young wife, both with a taste for rich living but lacking the wherewithal. So you put the bite on the poor old Brigadier. After all he'd done well enough – a decent pension and landing that job at Haldane's. Half their business was military stuff anyway, so having a Brigadier on the Board was good P.R., if nothing else. Trouble was, he was bright. Bright enough to put in charge of purchasing. Ironic isn't it? If he'd been a bit of a duffer he'd have lived a damn sight longer.'

I made the tea while Hallsworth and the girl took their cue from Albert, and said nothing. I carried the teapot to the table: 'The allowance he provided wasn't enough though was it? Not for your life style. So his job was your big chance, with him placing contracts worth millions and you living it up every night with Bruno Frascari. So you faked a failed marriage and Pamela Johnstone embarked on a life of business under her maiden name.'

Suddenly the girl banged the table, making us all jump. 'Shut up,' she snapped, looking at Hallsworth as if to tell him to make me. But he was hooked. There was enough curiosity in his eyes to have killed a dozen cats. And all at once I realized what I had seen in the girl's face. *Tension!* She was as taut as a coiled spring. Every ounce of concentration was being used to stop her nerves from coming apart. The discovery encouraged me and drove me on.

'The scheme worked fine didn't it?' I said to Hallsworth. 'Except for a nosey newspaperman. And the Brigadier knew his son for what he was. So when he found out, the pieces fell into place. Poor sod. Sensed a scandal and blew his brains out.'

His white face may have meant painful memories, or maybe he was acting. I neither knew or cared. I had memories of my own and twenty-seven hours left to protect them.

'Pinero sniffing around was just bad luck.' I buttered a slice of toast, not expecting him to comment and not waiting. 'Especially when he got on the German end. Meetings with the liquidator and so on. So Miss Johnstone had to disappear. Back to England for a timely death. Except that Pamela Johnstone, with all that money stashed away, wanted very much to live, didn't she?'

'You're guessing,' Hallsworth said, so quietly that it took someone who'd known him a long time to detect his uncertainty. And I'd known him just long enough.

'Only about where you found little Miss Ballantyne.' I turned to the girl. 'Who was she? An old school chum? A scholarship girl perhaps? Orphaned and living in what's called reduced circumstances.'

Her face wasn't motionless now. The vein I'd noticed standing out on her neck began to throb and drew an answering twitch from one corner of her mouth, while her eyes flashed messages to Hallsworth. 'He knows – ' she began, but he interrupted her. 'Nothing,' he snapped. 'He *knows* nothing.'

Her hands in front of her on the table were folded into tiny white fists with smaller spots of white marking her knuckles as they strained against the skin. She sat straight-backed and stared at me with frightened eyes. 'How – ' she began, but again he cut her short.

'How did I know?' I ignored Hallsworth, concentrating on her, watching the alarm signals of her body language. 'You told me.'

A hand flew to her mouth as if to stop words uttered long ago.

'Oh, not outright,' I admitted. 'You changed the story a bit. Swapped the roles around.' I jerked my head at Hallsworth. 'He probably seduced her. Easy enough, I'd think, girl like that probably imagined herself in love anyway. Then you arrived back at the crucial moment to catch them at it. Enstranged wife accuses lifetime friend of betrayal. And sets the scene for the final act. Sue Ballantyne's final act. Doused with petrol, your rings on her fingers, stuffed behind the wheel of a car, and –'

'No!' she leapt to her feet, her hands covering her ears. 'Shut up. Damn you, shut up!'

'What's the matter, Pamela Johnstone?' I jeered. 'Afraid of ghosts?'

Hallsworth cut in then, his voice rising almost to a shout: 'The whole things preposterous. A guess that's so bloody crazy that –'

'That it worked!' I shouted back, on my feet now, putting the table between me and them. 'You two murdered Sue Ballantyne, didn't you? Years ago. Then you –'

'Albert,' Hallsworth shouted. The giant took an uncertain

step forward, his path blocked by the table.

'Call him off,' I snapped. 'I'm no good to you if I can't even sign my name. And when I've done that you'll fake my death just like you did hers. Except hers was easy – Pamela Johnstone writing her own suicide notes, confirmed as authentic by heartbroken parents and shocked solicitors. Evidence enough to satisfy the police. It was about all they had – apart fom a body so badly charred that the only remains were the rings on its fingers. And after that no one paid any attention when little Miss Ballantyne left to live abroad. Except by then Susan Ballantyne was Pamela Johnstone.'

Albert had been denied long enough. The table went over, crockery crashed onto the floor and he was on me half lifting, half throwing me back against the wall. I managed two punches before collapsing under the fury of his onslaught, the floor spinning up to meet me as I rolled over to avoid his swinging boot. A glimpse of Pamela Johnstone's white face above me, her hands still at her ears; my gaze spinning to take in the kitchen clock. Eight o'clock. I had twenty-six hours left.

CHAPTER THREE

I lost the next two hours, and when Hallsworth came to my room at ten o'clock one look was enough to know he was still angry. He motioned Albert outside and let rip with his own version of the riot act. I got the lot – beginning with the bit about Jean's life hanging on the slender thread of my co-operation and ending with a vivid description of the fun Albert would have unless I stayed in line. It was a performance designed to cow me and it partially suceeded. Whatever happened in the future I would have to watch my step – for Jean's sake if not my own.

Afterwards Albert went to work with a clothes brush, for

once dusting me down instead of knocking me down. Fussy about marks was Albert. Even when he hit me he punched where the bruises wouldn't show.

Hallsworth and I went down to my office. A typewriter tapped in the next room and for a wild moment I imagined Jean at her desk and everthing normal, but seconds later the door opened and Pamela Johnstone came in with a letter for Hallsworth's signature. They worked swiftly, the sureness of their actions testimony to months of preparation, a chilling reminder that more than a year of my life had been used by others to set the scene for a single operation. The Pepalasis project.

Hallsworth unveiled a duplicate set of books, covering every transaction since the company's incorporation. Almost a duplicate set, but not quite. Entries converted his drawings to mine to create the illusion that I'd drawn more than my entitlement, whilst clients' accounts were credited with an additional fifty thousand pounds worth of earnings before the same amount was systematically syphoned off to my personal account at Barclay's Bank. But those were just the opening moves. On Hallsworth's instructions I drew a cheque for the entire amount of the company's cash reserves held at the Midland Bank in Piccadilly. Eighty-two thousand pounds. Payable to me. And then another cheque, drawn to 'cash' on my Barclay's account for a hundred and thirty-two thousand – the value of the reserves plus the fifty thousand transferred by Pepalasis. After which I telephoned Barclay's to tell them I would be sending a messenger to pay in the cheque drawn on the Midland and to collect the one hundred and thirty-two thousand. In cash. Hallsworth had reason enough to smile as he replaced the telephone extension and handed the two cheques to Pamela Johnstone. She and Albert went on their way rejoicing to the Bank while I sat and calculated how much of my freedom had just been sacrificed. It was almost lunchtime when they returned, and the four of us adjourned to the flat for a quick meal.

'When do I speak to Jean?' I demanded.

'Later,' Hallsworth stonewalled. 'At the end of the day.'

In the afternoon Pamela Johnstone went out, leaving Hallsworth and me to finish the job of painting me the biggest bastard the City's ever known. Specifically he worked, I watched. And worried about Jean. When he still refused to let me speak to her I adopted a policy of cautious non co-operation and refused to initial entries in his duplicate Minute Book until I was satisfied about her safety. It irritated him, but he did damn all about it except grumble, and I drew consolation from making small stands where I could.

The afternoon wore on. I answered a couple of calls, neither related to the Pepalasis project. But Hallsworth listened to both of them, grim faced and alert for any sign of foolishness on my part. And Seckleman continued to interrupt every hour on the hour. He had been in and out all day, relaying news of the export order. Pamela Johnstone had even been introduced to him, as a friend helping out while Jean had a couple of days off. And Seckleman's three o'clock appearance brought a real problem. I'd not paid much attension earlier, using his visits as thinking time to search for a way of getting Jean to safety. But the mid-afternoon bout of agitation caught my interest in a big way. And so did Hallsworth's reaction to it. He was worried sick.

'For God's sake!' he exploded. 'All the cargo's containerized. There can't be a delay. Understand? It's quite out of the question.'

Seckleman made a gesture of helplessness and repeated his story. The problem sounded simple enough – at least to my ears. All suppliers were delivering to a bonded warehouse in Liverpool, from which goods would be released when suppliers confirmed receipt of payment – on Thursday morning. The day would then be used for loading and the ship would be put to sea in the early hours of Friday morning. The hitch lay in the docks, and a snap decision by the employed labour to work to rule. Which meant that loading would take seven hours longer.

'There's absolutely nothing I can do about it,' Seckleman said miserably. 'We either load earlier by advancing payment to tomorrow morning, or the ship's master has to apply to the Port Authority for permission to remain in berth for an extra day. And that won't be easy. Not with half the ships hit by the same problem creating a queue of freighters half way to Ireland.'

'But earlier payment is *quite* impossible,' Hallsworth said furiously. 'Absolutely bloody *impossible*.'

Seckleman shrugged helplessly while Hallsworth gave vent to his views on dock labour and then lapsed into a long silence.

'Telex all suppliers,' he said eventually. 'We'll pay by direct bank transfer before closing of banking tomorrow. Get back to the warehouse and ask them to stand by for cargo release tomorrow afternoon. Find out if the extra half day and night gives them enough time.' He scowled angrily, and added, 'We'll undertake to meet any costs as a result of night shift working. Understand?'

Seckleman hesitated, thought better of it, nodded and hurried off to spread the glad tidings about early payment.

Something nagged at the back of my mind, but before it reached the front the telephone rang. It was Bob Harrison. 'Who's Harrison? Hallsworth wanted to know, after telling Muriel to hold the call.

Bob! My mind erupted with memories of Sunday's supper. 'A friend,' I said, trying to make it sound casual. 'Nothing to do with business.' Which was true. But Bob had heard enough on Sunday to put him on guard as far as Hallsworth was concerned. I wondered if I could get a message to him? *About Jean. About what was happening.* 'He's coming over tonight,' I lied quickly. 'I forgot – we're supposed to be having dinner together.'

Hallsworth reached for the extension. 'Put him off. Very carefully.'

Threats were unnecessary. I was convinced already. If the real Sue Ballantyne could be reduced to a cinder, an accident involving Jean would be child's play.

I picked up the phone. 'Bob, I'm awfully sorry but I can't make tonight.' I rushed on, speaking so quickly that he had no chance to answer, 'but we've got a bit of a flap on. My partner and I are sitting here re-arranging appointments like mad. Both of us. Er, together.' I took a deep breath and added quickly: 'By the way, great party Sunday. Say thanks to Barbara for me will you? You're a lucky fellow, having a charmer like that for a wife. And – those friends of yours – fascinating people, and so right about everything they said. Absolutely spot on.' Hallsworth's glare was so furious that I dried up. *Completely*. My mouth opened and closed but not a sound came out.

'Yes,' Bob said slowly. I held my breath and I felt beads of sweat form against the inside of my shirt collar and across my forehead. I *had* to shut him up, had to say something, anything, just a quick word before he gave the game away. My mouth opened but still the sound wouldn't come.

'We enjoyed the party too,' Bob said. 'Must do it again. How's Jean?'

I was so surprised that I almost fluffed it. 'She's fine. Er no, not fine – matter of fact she's a bit off colour. Not in today.'

'Sorry to hear it,' he said slowly, as if taking a long time to think. 'Give her my love won't you. And bad luck about tonight. Make it Friday shall we?'

Hallsworth was shaking his head violently and making urgent gestures for me to hang up.

'No – er, not Friday either, Bob. Sorry. This rush job. Must go now –'

'Just a sec! Amy, er Amy *and* Barbara, asked me to collect those encyclopedias you promised to lend us. You rememeber the ones. For Amy's school project. Okay if I pop in tonight – just to pick them up?'

The palm of my hand was so damp with sweat that I almost dropped the telephone. But I could have cheered. God knows who runs Army Intelligence, but the job rightfully belongs to a man called Bob Harrison.

'Not this evening, Bob,' I said quickly, and Hallsworth relaxed a second too soon to stop me adding, 'but the morning, eh? Early – say nine o'clock?'

'Fine – see you then – okay, Mike?'

But the line went dead as Hallsworth's hand came down sharp on the receiver rest of the extension phone. 'You crazy, bloody fool!' he stormed at me. 'What the hell do you think you're doing?'

'You heard him. About the books. What else could I do?'

He smouldered with suspicion, as agitated as I had ever seen him. 'Yes, I heard him,' he said. He lit a cigarette and puffed it nervously in between quick peeks at me.

Our moods contrasted for the rest of the afternoon – his decidedly nervy and irritable, mine almost cheerful as I blessed the day I had made a friend of Bob Harrison.

Pamela Johnstone returned at half-past six, letting herself in downstairs with a key I didn't even know she had. The office staff had left for the day, Seckleman only minutes earlier, and Hallsworth and I were as good as finished.

'Any problems?' he asked anxiously, as she came through the door.

'No,' she shook her head and walked to the sideboard. 'Everything's fine. Want a drink?'

I watched her carefully. Early this morning, over breakfast, she had been near to cracking apart, but she was a lot calmer now. Coolness itself, as she poured drinks, as if we were old friends preparing a quiet evening together. Thinking about it , I suppose we were. Old friends and new enemies.

'Jean,' I reminded both of them. 'When do I speak to her?'

'Oh, sorry, I forgot,' she reached into her handbag. 'A message for you.'

I wondered what she meant, holding a cassette in her hand, offering it to me. Then I understood and in the same split second remembered the other cassette, the one I had pocketed in Poignton's office. Remembered it and forgot it, as I snatched the one from the outstretched hand, hating the casual way *she* handled it, hating *her* for having anything to do with Jean. A minute later it was in the machine on the desk and the tape was running.

I felt sick. Jean began by reading the headlines from the day's issue of *The Times*. A copy was folded in my out tray and I grabbed it to follow every line as she read. Afterwards, in a halting, frightened voice, barely recognisable as hers, she dictated the briefest message saying she was unharmed and had been promised I was unharmed too. Her voice broke near the end, and the undercurrent of terror came to the surface in a series of gulps as she fought against the tears.

The recording lasted for less than two minutes and I rewound the tape and played it through a second time. My hand shook as I operated the machine, my guts turned to water at the fear in her voice. Then the black hate took over again. They must have expected trouble because when I looked up Albert had been summoned from upstairs and he was the first one I saw, standing in the open doorway like a jailer waiting to return me to my cell.

'It's not enough,' I said in a voice distorted with emotion that I didn't recognize as mine. 'It's not enough. I'm not signing anything. Not a *bloody thing*. Understand? Not a *damned thing*. Until she's freed.'

But I went upstairs without protesting. I was still shaking I think. I took a bottle of scotch and some fruit with me and allowed them to lock me in. It was seven o'clock. I stretched out on the bed to think, knowing that I had only sixteen hours left. Sixteen hours left to save Jean's life.

CHAPTER FOUR

I was a third of the way down the bottle of whisky when the answer came. No wonder Hallsworth had been so shaken by the hitch at the docks. The crisp new thought had me trembling with excitement. And it blew enough holes in Poignton's argument to make me wonder again just how much he knew? Of course he was right. All that stuff about Bank of England consent to transfer thirty million outside the U.K. It *could* mean delay. Weeks certainly, months possibly. *In extremis*, even outright refusal.

But exporting thirty million pounds worth of goods was a very different matter. No government interference. In fact the very opposite. It was the Frascari con all over again! Or at least a variation on the theme. Collect thirty million from the consortium, push it straight into the export company via the London-based company set up by Pepalasis, pay the suppliers and end up with goods *worth* thirty million on the high seas. The cash would never leave the U.K. *Not as cash*. But its value would have been moved out of the country as effectively as shipping gold bullion – while everyone believed that the Greek still held it in London.

Discovering *how* was one thing. Stopping it, another. And the nine o'clock chimes from St Mary's in Mount Street raised desperation to the level of panic. My brain hunted for something positive to cling to – and found Bob Harrison. Bob. Calling in twelve hours time and knowing damn well that something was wrong. All that gibberish on the telephone.

Christ, he'd played his end well. Maybe he was already working on something? Jean's name was in the phone book, perhaps he had gone to Fulham in search of her? And not

236

finding her was putting two and two together.

I left the whisky alone and fifteen minutes later had the idea about the cassette and hammered on the door to be let out. 'Hallsworth,' I said when Albert answered, pushing past him into the corridor. It was a mistake. For a big man he moved fast. A foot stuck between mine to upset my balance and two blows to the ribs fell like power hammers.

'Now what?' Hallsworth stood in the open doorway to the sitting room.

'Get this animal off for a start.' I struggled upright and felt my ribs cautiously.

Hallsworth nodded and Albert eased back enough for me to pass into the sitting room. Pamela Johnstone was there, an outdoor coat draped around her shoulders, as if she was coming or going.

'I've thought it over,' I said firmly. 'And it's not on. I'm not signing unless Jean's released first.'

'Out of the question.' Hallsworth's answer was equally positive.

'Then it's no deal.' I put everything I had into sounding confident, like a salesman of second-hand cars, pretending it was his loss if he didn't take me up on my offer.

'Co-operate and she's safe,' he said. 'If not?' he shrugged. 'I warned you what might happen.'

I wasted the next few minutes telling them both what I thought of them before finally asking: 'When does she go free then? If I sign.'

He hesitated. 'A week's time. Next Tuesday. After a sea voyage.'

'And me?'

'At the same time and place. You'll both be put on to a direct flight to Buenos Aires from an overseas airpoint. After that it's up to you.' He laughed humourlessly. 'But I wouldn't hurry back to London if I were you.'

I supposed it was a hint that news of my frauds would be leaked in a short time. That I believed. But not the bit about

237

being set free. If anything had sealed my fate, my outburst about the real Sue Ballantyne had. And if they killed me they wouldn't risk Jean's silence for long afterwards.

'Not good enough,' I shook my head, paused a moment and then began to pave the way for the idea I'd had earlier. 'But I'll give you a deal if you want one. Something guaranteed to make me sign in the morning.'

He was tempted and it showed. Pamela Johnstone watched us, not saying a word, her white face empty of expression as her teeth nibbled at her lower lip and the strain took its toll.

'I want proof that Jean is unharmed,' I said slowly. '*When* I sign. I want actually to *see* her.'

His lips tightened and he was shaking his head as I continued. 'The A.W.F. Boardroom overlooks Holborn. You can see as far as the junction with Gray's Inn Road from the window. About a hundred yards. There's a newspaper stand on the corner. And the entrance to the tube is opposite the A.W.F. office. Ten minutes before the meeting starts I want to be able to see Jean from that window. I want to see her walk down the street, buy a paper and then come back again. As simple as that. If she's there I'll sign. If not, you haven't got a prayer.'

I tried to say the whole thing in a take it or leave it fashion. As if their decision was of no consequence. And in a way that's how I felt. I don't profess to be a brave man but if violent death is inevitable twenty-four hours or so would make damn all difference. Especially if it gave Jean a chance to get free.

'I warned you that we'd made contingency plans,' Hallsworth threatened. 'Your participation tomorrow isn't absolutely vital.' He shrugged and then speculated on an alternative. 'A sudden illness in the night, preventing your attendance. Me arriving, with your signed power of attorney—'

'And risk postponement?' I countered quickly. 'You

238

wouldn't dare. A week ago, maybe. You could have prepared the ground, made it convincing. But to arrive at the actual completion meeting without me?' I left the question hanging in mid-air for him to think about, and then got the shock of my life as Pamela Johnstone tipped their hand.

'And if we agree?' she asked anxiously. 'You'll attend the meeting? Sign everything? Behave normally?'

'Subject to one other condition.'

That was too much for Hallsworth. 'You're making a lot of demands,' he sneered angrily. 'I warn you. Overplay your hand and . . .'

I ignored him and spoke to the girl. 'Are you leaving for Winchester?'

She glanced quickly at Hallsworth, as if frightened to answer. Neither spoke, so I sighed heavily and explained. 'You've taken Jean somewhere. And Albert the Terrible was gone long enough last night to have made Winchester and back.' I looked at the girl. 'So I presume you *have* got a cottage or something down there?'

Hallsworth answered with a question. 'Why do you want to know?'

'I want a message taken to Jean. In your interests as well as mine. She'll be more prepared to co-operate if she knows that tomorrow is my idea.'

They thought about that for a few seconds before the girl said with unexpected decisiveness, 'Very well. What do I tell her?'

'I'll record the message. It's better don't you think?' I held my breath. It the crucial that they agreed. The whole plan depended on it. They pondered and I've seen happier people, but in the end the offer of my co-operation was too tempting and they agreed. 'But just remember,' Hallsworth warned as Albert led me from the room, 'Pamela will be there when the tape is played.'

We went downstairs, propped together like amiable drunks. It took me no time to dictate what I wanted onto the

239

cassette on which Jean had recorded her message to me. Albert must have thought me a very cold fish. No pleasantries, just a recital of what was to take place in the morning, ending, 'Hallsworth promises that we'll be set free on Tuesday next at an undisclosed overseas airport.'

Then I switched off, rewound the tape, slipped the cassette into my pocket, and allowed Albert to hug me all the way back upstairs, but not before I had deftly palmed an extra, blank cassette without Albert noticing.

'There you are,' I handed a cassette to Pamela Johnstone. 'And thanks.' I went to the bookshelves.

'Now what?' Hallsworth eyed me suspiciously.

'Bedtime reading,' I grinned, clutching the two encyclopedias. 'Come on Albert, time to tuck me in.'

CHAPTER FIVE

Albert turned the key in the lock and from the inside I blessed the old mortice for creaking enough to warn me of anyone returning in a hurry. It would give me time. Time to get from anywhere in the room to the bed. Into bed. To where they would expect to find me. I waited impatiently, listening to his shuffling withdrawal down the corridor. Then I changed into pyjamas, expecting a routine inspection later and knowing suspicions would be roused if I was found to be still fully dressed. Hurriedly I set to work. There was so much to do in such little time.

From my jacket I retrieved the two separate cassettes from the two separate pockets, staring hard at the one taken from Poignton's office as I tried to remember how much blank tape had been left on the reel at the end of the meeting. I guessed ten minutes, which meant the last third of the tape. The other cassette was easier. Jean's message had taken less than two minutes and mine to her, dictated on to the same tape and immediately after hers, had taken even less. So the first third of the tape carried both recordings. I marked the cassettes to tell them apart and hunted for a razor blade and sticky tape. And a cylinder of lighter fuel to use as a pick-up spool. Quickly I stuck the leading inch of Poignton's tape to the cylinder and started winding, careful not to twist the tape in the process. Guessing where the recording ended was a hit and miss, but I banked on the hope that anyone hearing it would establish the point of the conversation, even without the last few words. So with two thirds on the cylinder I cut the tape and yanked most of the remaining footage from the cassette before cutting again, leaving just enough to receive tape spliced from the other cassette. That done I reeled the first third of the second cassette on to the cylinder, cut and spliced it with sticky tape to the tiny piece protruding from the mouth of Poignton's cassette. Rewinding was more difficult. The tape twisted as it approached the mouth of the cassette and the task put a strain on my trembling fingers. But ten minutes' careful work saw the job completed, and another twenty had the Poignton recording safety spliced and reeled in after it.

The whole story was on that tape. My accusations to Poignton in his office, his denials, Jean's frightened message. And a carefully precise description of the events planned for the next day. All I had to do now was to get the cassette to Bob in the morning. That was *all*.

I hid the mess of loose tape under the wardrobe, lit a cigarette and tried to think of a way of slipping the cassette to Bob when he called. Getting Jean into the open had been more than I dared hope for. There was a chance, if Bob listened to the recording soon after he left the office in the morning, that he could get her as she walked down Holborn. Maybe not much of a chance. But I wasn't exactly loaded down with alternatives.

I practised for half an hour. Trousers slipped over pyjamas and standing sideways on to the wardrobe mirror. The trick was to palm the cassette from my trouser pocket and extend my hand for a hand-shake. Without the cassette being seen. Bringing it out of the pocket was the easy part. The problem was as my hand opened and straightened, the cassette was a fraction too large for the curvature of my palm. And in twelve attempts I saw the cassette five times and *dropped* it twice! Experiment taught me to keep the thumb and index finger close together, and splay the other fingers like a claw. The hand looked unnatural but in the next dozen attempts I only dropped the cassette once, and barely glimpsed it at all. So by the time I had finished I was near perfect. Satisfied, I returned the cassette to the pocket of my suit jacket and turned my attention to the encyclopedias. Hallsworth was bound to inspect them. He had watched me take them into the bedroom and would never stand by in the morning while I handed them over to Bob. Not without inspecting them first. The question was, how thoroughly would he look at them?

I almost decided not to do anything with the books. But fear that I might bungle the sleight of hand with the cassette made me desperate for a second line of communication. So I worked until two o'clock. A code would be too flattering a description, but at least the message escaped superficial inspection. No page was obviously marked. No passage of print was underlined. Nothing was written in a margin, or in a flyleaf. But it was all there. A full account. More obvious to a blind man than a sighted one. A puncture made with a pin under the second letter of a word in every sentence for more than three hundred pages. Good enough, I hoped, to escape Hallsworth's scrutiny. Not good enough, I prayed, to elude Bob if I gave him some kind of clue.

I switched the light out and lay staring into darkness, thinking about the A.W.F. building. It stood cheek by jowl with others, one grand entrance on to Holborn, with no other door visible. But there would be a rear entrance or a side door somewhere. There had to be. I imagined arriving in the morning. By then Jean would be near by, no doubt guarded by one or other of them. It wouldn't be Pepalasis. He would be with me, going to the meeting. I pictured us passing through the doors, side by side, perhaps McNeil greeting us in the lobby. All three of us turning and moving towards the elevators. That's when I'd make my move. It had to be then. Wait for the elevator doors to open, turn quickly and race down the corridor, find another way out at the back somewhere. Hit the street with them yards behind me. Double back to Holborn. I'd be running up from the corner as Jean walked down from the tube station. Albert probably a pace behind her. Maybe Bob would make an appearance at the same time. A minute! That's all we'd need. A minute – to bundle Jean to safety somewhere. A minute – to break their hold on me.

I was desperately tired and longed for sleep. What plans I had were made, and I felt relieved to have made them. So I was almost lightheaded with fatigue as I drifted off, amused by my last conscious thought. Of Pamela Johnstone listening to the blank tape she had taken to Jean.

CHAPTER SIX

They came for me at four in the morning. Hallsworth and the Greek. And Albert. I opened my eyes and they were grouped round the bed, like pall bearers at a coffin.

'Get up,' Pepalasis ordered abruptly, before turning from the bed and moving across to the wardrobe. 'Which suit are you wearing today?'

'Today?' I blinked, barely focusing. 'What's this? Dress rehearsal?'

'Which suit?' he repeated.

Scrambling from the bed I pointed at the grey herringbone

and reached it before he did in case he searched it.

'Get washed and dressed.' Pepalasis was certainly giving the orders. He jerked his head at Albert who jerked his towards the bathroom. I followed him from the room, thinking there was nothing for it but to do as they said, and get back to the bedroom as quickly as possible. When I returned the suit appeared to be undisturbed where I had left it.

'I've had your new demands explained to me,' Pepalasis said briskly. 'And we'll agree to them.'

'You woke me to tell me that?'

'Subject to certain conditions,' he finished.

I told him where to put his conditions but he wasn't listening. 'You're going to have an accident,' he said with a glimmer of a smile. 'How painful it will be is up to you.' He turned to Albert. 'I'll need a bowl of cold water. Try the kitchen.'

I struggled into my clothes as Albert left, and Pepalasis opened a briefcase to produce a roll of bandages and cotton wool. And a paper bag which looked as if it contained flour.

'The story is that you fell downstairs,' Pepalasis said simply. 'Here at Hill Street. Last night. Fracturing your left wrist and right ankle. You were taken to St George's Hospital where the appropriate limbs were encased in plaster.' He shrugged. 'You'll be mildly uncomfortable, that's all.'

'That might be your story,' I said. 'But it's not mine.'

'It had better be. Because if it isn't, Albert will inflict enough damage to your wrist and ankle to make a visit to the hospital highly desirable.'

He was deadly serious. So was Hallsworth, standing next to him. Albert returned with a bowl of water and the three of them stood watching me make up my mind. Minutes later Pepalasis was bandaging my right ankle with cotton wool padding to provide a suitably swollen appearance. 'This stuff takes about two hours to set,' he said, turning the contents of the paper bag into plaster of Paris with a magician's flourish. 'So stay on the bed and think pure thoughts, eh?'

I voiced a dozen which were anything but, without even denting his smile.

'Why so bitter?' he asked. 'We're complying with your requests. Just taking a few precautions, that's all.'

'Who's Frascari?' I asked quietly, hoping to catch him off guard.

He straightened up at the end of the bed, and brushed the iron grey hair from his eyes. 'So? Questions now.' He sneered, while accepting from Hallsworth a clean towel to dry his hands. 'From the man who knows everything.'

I said, 'It's McNeil isn't it?' and tried to intercept the quick look of surprise which flashed between them. But they recovered fast, Hallsworth turning away to murmur something to Albert while Pepalasis hooded his eyes as he spoke to me. 'Miss Wilmslow,' he said slowly, and I jumped at the sound of Jean's name, 'Will keep the appointment you've arranged for her. But don't be alarmed when you see her.'

'What's that supposed to mean? By Christ, if you've . . .'

'We've done nothing,' he snapped. 'Yet. But when you see her she'll be in a wheelchair.'

I was speechless with horror that something had happened to Jean.

'There's nothing at all wrong with her.' He gloated at the fear in my eyes. 'The rug across her knees will be pure camouflage. To conceal the straps holding her legs to the chair.' He paused and let that sink in, then added, 'Just in case she's tempted to do anything foolish. And in case you are – remember – at the first sign of trouble Albert will shove that chair right off the pavement and into the road. Straight under the nearest bus.'

My voice came back then, and with it every swear word and bit of foul language I'd heard in my life. Not that they stayed to listen. Pepalasis had finished playing doctor for the day and he and Hallsworth retreated to the sitting room

– leaving Albert on guard in case I was tempted to interfere with their handiwork.

I just about hit rock bottom during the next couple of hours, engulfed in a suffocating depression. I was sick with worry about Jean. And bitterly disappointed that my carefully constructed plan had been so totally wrecked. Now *everything* depended on Bob Harrison. And I was in a cold sweat of anticipation about his call at nine o'clock. But the 'medics' returned before that. By seven-thirty the plaster casts on my wrist and ankle had set and Pepalasis and Hallsworth trooped back in to supervise the finishing touches to their window dressing. I complied meekly enough, my main concern that they didn't discover the precious cassette. They didn't, but Pepalasis came damn near to finding it when he was working on the sling for my left arm. When he finished we all adjourned to the kitchen for breakfast. And the phone call came about an hour later, when I was on my second cup of tea and sixth cigarette of the morning.

'That was Pamela,' Hallsworth announced when he returned to the kitchen. 'The tape you sent down last night. It was blank.'

I was astonished. First I called Albert as a witness to the message I had dictated, and then I claimed Pamela Johnstone must be misoperating the machine at her end. Altogether not a bad performance. Good enough to convince Hallsworth anyway. But the Greek watched slit-eyed with suspicion, not saying a word, and listening with every pore in his skin. When I finished he rose from the table and went to the bedroom, returning a minute later with the encyclopedias.

No respecter of scholarship was Pepalasis. The opening move was predictable enough. Holding each volume by its spine, he shook the pages open for any loose papers. But when he began searching the gaps between spines and covers, and progressed to slitting the leather bindings with a razor blade my stomach turned over. I knew it was only a

246

matter of time. I hobbled across to the sink to refill the kettle, complaining bitterly that they were deliberately withholding my message to Jean. Saying anything and everything to divert attention from the books on the table. But the Greek was oblivious to my ramblings. He began a page by page examination of each volume and twenty minutes later he found it. 'What's this?' he poked a stubby finger at the page in front of him.

'What's what?' I leant across the table, seeing the type on the page and pretending blindness to the rash of spots between the lines.

'*BASTARD!*' He caught me across the face with his open hand, knocking me sideways and scattering crockery everywhere. 'You *had* to try didn't you?' He turned to Albert. 'Search him,' he said, and the giant reached me before I was even out of the chair.

Maybe if I'd been twenty-eight and not thirty-eight, had stayed clear of booze and cigarettes and had taken an advanced course in karate, I might have been a match for Albert. And maybe the excess luggage on the end of an arm and a leg didn't help. But as things stood it was no contest. He threatened to break my neck from behind with one hand while his other ransacked my jacket pocket. The cassette was the very first thing he seized upon. Hallsworth went to get a dictating machine from the office while I glumly watched my possessions heaped on to the table in front of me.

They listened to the recording in silence. Apart from the clicking of the kombolois. And Hallsworth drumming his fingers on the table top. It wasn't a bad tape really. Oh, it wouldn't have won first prize in a sound studio or anything like that. But it was every bit as comprehensive as I'd hoped it would be.

'So now Poignton knows!' Pepalasis was badly shaken. It showed in his face and echoed in his voice. 'Who else for God's sake? I don't like it. The risk is now . . .'

'The same as it's always been,' Hallsworth cut in.

'Poignton knows nothing. You heard his reaction. A lot of vague theories. Christ, he discounted the whole –'

'He did *then*!' Pepalasis scowled. 'What if he's had second thoughts? He'll be at the meeting today. Another clue and –'

'Jean Wilmslow gets pushed under a bus,' Hallsworth rapped back. 'I'll see to that.'

I exploded. 'And get yourself caught at the same time?'

'In a street accident?' he raised an eyebrow. 'I don't think so somehow.'

I remembered the sick, helpless horror of my sister being knocked down by a corporation bus in Darlington. No one quite knowing what to do. People rushing in all directions. For a doctor, for an ambulance. For anyone who could help. And I knew Hallsworth was right.

'You'll have to see this man Harrison,' Pepalasis was saying to Hallsworth. 'And for God's sake get rid of him without any fuss.'

Minutes later I was back in the bedroom. I glimpsed my reflection in the mirror. Standing all lopsided, sock-covered toes protruding from a plaster cast, arm in a sling, and face as white as my bandages.

Pepalasis stood in the doorway. 'Here, you had better practise.' He handed me an aluminimum crutch. 'Otherwise you might fall and hurt yourself.'

The door closed and the lock turned. And I had less than three hours left.

CHAPTER SEVEN

Bob arrived promptly at nine. I watched as he moved with his soldier's stride up Chesterfield Hill from the direction of Piccadilly. It was odd seeing him like that. Knowing that he was coming to see me and yet wouldn't. As he crossed Hill Street his eyes lifted almost to the level of the fourth floor window. I moved backwards into the room, changed my mind and then almost pressed my face through the pane of glass. But it was too late. He had crossed and was directly below me, trotting up the steps and into the building.

I smoked another cigarette and thought about the meeting downstairs. It wouldn't be easy. Bob was already suspicious. Sunday's supper and our nonsensical telephone conversation had seen to that. And me being absent would take some explaining. Especially with Jean away sick as well. So I discounted Hallsworth's ability to talk the birds from the trees and allowed myself to hope, while Albert glared balefully at me from across the room.

But Bob left after half an hour, clutching a brown paper parcel under one arm, the size of a couple of books wrapped together. I couldn't see his face as he marched back down Chesterfield Hill, so I've no idea of its expression. But my hopes faded and died with every step he took. And when he turned the corner at the bottom of the hill the feeling of total despair which flooded through me was so painful that I groaned aloud.

Hallsworth unlocked the door a minute later. 'Charming man,' he purred, well pleased with himself. 'Gone away quite happily.'

I would have asked what happened but never got the chance. 'We're all going downstairs now, Mike,' he said pleasantly. 'There's the staff to see and your solicitor is arriving at ten. And we'll be leaving for Holborn at a quarter past.' He paused and fixed me with a conspiratorial look. 'It's all going to work, Mike. No doubt of it. And Jean and you will come through it. Alive and well. Play your part and no one gets hurt. That's all you've got to remember. And afterwards you'll have a new life ahead of you. Oh, not the City and what you're used to, I know. But imagine making a fresh start in South America? You and Jean. Plenty of scope there I'd say.' He took my elbow as if to help me across the room. 'And don't worry about money. We'll make sure that you get some kind of cut.' He grinned happily and I could feel his excitement. It almost tingled out of his fingers and into my arm. 'So everything's under control. It's going to be a breeze. A big day. So why not enjoy it?'

I was too astonished to reply at first. But at the door I stammered, 'It's a bit late isn't it? This sudden concern –'

'Believe me, I'm sorry. Sorry about some of the things that happened. But that's all over now. Everything's going to be fine. Believe me.'

Believe him was the last thing I did. But it was a good try. Good tactics. Get me to relax. Pretend we were all in it together. That Jean had never been humiliated. Never been kidnapped. Wasn't in danger – even now.

I said nothing, and he helped me down to my office like a boy scout with a little old lady. Pepalasis was on the chesterfield. Drinking brandy. 'Just one,' he said guiltily in answer to Hallsworth's warning look. He raised the glass in toast. 'To a successful day.'

Even through my own mood of despair I sensed his nervousness, keying himself up for the strain of the meeting ahead of him. Hallsworth sat me behind my desk and handed me the fake minute book. 'The entries which need your signature.' He smiled his old friend's smile. The intercommunicating door opened and Pamela Johnstone came in. She dropped a letter file into my tray and Hallsworth said: 'And some letters for you to sign.' He glanced at his watch. 'You've time now. If you hurry.'

I signed. The minute book and then the letters. Seventy-two letters, one to each of our clients. Due to the expansion of our business, I read, Townsend and Partner were moving to larger premises. Hill Street was to be closed down. The company was to re-open for business in two weeks' time at a new address, given as P.O. Box 2000, Croydon, and accompanied by an out-of-town telephone number.

'Good-bye Hill Street,' I said, as much to myself as to anyone.

'It served its purpose,' Hallsworth murmured, watching me sign my way through the pile of mail, while Pamela Johnstone went off in search of Seckleman.

I finished the last letter as Hallsworth gave Seckleman the news about his job. The export side was being closed down after this one shipment. 'But I want to stay in touch,' Hallsworth assured him. 'We'll have another big job next year and I'd like you running the team again. So meanwhile we're paying a year's salary as a sort of retainer. Of course, you're free to accept employment elsewhere, but I hope that . . .'

I stopped listening, vaguely aware of talk about six months' pay for the clerks and three months for the typists. Hill Street was being closed down! Quickly and quietly. All the loose ends were being tidied up. The bank account had been cleared already – thanks to me. And the magic million, Hallsworth's original stake money which had tempted me more than a year ago, had already been transferred to Poignton's client account as part of the purchase money to be paid to Pepalasis. I smiled grimly as I remembered how strongly I had argued that he should invest it all. How they must have laughed about that.

Seckleman was leaving. He came across to the desk to shake my hand, frowning at the sling and the plaster on my left wrist.

'Cut myself shaving.' I grinned at him. 'Nice knowing you – hope to work with you again one day, eh?' I doubted it, but he seemed pleased at the prospect. He shook my hand, said goodbye, and was ushered out by Hallsworth.

Pamela Johnstone returned to scoop up the pile of signed letters. Pepalasis asked for the sixth time, 'What time's this lawyer arriving?'

'Arranson? He'll be here at ten.' Hallsworth put the minute book in the cabinet along with the other financial records. His financial records. 'Relax. We're on schedule. It's going to be a breeze.'

I wondered if Drachman would show. After all, Arranson was his lawyer and attending on behalf of the three of us – Drachman, Emanuel and me. And bringing a banker's draft for four million pounds with him.

But Arranson arrived alone. He was an unprepossessing little man of about fifty wearing a perpetually nervous expression. As if everything he saw of life frightened him half to death. It probably did – with Drachman for a client.

I introduced everyone and Pepalasis suggested a drink while we waited for the cab to arrive. Arranson refused. So would I if my day hadn't started at four in the morning. So I had a brandy along with Pepalasis while Hallsworth muttered something about another appointment and left. And at ten fifteen we went too. The cab, ticking like a time bomb, at the front door. Pepalasis and Arranson on either side of me, crossing the lobby like a funeral procession. Me arranging stiff limbs and the lightweight crutch into some sort of sequence as I negotiated the steps to the pavement. Time had run out. We were on our way. To the biggest fraud ever committed in the City of London.

CHAPTER EIGHT

For reasons best known to himself the cab driver took us to Holborn via Green Park, a less direct route than Berkeley Square and Piccadilly which is the way I would have gone. Perhaps he had just come from there and the traffic was bad, who knows? And it hardly mattered. There was no hurry and for those who enjoyed it, the morning sunshine was delightful. Not that we gave a damn for the weather. We rode in silence, avoiding each other's eyes and nursing private houghts. I gazed grimly through the half opened window at he outside world and resented it. People laughing and joking s they enjoyed small everyday things, like not having to vorry about the person you love being mutilated and killed •y an animal like Albert.

Half way down the Mall a girl crossed the road fifty yards head, her legs brown under a white summer dress. Long, raceful legs. Like Jean's. And the same colour of hair. She •aused on a traffic island, her back to me as she watched the •ncoming traffic. Something in the way she stood seemed amiliar, one leg bent slightly, her right arm loose at her side, •er left clasping a bag to her waist. Suddenly, absurdly, it eemed she had to be Jean! I came alive, my head turning as ve approached, my right arm already rising to rap the •artition for the driver to stop. Pulling alongside. Almost here. Her head turning as if drawn by a compulsion to look ny way and into the cab. She did, and our eyes met across . gap a yard wide as I stared into the face of a total stranger, omeone I had never seen in my life before. Shock waves of lisappointment knocked me back in the seat. I felt sick with lisappointment. Physically sick. And cheated by another ruel joke, a torturer's trick to wring the last ounce of misery rom my despair.

I still ached with bitterness ten minutes later when 'epalasis led me across the pavement, and Arranson and the ommissionaire arranged themselves like sentries on either ide of the plate glass doors at A.W.F. Sunlight glittered •n the glass, the doors swung open, and I hobbled hrough.

Harry Smithers greeted me with a mixture of concern and ımusement, finding vague comedy in the thought of me alling head over heels down the stairs at Hill Street. And VcNeil was already there when we arrived. I gave him a nurderous look and made a point of avoiding his proffered tand, at which he looked shocked and offended, and more han a shade puzzled. So for that hundredth time I found

253

myself wondering whether I was right or wrong about his being Frascari?

A man called Henry Simpson arrived, the tame lawyer hired by Pepalasis to form the British-based company, and to comply with the niceties of the Companies Acts.

The room began to fill. Peter Emanuel hurried through the formalities of greeting others until he reached Arranson.

'Any problems?' he asked. Arranson flinched at the prospect of involving his client in even a minor difficulty, while I shuddered at the thought of Drachman's reaction to what would happen in this room within the hour.

'You're all right, aren't you?' Emanuel had seen my shudder.

'Shock, that's all.'

He nodded sympathetically at the plaster casts. 'Delayed.'

'Anticipated,' I corrected, and shut up as Pepalasis took the seat next to me.

Poignton made his entrance, greeting the other solicitors with the disdainful look he practised on his articled clerks. He was far and away the most senior lawyer present and undoubtedly the most capable, and his attitude served notice that if the others wanted a demonstration of his competence he would be happy to oblige.

'Changed your mind?' he murmured as we shook hands. 'Too much at stake?'

'That's an understatement. Even for you.'

Faded eyes crinkled knowingly and he turned away to greet someone else while I watched and wondered. Wondered just how much he did know? At times, I had been as good as convinced that he was in league with them however improbable it had seemed. But Pepalasis had finally convinced me otherwise. He was afraid of Poignton. His fear had been obvious when he listened to the tape. And it was evident again now. And for Poignton to involve himself had never made real sense in my mind. After all he had money enough for his comforts and he already had what he craved.

most from life – an untarnished reputation and universal approbation. I watched him move away, my head shaking slightly, thinking that the poor sod had been used and knowing the feeling.

Tommy Richardson waved from the other side of the room, his big farmer's face grimacing at my bandages. He was about to make his way over when someone caught his elbow and trapped him in conversation. I felt relieved. I was too wound up with worry about Jean to share in the general mood of celebration. And even now, torn with a terrible indecision about signing when it actually came to it.

About thirty people milled round the table, chattering like women at a church bazaar, sipping sherry served by frock-coated stewards while waiting for Harry to get the meeting under way. Their attendance was totally unnecessary. Harry and I would sign for the consortium and Pepalasis would sign for himself. But Harry wanted to make an occasion of it.

Pepalasis touched my elbow, and nodded towards the windows. Time already? My stomach turned over and I pushed him away angrily as he offered to help me from the chair, remembering only his striking Jean, and the look on his face as he had gloated at her nakedness.

I hunted the pavements opposite, my gaze sweeping past shop fronts to the station entrance. Seeing everything and nothing. Pedestrians, shoppers, office workers, tourists. But no sign of Jean. I turned to Pepalasis, dimly aware as I did so of someone in the background tapping the table to bring the meeting to order.

'You bastard!' I hissed. 'You promised. If anything's happened . . .'

'Look,' he said urgently. 'Down there.'

I looked, and not seeing what I expected, almost missed it. An ambulance parked, ten yards from the tube entrance. The driver was already at the back of the vehicle, opening the doors and lowering a ramp to the ground. Then I saw her. Jean in an invalid chair, a rug across her knees, being pushed

255

from the door of a shop, a woman holding the door open to make manoeuvring the chair easier. They progressed to the ambulance, the woman who had helped, Jean in the chair, and then the man pushing. The driver went forward to meet them. He stopped, gripped the underside of the chair and helped lift it into the road. Then he straightened and turned, facing across the road, looking up to the windows. It was Hallsworth. A bus passed between us, obscuring my view. Then it was gone and they were still there. Faces turned upwards. As motionless as a tableau. Jean's frightened expression contrasting with Pamela Johnstone's drawn defiance. And the glowering stupidity of Albert behind. Another bus passed and I remembered the threat, and imagined muscled arms tensing before sending the chair forward under the crushing weight of those wheels. It would be so easy. Then, as I watched, Hallsworth lifted his hand, very slowly, to the peak of his cap in a mock salute, holding the gesture for perhaps half a minute before returning his hand to his side. From the corner of my eye I saw a policeman approach, his hands clasped behind him while his eyes looked up towards the windows, as if he had been watching the whole performance at the kerbside. For a second I grabbed at the hope that he would intervene, stop them, delay them, until I could reach the street and explain what was happening. But when I looked back Albert and Pamela Johnstone were already in the back of the ambulance with Jean. And Hallsworth was hurrying round to the driver's door.

'Hallo?' Peter Emanuel stood at my shoulder. 'Some sort of accident?'

'Not yet,' I scowled at Pepalasis. 'And there'd better not be one.'

The official meeting only lasted fifteen minutes. I don't know whether Harry Smithers disliked Pepalasis instinctively, or whether it was a result of bits and pieces fed to him by McNeil, but dislike him he did. It was obvious from the way he ran the meeting. He saw it all as an elaborate joke, with everyone present knowing about the provisional contract with U.S. Steel except Pepalasis and his lawyer. It was spitefully meant and Harry must still be regretting it. But the actual business went smoothly enough, Poignton had seen to that. The members of the consortium presented bankers' drafts which were verified and accepted by Simpson. Then the contracts were produced, heavily bound documents already agreed between the lawyers in private session. And then came the moment of signing. Harry penned his signature with a flourish while I watched the smallest bead of sweat form on Pepalasis's forehead. I hesitated and looked at the men round the table. None of them would ever trust me again. They would swear and spit on my name after today. I would be finished in the City. And if Drachman had my balls on the end of a garlic knife they would laugh and say it was what I deserved. I felt sick. And tired. And very frightened. But the thought of Jean in the back of that ambulance with Albert made me tremble most of all. I reached for my pen, took a deep breath, and signed. There was applause and flashbulbs – and then champagne.

I got quite drunk. Not drunk enough, but certainly lightheaded. Lots of grinning faces, loud masculine laughter, plenty of people slapping my back. After half an hour of it, Pepalasis was making apologies about leaving and having to take me with him. Cheerful goodbyes all round. Beefy handshakes. Out to the lobby, with a few of the others who were also going. I got into the lift, slowly and clumsily, expecting Pepalasis to follow, but someone delayed him and he turned too late to catch the doors.

Peter Emanuel was in the lift with me. And Arranson.

'Very satisfactory,' Arranson was nodding. 'Very satisfactory indeed.'

'Your boss won't think so,' I said quickly. 'Not in a few days' time.'

His eyes widened in shocked surprise but before he could say anything I added: 'It's a con. Everyone loses their money.'

257

He dropped his jaw and his briefcase at the same time and floodgates opened to let fear into his eyes. Emanuel, next to him, might have been pole-axed.

'Not that I'm worried,' I said airily. 'I'm off on a long sea voyage. But perhaps you'll deliver a message to your client for me?'

Arranson's expression beseeched me to make it a good one, so I remembered the meeting at Paddington and said: 'Why don't you tell him to go fuck himself?'

Before either of them could answer, the doors slid back to reveal the ground floor entrance hall. I heard the clatter of footsteps from the stairs and a second later Pepalasis came into sight, struggling to retain his balance on the polished marble.

'Good exercise,' I nodded at him approvingly. 'Wish I could do it.'

He got his face into some kind of muddle, scowling at me and smiling at the others simultaneously. It's no easy trick, and he had difficulty with it. But his legs worked well enough to get both of us out into the street a minute later. The commissionaire already had a cab waiting and we were away, Arranson and Emanuel looking after us like whipped dogs.

'So, we sold your island for you.' I slurred the words slightly, pretending to be more under the influence of the champagne than I was. 'Tell me, now it's all over, just how much nickel is there in that place?'

His roar of laughter had the cabbie turning and wanting to join in, until sight of my sour expression turned him back to his steering wheel.

'Well?' I prompted, watching him closely, thinking that the exaggerated laughter was an expression of his relief at getting the meeting over with.

'There's some,' he smiled craftily. 'But most of what's there we put there.'

'You *put* there?'

He grinned hugely, while I wondered why they had bothered. After all McNeil could have reported finding

258

almost anything without fear of contradiction from me. And then another struck me, 'You got rocks onto that island? Through the barrier reef?'

'There's another way,' he confided artfully. 'From the other side. It's very much easier.'

'I get it. You took me the scenic route.'

He had another good laugh at that and let his nerves out another notch. When he had finished chuckling he said, 'We lived in that Godforsaken hole for six months.' His smile faded at the memory. 'And worked like slaves to salt that mine. Almost every passage in the place is lined with nickel deposits.'

I tried to take it all in. 'Why nickel? I mean, why start with diamonds and end with nickel?'

He seemed surprised. 'You really don't understand, do you? Even now. You're a fool, Townsend. A fool disguised as a clever man.'

That about summed up what I thought anyway, so I gave him no answer and a moment or two later he added, 'You had to discover something. Don't you understand? Something I didn't know about. That way you were the art collector getting a Rembrandt for the price of a cheap etching.' His smile overflowed with self-satisfaction, 'That way you and your clever friends back there could all have a good laugh at my expense.'

'Some joke,' I murmured, and was about to ask something else when he leant forward and told the driver to stop. Through the window I saw Hallsworth standing at the top of the steps to his club. His eyes sought us out as we drew alongside and a grin lit his face as Pepalasis raised the briefcase to the level of the window. 'Okay?' he asked as he climbed in.

'It was a breeze,' I said. 'Where's Jean?'

'In a safe place,' he answered, dismissing me as a parent would a child, his eyes flicking a glance of enquiry to Pepalasis who nodded.

The cab took us to Hallsworth's bank where I joined

them in the manager's office. I doubt that they wanted me there, but they could hardly ask me to cruise round the West End until they had finished. And maybe they weren't that bothered – after all there seemed to be damn all that I could do about anything.

The manager showed the kind of deference bankers the world over reserve for very large sums of money. Even at the Bank of England, thirty million would warrant an extra biscuit with the afternoon tea.

Hallsworth handed him a list of payees. 'Those are our suppliers' bank accounts,' he said briskly. 'The total transaction, including your fees, amounts to an exact total of twenty-nine million, nine hundred and ninety-one thousand.'

I thought nine thousand was a lot to leave as a tip and then remembered that the cheques given to the Hill Street employees would have been drawn on the trading company's account.

The manager looked at his watch. 'You're running early, which helps.' He nodded at the two assistants and handed them the bank drafts. As they left the room he smiled at Hallsworth. 'Rest assured – all of the banks will be in receipt of the bank transfers within the hour.' He gave the faintest of shrugs. 'After that of course, it's between them and their customers.'

Hallsworth nodded. 'All of the banks are co-operating. They'll confirm receipts to their customers immediately.'

After that, Hallsworth and Pepalasis signed a couple of authorizations and we left. On the way to the door the manager must have felt I'd been left out of things long enough, because he said, 'You've had an accident Mr Townsend?' Considering the aluminium crutch and the plaster casts it seemed an especially inane remark, but perhaps banks don't select their managers for their powers of observation.

'No,' I surprised him with, 'I'm trying to avoid one.' But I didn't give much for my chances.

Part Six

CHAPTER ONE

We were back at Hill Street by one o'clock. My eyes searched the row of parked cars but that's all they were, not an ambulance anywhere to be seen. I was told to pack a suitcase which included my passport and was locked in my bedroom to get on with it. It all seemed an elaborate farce when I knew they would kill me. But packing a suitcase with one arm in a sling isn't easy and it helped me take my mind off Jean for a while. For almost half an hour. Then I stewed until seven o'clock when Pepalasis opened the door and motioned me to follow him to the sitting-room.

'Help yourself,' he nodded at the coffee pot and the plate of sandwiches.

Breakfast had been twelve hours earlier. Twelve hours, sixty cigarettes, a glass of brandy and a few more of champagne. I helped myself and watched him pack a suitcase with financial records brought from my office.

'Where's Jean?' I asked, almost mechanically.

'For Chrissakes – ' he began, but the telephone interrupted him.

'Who's Drachman?' he asked, one hand over the mouthpiece.

Dear God, he didn't know! Arranson had used the expression 'my client' all morning and Emanuel and I had kept as quiet as the grave about the source of our funds.

'A pain in the neck,' I pulled a face and held my hand out for the phone. 'Been pestering me for weeks about some advice. Small stuff, not important. Give it here – I'll speak to him.'

But he swayed back beyond my reach, his eyes narrowed with suspicion, his grip tight on the telephone. For an instant he stared at me, as if trying to decide the truth, then maliciously he leered as he spoke into the mouthpiece. 'I'm sorry Mr Drachman, but Mr Townsend's too busy. Er, he's packing to go on a trip.' Without waiting for a reply he slammed the receiver back into its cradle, no doubt delighted to have foiled a suspected escape attempt.

'I couldn't have put it better,' I said, while my mind gagged at the thought of Drachman's reaction.

Hallsworth joined us an hour later. Apparently all of the staff had gone happily on their way, clutching their newfound wealth, and we were alone in the building. He nodded at the suitcase. 'Everything ready?'

'Up here, yes,' Pepalasis nodded. 'Downstairs?'

'Finished.' Hallsworth turned to me, 'And you?'

I hoped that wasn't meant as it sounded. I patted my jacket pocket. 'Even got my passport. What about Jean's?'

He smiled. 'Flat twenty-eight, Sutton Mansions, Fulham. Don't worry, she's got it.'

'I'll fetch the car,' Pepalasis hoisted a suitcase and looked at me. 'What about him?'

'Wait in the lobby downstairs,' Hallsworth instructed, and then turned to go into the bedroom, no doubt to search it before we left.

It was a strange feeling travelling down in the lift with Pepalasis, neither of us speaking, both knowing we were leaving the building for the very last time. When we reached the entrance hall he said, 'Wait here. And no tricks.'

I prodded the plaster cast on my foot with the crutch. 'Like running for help?'

There was no sign of Jean. Or Pamela Johnstone or Albert. Or of Kirk McNeil. I wondered if I would get to know Frascari's identity before they killed me. Not that I had long to brood over it. Hallsworth was down within a minute or two, and moments later the boot of the car was full of suitcases, Pepalasis sat behind the steering wheel and Hallsworth got into the back with me. As we stopped for the lights at South Audley Street I glanced back for a final look at the building which had played such a big part in my life. And my heart missed a beat as a long Cadillac slid into the line of traffic three cars behind us.

For some reason I imagined we were going to Winchester. I expected Pepalasis to make for Chiswick and the beginning of the M3. But instead he went north, through Camden Town and on to Hampstead. We even passed Jack Straw's Castle, and I remembered stopping there for a drink with Sue on the way back from Barmouth. Sue? I laughed aloud at the thought.

'What's so funny?' Hallsworth snapped, and it came as a surprise to realize how nervous he was. I took a hurried look at the grim expression and thought about the car trailing us and my sense of humour vanished.

Pepalasis stopped for fuel at Scratchwood and just before we pulled back on to the motorway I saw the ambulance. Ambulances look much of a muchness really. See one and you've seen them all. But this one was parked when we arrived, blinked its headlights in greeting, and pulled out ahead of us as we left. I felt close to Jean at that moment and prayed that she was still unharmed, shifting in my seat to get a better view. But the ambulance stayed fifty yards ahead and the smoked glass of the window defied all efforts to see inside.

We were north of Birmingham before I guessed where we were going. It had to be Liverpool. To the cargo. To a ship putting to sea tomorrow night. Pepalasis had mentioned a voyage and Hallsworth had promised to put us down in another country. Promised? A sideways glance at his set expression convinced me otherwise. I peered back at the road behind. The Cadillac was still there – four cars away and keeping formation like a fighter pilot. It passed us once. On a long open stretch without any exit points – only to slow down after a couple of miles to allow us to pass. I squinted through the windows, trying to glimpse its passengers. But my glances had been secretive. I was afraid that any obvious interest would draw the attention of the others. So the hasty peering had proved nothing. But I was sure that Drachman was in that car.

Turning off to Nantwich worried me. True, it's one way of getting to Liverpool, but it's a roundabout route adding thirty miles of bleak, open countryside to the journey. Dusk was settling fast, and as the light faded, so the tension seemed to grow between Pepalasis and Hallsworth. As if they were keying themselves up for something. Not a word passed between them, but I could sense their nervousness. Then, abruptly, the ambulance swung off the main road and we followed through what were little more than country lanes. I glanced over my shoulder. Twice I thought I saw the lights of the Cadillac. Then they were lost behind the twists in the road.

We skirted Nantwich, and Timperley afterwards, using secondary roads all the way. I guessed our position as somewhere at the base of the Wirral, with Chester away to our left and Ellesmere Port miles to the right. Whoever was driving the ambulance was going more slowly now and we closed up until we were barely ten yards behind. Trees crowded the edge of the road. An occasional gap in the hedges revealed the stark mounds of gravel pits, black with shadows under a darkening sky. Then the ambulance stopped.

Pepalasis had expected it and he halted two yards behind. We were pulled off the road, both vehicles facing up a long drive, flanked left and right by a tall beech hedge. A derelict gatekeeper's lodge squatted to one side, its crumbling masonry ghostly in the light of a pale moon. But there was no gate across our path. No reason to stop that I could see. Yet something told me we had reached the end of the line. This was the place where they would kill me. And Jean. I strained forward in my seat, noting the rutted surface of the drive, and the general air of neglect. Untrimmed hedges, the disused stone lodge. Pepalasis cut the engine and switched off the headlights. I watched to see if the ambulance would do the same. It did. The darkness deepened in silence. Inside the car no one spoke, until I said, 'Funny place for a picnic.'

'Shut up!' Pepalasis hunched his shoulders and a second later I heard the click of the kombolois.

'We're two minutes early,' Hallsworth said, looking at his watch, a green phosphorous blob in the darkness. A fast moving blob as he grabbed my wrist.

'Christ, you're jumpy.' I pulled the pack of cigarettes clear of my pocket and felt his grip relax. 'You searched me. Remember?'

'Shut up!' Pepalasis repeated urgently, without turning in his seat.

Hallsworth released his grip and I put a cigarette to my lips before fumbling for my lighter. If the Cadillac was still with us it would pass the entrance to the drive at any second. Except pass was the last thing I wanted it to do. I flicked the lighter, adjusted the flame to maximum, turned sideways to make it clearly visible through the rear window – and lit the filter end of the cigarette.

'Blast!' I spat it out with all the simulated surprise I could muster, transferred the still burning lighter to my plastered hand, and reached for another cigarette.

'Put that blasted thing out!' The agitation in the front seat increased by the second.

I shut the lighter off, leaned forward with a fresh cigarette in my mouth, and flicked the lighter again. Long enough for its flame to stab the darkness and the end of the cigarette. Car headlights flitted past the end of the drive behind us, one second there, gone the next, the engine note a low purr, travelling no faster than cruising speed.

Simultaneously Hallsworth said, 'There's the signal.' He was straining forward in his seat, looking over Pepalasis's shoulder and up the drive. I saw twin pinpricks of light at the far end. Headlights. Switched on and off. And on and off again.

'Right.' Pepalasis was getting out of the car.

Hallsworth spoke without looking at me. 'You travel by ambulance the rest of the way.'

Pepalasis opened my door. I looked at Hallsworth. 'Shouldn't you douse me with petrol first?' He made no reply, not even looking at me, his eyes still fixed on a point at the far end of the drive. I heaved my plastered foot out of the door and on to the ground. The ambulance door opened and even in that poor light there was no mistaking Albert's bulk as it bore down on me.

'Hurry up,' Pepalasis said to me, then more loudly to Albert. 'Over here – give me a hand.'

It was now or never and I knew it. Holding the top of the door with my right hand I pivoted quickly, swinging my left arm clear of the sling and crashing the plaster cast across his face. The full weight of my body was behind that blow. Even through the plaster I felt the bridge of his nose crush under the force of it. He staggered backwards, his scream shattering the night air as his hands clawed at his face. Blindly he fell into Albert's path as I scrambled towards the edge of the drive, stumbling on the rutted surface and turning as Albert recovered to come after me. I jabbed the crutch, aiming for his face, missing wildly and swinging it like a sabre. I missed again and staggered off balance. Straight into his fists. His first punch sent me sprawling in the dirt. I rolled to one side as his boot kicked viciously and by the time he kicked again, I was up on one knee. I parried the next blow and rose to a half crouch, my eyes on his face above me. Then the drive blazed suddenly with light and the night came alive with the noise of a high revving engine as the Cadillac rounded the corner at full speed. Albert's hands flew to his eyes to shield them from the glare. For a moment I was forgotten amidst the sounds of wheels skidding and doors slamming and voices shouting. Then the unmistakable sound of a shot. I didn't look back. Half hopping, half dragging myself around the ambulance to the driver's door, stubbing my toes and cursing the clumsiness caused by the plastered foot. I was behind the wheel a second later, a hand fumbling for the ignition keys while my plastered foot tried to distinguish brake from accelerator. Albert was alongside then, wrenching the door open, a huge hand reaching for my face as the engine sprang to life. Bracing myself against his grip, I slammed the gear lever forward, and the vehicle lurched, throwing him off balance. He recovered for an instant, staying alongside, one hand gripping the door as he staggered backwards, his head turned towards the rear of the ambulance. Then the entire lower half of his face burst open like a ripe melon hit by a baseball bat. And he was gone. I never even heard the shot that killed him. Not with my foot slammed hard down on the accelerator and the door swinging open like a bird's broken wing.

I'll never forget that drive. The ground so badly pitted that the ambulance bucked wildly in the holes. Or reeled drunkenly from side to side as its wheels caught in the rutted tramlines. It seemed to go on for ever. I prayed it might lead to another exit point. Another way of getting back on the road. But it didn't.

I saw the car first. The one that had signalled. A red mini – empty now as my headlights washed its windscreen. Another car behind it, both parked beside a house which might have made House and Gardens. A hundred years ago. Now it was a ruin. Ground floor windows boarded up, only the double doors at the entrance swinging wide open. The drive swept past the front of the house and round behind it. And so did the ambulance as I hunted for another way out. But the rear of the house brought bitter disappointment. A dead end. Parking space. Surrounded by the beech hedge which gave way to a crumbling wall ten feet high. And no way out that I could see. I slewed in an arc, every nerve in my body taut, expecting to see the Cadillac in hot pursuit at any second. But nothing happened. I killed the engine and listened. Still nothing. Then I recovered enough to look around the cab and to discover the communicating door to the back of the ambulance. Jean! Her name had already passed my lips as I grabbed the handle and pulled the door back on its runners. Jean! Jean! Oblivious of anything and everything. But then the shouts stifled to a sob, as I looked into an empty interior. No Jean. Just me. Alone on a dark night. Waiting for a man to kill me.

There was nowhere to go but the house. The yard offered no cover and Drachman was likely to round the corner any second. But I hesitated. Remembering the front doors as I passed. Swinging open on their hinges. Whoever had signalled from the top of the drive had seen the commotion and gone somewhere. And they certainly hadn't passed me. Which left only one place to go.

The sound of a car's engine had me out of the ambulance and hobbling towards the house. The first two windows were boarded up like the ones at the front. Inch thick timbers too close together to prise apart. But the old-fashioned french windows offered a chance. Some of the planks had fallen away, and those remaining were held in place by rusty nails loose in the rotted wood. I tore two away and climbed through to an empty room, as big as the yard outside with about as much protection. Thin white fingers of moonlight reached across the dusty boards to a door in the far wall. I shuffled over, bumping the plaster cast on the uneven floorboards with enough noise to waken the dead. The door opened into total darkness and for a moment I just stood there, frightened to turn back and fearful of what lay ahead, as my eyes adjusted to the heavy gloom. I was in a corridor. About six feet wide and maybe twice as long. Tall double doors to my right, a single door opposite, and another to my left on the other side of the passageway. I tried one of the curved handles on the double doors until it loosened in my hand, and with the pressure of my shoulder I inched the door open enough to see into the room beyond. A big square entrance hall, menacing with shadow and threatening in silence. The big front doors almost opposite, still open. A curved staircase sweeping gracefully up from the left hand side. It seemed important to get upstairs. But not that way. Whoever had reached the house ahead of me had used the front door. And almost certainly the staircase. To repeat the journey now would offer a certain target to anyone hidden in the gallery. I closed the door with my fingertips and edged back down the corridor. The door at the bottom led to a scullery, two chipped enamel sinks and some wooden cupboards hanging uncertainly from the window wall. I passed through to another room, and yet another beyond that, cursing the noise made by my plastered foot. Then I found what I was looking for. A back staircase. Not as grand as the one at the front and these stairs were narrow and enclosed on both sides by walls scruffy with flaking plaster. But the treads looked sound and the light was good, a gutted window at the top showing itself as an oblong patch of night sky. So I went up.

One stair at a time. As quietly as possible. Taking care to lift my plastered foot well clear of each riser I climbed. Fearful that any sound would be carried upwards by the funnel of the stair well. And I was half way up when all hell broke loose. A shout. A shout of warning followed by a shot, then two more shots in rapid succession. A scream of agony, interrupted by yet another shot and another scream. And from above the sound of running feet. Heavy feet, too solid to be a woman's. I braced myself against the wall – caught midway on the staircase – unable to hurry, unsure of which way to go. The footsteps grew louder. Sliding and stumbling, scrambling to a halt, panic stricken, right above me. A shadow fell between me and the open window, and I looked up to see the bulk of a man on the landing, his left hand clasped to his right shoulder as if he had been hit. Gasping for breath, he shifted his weight, backing himself against the window wall, his right hand lifting slowly and pointing back in the direction he had come from.

Then he saw me. And in the same second I recognized him. The light from the window fell full on his face as he turned towards me. It was Vince Pickard! Vice President of U.S Steel!

'You?' he croaked, his right arm turning towards me, moonlight catching the metallic glint of the gun in his hand. 'You? For Chrissakes, if you're here who the hell's back there?'

He was no more than five yards away and his gun arm had almost reached the level of his eyes when I threw myself down the stairs. The shot sounded in the same instant as my head collided with the bottom step and my mouth filled with blood. I was convinced I was dying. But I was still conscious. Conscious enough to feel pain in my body and terror in my heart. I looked back up the stairs expecting to look into the grinning face of death itself. And I did in a way. Pickard was already past the point on the stairs I had climbed to. And coming down fast. And very dead. His body stopped short of me, spread-eagled across the bottom three stairs, his gun clattering to a rest behind him on the fourth stair up. My brain cleared enough to register the blood streaming from my nose, and instinct had me reaching for the gun.

'Leave it!'

I didn't need telling twice. All I moved was my head. Even that very slowly. I knelt at the bottom of the stairs and forced my gaze upwards until it rested on the man on the landing.

'Townsend, I think you owe me,' Drachman said. 'And I've come to collect.'

I thought he had as much chance of doing that as I had of leaving the place alive, but it seemed inopportune to tell him. So I said, 'Do we talk like this? Or do I come up there?'

I went up and together we went to find Miss Pamela Johnstone. And a friend of mine.

CHAPTER TWO

Pamela Johnstone lay as limp as a rag in the corridor, less than twelve feet from the head of the stairs.

'Is she dead?'

'Doubt it,' Drachman's indifference was chilling. 'I belted her on the way to that guy at the foot of the stairs.'

Desperately, and without knowing if I was right or wrong, I said, 'There's someone else in the house.'

'Not alive there ain't.'

'A girl. She must be here.' I had another idea. 'Or perhaps in one of those cars in the drive.' I turned and seeing him behind me realized how good a target Pickard had presented against the gutted window at the head of the stairs.

'Quit stalling, Townsend. I checked the cars before we hit the house. There's no one, and anyway –'

'Listen!'

In the same split second he heard it. 'On the floor!'

'But it must have been Jean.' I took a quick step forward. Too quick for his liking. A bullet smacked into the floorboards a yard ahead of me.

'Get down.'

I dropped clumsily. Dreading the next bullet. The one to shatter my spine.

'Whoever it is ain't one of mine,' he hissed. 'The room on your left – ease it up a bit and push the door open. Slowly. And Townsend – move wrong and the next slug gets you behind the left kneecap.'

I covered the two yards on my belly, reached for the bottom of the door, and pushed. It creaked slowly back against the inside wall, the sound suddenly obliterated by the rush of feet as Drachman closed the gap and stood above me, his gun already describing an arc around the room. Moonlight flooded in from a broken window and from a hole in the roof high above. Jean sat propped against the far wall, her hands bound behind her back and her mouth taped with sticking plaster. Her eyes were wide with fright as Drachman levelled the gun at her.

'No!' I half threw myself across the room to reach her, shielding her body with mine, expecting all the time that Drachman would shoot me. My hands reached for the thin rope at her wrists and I attacked the knots in a cold sweat of panic, my fingers numb and clumsy with fear, my movements awkward from the plaster cast on my wrist. I risked a glance over my shoulder at Drachman. And felt an overwhelming sense of relief as he sat down just inside the door, the gun for the moment not pointing at us but resting in his lap.

I removed the sticking plaster. Even the best way was a brutal business. Two quick tugs to rip it clean away. She was already crying, 'Oh Mike, what have they done to you?' as she reached for my face. I realized I was streaked with blood from my fall down the stairs. 'And your hand?' she said, but I pulled her close to me, my right hand stroking her hair as I whispered reassurances. Not that she took much in. She was in a state of shock and the sight of Drachman's gun wasn't helping. But I held her trembling body in my arms until Drachman interrupted us. 'That's enough, Townsend. Now talk.'

I sat on the floor next to Jean and talked. And in the talking made a discovery. The identity of Bruno Frascari. Bruno Frascari was Vince Pickard. Vince Pickard was Bruno Frascari. I was stunned. That a man called Vince Pickard was Vice President of U.S Steel was a fact. Emanuel had checked it from the company's records. And Poignton had verified it from another source. Checked and verified? Strong words for the scant attention we had paid the matter. We had been mesmerised by Marlborough House.

And all those people. The teleprinters and the satellite link with Pittsburgh. The computers and the non-stop flow of telex messages. I wondered what had happened to the real Vince Pickard and how Frascari had substituted for the Vice President of one of the largest corporations in the world. And my muzzy head tumbled over another thought. That Smithers and Emanuel would be in for quite a shock. If they ever got to Pittsburgh.

'So where's the money now?' Drachman persisted.

I swallowed hard, anticipating his reaction and wishing that he'd put the gun away. 'It's been spent.'

'Thirty million pounds! Which they had for a *few hours*? Come on, Townsend, what are you giving me?'

I told him about the export deal.

'So, okay, when do they get paid? And where?' he asked, convinced that I had all the answers, despite all I had told him about Jean being held hostage. I repeated my ignorance and the gun loomed large in his hand. 'So who does know?' he asked.

'Hallsworth,' my mouth went dry. 'And Pepalasis.' I jerked my head at the window. 'The men out there.'

'Huh, you wanna know what's out there? My driver and the three clowns you were with. All dead. And in here there's me and you and her.' He jerked his gun at Jean. 'An' Larry Baines just inside the front door. As cold as that creep on the back stairs. An' that's all, Townsend. Understand?'

'And the girl in the corridor,' I said desperately.

'*She* would know?'

Oh God, I hoped so. I nodded.

'Get her.' His voice rasped like a file on steel. 'And you're going to die, Townsend. You got me into this and you're going to get me out of it. Then you're going to die.'

I nodded again and rose slowly to my feet to walk carefully past him and out of the door. Into an empty corridor.

I couldn't believe it. She had been on the floor a few yards away. Not fifteen minutes before when we had gone into the

273

room. Disorientated, I swung my gaze in the opposite
direction. But the corridor was quite, quite deserted. There
was no sign of Pamela Johnstone anywhere.

CHAPTER THREE

It didn't take us long to find her. Drachman used Jean and
me as human shields and marched us ahead of him down the
corridor towards the front of the house. Down the corridor
and along the gallery and down the grand staircase I had
glimpsed earlier. Except earlier a body hadn't lain at the foot
of the stairs in a pool of blood like black oil in the moonlight.

Pamela Johnstone was standing a few yards from the front
of the house. She must have heard us. My plastered foot had
banged its way down the stairs and scraped on the gravel
behind her. But she neither turned nor looked up as we came
and stood alongside her. The car door was open and
Hallsworth was sprawled in the back, his head falling
drunkenly over the edge of the seat. Blood from a chest
wound covered the whole of his trunk so that only his face
remained unmarked. And his open staring eyes accused all
of us as we formed a semi-circle around the car.

'I told you once that he was a genius, didn't I?' she said
to me, while still looking at him. Her voice was as soft and
as gentle as I had ever heard it. 'He planned the whole thing.
It was his game, don't you see? The others really only cared
about the money. But not him. To him the excitement was
pulling it off. And he did, didn't he? He pulled it off
beautifully.'

She leant forward and closed his eyes, and for the
hundredth time I wondered about the strange relationship
which had existed between her and Hallsworth. She was a
ghost from my past. Someone I had made love to, lovers

274

without love. But there had been *something* once. I had felt for her. I had enjoyed her companionship, been grateful for the pleasures of her body. Now, seeing her alone, small and vulnerable, a bruise darkening her cheekbone where Drachman had hit her, I felt a moment's pity. Until I remembered her standing by while I was beaten and Jean was humiliated and terrified to the edge of hysteria.

'He brought Jean and me to this place to die,' I said harshly.

'No! You're wrong. We only needed another few hours. He wanted to leave you here – both of you, tied up and drugged.'

'*He* wanted to?' I detected the inference. 'But you didn't?'

'It was a split vote.' Her eyes flickered. 'Does it matter now? Who was for and who against?'

Drachman had been quiet long enough. 'Nothing matters,' he snapped. 'Except the money. Townsend reckons you know where it is?'

'I know where there's a great deal of money,' she said coolly. 'And the irony is I can't touch a penny of it. Without your help.'

We waited for an explanation, but instead she turned and walked to the Cadillac parked ten yards away. I remained where I was. Even from there I could see the bodies piled in the back like carcasses on the butcher's truck. Pepalasis, Albert, and another man. Jean shuddered and turned her head away from the carnage. But I couldn't tear my eyes from Pamela Johnstone as she stood looking down into the bruised, dead face of Pepalasis. Nor could I repress the long hiss of surprise a moment later. When she pressed her mouth to his lifeless lips in a lingering kiss of goodbye. Then she walked back to join us, ignoring the question in my eyes.

'Very well.' She looked at Drachman. 'You've heard enough to know what's going on. By lunchtime tomorrow the cargo will be fully loaded. The buyer's agent is already in Liverpool and payment has already been made to a bank in Switzerland. I meet the buyer, hand over the ship's manifest and in exchange he authorizes the Swiss Bank to pay ten million pounds into each of three numbered accounts.' She shrugged and gave a wintery smile. 'Unfortunately I can't change the arrangements. I must complete by noon accompanied by two men. We each sign for one account. So, Mr Drachman, it would seem we are mutually dependent. If I am to get my money, you will get yours.'

'Ten million?' he sounded awed for the first time since I'd come into contact with him.

'Third shares?' I queried. 'But there were four of you?'

'Two shared,' she said simply. 'That's all you need to know. Now, I would suggest that we've plenty to do here and –'

'How do I know I can trust you?' Drachman complained.

'You don't!' She spat at him, suddenly very angry. 'But you've very little choice in the matter. Kill me and you get nothing. Accept my deal and be bloody thankful you've got it. And I'll give you a piece of advice. Spend some of the money buying yourself a hole, Mr Drachman. Because some day I might just come looking for you. For what you did here tonight!'

It was an astonishing outburst from a girl five feet tall, trembling like a leaf as she stared into a killer's gun. But no one doubted she shook from temper, not from fear. Afterwards there was little doubt, gun or no gun, that Drachman had forfeited control to Pamela Johnstone. The gun was only used for my benefit, one wave of it in Jean's direction being enough for me to do their bidding.

We worked quickly. The bodies we searched first. That was my job. I stripped them of their wallets and cigarette lighters and pocket books – 'the dead men's effects' as old Poignton might have said – tossing everything into an open bag held by Drachman standing alongside. It was a grisly business and I worked clumsily, hampered by the plaster casts which Drachman insisted remain on.

Then the surplus vehicles were disposed of in a way which convinced me that Jean and I had been taken to that remote spot to meet our deaths. Part of the surrounding wall at the back of the house was camouflage. A section had been collapsed and the chunks of brickwork had been placed back together again without the binding of mortar – so that one good shove from the ambulance brought the whole lot down like a pack of cards. Beyond the wall the ground sloped sharply away for forty yards or so before disappearing into old quarry workings, the sides a mass of tangled undergrowth and the bottom hidden in darkness a hundred feet down.

Drachman and I ran all the vehicles except one over the side of the open pit. Even the Cadillac went, carrying its grim cargo with it. And the two bodies from the house were loaded into the ambulance and then that too was pushed to the edge and beyond. Only the grey B.M.W. seen earlier behind the mini in the drive was retained for our journey.

Pamela Johnstone supervised throughout, her face marbled by moonlight and her eyes as cold as stone as she gave her orders. Drachman and I spent an hour 'rebuilding' the wall and then we had finished, close to exhaustion as we clambered into the car, me in the driving seat, Pamela Johnstone next to me and Drachman in the back with Jean.

And so we left the house and its grounds in which six men had died and Jean and I had nearly joined them. Down the long rutted drive and back into the tiny lane. I drove as Pamela directed. Through country lanes for twenty miles, into Chester and out again, and on to the Liverpool road. Until we reached the motel where three rooms had already been booked and paid for.

Jean was sent to collect the keys. Drachman and I were too dirty and blood-stained and dishevelled not to have invited comment, even at that late hour. And Pamela Johstone remained in the car at Drachman's insistence. Jean would be free for the first time since Sunday. As I listened to Drachman telling her what to do, I toyed with the idea of slamming the car into gear as soon as she got out. But he forestalled me. Before she was even out of the car I was told to switch off and hand him the keys. And she was told I'd have a hole in the back of my head if she was gone longer than five minutes. White-faced and anxious, she hurried away into the darkness. And I realized that I'd swapped one prison for another.

CHAPTER FOUR

I woke early that Thursday, stiff from sleeping on the floor of the motel room, having been denied the comfort of a bed as we were all crammed into only one of the three rooms reserved. But I felt a hundred per cent better for the rest. Jean and Pamela Johnstone, both fully clothed, remained asleep on separate beds, while Drachman sat with his back to the door watching me. It took a second or two for it all to flood back but when it did it terrified me. A week ago I had been leading a normal life as a moderately successful businessman. Now I shuddered at the crimes I'd be accused of. Embezzlement. Fraud. Conspiracy. Even murder if no one believed my story.

I struggled to the bathroom and removed the plaster casts, cracking them with blows from the heel of a shoe so forcefully applied that I was almost in geniune need of them. Then I collected fresh clothes from my suitcase and soaked in the bath before dressing, so that by the time I joined the others I felt less edgy than I had done for days. After all, Jean might still be in danger but at least she was here where I had a chance of protecting her.

As soon as Pamela Johstone went to the bathroom, I went to work on Drachman. 'Relax', I told him cheerfully. It's time you realized that you're here by invitation.'

He transferred the gun from one hand to the other and watched me through eyes red-rimmed with tiredness. I guessed that having insisted we all slept in the same room he'd spent the night guarding the door.

'My invitation,' I stressed. 'Giving Arranson that message when I did. And getting it confirmed when you phoned Hill Street.'

His dull look failed to register even a flicker of comprehension, so I tried again. 'It was all I could do. While Jean was in danger.'

'And she's safe now?'

'Why not?'

He jerked the gun for an answer. Last night it would have frightened me but I'd had time to think since then.

'Listen, Drachman, yesterday you were ripped off for four million, today, you can pick up twice as much. Thanks to me.' When he remained silent, I shrugged and added: 'Have it your own way. But you heard the girl. We're mutually dependent. And you wouldn't even be in line for a share if I hadn't got my message to you.'

'So we're allies?' he said, as if getting used to the idea might take him quite some time.

'We always were. I got you into this, remember? So I'll get you out of it.'

I persisted until he succumbed to my next idea. That we all transferred to the next cabin and have breakfast delivered to the room. By now both of the girls had bathed and changed and were looking quite presentable, whereas he looked tired and bedraggled.

Over tea and toast I concentrated on finding out all I could from Pamela Johnstone.

'We're due at the bank at eleven,' she said. 'Van Hoffman –'

'The bank?' Drachman was hostile with suspicion. 'You said a Swiss bank?'

'They have agents in Liverpool,' she explained wearily,

279

giving him a look of contempt. 'Look, everything's arranged. Just don't interfere, that's all. And for God's sake don't try to alter anything. A wrong word to the people we're meeting and –'

'People?' he queried. 'What people?'

He was pushing her too hard and she almost screamed at him. 'Just leave it alone will you? I know what I'm doing and –'

'You know what you're doing,' he snapped back. 'But I don't.' He turned to me. 'And you don't either I suppose?'

'No more than you do.' I turned back to her. 'Which bank is agent?'

'The Bank of Liverpool and Sao Paulo.'

I knew it by reputation but had never had dealings with it. But it was well established. Maybe not as prestigious as the Bank of London and South America but after financing Liverpool's trade with South America for a hundred years it was damn near as big. And the Bank of Liverpool and Sao Paulo was agent for Suisse Commercial of Zurich. Which is where the money was.

'Who's the customer for the cargo?' I asked.

'His name is Van Hoffman,' she glanced at her watch. 'He'll be waiting for us at the Bank.'

'Van Hoffman? Dutch?'

'South African,' she smiled craftily. 'I believe you spoke to him once. On the telephone.'

I was at a loss at first, but then I remembered. It seemed a long time ago. Late one night at Hill Street, with Jean listening on an extension. And if *that* was the man, then we had problems. 'But he must know Hallsworth?' I said, alarmed, correcting myself a second later. 'Must have known Hallsworth.'

She shook her head. 'He knows I've got partners. Male partners. But he never met them.'

Baffled, I searched her grey eyes for trace of a lie before saying, 'But if he made that phone call to me, he knows who I am. Knows damn well that I'm no partner of yours.'

She hesitated about that and had the grace to think about it. Or at least pretend to think about it. Finally she said, 'Van Hoffman won't look for reasons to hold things up. It's his money on the line in Switzerland. All he wants is that cargo.' She could see that I was still doubtful because in an effort to convince me she added, 'Beside Van Hoffman's known me to change partners before.'

I wondered what the hell that meant? And found myself wondering why she had kissed Pepalasis but not Hallsworth. But I'd no time to work on it. Drachman was getting impatient and impatient men with guns make me nervous. But I wanted to find out a bit more about who we were going to meet, so I asked, 'And Van Hoffman's the customer?'

'He's *our* customer.'

'Meaning he's a middle man?'

'What does it matter?' she pretended to be bored with the whole conversation.

'Because it's usual to make a profit,' I said coldly. 'Thirty million ex-works U.K. should fetch considerably more overseas.'

'Oh, so that's it?' Her eyes flashed with temper. 'You're getting greedy.'

'Not greedy. Cautious. The more I know, the less chance you've got of selling Drachman and me down the river.'

He threw me a grateful glance while her eyes buried me. She shrugged. 'So Van Hoffman takes a profit.'

'From whom?'

'Oh, God Almighty! Who cares? The Rhodesians I should think. Van Hoffman's been running goods through that embargo since the day it started.'

It was all beginning to make sense. No straightforward buyer would transact business Van Hoffman's way unless the deal was complicated by some factor. And South African businessmen had kept Ian Smith's Rhodesia going for years. I was still staring at her, working it out in my mind, when she obviously misinterpreted my look for one of disbelief because, quite gratuitiously, she added, 'And Van Hoffman took care of some expenses for us.'

I pricked my ears up. 'Such as?'

She shrugged. 'That place at St Albans for a start. That cost a fortune to set up. And Bruno's crowd from New York weren't cheap.'

'Bruno Frascari,' I said very quietly, thinking of the apology owed to Kirk McNeil if I ever saw him again.

She nodded and gave a funny sort of half smile. 'Vince Pickard to you.'

I pieced a few more details together, cross checking where possible until deciding that the story was as near to the truth as it ever would be with a girl like Pamela Johnstone. And after that there was nowhere to go but the Bank of Liverpool and Sao Paulo itself.

'What happens after the Bank?' Drachman wanted to know.

She spat at him. 'We each go our separate ways to hell, Mr Drachman. And remember what I told you about that hole.'

'I could reach you first,' he snarled back.

'Just you damn well try!' she hissed.

It seemed a pity to break it up. But my one remaining hope of seeing old age lay in finding Drachman his money. I felt better though. Better than I had for days. I had a bargaining position for the first time since Monday. Manipulating the balance of suspicion between Drachman and Pamela Johnstone.

The journey to Lime Street took only half an hour. But it seemed longer. Jean drove, with Drachman coiled like a spring beside her, while Pamela Johnstone sat as taut as piano wire in the back with me. The atmosphere between them fairly crackled with suppressed hostility. And their mutual aversion made me, if not the leader, then at least no more of a prisoner than they were. So we rode in suffocating silence while I thought things over. And reached the decision that was to change the rest of my life.

'Jean, did you put that lighter in your bag?' I leaned forward, as if to reach for the handbag on the seat next to her. But Drachman was as suspicious as ever and he got there first, his thumb flicking the clasp open and his fingers fumbling inside the bag. Not that he found the lighter. But then he wouldn't. Not when it was in my pocket all the time. But my view of the bag's contents told me all I wanted to know.

The Bank of Liverpool and Sao Paulo greeted us like visiting royalty. The local director was a man called Hughes, who bowed and nodded his silver-haired head all the way from the lobby to the board room, where a line of assistants stood waiting to slip chairs out from the table then in again as we took our places. And where another man was already waiting for us. A man who introduced himself as Mr Piet Van Hoffman.

After each of us had accepted a glass of madeira, Pamela Johnstone made a brisk start. 'You've been to the warehouse this morning?' she asked Van Hoffman.

He nodded and took his curious eyes away from me long enough to answer her. 'Yes. Everything's in order.' I recognized the accent all right.

Hughes cleared his throat importantly. 'And I've received copies of the ship's manifest and bills of lading.'

'Good,' Pamela Johnstone's eagerness betrayed her anxiety, despite her apparent calm. 'Then we can proceed with completion?'

Hughes looked to Van Hoffman as if for guidance. The room went very quiet. A tug hooted on the Mersey half a mile away and traffic sounds struggled up from the street below. Van Hoffman looked around the table. From Jean to Drachman to me. And then his gaze settled on Pamela Johnstone. The vein pulsated in her neck and the bruise on her cheekbone glowed through make-up she had applied so carefully earlier. Almost imperceptibly she nodded back at him. It was the faintest of movements. As much with her eyes as her head. Van Hoffman hesitated a half second longer, smiled and said, 'Yes, we can proceed.' And Drachman's hiss of relief was heard all round the table.

Like everything well organized it didn't take long. Van Hoffman signed an acceptance for the cargo and a letter of authority to the Bank to release the funds in Switzerland. And we had another madeira while the information was relayed to Zurich by closed line document transmission. Then the messenger returned and handed Hughes the reply from Suisse Commercial, together with three large sealed envelopes. I looked at the envelopes. They looked plump, secret, and very important. And Hughes almost caressed them as he spoke to us.

'The arrangements are complete,' he smiled. 'And the funds have now been transferred in equal lots of ten million to three numbered accounts.' He let the full significance of that sink in and then added, 'I'm sure you'll find everything you need for the management of these accounts in the envelopes here. As you see, each of them bears the unbroken seal of Suisse Commercial and we have held them in trust until this moment.'

Slowly, almost reluctantly, certainly reverently, he released possession of the envelopes to an assistant, who placed the first in front of Pamela Johnstone, the second in front of Drachman, and the third in front of me. I sat staring at my ticket to ten million while the room filled with the noise of crackling parchment as the others broke the seals and spread papers on the table in front of them.

'My colleagues and I appreciate that you may wish to instruct us individually,' Hughes was saying. 'Should that be the case, private interview rooms have been set aside and . . .'

'I'd appreciate that,' I heard myself saying. 'Perhaps if the rest of the meeting would excuse us, Mr Hughes? You and I could . . .'

'But of course.'

284

He rose as I did, one hand reaching for Jean's elbow as the other hand closed on the envelope. I was vaguely aware of the others. Of Van Hoffman watching with enough mockery to have rivalled Hallsworth. Of Pamela Johnstone's white face and wide-eyed unblinking stare. Of Drachman still poring over the contents of his envelope. But only vaguely aware of them. I felt myself walk to the door, sensed Hughes stand to one side, barely heard his murmur about the first door on the left. I might have been dreaming. Or in a trance. Jean's questioning eyes looking up at me, her hand finding mine as we sat together in the manager's office. I heard myself talking to him, knew what I said, was conscious of his reply and aware of my answer. But it was as if I were listening to my voice from a long way off, each word clear and distant but rounded and hollow-sounding. Like in a tunnel. A long, dark tunnel. And that's where I was. At the end of the tunnel.

We left twenty minutes later. Hughes took care of everything. From the taxi at the side door to ready cash for the journey. But I still felt as if I was watching a film shot in slow motion with a badly synchronized soundtrack. Jean's anxious questions. My reassuring answers. Telling her that we were doing the right thing. It was all too dreamlike to be exciting. Her handing me her passport from her handbag. Us taking the first plane out of Speke Airport. Watching Liverpool and the Mersey drop away below us. Flying Lufthansa to Hamburg and then on from there. To our place in the sun. The sun we found. At the end of our tunnel.

POSTSCRIPT

Thameside Mansions,
Putney, London, England.
23 December 1977.

Bob Harrison woke first. He always woke first. Amy would sleep until lunchtime if he let her. But this morning something had disturbed him. He yawned, stretched, grunted, scratched himself – and waited. Perhaps whatever, or whoever, had roused him would go away again and let him sleep? Turning in his bed he drew his wife into the curve of his body and closed his eyes. But even as he did the door bell rang again. This time a steady, relentless, unremitting buzz. As if someone had jammed a finger in the bell push and couldn't release it.

It was the postman. Harrison took the parcel and the handful of Christmas cards to the kitchen to make tea. He was up now and from bitter experience knew he wouldn't get back to sleep again. Mechanically he loaded cups, milk and a sugar bowl on to a tray, reminded by the pain at the back of his eyes that last night was the fifth in succession he'd reached his bed with a drink too many under his belt. He grumbled about its inevitability. This time of the year, some damn function every night of the week. He looked through the post while waiting for the kettle to boil. The parcel was about the size of a shoe box, but his attention was caught less by its shape than by its postage stamps. Brazilian. He frowned, and tried to remember which army pal had secured the soft advisory posting to South America. But no name came to mind. The kettle boiled, he made the tea, put three spoons of sugar into a cup, added milk and poured tea over it. It rankled, not guessing who'd sent the parcel, so that seconds later speculation gave way to curiosity as he unwrapped the brown paper cover.

It *was* a shoe box. Sealed on every side with tape, and a letter stuck to the top. He began to stir his tea as he read the letter.

'Dear Bob,

I've been meaning to write for a long time. The problem was knowing where to begin. And once, having started, being determined to leave nothing out. To tell exactly the way it happened. Because if anyone's owed an explanation, you are, together with my thanks for persuading the police to raid Hill Street when you did. Unfortunately, or otherwise as things turned out, by the time they forced entry I was already on my way out of the country.

I've read your defence of me in the Press and what can I say? Except thank you. And to tell you what happened. At least now you'll know how and what was done. Or at least as much as I do. And if you ask WHY, let me tell you. I could never prove this story. My witnesses are dead, except for Pamela Johnstone, and she had committed suicide years before – ask Poignton at Durbeville's and he will prove it to you. It took Jean a while to see it but she did in the end. I was a wanted man in London without a chance of clearing my name. So I *had* to make a start elsewhere. Which takes money. Maybe not ten million but I could hardly keep some and hand the rest back. So I kept it all. Now it's as though we've always been rich. Rich and happy.

Sometimes – late at night, when we're alone – Jean and I still talk about them. Hallsworth and Pepalasis, Drachman and the man I knew as Vince Pickard. But mostly I remember a girl called Sue. Sue laughing, Sue serious, Sue as an angel, Sue as a bitch. Sue whose real name was Pamela Johnstone. I wonder where she is now? I wonder WHO she is now? But most of all I wonder if she meant it, that night at Windsor, when she said: 'I'm sorry, Mike. Sorry now that it was *you*.' And do you know Bob . . . I really think she was.

Affectionate best wishes, M.T.'

Harrison had ceased to stir his tea long before he finished reading it. For a minute or more he just stared at the letter, remembering the man who had written it. Then he dipped both hands into the shoe box and drew out the bundle of papers. He would let Amy sleep for once. Dammit, it was Christmas! So, after making sure that his cigarettes were to hand, he sipped his tea and began to read *The Money Stones*.